BONESMITH

BONE SMITH

HOUSE OF THE DEAD DUOLOGY

NICKI PAU PRETO

MARGARET K. McELDERRY BOOKS
NEW YORK · LONDON · TORONTO · SYDNEY · NEW DELHI

MARGARET K. McELDERRY BOOKS • An imprint of Simon & Schuster Children's Publishing Division • 1230 Avenue of the Americas, New York, New York 10020 • This book is a work of fiction. Any references to historical events, real people, or real places are used fictitiously. Other names, characters, places, and events are products of the author's imagination, and any resemblance to actual events or places or persons, living or dead, is entirely coincidental. • Text © 2023 by Nicki Pau Preto • Jacket illustration © 2023 by Tommy Arnold • Jacket design © 2023 by Simon & Schuster, Inc. • Map copyright © 2023 by Robert Lazzaretti • All rights reserved, including the right of reproduction in whole or in part in any form. • MARGARET K. McELDERRY BOOKS is a trademark of Simon & Schuster, Inc. • For information about special discounts for bulk purchases, please contact Simon & Schuster Special Sales at 1-866-506-1949 or business@simonandschuster.com. • The Simon & Schuster Speakers Bureau can bring authors to your live event. For more information or to book an event, contact the Simon & Schuster Speakers Bureau at 1-866-248-3049 or visit our website at www.simonspeakers.com. • The text for this book was set in Ten Mincho Text. • Manufactured in the United States of America • First Edition • 10 9 8 7 6 5 4 3 2 1 • Library of Congress Cataloging-in-Publication Data • Names: Pau Preto, Nicki, author. • Title: Bonesmith / Nicki Pau Preto. • Description: First edition. | New York : Margaret K. McElderry, 2023. | Audience: Ages 14 up | Audience: Grades 10–12. | Summary: Seventeen-year-old failed ghost-fighting warrior, Wren, journies to the haunted wasteland of the Breach to rescue a kidnapped prince and must team up with the very person responsible for the kidnapping. • Identifiers: LCCN 2022029759 (print) | LCCN 2022029760 (ebook) | ISBN 9781665910590 (hardcover) | ISBN 9781665910613 (ebook) • Subjects: CYAC: Fantasy. | Ability—Fiction. | Adventure and adventurers—Fiction. | Princes—Fiction. | Magic—Fiction. | LCGFT: Fantasy fiction. | Novels. • Classification: LCC PZ7.1.P384 Bo 2023 (print) | LCC PZ7.1.P384 (ebook) | DDC [Fic]—dc23 • LC record available at https://lccn.loc.gov/2022029759 • LC ebook record available at https://lccn.loc.gov/2022029760

TO JESSI RAE FOURNIER,
the best semiprofessional
hype-woman a girl could ask for.
I can't wait to return the favor.

BONELANDS

Marrow
Hall

Severton

The
Bonewood

Landon
Point

Astoria Peninsula

North Road

Aspen
Ridge

SPEARHEAD MOUNTAINS

HIGHLANDS

Stonespear

Brighton

South Road

Westway

Granite
Gate

Southbrook

RIVERLANDS

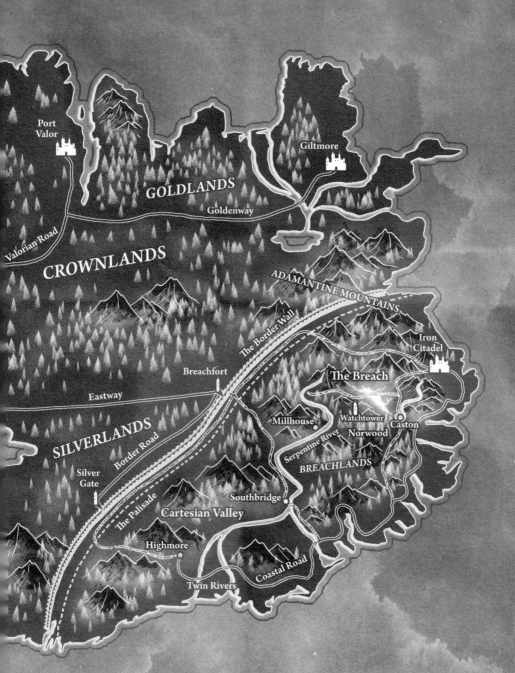

GOLDLANDS

Port Valor

Giltmore

Goldenway

Valorian Road

CROWNLANDS

ADAMANTINE MOUNTAINS

The Border Wall

Iron Citadel

Breachfort

The Breach

Eastway

Watchtower

Caston

Millhouse

Norwood

SILVERLANDS

Serpentine River

BREACHLANDS

Border Road

Silver Gate

The Palisade

Southbridge

Cartesian Valley

Highmore

Coastal Road

Twin Rivers

ONE

"Ready your blade."

As one, the novitiates knelt in the snow, their weapons held high on upturned palms. For valkyrs like Wren, it was a blade fashioned from dead bone. For reapyrs, a scythe of gleaming steel.

The sun had set, the sky inky black and riddled with stars—the Gravedigger's hour was upon them. Any moment now, the sickle moon would crest the would-be trees.

Any moment now, the trial would begin.

Wren's heart thundered in anticipation.

The branches of the forest stood pale and stark before them, sharp with reaching hands and gaping mouths. With splintered spines and cracked ribs.

This was no ordinary forest, after all. This was the Bonewood.

Arms and legs soared up from the ground, twisted and warped. Bent and broken.

Dead, soulless bones.

Undead, haunted bones.

Human bones, yes, but other creatures too. Reindeer with spiky antlers and great woolly mammoths with arching tusks. Ancient bones from unknowable beasts. Bones from the dawn of time.

The Bonewood was at once a graveyard and a training ground. It was here that bonesmiths tested their skills, extended their magic . . . and showed their mastery over the undead.

Now, after years of training and a lifetime of living in its shadow, Wren would traverse the Bonewood and compete in the Bonewood Trial.

She lifted her head slightly, considering the novitiates kneeling on either side of her. There were ten of them total, each dressed in Bone House black and with black grease lining their eyes, making their sockets look sunken like skulls. Ghostlight was bright enough on its own but turned blinding when it flashed against the snow, so they used the wax-and-charcoal mixture to reduce glare. It also made the mark of their magic—their pale, bone-white irises—stand out all the more.

Sometimes Wren extended the eye black into her hairline or painted her lips for a more dramatic effect, though her teachers usually told her to wipe it off.

Sometimes she spread it on her teeth and smiled wide, just to give them a fright. There wasn't much to entertain in the House of Bone, frigid and isolated on the northernmost tip of the Dominions, so Wren had to make do.

Not tonight, though. Tonight Wren would play by the rules . . . for once.

If she passed the trial, she would serve for life as a valkyr of the House of Bone. In the Dominions, where magic welled up from deep in the earth, the dead lingered—violent and unpredictable—unless a bonesmith severed the ghost from its earthly remains. That was the duty of the reapyr.

But not all ghosts went quietly. Some put up a fight, so it was the valkyr's task to defend the reapyr from the undead.

Without the House of Bone, ghosts would overrun their land, making it uninhabitable, as it had been for centuries. Their work was more than a job or a calling. It was a *necessity*.

But that didn't mean Wren couldn't enjoy it.

In contrast to their blacks, the valkyrs also wore bones. They wore them fastened to their forearms as gauntlets and their chests as breastplates, and bone weapons were strapped across shoulders and in belts or loaded as artillery into bandoliers.

They all had their favorites—Wren wore twin swords in sheaths on her back, while Leif had a broad ax made of sharpened pelvic bone and Inara carried a flail with a spiked skull on the end.

In short, they were dressed for war. The battlefield was the Bonewood, and the enemy was the undead.

Though they would one day be allies, tonight the other valkyr novitiates were Wren's rivals, her competition—sons and daughters of the House of Bone and its various branches, or upstart nobodies from across the Dominions who somehow found themselves with bonesmith blood. Cousins and distant relations, strangers and outsiders, but not friends. Not family.

Her father had explained it to her during one of their rare conversations: They were linked by *magic*, not love. *Duty*, not affection.

That was the way of the House of Bone.

Wren had worked hard, had scraped and clawed to get here. She was the best damn valkyr novitiate her house had seen in years, and tonight she would *prove* it in front of everyone: her teachers and instructors, Lady-Smith Svetlana Graven—head of the House of Bone—and most of all, her father.

"Psst," whispered a voice from her right.

Inara.

Of all Wren's cousins, Inara Fell was the biggest threat to her superiority among the valkyrs—and her only worthy adversary. They were of an age and had comparable height and build, so they were often paired together for lessons and exercises, though the similarities ended there. Inara had coarse black hair, carefully arranged in rows of tight braids, while her ivory bonesmith eyes stood out starkly against her brown skin. Wren, meanwhile, had wild bone-white hair—always tangled and unkempt—and eyes to match, her skin equally pale and colorless. Inara was organized, by the book, and always on time. Wren was more *intuitive*, coming and going as she pleased, and considered rules as *suggestions* more than laws to follow to the letter.

The two of them had been at each other's throats for as long as she could remember, but after tonight, they'd go their separate ways. Once they passed their trial, they'd each be paired with a reapyr and sent to travel the Dominions, performing death rites and battling dangerous ghosts, ensuring *all* the dead were reaped. Elsewise, they might be lost and forgotten for centuries until some hapless fool dug them back up and unleashed an undead horde.

Like what had happened at the Breach—the darkest challenge the bonesmiths had ever faced. But it was in such times that heroes were forged and legends were made, like Wren's uncle Locke Graven.

She longed for such notoriety, and one day she would achieve it. But first she had to pass the Bonewood Trial.

"Shut up," she said to Inara, not turning her head. She was generally in favor of whispered conversation—the more inopportune the time, the better—but tonight was far too important for Wren to allow herself to get distracted.

The terms of the trial were simple: Each valkyr and reapyr pair must pass safely through the Bonewood, reaping three ghosts along the way. They had until dawn.

But the Bonewood did not suffer travelers lightly. There were ghosts there that did not sleep, undead that would never find peace.

And that was to say nothing of the living.

Wren had to protect her reapyr from violent ghosts *and* contend with the other valkyrs making their way through the trees. Valkyrs like Inara, who would love nothing more than to see her fail.

"Want to make things interesting?" Inara pressed. For someone who loved to toe the line, she was being surprisingly insistent tonight.

"I'm talking to *you*," Wren drawled. "I'm not sure that's possible."

Yes, Inara was worthy competition . . . but she was also a constant thorn in Wren's side and always nipping at her heels. Second place in everything, except rule breaking.

In that regard, Wren had no equal.

Inara was unfazed. "You might make things more interesting for *him*, then," she said softly. She spoke to the ground, the pair of them still poised on their knees in the snow, but Wren heard the words clearly. There was only one "him" she could mean.

She glanced up at her father.

Lord-Smith Vance Graven stood next to his mother, Svetlana, atop the podium with the rest of the trial's judges. As heir to the House of Bone, he was required to witness certain events—whether his only child participated in them or not.

He gave her the subtlest of nods. Acknowledgment, yes, but also a reminder.

"I'm counting on you today," he had said to her mere hours before. They'd stood inside the training grounds of Marrow Hall, bone-white pillars arching over them and black sand underfoot. "Make me proud."

To Wren, it sounded like a challenge. She hadn't seen him for three months, and she was determined to make him *more* than proud. She wanted to make him *stay*, even just for a little while.

She lifted her chin. "Yes, Father."

He'd surveyed her for several silent moments, then given her a reluctant, indulgent smile. "They tell me you spent half the night sweeping bonedust from the librarian's bookshelves. Why?"

Wren couldn't help but smirk back at him. She shrugged. "I was bored."

Technically true. She'd climbed the bookshelves on a dare because she'd been bored during lessons, and when the librarian caught her three stories high with her dirty boots perched on a first edition of *The Gravedigger's Watch*, the cleaning had been the eventual punishment.

Her father's pale eyes danced, reading between the lines as he often did. Whenever he came home for a visit, however rarely, he asked Wren about her various studies—and accompanying punishments—with a serious air, like he was *looking* for something. For proof of her abilities? Or lack thereof? The topic was dull, even to her, so it seemed only proper, then, that her antics should entertain him. It was the least she could do.

He sighed, going for stern, but the amusement was still there in his gaze. Wren lived for that spark. Though he'd never own up to it, Wren had heard stories of Vance Graven as a young bonesmith, and he was at least as much of a troublemaker as she was. In fact, given Wren's problematic origins, he was more so.

"I do hope the lack of sleep won't affect your performance in the trial," he said, the smallest amount of censure there.

Wren shook her head resolutely. "Never."

He nodded, then turned to survey the rest of the novitiates who continued to practice in the training sands. Forgetting her already.

"In fact," she added, reclaiming his attention. "I'd been planning on staying up anyway—acclimate to the night trial, you know—so the librarian did me a favor."

His lips quirked. "I suppose that also explains why you slept until noon and missed morning lessons?"

Wren beamed. "Exactly."

His focus shifted back to the other novitiates, Inara among them, and Wren had the sudden urge to tell him about the things she *hadn't* screwed up lately. "I'm undefeated in our sparring class, and—"

He spoke over her as if he hadn't heard. "Your grandmother is watching you, Wren. You must be careful. She will take any excuse to fail you." His gaze returned to hers. "Do not give her one. You cannot simply pass tonight. . . . You must pass *spectacularly*. Do you understand?"

Now, with the Bonewood Trial mere moments away, Wren tilted her head toward Inara. "What did you have in mind?"

Inara smiled, and behind her, Ethen—her reapyr novitiate for the trial—exchanged a look with Wren's novitiate, Sonya. This was not Wren's and Inara's first time going toe-to-toe, and their conflicts rarely ended without some form of collateral damage. Both reapyrs likely feared they might be it.

"A race," Inara said, darting a glance up into the trees before looking down again. "First one through wins."

That was already, more or less, the purpose of the trial. It was not timed, but being last to finish would not look good. Everyone wanted to be first, Wren most of all.

"And the second one through?"

Inara turned her head enough to frown, as if the answer were obvious. *"Loses."*

Wren smirked. It was sufficient motivation for both of them, but . . . "That hardly makes things interesting. I plan on winning whether you dare me to or not."

Inara licked her lips, her gaze fixed on the ground. "If you win, I'll give you Nightstalker."

That caught Wren's attention. Nightstalker was the Fell ancestral dagger, currently sitting in Inara's open hands and gleaming in the moonlight.

Like Wren's own blade, it had a long history within the House of Bone and had belonged to dozens of talented valkyrs over the years—most recently, Inara's mother. She had been Wren's father's schoolhouse rival, just as Inara was hers.

How sweet would it be to lay claim to such a weapon? To show her father that she had not only outclassed her greatest competition—and in a lesser way, *his*—but now possessed *two* valkyr blades?

They were more than just practical weapons; they were symbols of the valkyr order itself, representative of their place within the House of Bone. They were not given lightly and could only be taken by a worthy opponent during a formal challenge. Or by the head of the house if a blade bearer was deemed unworthy.

Wren couldn't imagine a more powerful way to prove herself. To be spectacular.

There was, however, a flip side to the arrangement.

"And if I win," Inara continued, "you give me Ghostbane."

Wren's dagger, and her father's dagger before her. It felt heavy suddenly, sitting in her palms, causing her arms to tremble with the weight.

Once this night was through, Wren would either have two ancestral blades . . . or none.

But with or without the bet, she had no intention of *losing*, as Inara put it, and not coming first. Then again . . .

You cannot simply pass tonight. . . . You must pass spectacularly.

"Oh, one more thing," Inara added, with the superiority of someone who has set the bait and is ready to release the trap. "We have to take the Spine."

The Spine. It was the hardest path between the trees, slicing right through the middle of the forest. It was the shortest way, but also the oldest and most severely haunted, traversing the very heart of the Bonewood.

It was the surest way to run into trouble, even if they weren't traveling together. But they were. They'd be directly in each other's path the whole way through, which presented its own opportunities and obstacles. Much as Wren flouted the rules on principle, she didn't intend to *sabotage* Inara. But if they traveled together, she *could*.

And, of course, Inara could sabotage her, too. Doubtful, since Inara was a teacher's pet who loved the rules, but this was the Bonewood Trial. The stakes had never been higher.

It would be risky, and reckless, and make what was already a challenging test twice as dangerous.

You cannot simply pass tonight. . . . You must pass spectacularly.

A horn call sounded, making Wren jump. She looked up at the moon, just now cresting the highest branches. She lurched to a standing position along with the others, her grip on her dagger achingly tight.

She glanced at her father once more; then her gaze shifted to Inara. "You're on."

The moon cleared the bonetrees.

All eyes fell on Lady-Smith Svetlana. It was she who had called them to arms in the first place.

Ready your blade.

And it was she who spoke again now.

"Defeat the undead."

The Bonewood Trial had begun.

TWO

The forest was ten miles wide and another ten deep. Some said the ancient bonesmiths had been giants, their limbs as long as Wren was tall—but it was more likely that they had stretched and distorted the bonetrees, making them narrow and spindly or thick as oaks.

That was the magic of the bonesmiths, the ability to sense, move, and manipulate dead bones without touch. Within a ten-foot radius, bonesmiths could summon a bone to their hand, guide its movements in midair, or heft bones much heavier than their muscles alone could bear. Valkyrs like Wren carried bone weapons, their magic lending them extra speed and strength, as well as pinpoint accuracy.

Bonesmiths could also see spiritual tethers—the fibers that connected the ghost to its bones—that were indistinguishable to the non-bonesmith eye.

If Wren was totally honest, they were often invisible to *her* eye as well. It came down to training and natural talent—the former of which Wren hadn't bothered with, knowing that it was the realm of the reapyrs and she was meant to be a valkyr, and the latter she'd simply been born without.

Reapyrs had a more delicate touch, able to detect and label every bump and groove, and were better at sensing and locating the anchor bone—the bone that connected the ghost to the body. While all bones in a dead body contained some trace of the spirit, the anchor bone was the strongest. It was usually the bone nearest the mortal wound that had killed the person, or in the case of death by illness or age, the bone nearest the ailment or first organs that started to fail.

The anchor bone was also the most coveted by bonesmith fabricators, who used a combination of tools and their magical touch to create armor, weapons, and talismans. They could shape rib cages into breastplates and carve femurs into longswords, or pulverize knuckles into bonedust. The possibility of crafting her own weapons certainly held some manner of appeal for Wren, but the idea of being locked away inside Marrow Hall's catacombs for the rest of her life did not.

As such, it was valkyr or bust for Wren. Their job was the most dangerous, and Wren loved nothing more than a challenge.

And for valkyr novitiates, there was no greater challenge than the Bonewood.

It was filled with *undead* bones, haunted by ghosts and beyond a bonesmith's magical reach. Only by fighting back their spirits and allowing the reapyr to cut the tether to their bodies could the bonesmiths use and manipulate their bones. In one swift move, bonesmiths made the world safe from ghosts and acquired the materials to do so. After all, there was nothing that ghosts hated more than dead bone. It was the bonesmith's first and best protection against them.

It was a tough job, but *somebody* had to do it, and Wren was only too happy to oblige.

But the Bonewood was more than a haunted forest—it was a maze, dense and confusing. Marking the barrier to the House of Bone's lands, the Bonewood doubled as a line of defense and was filled with the bodies of would-be attackers and trespassers.

And just because there were trails through the wood did not mean those routes were safe. Stray off the path to find a shorter road—or one less haunted—and risk never finding your way again.

Many novitiates would rather travel twice as far and take twice as long than have to encounter a ghost higher than a two on the undead scale.

But not Wren.

She smiled fiercely at Inara before striding toward the bonetrees. Her reapyr followed, while Inara and her reapyr—as well as the other pairs on either side—did the same. When Wren moved toward the entrance to the Spine, Inara close behind, the other pairs balked and shook their heads, choosing safer routes.

Wren thrived off their doubt, but the instant she stepped into the trees, her attention sharpened and her focus was honed.

The Spine was not, in fact, a real path, but rather a rough route through the forest, demarcated by old smears of red paint against the pale trees. That meant Wren and Inara would not actually be walking *together*, hand in hand like lost children from a fable, but following their own instincts and choosing their own way, ever heading toward the next flash of red.

The only light came from the moon above, obstructed by soaring bone branches that creaked and rattled together, drifting in an undead wind Wren could not feel—and, of course, from the ghosts.

There were surely thousands of them, some bright as the sun but with an eerie, green-white light and others as soft as a guttering

—13

candle, begging for release. Some were mere wisps of vapor without shape or form—tier ones—while others were nearly solid, their edges sharp and clearly defined. Tier twos. No matter how dense and substantial, there was no way to mistake any of them for the living. Their bodies rippled in the same, unearthly wind as the bones, and their features were stretched and distorted or flickering in and out of existence like flashes of lightning. There were animals among them too, swooping bats or stalking snow cats, and the lot of them blurred together between the trees.

With a small amount of distance now between herself and Inara, Wren turned to Sonya. It was the valkyr's job to lead, to choose the safest path and soundest strategy, but the most successful pairs worked together in well-balanced harmony. While Wren had never been the best team player, she tried to include Sonya so the reapyr could do her job properly.

Wren needed her, after all.

"How do you want to play this?"

There were numerous different strategies they could implement for the trial. Tier-one ghosts were virtually harmless, but that was because their tether to their bones was weak. That made finding their earthly remains more difficult, even if trying to do so was safer. The higher on the undead scale, the more corporeal the ghost—and the stronger the connection to their bones—but it also made trying to reap them more dangerous.

Targeting tier ones would mean a nice, safe trial . . . but the reapings would be slower. Not ideal in a race that had an extra bet with a lifelong rival tacked on. Targeting more dangerous ghosts would be faster, but the likelihood of mistake and injury higher.

The likelihood of *failure* higher.

It wasn't terribly common, but it *did* happen—a reapyr and valkyr pair got lost and failed only the previous year—and would mean another year of study at Marrow Hall before the next trial began.

Wren was generally a fan of the chaos approach: barreling through at top speed and choosing targets on the fly. She didn't like to back down from a fight, but if a ghost was too volatile, they'd leave it and move on. If a ghost was too weak, it likely wasn't worth the time and effort.

"Take them as they come?" she prodded as Sonya chewed on her lip, uncertainty written on her face. "Avoid ones and fives?" Wren quirked a smile. There were no fives in the Bonewood. In fact, they shouldn't even exist. Only in the Haunted Territory to the east, behind the Border Wall, did the bones of the undead walk *with* their ghosts—and that was because of the Breach. Apparently, if you dug deep enough, like the ironsmiths had, you could unearth all manner of surprises . . . including hundreds of buried corpses flush with dark power and happy to be set loose.

Those walking undead—or revenants—had been the work of ancient ghostsmiths, a long-extinct order of necromancers shunned by the rest of society for using their magic to command and control the undead. Even Wren, who loved nothing more than a good fight with a ghost, suppressed a shiver at the thought of them. Thankfully, the ghostsmith civilization had been buried by some sort of cataclysm centuries ago, and anyone who possessed their abilities was buried with it. Unfortunately, just before Wren was born, the ironsmiths' mining had dredged their lost world back up along with their undead creations. It was because of the Breach that bonesmiths had to come up with the undead scale in the first place.

While the *idea* of tier fives in the Bonewood might make her smile, Wren had no desire to face one tonight.

Sonya's gaze flicked over Wren's shoulder—in the direction of Inara and Ethen—and she nodded. "S-sure. What you said. Take them as they come."

Like the valkyr novitiates, the reapyrs also dressed in black, but while Wren's blacks consisted of formfitting leather and thick, padded layers, the reapyrs wore long, sweeping robes that dragged across the snow—a bit dramatic, honestly. They bore no weapons save for the scythe: the curved, handheld blade used to make the final cut. Each bone in a body contained a complex web of ley lines—these were the seams, the places where ghost met bone, the junctures that could hold the two together or the fissures that could wrench them apart. It was the reapyr's business to identify the ley lines and sever them, releasing the spirit.

"Stay behind me," Wren advised, sheathing Ghostbane and withdrawing one of the twin bone swords strapped across her back. It gave her a longer reach and was better suited for the task at hand.

As Wren and Sonya moved through the trees, the sound of the others faded, and a tense silence rose to take its place. Not true silence, but the heavy, weighted silence of the undead.

Wren's magic could sense the bones all around—humming like a current against her skin—and her eyes caught every shift and movement, waiting, watching . . .

When a bowed arm—no, *arms*, twisted and fused together with three or four elbows—leaned precariously over their path, Wren held out her sword to stop their forward progress.

She approached the monstrous tree warily, but closer inspection revealed the bones were dead and unhaunted, as she'd expected, crafted by some creative and slightly disturbed bonesmith long ago. Bone transformations undertaken while the ghost was still attached, performed on undead or even—Wren shuddered—*living* bones, were impossible.

"Don't tell me you're afraid of a few extra elbows," called Inara, who was closer than Wren realized and watching them through the trees.

Wren smiled stiffly and used both hands to bring her sword down in a flashy move, cutting through the many-elbowed tree with one fell swoop. Her blade might have been made from the same material as the tree, but it had been sharpened and hardened under a fabricator's careful touch and was almost as strong as steel.

Splintered bits of bone littered the ground at her feet, combining with the fresh snow to create a pale and brittle forest floor that crunched and crackled underfoot.

A cloud of bonedust settled onto Sonya's pristine black robes.

"Whoops," Wren murmured in false concern, reaching out a hand to swipe at it.

Sonya stepped out of reach and rolled her eyes, flicking her wrist and causing the dust to rise from the fabric and disperse in an instant. It was the kind of delicate work Wren could never have achieved and that characterized a reapyr's talent. Wren was fairly average for a bonesmith in terms of magical ability, and while she was capable of powerful bursts, she was not much good at subtlety or finesse.

Sonya wasn't a friend, exactly, but hardly anyone in the House of Bone really was. Wren had enemies like Inara and then people who tolerated her like Sonya. Her father was her only emotional touchstone, and he was never there.

It was tempting to wish for more—and certainly she had, when she was younger. Looking for a mother who was alive or a father who would stay, but any time someone started to fill the hole her parents left behind, her father would turn up again, and she'd forget whatever surrogate she'd attached herself to. The truth was, she wanted something real, even if it was painful.

That was the point of all this. *Pass spectacularly* and be named a valkyr. Then she'd actually get to leave Marrow Hall and travel—sometimes *with* her father—fighting ghosts in every corner of the Dominions, from Giltmore to Granite Gate and everywhere in between.

They were about to press on when something raised her hackles.

She whirled around just in time to see a silver-green mist rise. A ghost, floating mere feet away and with a direct path to Sonya, called into existence thanks to their presence and drawn, as all undead were, to the living.

The disfigured arm had been keeping the ghost at bay, but now that it lay in broken pieces upon the ground—perhaps Wren *shouldn't* have hacked that arm to bits just to show off for Inara?—the spirit had free rein to move across the path.

Wren didn't wait to see what it would do next. She jerked Sonya aside and stepped forward, reaching into the bandolier across her chest, releasing a handful of knucklebones. They shot out in a small burst of magic, piercing the vaporous form and causing it to slow its pace, swirling and undulating in the air.

It was probably a tier-one ghost, incorporeal to the point of almost being no threat at all, but Wren couldn't risk being fooled by a two or three that had yet to take its shape. She waited a second more to see what it would do, and much to her satisfaction, it began to coalesce into something human-shaped. Or at least, it had a face, with a wide, gaping mouth—stretched and distorted—and long, trailing limbs.

"What do you think?" she called over her shoulder.

While Wren's attention was on the ghost itself, Sonya's attention was lower, on the ground, seeking the body the spirit was still tethered to. She dropped onto her knees in the snow, a small spade in her hands.

The shovel hit the dirt below with a soft thump and scrape, but it wasn't long until Sonya was scrabbling through the snow and soil with her bare hands, relying upon touch and magical senses as she sought the ghost's bones.

Wren watched, itching to help dig and speed things along, but that went against a cardinal rule of valkyr-reapyr training. No matter how seemingly benign, never turn your back on the ghost. Never let your guard down.

It was also why she didn't just slash at the specter as she had that many-elbowed arm.

She might get the ghost to disappear entirely as it recoiled from the dead bone, but such a reprieve was only temporary. There was no telling how quickly it would return . . . or *where*. Better to keep it trapped in her line of sight than to dispatch it now and have it turn up behind her back or directly on top of them.

So Wren did as she had been trained and withdrew her second bone sword, holding them before her like scissors, trapping the spirit within. A stronger ghost would fight back, but this one only ebbed and swirled with mild and uninspiring menace.

To Wren's delight, Sonya made a soft exclamation of pleasure and lifted a muddy femur from a pile of bones in the dirt.

The anchor bone.

With her attention split between the wobbling, silently trembling ghost and the reapyr at her feet, Wren watched as Sonya lay the mottled, off-white bone against the stark white snow. She withdrew her scythe and closed her eyes. Her muddy hand ran the length of the bone once, twice, three times. On the fourth she brought the weapon down on the invisible ley line, cracking into the bone and severing the connection between the ghost and its earthly remains.

There was a familiar, sucking sensation, leaving the air in Wren's lungs sparse, and a heartbeat later, the ghost disappeared in a puff of cold air and ether.

As Sonya collected the now-dead bone and got to her feet, Wren cleared the area, swiping her blades through the air to make sure nothing remained, then gathered her scattered knucklebones for later use.

As she did so, she caught sight of a spectator between the trees.

"One already," she said, smiling smugly at Inara. "Try to keep up."

THREE

The deeper they moved into the Bonewood, the more tightly packed the trees became, their swaying branches knocking together and snagging the fabric of Sonya's robe. She brushed the bone aside with a casual wave of her hand, while Wren preferred to keep her swords raised to discourage their grasping reach.

The ghosts, too, were more plentiful, though the majority were tier ones, hanging in the air like fog or swirling in an unseen current like woodsmoke. They spotted what looked like a tier two, but it was too far off the path—trying to lure them into the darkness like a will-o'-the-wisp—and a tier one that glowed so brightly Sonya had to look away until Wren dispatched it.

Their next reaping came nearly an hour later.

They spotted the bones before they saw the ghost, so when the glowing form suddenly appeared out of nowhere, angry and violent, both Sonya *and* Wren—much to her embarrassment—leapt back in alarm.

Wren recovered first, swords raised, but the ghost wasn't interested in her. It had surely been a bonesmith in life, its vaguely human shape draped in a wispy fabric that could have easily been a reapyr's robes, and it focused on Sonya with single-minded intent that suggested it knew exactly what they were about. Reaping might provide peace, but the undead wanted to *live*, just like everything else.

When it crashed against Wren's swords with a physical impact strong enough to make her boots slide in the slush beneath her feet, Wren realized it wasn't just a self-aware tier three. It was able to affect the world around it. Only a tier four—also called a geist—and higher could do that.

Sonya quailed, neglecting her task as the ghost drew nearer.

"Hey," Wren barked, glancing away from the ghost for a split second—but that was all it needed. The next time it slammed into her bone blades, heedless of the damage such contact did to its form, Wren *dropped* one of her swords thanks to her distraction.

Sonya cried out and took a hasty step backward, ready to bolt in fear, forgetting another fundamental rule of the death trade: Never run.

The simple, terrible truth was that tier-three and higher ghosts were *fast*. They were able to disappear and reappear in the blink of an eye, or streak across an open field in half the time it took a horse galloping full tilt.

Running was far too dangerous and risked the person running directly *into* the ghost, which would mean instant death or such severe deathrot that they'd be a shell of a person, immobile and in constant pain until they eventually succumbed. Wren had seen the victim of such an attack once—her father had, on Lady-Smith Svetlana's orders, dragged her out of bed and hauled her to the infirmary to witness it firsthand. Wren had hardly ever spoken to her grandmother before then—she hardly ever spoke to her now, either—and had approached with wary fear.

"I'm not sure—" her father had said, trying, perhaps, to protect Wren, but Svetlana quickly shut him down. Then he just stood there, silent and unflinching, while the woman's clawlike hands gripped Wren's narrow six-year-old shoulders and forced her to hover next to the bed until the dying man's last, choking breath.

After, her father's voice had seemed kind, almost gentle, as he said, "This is the price of failure in the House of Bone."

Wren would not fail now.

"Sonya," she snapped, using her now free hand to dig into her bandolier. The reapyr halted, her gaze fixed on the quivering spirit. "The bones."

Turning back to the ghost, Wren sent more knuckles hurtling outward, slicing holes clean through the misty shape, but the attack seemed only to enrage the spirit further.

Wren cursed and picked up her fallen sword just in time for the next impact. The ghost's form hissed and crackled like a flame against water as it connected with her blades.

It was time to try something different.

Before it could gather itself for another violent surge, Wren went on the offensive. Instead of fighting defensively and protectively, as valkyrs were trained, she angled her body and stepped *forward*, her swords outstretched. The movement drove the ghost back and away. Creating space between it and its bones.

The spirit did not like this. It was like separating a shoulder from a socket—unnatural and uncomfortable.

In response, the ghost fought harder and more erratically, but

Wren could take it. *She* drew its rage and attention, not her reapyr, allowing Sonya to work.

The move was risky, of course. There could be other ghosts nearby, waiting to pounce, and valkyrs were taught to never let their reapyr out of arm's reach.

But it worked. Sonya gripped the haunted bone—the clavicle, in this case—and performed the cut with a somewhat shaky hand. The scythe fractured the bone and severed the ley line, and the ghost disappeared.

Wren whooped in delight. Sonya looked like she wanted to be sick.

"Almost there," Wren said cheerfully, already imagining Inara's sour expression when she handed over Nightstalker. Then she thought of her father's face, glowing with pride when Wren held two blades before Lady-Smith Svetlana and swore her fealty.

She had lost sight of Inara and Ethen, but she and Sonya were already two-thirds of the way through their task, and they'd yet to hit the midway point of their journey—or their timeline. Judging by the moon above, they had at least three hours left until dawn, and they'd been at it for about two.

To her surprise, it was Sonya who pushed hard to find their next reaping, forgoing Wren's offer to take a short break—not that Wren minded. The sooner they had Sonya's task done, the sooner they could focus on speed. Wren would go all night if it were up to her, and she was eager to reach the center of the forest. She had heard all manner of rumors about the deepest parts of the Bonewood. Cook said the very first bone in the entire forest was "planted" there by the Gravedigger himself, founder of the House of Bone and the first-ever bonesmith, and the hostler swore there was a dragon skeleton deep in the trees, the ghost unreaped, though Wren's father insisted that was nothing more than peasant superstition. No one had ever seen such a creature, nor was there an official record of one. The largest bones they had were from mammoths or whales. Still, Wren imagined fighting some great beast's spirit and carrying *that* skull back to her father as their third and final reaping, and swelled at the thought.

As it turned out, their third reaping *was* an animal, but nothing so fantastic as a dragon. The elk had impressive antlers though, jutting from the ground where Sonya had unearthed it.

The deer's spirit was utterly peaceful in comparison to the bonesmith ghost they'd just reaped, and while Wren enjoyed fighting human spirits, she found the animal undead almost soothing. They didn't understand life and death, like people, and seemed to exist much as they did when they were alive, without all the angst and torment. It also meant their spirits didn't linger long in this world. Most animal ghosts would disappear on their own over time—even those that had been domesticated or kept as pets would rarely last longer than a few months after their corpse had decayed—and since they provided little threat to the living, they were rarely properly reaped by a bonesmith. Instead, they could be found scattered across the Dominions in forests and fields, like fireflies, carefully avoided by the living until they eventually winked out.

As such, the reaping was swift, and while an animal was as easy to deal with as a standard tier one, it still counted toward the trial, and Wren wasn't about to be picky. Not with so much on the line. She helped Sonya load their third and final bone—the long, narrow-faced skull complete with antlers attached—into the reapyr's satchel, and they pressed on.

Triumphant and flushed with adrenaline, Wren perked up when

they reached a clearing. Could it be the center of the Bonewood? The entire place was hazy and lit with the barest hint of ghostlight, as if whatever undead lurked here were so incredibly ancient that they existed only as the tiniest of molecules, barely discernible to the naked eye.

They approached a gigantic rib cage, the cartilage gone and the bones open and gaping like some monstrous flower, reaching for the moon. It must have belonged to a mammoth, each individual rib longer than Wren was tall.

And standing in the middle of it was Inara. Ethen was next to her, sitting on a moss-covered stone, and they both had pieces of dark bread in hand.

At Wren and Sonya's approach, Ethen leapt to his feet, his wary gaze flicking to his valkyr.

A knot Wren hadn't realized was there eased at the sight of them. She was relieved to know that Inara hadn't managed to get far ahead—and better yet, judging from the two bones poking out from Ethen's satchel, they had yet to finish their third reaping.

"Come on, Sonya," Wren said, smiling victoriously, as if she had already won. Forget the dragon—this was their chance to make some headway. They could eat as they walked.

She made for the far trees without a backward glance.

Footsteps crunched behind her, but it took Wren a second to realize they were moving away from her, not toward.

She whirled back around. Inara had taken several steps toward Sonya, though she halted well short of her.

"Did you get them?" Inara asked the reapyr. Sonya nodded, gaze fixed on the ground.

"Sonya," Wren said, brow furrowed in confusion. Sonya ignored her.

"Come on, then," Inara said.

Then, to Wren's surprise, Sonya obeyed. Instead of going to Wren's side, she went to Inara's, skirting the edges of the massive rib cage to stand next to Ethen.

Wren's gaze went to Inara's, realization dawning. "What do you think you're doing?" she demanded. Inara's face revealed nothing, and both Ethen and Sonya refused to look at her. "You think you can just—what, hold my reapyr hostage?" She laughed incredulously and shook her head. "*Sonya*," she said again, keeping her voice calm and reasonable as she spoke over Inara's shoulder. "We're almost there. Let's finish this. Whatever she's promised you, whatever she's said . . . it's not worth it. They could exile you for this."

Sonya wavered, fear flashing across her features, but Inara's hand shot out, holding her in place. Wren wondered what threats or promises had gotten Sonya to her side. The Fells were rich and influential. Ruthless. But not stupid.

This was a bold move for Inara. Risky to the point of reckless. It was, admittedly, something Wren might do.

"Fine. I'll just tell them what happened when I get there." She shrugged, hoping she looked more unconcerned than she felt.

"Who would ever believe you?" Inara said, smiling sweetly. "I'm a model student and bonesmith. *You're* the rulebreaker in this house, not me."

The validity of that caused unease to flicker inside Wren's chest.

Inara's smile stretched wider, as if she could see it. "Poor Wren," she said with mock sympathy. "Daddy will be so disappointed in you. Not only will you fail, but you'll have bargained away his precious ancestral blade. The one thing in this house he *actually* cares about."

"Shut your mouth," Wren snapped, her heart pounding. She

withdrew Ghostbane and took an angry step toward her cousin. "You want this blade? You'll have to pry it from my cold, dead hands."

"It would be my pleasure," Inara said, her hand dropping to the hilt of Nightstalker.

Inara was goading her—that much was plain. They were several feet apart, and it was taking all Wren had *not* to attack her. But while Inara's sabotage left no visual evidence that Wren could discern, if Inara returned with a bloody nose—or worse—it would be far too easy to point the finger at Wren. Backstabbing happened all the time in the Bonewood Trial, but those who did it were smart enough not to *actually* stab anyone in the back. Tricks and traps, bargains and mind games—these were the weapons most bonesmiths wielded against each other.

Most, but not all.

Wren sheathed her dagger, took a slow, steadying breath—then swung her clenched fist and punched Inara hard in the gut. If Inara wanted to hurt her where no one could see, Wren would do the same.

Inara keeled over, scrambling backward in a surprising show of cowardice. Blood pounding in her ears, Wren pursued.

One step, then another, until suddenly—the ground gave way.

Her breath caught in her throat as she fell, crashing into a heap of dead bones and sliding snow. Once the initial shock wore off, pain radiated through her body, stinging across a dozen cuts and scrapes and aching bruises sure to come. Coughing, she got gingerly to her feet.

She was in a small pit, rising several feet over her head and a foot or so wider than her arm span on either side. But the sloping ground was slick with mud and snow, and when Wren tried to scrabble upward, more of the soil gave way, cascading down upon her . . . along with the truth.

Inara had dug this hole—had set her up from the very start. She had initiated the bet, dictated the route, then waited here for Wren's arrival. She'd lured her close—taking that punch and scampering away like a dog with its tail between its legs—just so Wren would follow, would step in this exact place. . . .

"*Inara*," she growled, swiping at bits of mud and bone stuck to her face. In fact, there were bones everywhere, small and large, broken and whole, saturating her senses and humming against her skin.

Inara leaned over the edge of the pit wearing a gloating smile, though she was still hunched from the blow to her stomach. "What was that? I can't hear you from all the way—" She froze, and a second later, Wren felt it too.

There was a creaking sound, a rumble, and then the ground beneath Wren gave way *again*, bringing the sides of the pit along with it. Inara cursed and stumbled backward as the hole widened, while Wren threw her hands over her head and braced for impact.

When she opened her eyes, it was to see that she'd fallen even deeper underground, landing in some kind of cavern, cold and musty and untouched by snow.

Inara wore an expression of shock as she squinted down into the darkness. Wren's anger was hot, but surely Inara hadn't dug *this* deeply.

"Now what are we supposed to do? We can't just leave her down there," Sonya said, somewhat shrilly.

"I told you this was a bad idea," Ethen said, his face chalky and pale.

They were cowards, both of them. At least Inara had the stomach for what she was doing.

"She'll be fine," Inara said, though her voice was slightly breathless. "Won't you, Graven? Best valkyr of our generation, aren't you?" Wren bared her teeth in frustration. She *had* said that, dozens of times, to anyone who would listen, and often to Inara's face.

"You won't get away with this," Wren said, fear tightening her belly as Inara prepared to leave. "My father—"

"Is not the hero you think he is," Inara said softly. "See you on the other side. Don't forget to bring my blade."

Then she walked away, the two reapyrs following close behind, leaving Wren alone in the dark, with a view of nothing but stars and bones and the moon's unwavering progress through the sky.

FOUR

"Fuck!" Wren shouted, the word reverberating off the cavern walls and echoing out into the night. She clenched her hands into fists to stop them from shaking.

It didn't work.

She kicked and punched and spat, raging at everything and everyone, but at herself most of all. How could she have let this happen? She had been halfway there, her victory within reach, and she'd allowed Inara *fucking* Fell, perpetual second-best and shameless bootlicker, to snatch it away from her.

Wren halted, her chest heaving. She stared up at the sky, and the moon stared back at her.

There was still time.

She had until dawn, and Inara and Ethen needed to do one last reaping, which gave Wren a chance to catch up. All she had to do was get out of this Digger-damned *grave* Inara had somehow managed to drop her into.

She examined her surroundings more closely. The opening above was at least twice her height, and the earth was surprisingly muddy and wet underneath the snow that had fallen down with her. It was early winter, and though the cold never really left the Northern Dominions, the ground was soft enough to allow Inara to dig this hole and set her trap.

But how? As Inara had pointed out, Wren was the rulebreaker in the House of Bone, and even she had never managed to get into the Bonewood on her own. Had Inara gotten outside help? And from whom? Her mother, perhaps? Ingrid Fell hated Wren's father and had been vying for power and influence alongside him for most of their lives.

Pushing those thoughts aside, Wren considered all she'd brought with her. She carried her swords and her dagger, knucklebones, and pouches of bonedust, but she had, unsurprisingly, not brought any climbing or grappling tools. In her defense, of all the things she'd thought to prepare for, her conniving cousin burying her alive wasn't one of them.

But Wren was resourceful. She pressed her hands into the muddy sides of the pit, feeling a distant tingle from bones embedded within, and while the outer layer was indeed soft and slick, the deeper she pushed, the more solid the ground became. The digging was what had made the earth so unstable, but just past the surface, firm, semi-frozen soil remained. It was, however, impossible to get a proper hold with her bare hands.

She grinned. It was a good thing she had her blades.

The first sword sank nearly to the hilt into the muck, just above Wren's right shoulder. She did a cursory tug, then let it take her full body weight.

It held.

She fixed the second sword higher and to the left. The angle was more difficult, but she pushed and hammered on the grip, using her magic to help the blade along until it, too, was stable enough to bear her weight.

Wren was a good climber, light on her feet and agile—she had proven that on the library bookshelves. But the hard part was yet to come. She would have to remove and reinsert one blade while dangling from the other, repeating the action several times if she wanted to make it to the top. She could shove her booted feet into the holes the swords left behind, but it would still be a tall order.

As she stepped back to admire her handiwork and wipe her slimy hands for the climb, she stumbled over something. Not solid and firm, like bare bone, nor slick like melted snow or mud. Instead, it was soft and . . . squishy.

She looked down.

It was a body.

Not a skeleton, ancient and eroded. No, this was *fresh* . . . or at least, fresher than it should be. Too fresh to make sense. They'd stopped disposing of bodies in the Bonewood decades ago. It had originated as a way to defend their borders and ward off attack, but that was in the time before the Dominions, when dozens of rulers vied for power and control over these lands. Now, in times of peace, such protections were no longer necessary.

The corpse Wren was looking at now, though partially preserved thanks to the cold, could not have been there much longer than a few years . . . five, tops.

The flesh was mottled, the features gaunt but not fully decomposed. Even the clothing was well preserved, the thick layers of wool and leather and mud-spattered boots telling her this person had undertaken a long journey before they'd arrived here. Had they been a wayward traveler? A messenger? There was nothing else to indicate who they were or how they'd wound up here.

Well, that wasn't true. There was *one* piece of evidence that pointed to how this person had wound up dead in the Bonewood.

The back of their head was caved in.

It was certainly the death blow, but the more Wren looked, the more unease she felt.

This person had not wandered into the wood and gotten *lost*—the crushed skull was proof of that. They had been killed and disposed of in the one place in the Bonelands where a dead body might go unnoticed.

No death rites. No reaping. And hidden in the Bonewood.

Lost, never to be found again.

Until now.

The manner of death fueled a ghost's spiritual existence. A peaceful death meant a peaceful ghost. An old, tired death meant an old, tired ghost.

A death on a battlefield amid violence and hatred left behind a violent, hateful ghost.

But there was nothing more violent or hateful than cold-blooded murder.

It was clear to Wren that this death had not been peaceful or tired, and a blow to the back of the head meant a surprise attack—a cowardly attack. The Bonewood was no battlefield . . . at least, not for those outside the House of Bone, which this person surely was. They carried no bones, wore no armor; they had no weapons of any kind that she could see.

For a moment Wren just stood there, frozen, wary of disturbing the body further than she already had.

Ghosts didn't instantly detach from their bodies with death. That separation took time. How much time usually depended on the state of the body, which acted as a sort of container and camouflage for the soul.

Not only did it trap a ghost, but it obscured a bonesmith's ability to detect bones. It was one of the reasons why bonesmiths couldn't sense or manipulate the bones inside a body, because their flesh acted as a shield.

But a body didn't need to be fully decomposed for the ghost to rise. If the anchor bone was exposed—likely the skull in this case, given the obvious death wound—then the spirit could detach. Just because it hadn't yet didn't mean it wouldn't, either, which made the prospect of turning her back on it in order to climb even more precarious.

But there was nothing for it. She had already lost too much time.

As she turned to go, her gaze landed on a flash of pale white against the muddy ground.

She shifted a piece of stiff, partially frozen fabric to reveal a ring.

It hummed powerfully in Wren's senses, telling her it was made of bone, except . . . bonesmiths didn't make jewelry.

She carefully lifted it from the ground, seeing designs carved into the band's smooth surface—another thing bonesmiths never did. She thought it was a pattern at first, but the odd shapes and lines were actually glyphs of some sort, spanning the entire band. The images nagged at Wren, and she had the feeling she'd seen something similar before.

Turning the object in her hands, she spotted additional carvings. There were two spread-winged birds, one on either side of the flat bezel top, and where a signet or gemstone might be, something dark and polished flashed in the moonlight.

It looked almost like metal, pointed in a spike, and it protruded from the surface of the ring like a nail through a board of wood, its flat head visible on the underside.

It was too small a point to be much good as a weapon, and the longer she examined it, the more confused she felt. There was something distinctly off about that small black spike, the way it pierced the bone. Something *wrong*.

Wren knew of only one kind of material that shone black like that. *Ironsmith* metal.

But the thought of bonesmith and ironsmith artisans coming together to construct such an artifact was difficult to imagine. The Houses of Iron and Bone had been enemies for decades—ever since the ironsmiths had caused the Breach. Wren's father hated them with particular vitriol, but she supposed that was to be expected. He'd been on the front lines of the battles that had followed, and his older brother, Locke—the original heir to the House of Bone—had died in the fighting.

The House of Bone was the Dominions' only chance to stem the flow of walking undead that had poured forth from the Breach, but the bonesmiths had never faced such a threat. There was a reason the ghostsmiths had been exiled in the first place—their necromancy was not only unnatural, but it was a danger to the very survival of the Dominions. The same things that limited ghosts—their incorporeal state and the fact that they couldn't move far from their bodies—were negated by undead that could carry their bones with them.

Tier fives had always fascinated Wren, who loved the idea of testing her skills against the revenants, but as her instructors constantly reminded her, it wasn't all fun and games. Countless people had died at their undead hands, including bonesmiths and ironsmiths, as the lands to the east had been lost one by one to the ever-growing Haunted Territory.

In fact, the Border Wall had been built in an attempt to save the rest of the Dominions from being overrun. It was a massive structure spanning the entire island from north to south, and unfortunately for them, the House of Iron was trapped on the wrong side of it. Even though they had caused the Breach in the first place, the king had offered the House of Iron the chance to relocate to the safe side of the Border Wall, but they'd refused.

Then, barely five years afterward, they staged an uprising, determined to destroy the Border Wall and have both their lands *and* their place in the Dominions—by any means necessary. Once again, the king called upon the House of Bone. Now they were fighting living foes as well as undead ones and were integral in putting the rebellion down and keeping the Border Wall intact.

The ironsmiths had been all but obliterated, the Knights of the Iron Citadel—their ruling bloodline—wiped out, and the House of Bone had lost their shining heir, plus hundreds of other bonesmiths besides.

Wren sometimes wondered if her father had been different, before. Before all the fighting. Before his brother had died. But that was also before Wren had even existed, so she supposed it didn't matter, and he sure wasn't going to tell her.

Needless to say, there was no love lost between their houses. And yet here, in the depths of the House of Bone's territory, was a ring that was at least partially ironsmith-made.

It could easily predate the Iron Uprising and the Breach, of course, but it was still a strange object, and Wren couldn't help her inquisitiveness. It was a character flaw, she'd been told, by her grandmother, her father, and several of her teachers.

She stared at the ring in the palm of her hand—then pocketed it.

Getting to her feet, she moved toward the wall and her swords.

She had barely taken a step when something stirred in the air behind her. An almost-wind brushed the hair along her neck, the slightest touch of cold against her sweat-dampened skin.

She turned her head slowly, hardly daring to breathe, and found herself face-to-face with a newly risen ghost, hovering in the air above the corpse she'd just been examining.

They were barely a foot apart.

Dead spirits took on the last shape they'd known in life, wearing the same clothes, hair, and flesh.

However damaged.

This ghost wore the same travel-worn clothing that lay on the ground at Wren's feet, stained with brightly glowing drops of blood. Light poured from the death wound on the back of its head, causing Wren to squint in the sudden, fierce glare. Ghostlight also emanated from the eyes—windows to the soul, or so her tutors claimed—but thanks to the head wound, the entire face had become little more than a gaping maw of sickly green glow.

But while they might look as they had in life, ghosts did not move like living things.

No, they streaked and exploded into motion, only to halt suddenly, trembling with agitation and pent-up aggression. In many ways, ghosts behaved like fire buffeted in a breeze—just as likely to flicker out as to be stoked to blazing brightness.

Wren blinked furiously, cursing herself for her foolishness—both in exploring the corpse and in leaving her bone blades several feet away and out of reach. She gave several hard tugs with her magic, but they were just at the edge of her range, and the mud held them hostage.

Some ghosts, once unleashed, took time to acclimate to the living world.

This ghost did not.

After a breathless, still moment, it set upon its nearest living target—Wren—with rapid, malicious intent, streaking forward in a terrifying blur.

Wren did the only thing she *could* do: She cried out and fell backward.

The spirit swooped toward her, *over* her, missing her body by inches as it ripped past. The momentum took it careening toward her swords, cutting Wren off from her best weapons.

She scrambled to her knees, jostling more bones.

No, not just bones.

Bodies.

There were others there, in the mud.

With a sinking feeling, Wren realized that of course this giant hole hadn't been dug to bury a single body. It had been dug to bury many. Then years later, this fresh one had been unceremoniously thrown on top.

She had stumbled into a mass grave.

Panic seared her chest. Surely Inara hadn't meant to *kill* her? Not that it mattered. Whether Inara had intended it or not, Wren was in a fight for her life.

There were five at least, maybe closer to ten, though it was difficult to tell with all the random bones that had shifted during her slide down here. Their bodies were older than the first, their bones broken and scattered, but their ghosts would be no less malevolent.

Hand shaking, she withdrew Ghostbane, but it would be of little use.

Already the other undead were rising, filling the cavern with light.

Wren might have had a chance against one ghost, or a handful of tier ones or even twos, but judging by the attentive, violent stares of the undead she had uncovered, they were tier threes at least.

She'd managed to get into a crouch, putting the wall of the cavern behind her, but she was trapped. To her left were her abandoned weapons and the first ghost. To her right, the rest of the steadily rising undead.

Her knucklebones would not stop the ghosts, only anger them, and her bonedust, while having the same ghost-repelling properties as any intact bone, was less powerful. The dust dissipated in the air, making a flimsier barrier than true bone, and was best used in a fight as a distraction or deterrent. It was, however, more versatile, and it *did* have other uses. . . .

While the undead continued to swirl and coalesce into more glowing specters, the first ghost flared brightly, growing in strength.

It was ready for a second attack, which was both good and bad.

Bad because, well, it was a ghost, and one touch would be enough to land her with deathrot and a slow, agonizing death.

Good because it meant the undead would move *away* from her swords—and her best chance for escape.

When it came streaking at her again, its features blurred and distorted, Wren threw herself forward into a roll, avoiding it once again—but only just. The movement also brought her dangerously close to the other ghosts that were stirring but had not yet taken full form.

Staggering to her feet, she made for the newly vacated space across the cavern, near her swords.

For all their speed and supernatural movements, ghosts couldn't fly or climb. They were tethered to the earth the way they had been in life. She just had to get out of their reach, to climb high enough that they couldn't touch her.

So what she needed wasn't to defeat the ten or so undead she was trapped with; she merely needed to stall them, to buy herself time—and space—to climb.

And her bonedust could give her that.

Keeping her eyes on the ghosts before her, Wren withdrew a pouch and poured a hasty half circle in the mud, creating a protective ring around herself.

The magic that enabled a ghost's existence came from the earth, so no matter that they hovered above the ground, they couldn't cross certain barriers. Water, for one, and bones for another. Both were tied too strongly to life, their very nature repellent to the undead.

It was still a risky move. She couldn't enclose herself fully, thanks to the mud wall she was about to climb, and theoretically, a ghost could just pass through the wall and circle around. But that would require problem-solving skills that the undead didn't have. Their attacks were never sneaky or strategic—they were blunt and direct.

That didn't make it any easier for her to stand, sheath her dagger, and turn her back on them.

It felt wrong deep to her core—it went against her training and her instincts. But Wren *needed* to get out of this pit as fast as possible.

She tore the first sword from the soil and jumped to grab the second, hauling herself up and using the momentum to swing her body and reinsert the first sword. Her feet scrabbled in the mud, searching for purchase, when she felt a tingling against her back, followed by stuttering, flickering light. One of them had charged her and made contact with the bonedust barrier, and it held. For now.

Everything inside her wanted to turn, to look, but she feared what she might see—all of them ranged behind her, maybe, ready for attack. The last thing she needed was to stumble in shock, landing in the dust and disturbing the circle. Instead, she heaved, climbing with all the strength she had.

When the top of the pit was within reach, she embedded her swords side by side, and with both arms she managed to drag herself upward, muscles trembling.

Her left toe found one of the vacated sword holes, and it was the leverage she needed. She pulled and then pushed, climbing up and over the swords and cresting the edge.

She gasped, flopping onto her back. With one last shuddering breath, she crawled back to the pit. It was as she'd imagined, the lot of them clustered together just outside the ring of bonedust, ghostlight crackling in agitation as they charged and recoiled again and again.

With shaking hands, she reached over the edge and yanked out her blades, then got wearily to her feet.

She glanced up at the moon, making its relentless progress across the sky.

Time was running out, and she had her reapyr to find.

FIVE

When Wren finally emerged from the Bonewood, filthy and exhausted, dawn was a not-too-distant promise on the horizon.

She stepped from the trees, a pair of torches marking the finish line and burning too bright after hours of ghostly darkness.

Wren was the last to cross . . . and she had to cross alone.

Silence descended as she approached the judge's podium, every novitiate from the trial—including Inara, Ethen, and Sonya—standing there except for her.

Wren's heart pounded in the base of her throat.

While everyone stared at her, Wren stared unblinkingly at Inara. She had ruined *everything*, and yet she met Wren's gaze shamelessly, her hand settling, almost absently, on the hilt of Nightstalker.

Wren bared her teeth. She wanted to lash out, to strike her, but she knew her situation was far too tenuous. Panic threatened to overwhelm her, but she squashed it.

It wasn't over. She could still fix this.

She strode to the front of the group, ignoring the whispers and stares that followed her. She undoubtedly looked a mess, and while several of the others were spattered in mud or bore shallow scrapes, Wren looked like she'd been swallowed by the Bonewood and spat back out.

She lifted her attention to the judges' table. Her father looked alarmed by her appearance, though he'd schooled his features into an approximation of his usual, confident expression. The others studied her with more open and obvious rebuke.

Their disapproval was, unfortunately, something Wren was quite used to, so she blocked them out and focused entirely on the person whose opinion mattered most.

"My lady," she began. Her mouth was suddenly as dry as bone-dust, while her palms and the back of her neck were damp with cold sweat. Everyone turned at the sound of her voice, Inara among them, eager to hear what she would say. "I—"

Svetlana ignored her and got to her feet.

"Reapyr novitiates, come forward and present your bones."

The reapyrs opened their satchels and laid their reaped bones at the foot of the podium for inspection. The judges counted the offerings and looked for skill and accuracy in the scythe's cut, but also checked to ensure the bone was recently reaped and not scavenged from the forest floor or smuggled into the trial.

Afterward, all the novitiates ranged themselves in a line and stood at attention.

"Tonight you faced the Bonewood Trial," Svetlana said, looking down her nose at the collected novitiates. "A rite of passage for all who wish to serve the House of Bone in its battle against the undead. Your task was to reap three ghosts and make it through the forest unharmed"—her pale gaze paused for a moment on each of them, though it lingered on Wren—"*in your assigned pairs.*"

Wren bowed her head. If she could just explain . . . Sonya was fine, and they had performed three successful reapings *together*. Yes, they had gotten separated, but Wren had recovered from that bullshit betrayal, had fought off a swarm of tier-three ghosts, had climbed out of a sunken cavern in the deadliest part of the Bonewood, and *still* made it back before dawn. If that didn't prove she deserved to be a valkyr, she didn't know what did.

"Smith Colm and Smith Eiryn," Svetlana said loudly and clearly. "Ready your blade."

Both dropped to their knees, weapons unsheathed and held high in the exact pose they'd taken at the start of their trial.

There was no sound save for the wind in the bonetrees and the crackle of the torches.

"Do you offer it and yourselves, now and forever, in service to the House of Bone?"

"Yes, Lady-Smith Svetlana," they said in unison.

"Stand, valkyr and reapyr. Death is as certain as the dawn, and just as a new day will come, so too will the new dead rise. And we will be there. To find. To fight. To free. So the living may thrive, and the dead may rest in peace."

They were the House of Bone words, their most sacred purpose and rallying cry. Colm and Eiryn had passed the trial. They shared a grin, their shoulders rounding in relief before they moved to the side.

Then came Kalisen and Ginevra.

Leif and Imogen.

Finally Inara and Ethen.

"And Smith Sonya," Svetlana added.

Wren's head jerked up, and she stepped forward too, but her grandmother's cold look stopped her short.

"Ready your blade," Svetlana said, and all three went to their knees. "Rise, valkyr and reapyr . . . and reapyr."

There was a buzzing in Wren's ears as Svetlana spoke the rest of the words, and she could only watch numbly as her reapyr and the valkyr who had betrayed her accepted their victory.

"I would like to call special attention to Smith Inara," Svetlana continued. Wren's stomach twisted while Inara flashed her perfect white teeth. "For not only finishing the Bonewood Trial first among her fellow valkyr novitiates but for acts of bravery above and beyond the call of duty and for getting *two* of our precious reapyrs home safe."

She gestured to one of her retainers, who stood on the ground next to the dais. He hurried forward, placing something on Inara's head—a champion's wreath, crafted from linked finger bones and dipped in gold.

Wren had never seen one before, though she'd heard tell of them. She glanced at her father—surely this was the sort of thing he'd been hoping for *her* to achieve. Something spectacular.

The three of them stepped aside, leaving Wren alone in front of the dais.

Silence fell once more, and it seemed to grow and shift, like a ghost gathering its strength.

She couldn't take it anymore. "Lady-Smith Svetlana, I—" she tried again, but a raised hand was all it took to make the words die in her throat.

"Your blade," Svetlana said. Hope flared inside Wren's chest. They were so very nearly the words she wanted to hear . . .

She withdrew her dagger, uncertain. She dared a look at her

father, but his expression told her nothing. Did he know what was coming? If he did, and it was bad, he'd try to warn her, wouldn't he?

"Onto the ground," Svetlana continued.

Wren moved to kneel, hardly daring to breathe, but a harsh burst of cold laughter made her falter.

"Oh no, not *you*," Svetlana said, whatever humor had flickered there already gone from her face. "The blade."

Wren's fingers clenched convulsively on the hilt of Ghostbane. She glanced at Inara. Even *she* looked uncertain about what would come next.

Despite their bet, Wren had never really intended to part with the dagger because she had never intended to lose. Ghostbane was her most prized possession, the only gift her father had ever given to her.

But Wren pushed past that sentimental attachment to consider what Svetlana's words truly meant. Every valkyr had a bone blade dagger, either inherited from a family member or gifted to them by the House of Bone when they began their training.

Without it, Wren wasn't a valkyr . . . *or* a valkyr novitiate.

"But I need it," Wren said blankly, still clutching the weapon.

Lady-Smith Svetlana was unmoved. "No, you don't."

Those words woke Wren up. "Yes, I *do*," she said, taking a step forward. "My lady, please, you have to let me explain—"

"Wren," came her father's voice, sharp with warning.

Wren ignored him. "Grandmother," she said daringly—desperately. She had never addressed the head of her house so informally before, and certainly not in public, but Svetlana *was* her father's mother, her *blood*, and Wren needed the woman to remember that. Svetlana had always been a distant presence in Wren's life, a figurehead, not family, but it was all she had left. "Please."

Svetlana's eyes flashed. "Bone blade daggers are for Bone House valkyrs, and you are not worthy of such a title." The words cracked like a whip, shattering Wren's barely held composure. "Not only did you fail to finish the trial *with* your reapyr, but you left her to traverse the Bonewood alone. If it weren't for Inara, I shudder to think what might have happened."

"If it weren't for *Inara*, we never would have gotten separated in the first place," Wren said furiously. "She was the one who—"

"Silence," Svetlana hissed. "You, Lady-Smith Wren Graven, have no one to blame but yourself. You are rash and reckless, and I am confident that whatever predicament you found yourself in was entirely of your own making. The fact of that matter is, you *abandoned* your reapyr. You have dishonored the valkyr order, your Graven bloodline, and the House of Bone. Your actions cannot be ignored or excused, and I cannot allow such shame to fester under my roof."

Wren's vision was closing in. This was more than just failure. . . .

"You are no longer welcome in Marrow Hall. You are no longer welcome in the Bonelands. You will travel south at once and serve as a bonesmith tribute at the Breachfort."

"The Breachfort?" Wren repeated faintly. The Breachfort was the main fortress along the Border Wall. While it had once been a dangerous frontier, since the end of the Uprising, it was a backwoods posting, a place where third-rate smiths went to earn a meager living or where noble families sent their embarrassing children and spare heirs as "tributes" to serve in obscurity.

This was more than just punishment.

This was exile.

"Guard the Breachfort and the Border Wall the way you have

guarded your own selfish interests, and perhaps you will not disgrace yourself utterly." Lady-Smith Svetlana nodded her chin at the ground. "The blade."

Wren held Ghostbane before her in a shaking hand. Her fingers refused to move.

She looked at her father again, pleading silently. There was no response. She looked at Inara, who wore an intent expression Wren couldn't place. Had this been her goal all along? Had she meant for things to go this far?

The blade landed with a thump onto the snow.

New-made valkyrs and reapyrs stood on either side of her, but Wren remained standing alone.

She refused to pack, even though the ship would leave first thing the following morning.

It was called *Castaway*, and Wren couldn't help but wonder if it was the universe laughing at her in general or her grandmother laughing at her in particular. She had always known Svetlana had no love for her, as a granddaughter or as a bonesmith novitiate. She had been cold bordering on cruel for all of Wren's life, never really *looking* at her unless it was to call out or criticize. Still, a part of Wren had believed her father would shield her from the worst of it. But he hadn't. His own place in his mother's heart was tenuous. It seemed that no one was good enough for her, save for the dead.

She was pacing when a soft knock came at her door, and she whirled. She knew who it would be.

"I can explain," she said, hands raised in placation as her father strode into the room.

His face was darker than Wren had ever seen it, the spark in his eyes gone. "I told you to be careful!"

Her mouth fell open in outrage, despite her fear. "You also told me to be spectacular!"

"I told you to *pass* spectacularly, not to *fail* so."

Wren's mouth snapped shut.

Her father looked around the small room. He decided not to comment on the mess she had made, her clothes strewn about and her bags open and unpacked. "You let a *Fell* best you for the first time ever during the most important test of your life?"

Wren swallowed. "She tricked me. There was a pit—a cavern, really—and she set a trap. Then they just left me there. I . . ." She trailed off. In truth, she'd barely survived, but that seemed unimportant now.

"Sabotage and subterfuge have always been a part of the Bonewood Trial." He straightened, his gaze roving her critically. "I thought with all the nonsense you pull, you'd be well equipped to handle such hijinks."

"Hijinks?" Wren spluttered. "I fell into a fifteen-foot-deep *mass grave* filled with at least ten corpses and their tier-three ghosts! I am the *only* valkyr novitiate that could have made it out of there alive— and I barely did."

He was unimpressed. "You are not a valkyr novitiate anymore."

A surge of impotent frustration rose up. "Father, please. You have to talk to her for me. You—"

"It's too late, Wren," he said simply. "I told you Lady-Smith Svetlana was looking for any reason to fail you. You have never been your grandmother's favorite."

The bluntness of it hurt more than it should have—it was no surprise to her, but it was unfair nonetheless.

After all, the circumstances of Wren's birth weren't *her* fault.

Wren was conceived during the Iron Uprising. Apparently, her father had dallied with a fellow soldier while defending the Border Wall, and Wren was born as the war came to a close. Her mother had died in childbirth, and Vance had returned home to Marrow Hall with Wren in his arms. That in and of itself might not be enough to earn her grandmother's ire . . . except for the fact that he'd been betrothed to the king's daughter at the time.

The resultant scandal brought their engagement to a swift and bitter end, along with her father's—or, more accurately, Wren suspected, her *grandmother's*—royal ambitions. Everything Lady-Smith Svetlana Graven did was for the glory and prestige of the House of Bone, and Wren's existence was a strike against that. A constant reminder of it. Vance had disappointed his mother—first by coming home *without* Locke, heir to their house and her obvious favorite, and second by having an affair that resulted in fathering a bastard child on a random soldier.

It was no wonder her father rarely discussed his time serving at the Border Wall or anything to do with Wren's mother. It was no wonder he'd wanted her to do particularly well tonight.

And she'd been exiled instead.

She crossed her arms, jutting out her chin petulantly. "You're heir of our house. One day you'll be head. Surely you have a say?"

"You know it's not that simple," he said, looking away. "I have a responsibility to the entire House of Bone, not just you. I can't break the rules whenever it serves me."

She gave him a look that said, quite plainly: *Clearly you can and have—I'm living proof.*

"And look where that got me," he said quietly, correctly interpreting her expression. "Living in the shadow of a dead man, without the authority to stand up for my own daughter."

Despair welled up inside her. It felt as though the conversation was over, and she searched desperately for a way to extend it. "I found a fresh body down there," she blurted.

He stilled. "A fresh body?"

"Well, I mean, *relatively* fresh. No more than five years old."

His gaze roved her face for a moment—she fidgeted under his stare. "Did you find anything else?"

The ring in her pocket seemed to get heavier as soon as he said it. She wished she could show it to him—ask him about it—but she could already hear the reprimands and imagine the blame he might lay at her feet. Was *this* why she'd taken so long? Might she have saved the situation if she'd not dallied?

"No," she lied smoothly. This wasn't her first interrogation.

"No . . . ?" he repeated, dragging out the word. When she didn't contradict him, he finally turned away and shrugged. "I'll look into it. A mistake by a new digger, perhaps—or the body was just extremely well preserved."

"I know how to date a body," she snapped, arms crossed. She might have failed the Bonewood Trial, but she had been studying dead bodies in various states of decomposition since she was eight, when her bonesmith training had begun.

"As you say."

Wren scowled.

"Are you determined to fight? I came to say goodbye, not argue."

How did he always do that? Make her feel like she was the one being unreasonable, like she'd started all this, when *he* was the one who refused to listen.

When she didn't respond or remove the frown from her face, he laughed. He put his large hands on her shoulders and squeezed. They were almost at eye level, but the gesture made her feel small. "Come now, little bird. I don't want us to part in anger."

She clenched her jaw, refusing to look at him as sudden moisture pricked her eyes. Little bird. He'd not called her that in a very long time.

She was leaving, and she didn't know when she'd see her father again. She never really knew, with the way he was always coming and going from Marrow Hall, but this time, things were far more precarious. Her assignment as tribute at the Breachfort had no end date. It could be two years, two months . . . or the rest of her life.

She caved, uncrossing her arms and meeting his gaze.

"Attagirl," he said, nodding his approval. Wren hated the way her chest glowed with it. "Now, do your duty and serve honorably at the Breachfort."

"Serve honorably?" she repeated flatly.

"Yes. That means no more mischief, Wren. Despite what you may have heard, it is still an *active* fort on a strongly contested border. The war might be over, but that could change at any moment."

Wren frowned at that. "It could? I thought the ironsmiths had been wiped out and the undead beaten back?"

"Well, yes—our enemies were defeated," he said, "but what are our words?"

Wren had just heard them hours before. "Death is as certain as the dawn, and just as a new day will come, so too will the new dead rise."

"Exactly. We must always be ready. The Breach was never sealed, and though their numbers have diminished, the undead have not

NICKI PAU PRETO

been eradicated entirely. Besides, there are other dangers east of the
Wall. Bandits and brigands. Thieves and poachers. People have died
in the line of duty while posted there. Your uncle died while posted
there." He paused as he always did whenever his brother came up.
"Your name, your position . . . They will not be able to protect you.
I will not be able to protect you. Do you understand?"

Wren nodded, fighting back a rush of emotion. It was a relief to
know that he *did* care, despite his lack of reaction after the trial and
his insistence that there was nothing he could do to help her. That he
wanted to protect her, even if he couldn't.

"When you arrive, you'll be serving under Odile Darrow, who
is their highest-ranking bonesmith. She was Locke's reapyr, and we
all fought together in the aftermath of the Breach and during the
Uprising. She'll look after you." He released her shoulders, stepping
back. "Play by the rules, follow orders"—his eyes sparked at that,
regaining some of his usual humor—"and prove yourself worthy."

He kissed her on the forehead, lingering for half a heartbeat, and
then he was gone.

Alone, she packed in a daze, replaying her father's parting words.

Play by the rules.

Follow orders.

Prove yourself worthy.

While Wren had never bothered herself much with the first two,
it seemed she'd spent her whole life trying, apparently fruitlessly, to
do the third.

Now her father was telling her to *continue* to try, hundreds of
miles from home.

Her hand landed on her belt, on the empty sheath that had once
held Ghostbane. At least she'd not had to give it to Inara.

"You owe me an ancestral blade, Graven," her cousin had said after the trial had officially ended and Wren had received her fate.

"I'll give you one in your throat," Wren had snarled in reply, but Inara didn't hear. She'd already been out of earshot, basking in glory as she headed toward her new life as a valkyr, golden champion's wreath upon her head.

Wren sighed.

She had known their paths would diverge after tonight, but she'd not expected it to go quite like this.

SIX

The *Castaway* ferried Wren from Severton, the largest city in the Bonelands and closest port to Marrow Hall, down to Landen Point, a fishing town on the northernmost tip of the Astoria Peninsula, which was officially part of the Crownlands.

From there, it would be a five-day ride in a rickety old wagon, pulled by a pair of stout draft horses and driven by a sour-faced man who didn't even bother to look at her.

The man in charge of their journey was a soldier-turned-sell-sword called Ralph, and when Wren handed over her travel papers, he did an almost comical double take.

"Vance Graven's ba—uh, child?" he asked, blinking at her. *Nice recovery*, Wren thought blandly. "And he's shipping you off to the Breachfort? What for?"

Wren's scowl deepened as she climbed wordlessly into the wagon and threw herself onto the bench, pulling her hood down over her face. She would rather ride a saddle than a hard wooden seat that bumped and jostled as they rolled down the cobblestones and made for the road, but at least she could lean back, close her eyes, and ignore Ralph for the rest of the day.

Well, that was the idea, anyway.

"I might be a sell-sword now, but I was in the army before," Ralph said, not taking Wren's hint and continuing to chatter on. "I know your father, if you can believe it! Lord-Smith Vance and I were stationed together at the Breachfort during the Uprising. Well, not *together* together, him being a bonesmith and I, a simple soldier . . ." He paused, and Wren thought that was the end of it. She was wrong. "Those were the glory days for your house, weren't they? Back then, getting shipped to the Breachfort was the highest honor. Bonesmiths were cheered in the streets! Now, though? Well, unless there's a second uprising, I'm afraid your lot is back to funeral rites and village hauntings, aren't you? Not much renown to be found in that, is there? Of course, work is work. Why, just the other day . . ."

While Wren let most of his words go in one ear and out the other for the next few hours, she did, at one point, catch the phrase "first passenger," which meant they would be traveling with others.

Indeed, Ralph journeyed to the Breachfort four times a year—or so he shouted as they made their way down the busy road, which Wren assumed must be for *her* benefit, though she hadn't asked—traveling from Landen Point down through several smaller villages and towns before circling Brighton in the Silverlands to the south and then making for the Breachfort to the east, gathering up tributes along the way.

Brighton was where the House of Silver trained their smiths, and besides Marrow Hall, they sent the most tributes to the fort. Silversmiths were primarily healers, and therefore always in demand at military postings. Silver was antibacterial, so besides using it to clean wells or keep casks of wine fresh and free from germs, it had long been used in medicine. They used silver thread in bandages to wrap wounds, silver sutures to close deep cuts, and silver instruments to perform surgeries. Wren had even heard they could use silver to stabilize broken bones while they mended.

The stonesmiths, on the other hand, had helped build the Border Wall, and often did contract work in its maintenance, but they weren't a formally recognized smith house, so they didn't send tributes. Decades ago they had allied with the southern kings during the conflicts that eventually saw the northern Valorians gain sole rule over the Dominions and had lost everything in the aftermath. Now there were only a handful of families scattered across the Dominions who maintained the traditions, but they had no central house or lands. Still, the castle at Stonespear—built two centuries ago—was said to be the most magnificent in the Dominions, even grander than the gold-encrusted monstrosity that was Giltmore, seat of the House of Gold.

Wren had long wanted to see Stonespear for herself, after she finished her training and became a valkyr. Now that she was exiled, she realized with a pang that she might never get the chance.

Goldsmiths had little to offer in wartime, so they didn't bother with tributes and just sent gold instead, while ironsmiths were all but extinct. Thanks to the Breach, their craft had been outlawed and their schools shut down, though they certainly weren't the *only* smiths to receive such treatment. The ghostsmiths had been the first smiths to be exiled.

Wren tuned back in to Ralph's incessant chatter in time to learn he wasn't the only person to make a business of transporting tributes. Indeed, before long he was disparaging the competition.

"They might have cheap steel and horses and know the roads, but they never saw *war*. I'm the best protection money can buy," Ralph said proudly. He had decided, much to Wren's dismay, to ride *beside* the wagon rather than in front so he could more easily speak to her. He smiled down at her expectantly—did he want praise?—and there was no pretending she hadn't heard, as she had done several times before.

"Is the road so very dangerous?" she asked uncertainly. She didn't really care; she wanted to stew in silence and self-pity. She still couldn't believe she'd allowed herself to be tricked and trapped and carted off to the edge of the world by a man named Ralph, who didn't know when to shut up.

"Any road that cuts through the wilderness is dangerous!" he warned. "Outlaws roam the Riverlands to the south, no matter how hard His Majesty tries to keep them in check, and pickpockets and thieves will lay traps outside the cities, setting upon weary travelers. Not to mention other soldiers who've not found honest work after the war . . . or decided never to bother to try."

Wren perked up slightly. "Have you often had to fight?" A highway robbery would certainly shake things up.

"Never," the driver chimed in helpfully, causing Ralph's puffed-up chest to deflate.

"Not *yet*," he clarified, peering around ominously.

Wren sank back into her seat.

Like most in the Dominions, Ralph refused to travel after dark, misunderstanding the undead. They could rise and attack in daylight as well as at night, even though they preferred the darkness. It had to do with the warmth of the sun, which made it difficult for their ghosts—cold in nature—to take shape. Like cool morning mist, their spirits would be steadily burned away by the heat of the day.

Regardless, all the major roads had bonesmith-installed protections anyway. They would be totally safe, especially since Wren was with them, but when they arrived at a small roadside village, she was told to exit the wagon and sleep in the stables Ralph had secured for the night, so she did. With distaste.

Backwoods places like this would be unable to afford to keep a bonesmith in residence, so they had likely paid for one to see to their protections. Wren could sense the bones that surrounded the village, as well as the additional talismans that had been set into several of the larger buildings, including the stables. Perhaps they'd had a ghost attack their expensive horses at some point, making them wary. Or perhaps this allowed them to house visitors in a place with no inn.

When they departed the following day, they had three additional passengers. They stopped several more times in smaller villages before they reached Aspen Ridge, a large town with a full bone palisade outside the stone walls that enclosed it. It was a highly frequented crossing, with a dedicated bonesmith temple. Homes and villages could erect whatever protections they wished to guard themselves from what lay beyond their borders, but they did nothing against the undead *within*. All it took was one citizen too poor to pay for proper burial rights, or a tavern brawl gone awry and an unchecked body in a gutter, and there could be a ghost haunting their streets. That's why the larger towns kept at least one reapyr and valkyr pair on hand, or if they could afford it, a temple in charge of all burials, death rites, and defenses.

The capital had a full embassy housing dozens of bonesmiths. It was where Wren's father spent most of his time when he wasn't visiting Marrow Hall and being disappointed by her. However, it was her father's travels across the Dominions to inspect local temples or dine with important nobles that most interested her. Not for the chance to rub elbows with high society, of course, but for the sights. For the adventure. Despite the circumstances, this trip to the Breachfort was sadly the most exciting journey Wren had ever been on.

Most of the passengers they collected were poor villagers in search of paid positions as Breachfort guards, looking for regular meals and a roof over their heads, but they did pick up another tribute, a silversmith healer fresh from Brighton's academy.

They also picked up a pair of stonesmiths, hired on for temporary work, and a girl who claimed her father was a woodsmith.

"I've seen him call up trees myself."

The others shared dubious looks at that. The woodsmith craft had all but disappeared from the Dominions, along with some of the other lesser smith abilities like tin, lead, or copper. The stonesmiths, too, might have followed them into obscurity, if not for the fact that their craft was still useful. As such, they could support themselves with good pay and steady work, if not status. But training to become a tinsmith or coppersmith was seldom worth it, their wares not valuable enough and their careers less lucrative. Most learned at the knee of parents or grandparents and were considered hedgesmiths or base-level conjurers in comparison to nobly trained smiths.

If the girl's father *was* a woodsmith, he was part of a dying breed, and if any of them had been powerful enough to raise trees from the ground, they weren't anymore.

All smiths had been more powerful once. There were stories of stonesmiths calling up the Spearhead Mountains from flatlands and goldsmiths drawing molten streams of gold straight from riverbeds. The librarian at Marrow Hall said the Gravedigger could sense bones from miles away, but apparently magic faded over time, bloodlines watered down and abilities weakened generation after generation.

In the case of the woodsmiths, there wasn't a lot of forest in the Dominions to begin with, so it was probably difficult to maintain the connection to the material their magic required.

Luckily—for bonesmiths anyway—as long as there were people living in the Dominions, there would always be bodies and bones.

They arrived at the Breachfort the following afternoon.

Wren spotted the Wall first and stood in the wagon to get a better look at the massive granite barrier that marked the Border. It snaked across the landscape, over steep hills and rocky ground, disappearing in both directions. As they grew closer, the fort itself became visible, nestled against the base of the Wall and made of the same gray stone. Its highest tower was built directly into the Wall behind it, rising several stories above, giving the best view of the land beyond. Matching towers were spread along the rest of the Wall, acting as lookout points and housing smaller garrisons. There was a gate within the Breachfort, allowing crossing to the other side, and another farther south called the Silver Gate, though the accompanying fortress was small and more lightly guarded.

The Breachfort was the main defense, and larger than Wren had expected, though less grand. It was roughly built, made of large stonesmith-hewn blocks without decoration or artifice. She reminded herself that when it had been raised, undead had been wandering freely across the Dominions, and it was required to serve a dire defensive purpose. The Border Wall, too, was similarly constructed, with function superseding form. This was truly a structure made for war, and the effect was brutish and bleak. A solitary Dominion flag, featuring falling stars on a dark blue field, snapped in the breeze.

Guards ranged along the fort's battlements as Wren's party rode through the western gate, though it was too high for her to see which way they looked—east, toward the Breachlands and the Haunted Territory beyond, or west, at the newcomers.

The courtyard, however, was a different story. Breachfort servants and stable hands milled about, staring openly at the arriving wagon, while guards halted in their training exercises or paused on the way to their postings.

Wren raised her chin instinctually—it wasn't her first time being openly stared at—and busied herself leaping from the wagon and unloading her bags. She hadn't gotten far before she and the others were directed to stand at the foot of the wide steps that led to the main hall and await Commander Duncan, the Breachfort's leader.

Ralph and the wagon driver cleared out, and panic, sudden and fierce, pinned Wren to the spot. She had the mad urge to chase after them. Maybe she hadn't tried hard enough to convince her father to let her stay. Maybe if she *really* begged, he'd take pity on her.

Commander Duncan descended the steps, an older man dressed as a steward standing beside him.

The commander was a tall, broad man with ruddy brown skin, who looked like he might have made an impressive warrior . . . once. Now his shoulders were rounded, his hair receding, and his belly straining against the buttons of his jerkin.

He still dressed as a soldier, but one who was off-duty, with tall boots, thick gloves, and a sword at his waist. Wren doubted he had seen any real action in years.

He didn't bother with welcomes or pleasantries. The steward, a pale, reedy man with white hair, handed over a list, and Commander Duncan called out assignments.

The villagers would be heading to the guard captain to start their basic training, while the silversmith would report to the infirmary and the stonesmiths to maintenance.

"Lady-Smith Wren Graven, of House Bone?" he called out finally, easily identifying her in the crowd. "You'll report to Smith Odile Darrow at the bonesmith temple."

Ah, yes, Odile Darrow. Highest-ranking Breachfort bonesmith and former reapyr of Locke Graven.

Also, Wren was quite certain, her new babysitter.

SEVEN

The bonesmith temple was underground, at the bottom of a flight of stone steps. It consisted of a single workroom with a long table, its surface smooth black stone and scattered with various bone weapons in need of repair, jars of bonedust, and a couple of scythes with dulled edges or rusted grips.

Guttering candles were set in sconces or shoved into darkened recesses. The entire place was unnecessarily spooky, even for a bonesmith, and Wren tripped over several stacked chairs that were impossible to see in the darkness. She realized this space had likely once been a meeting room or council chamber, the long table meant to seat at least a dozen bonesmiths. Closed doors led into additional chambers, though she suspected they were no longer in use.

Only one door was open, a faint glow spilling out into the main room.

Wren edged around the remaining chairs, dumped her bags on the ground, and knocked hesitantly on the open doorframe.

"Yes?" came a woman's distracted reply. Wren could just see her seated behind a desk, head bowed, her nose in a book.

Wren sighed, speculating how far Ralph had made it at this point, and wondering again if her father would take her back if she pleaded hard enough.

Instead, she squared her shoulders and lifted her chin. "Commander Duncan sent me. I'm your new bonesmith tribute."

There was a pause, and finally the woman—surely Odile—looked up. Her pale-eyed gaze raked over Wren with surprising intensity. She blinked, then seemed to come back to herself. "Of course. Come in."

Wren strode into the room, which was set up like an office, with a desk in the center, where Odile was seated, the surface littered with papers and leather folders. The walls were lined with shelves stacked with books, bones, and more candles, and there was a fireplace, darkened with soot and burning low.

Wren paused before the desk, the woman's gaze still unnerving as it took her in. Finally, Odile smiled, but it seemed a resigned sort of expression, like she was amused at her own expense. She leaned back in her chair, hands steepled across her stomach. She was around Wren's father's age, her copper-colored hair sleek and cut in a severe line at her chin.

"Lady-Smith Wren Graven, I presume?" she said.

Wren nodded. "Call me Wren."

"You certainly look like him."

"Like Vance?" Wren asked, assuming Odile meant her father.

The woman's smile tightened, and Wren recalled that while her father had said they'd served together at the fort, he'd never said they were friends. "I was thinking of Locke, actually." Her expression softened, turning almost wistful, before she continued. "But I'm sure there is a resemblance to Vance in there too, somewhere. . . ."

"If you find it, you'll have to let me know," Wren said. "And my grandmother, while you're at it. When she looks at me, all she sees is my mother—though she never even met her."

While Wren had the same eyes as her father, with pale bonesmith irises and stern, straight brows, it seemed that there was little else to connect them. His hair was a light ash-brown, thick with curls, his nose proud and prominent, and his olive skin easily tanned. Wren's hair, meanwhile, was silvery blond and scraggly, her nose small and delicate, her skin more likely to burn than brown.

Odile's lips quirked. "Lady-Smith Svetlana is better at seeing faults, I think, than family traits. Though the two are often one and the same."

Had that been a joke? "My father said you were my uncle's reapyr—that all of you served together here at the fort."

"Is that all he said about us?" she asked. "About me?"

Wren shrugged. "He said you'd look after me."

Odile looked disappointed, for a moment, before she snorted. "Forgive me," she said, seeing Wren's startled expression. Odile shook her head—again with that same rueful smile.

"I assumed you'd be expecting me . . . ," Wren said awkwardly. How else had she known Wren's name?

"Oh, I was. Your father sent me a letter." She paused. "It's just so very typical of him. Charging *me* with your care when he's done such a piss-poor job of it himself."

Wren reared back in surprise, but Odile wasn't done.

"The man spends half his time gallivanting across the Dominions, leaving his only child behind in that frigid, barren crypt they call

Marrow Hall, and then when the time comes to see you safely settled in your career, he lets his mother ship you off to the Breachfort? The only child of the heir of the House of Bone?"

"I f-failed the tri—"

"Do you want to know who else failed the Bonewood Trial?" she interjected. "Locke Graven."

"What?" Wren gasped. According to everyone she ever spoke to, Locke Graven was the perfect son, heir, and valkyr. He led the final charge that brought the terrible, bloody Iron Uprising to an end. He was practically a saint, his name said with more reverence than the Gravedigger himself—the closest thing the House of Bone had to a deity.

Odile smiled. "He was a year ahead of me, but even then, he was the darling of our house. He was top of his class, popular and beloved. But kind, too." She looked wistful again, before her soft smile turned sardonic. "That meant he was always trying to do the right thing. Always trying to be the hero. Apparently, during the trial, one of his weaker classmates fell prey to a pair of geists, and Locke stopped to save him, making him miss the dawn cutoff. Of course, his actions only further endeared him to his mother and the rest of the house. His failure meant another year of study until the next trial, but there was no further punishment. I think she was only too happy to keep Locke close, especially with her husband dying only months earlier. I suppose it worked out well enough. . . . We passed together the following year, and were paired up. We served for two years before the Breach, when we were shipped east."

Wren scowled. She had been stripped of Ghostbane and *banished*, while Locke just got a pat on the head and another year of adoration at home?

Odile nodded, seeing Wren's angry expression. "Lady-Smith Svetlana bent every rule in the book when it came to her precious Locke. She bent a few for Vance, too, despite never quite forgiving him for living when her firstborn died. Still, she didn't exile him for the mess he made of that royal betrothal, did she? No, because she needed an heir, and he was all she had left. But now here you are, paying for the sins of your father, and somehow it's up to *me* to protect you."

Wren just gaped at her. No one had ever spoken so plainly, so bluntly, to her in her entire life. Her muscles went lax with an immense surge of relief. She felt understood, suddenly, and not so very alone. Her knees buckled, and she dropped into the nearest chair.

"You're right," she said. "It's bullshit."

There was a pause, and then Odile laughed—a deep, full-belly laugh. "Well said, young Graven. Well said." She cocked her head, surveying Wren a moment, then got to her feet, making for the sideboard. There was a clinking sound. Then she turned back around with a bottle and two glasses.

"Yes, it *is* bullshit," she said, pouring a good measure of clear liquid into each cup. Wren took hers, sniffing experimentally, and felt her eyes tear up at the familiar pungent scent. It was alka, a spirit distilled in the north and her father's preferred alcohol. Odile, meanwhile, had tossed back half of hers in a single gulp. She sighed, leaning back in her chair once more. "But who are we if not loyal servants to our house, hm? So I will do my duty. I will look after you and keep you as safe as I—"

"But that's the thing," Wren said, cutting her off. She took a quick sip of alka and gasped as it lit a fiery track down her throat. She coughed, but the words still came out as little more than a croak. "I don't *want* to be safe."

"What *do* you want?"

"I want to be a valkyr—failed trial or not. I don't know how long I'll be here, but I want to make the most of it while I am."

Something flickered in Odile's gaze, and it looked almost like approval. "Indeed. And so we shall. Come, let's give you a tour."

"Of the fort?"

Odile turned in the doorframe and smiled. She shook her head. "The world beyond."

They armored up, Wren digging her bones from her bags in the adjoining room and Odile stepping into a side chamber. As she was a reapyr, not a valkyr, her protections sat under her long, sweeping black robes. Wren, meanwhile, had both armor and weapons strapped to every inch of her body.

Odile quirked an eyebrow. "Twin blades," she murmured, nodding at the swords that poked out over her shoulders from their place in her baldric. "Like Locke, though he wore them on his belt. Vance preferred long-range artillery. Didn't like to get his hands dirty."

Wren grinned, relishing every scrap of information Odile gave her about her family, particularly her father. She had to admit that she'd often put him on a pedestal, despite his shortcomings—especially as they related to her—and it was grounding to know he was every bit as flawed as Wren. Perhaps even more so. Locke, too, wasn't perfect, and the information made them feel more like real people. Like family.

When they arrived at the gate, one word from Odile had the guards hurrying to let them through.

First they raised the portcullis—made of bone—and then the wide wooden doors creaked open.

The land beyond was gray and barren, whatever trees or greenery that might have once grown here hacked away to maintain their defenses.

There was a road underfoot, a remnant from before the Wall, though they had clearly built the gate overtop with its usage in mind. It would make for easy riding in and out on patrols, especially as it split not far ahead of them, running north and south along the Wall in both directions.

And the *Wall* . . . Wren gaped at it, soaring above them and blotting out the sky. It was impressive enough when viewed from its western front: easily fifty feet high—not including the crenellations—and twenty deep, made of massive blocks of granite that were as tall as Wren, each movable only by a team of stonesmiths. As a rule, a smith couldn't use their magic to lift an object that was heavier than their own body weight. They called it the law of ratios, which could be no more than 1:1. It must have taken ten burly stonesmiths combined to lift each brick, and there were thousands of them stretched out before her.

The view was even more astounding from the east. The blocks no longer glowed dull gray in the day's watery sunlight. No, they shone pearly white and emanated a powerful presence in Wren's magical senses.

Bone. Ground down into bonedust and shaped into bricks.

It gave the Wall a polished, slightly elegant look—and could easily be mistaken for marble from a distance—but the closer one got, the more that effect eroded. The color was not quite as lustrous, the finish not quite as smooth. It caused a chill to run down Wren's spine, and she regularly handled bones and bodies.

"I was here when it was built," Odile said idly, coming to stand next to Wren as she stared up at the structure. "Once the king officially decided to demarcate a border and erect a barrier, it went up alarmingly fast. Dozens and dozens of stonesmiths working around the clock. The bone facing took longer—we had to collect the bones and grind the dust first, then create the bricks—but it was finished before the Uprising. They say it took a hundred thousand bones to create enough bonedust for the job."

The number was almost beyond comprehension. "Where did they get them from?" Anyone killed by the undead from the Breach would have succumbed to deathrot, which rendered their bones soulless and without magic. They'd be useless for protection.

"Marrow Hall emptied its stores—the catacombs beneath the castle were stocked full of bones they'd been collecting for centuries—and every crypt, coffin, and mausoleum from Giltmore to Granite Gate was cleaned out. They weren't all anchor bones, of course. We'd never have enough to manage such a surface area. Instead, they used keystones"—she pointed to a smaller brick set among a cluster of larger ones—"carefully spread throughout. They're the true protections, while the others simply amplify their magic."

"Like a body," Wren mused. While the anchor bone held the soul and the most powerful magic, every bone connected to it shared in that power. One of her teachers had said it was like a fire in a hearth. The flames were the source of the heat, but the surrounding stones absorbed the warmth all the same.

"Exactly. But the Wall is a last resort. The first barrier is the palisade."

She stepped off the road and headed east, deeper into the Breachlands, where roughly fifty meters away stood a second wall—

technically the first one built—made up of a series of animal bones poking straight out of the earth, like jagged teeth.

Wren recognized this type of fortification. It was the more traditional bonesmith method, as she'd seen in towns and villages all over the Dominions. Each bone, depending on size, provided a certain radius of protection, and the bonesmith fabricators who built these structures had it down to an exact science. Massive bones, not unlike the rib cage Wren had seen in the Bonewood, protruded from the soil every ten feet, with smaller bones used to bridge the gap between the harder-to-find and much more valuable mammoth and whale bones.

It was a truly haunting sight, more primal and unnerving than the stone-and-bone Border Wall behind it. Wilder and less civilized, maybe, it harkened back to simpler times.

"Unfortunately, it didn't hold up on its own," Odile said. "Heavy rain, the freezing and thawing of the ground . . . They cause the bones to shift over time, creating gaps and weak points. And on a Wall that traverses nearly a hundred miles of wilderness, it was impossible to catch every variance. Now it acts more as a deterrent than an actual barrier. Stronger undead can sense the holes and pass right through, and tier fives . . . Some of them can even touch it."

Wren stared out past the palisade, imagining what it would be like to see a walking corpse. To fight one. "What are they like?" she asked. "The tier fives? The revenants?"

Odile cocked her head at Wren, considering. "Didn't your father . . . ?"

Wren shrugged, kicking at a stone on the ground. "He doesn't talk much, about the war. About any of it."

When she looked up again, Odile had glanced away. "I suppose not." She sighed. "It's difficult to explain. Some of them look almost human. Fully intact, moving with the lingering familiarity of the living. Those are the hardest to deal with." She cleared her throat. "Others, they're so badly decomposed, the spirit shines through their bones and barely there scraps of flesh, turning them into something more akin to a puppet on strings. Either way, our usual methods don't work against them." She reached up and tapped Wren's temple. "Use this, if ever you should face one. And this . . ."

She lowered her hand, and Wren thought she was going for her chest. "My heart?"

Odile rolled her eyes and then used the back of her hand to smack Wren in the stomach.

"Your gut, Wren Graven. Listen to your gut. Your instincts will know what to do, even if your training fails you."

The tour didn't last long after that. Odile pointed out the distant towers, how far Silver Gate was, and various other features.

"You said *if* . . ." Wren began as they strode back to the fort. A distant patrol could be seen riding from the south, back toward the gate. "Does that mean—do you not see any action here anymore?"

It's what she'd heard, but better to find out firsthand. Her father seemed to believe things could go bad again at any moment, and she wanted to know if there was merit in that or if he was just being paranoid.

"Not of the sort you're imagining. Our patrols"—she gestured to the riders who'd beaten them to the gate up ahead—"are more likely to encounter *living* problems than undead ones."

"What about the Haunted Territory?"

"We haven't journeyed past the palisade for ten years. And no one has entered the Haunted Territory since the Uprising."

Since the final battle, when her uncle—and hundreds of others—had died.

"You look disappointed," Odile observed. "When I first arrived at the temporary camp that would become the Breachfort, it was with a dozen other bonesmith tributes. Only half of us survived the week."

Wren looked up, shocked.

Odile nodded sadly. "This was in the immediate aftermath of the Breach, back when we used to send patrols deep into the Haunted Territory. We were still trying to understand what had happened. What we were dealing with."

"It's just . . . ," Wren began, hating the whine in her voice but unable to master it. "He told me—my father—he told me to come here and play by the rules, follow orders, and prove myself. But if we don't patrol beyond the palisade, if there's no real danger from the undead . . . I won't get the chance."

"I never said there was no real danger," Odile clarified. "Merely that we no longer patrol beyond the palisade. Ignorance is bliss, as they say, and Commander Duncan is only too pleased to report the lack of activity on his watch."

Wren considered that, frustration building inside her. "So it doesn't matter either way? Even if there *is* danger beyond this border, I'll never see it?"

"Not necessarily," Odile said carefully. "Besides, there are other ways to prove oneself than in combat."

"How?" Wren asked desperately.

Odile laughed, shaking her head. "Gravens," she muttered. "I'm certain you'll have your chance," she continued, expression growing more serious. Then she smiled. "And in the meantime—*I'm* the one who reports back to your father. We'll make a hero of you yet."

"But—why?" Wren asked, totally taken aback. "Why help me?"

Odile looked at her for a long time, but it wasn't her father's measuring stare or her grandmother's cold evaluation. It was soft and gentle and maybe a little sad.

"Because somebody should."

EIGHT

Despite Odile's promise of other ways to prove herself, Wren's first weeks at the fort passed in a blur of boredom—and no undead. She didn't know what Odile wrote to her father in her reports, but unless she invented tales of intrigue and danger, the details of Wren's activities at the fort would be very dull indeed.

Still, she *tried*. She did as she was told. Played by the rules. Followed orders. Showed up for training, was never late for patrol, and stayed out of every kind of trouble.

For all the good it did her.

She was doing everything right for the first time in her life . . . and it didn't matter.

They weren't soldiers in the midst of a battle for their lives—they were security guards watching a boundary line that nobody crossed.

It was a far cry from the glory days her escort Ralph had talked about. Wren and Odile were the only two permanent bonesmith tributes at the Breachfort; any others were there on temporary contracts, and all of them were fabricators—meant to repair damages and move on. As such, Wren went out on every patrol, though she supposed if they actually found any undead, they'd have to send for Odile to finish the job.

But, of course, they never did.

There were no run-ins with the undead, no skirmishes with the promised bandits and raiders. They were more likely to run into regular people who lived east of the Wall, trying to sneak over the Border or buying and selling contraband.

"Some of the guards will do business with them to supplement their wages," Odile explained when Wren returned from patrol one night after turning away a group of Breachside locals and their wagon filled to the brim with items for trade. She was standing in the main workroom, organizing jars of bonedust and other smithing supplies. "Whether Commander Duncan likes it or not."

"I didn't realize there were so many people living east of the Wall," Wren admitted, leaning against the table. "Or that they had anything of value to trade."

"Oh, they have items of value," Odile said without looking up from her task. "There are whole towns along the coast. They are not thriving as they once were, but they are *surviving*, at any rate. Not everyone got out when the Wall went up, as you well know. The Haunted Territory that surrounds the Breach spans less than half of the region trapped behind the Border." She indicated a large map mounted on the wall, depicting the Dominions and the land beyond the Border Wall. Wiping her hands on her robes, she walked over to the map, indicating each region in turn. "The Adamantine Mountains, the Serpentine River . . . there are natural barriers that keep the worst of the undead activity trapped in the northeast. The coastal towns are relatively safe, if isolated. Their shallow shores and dangerous currents make it impossible for ships to dock, not that any would dare, given the state of things. They struggle more for food and supplies—that's what they trade the guards for—than against undead, though they are troubled by them often enough. Without bonesmiths east of the Wall to perform burials and death rites, even those who die peacefully in their sleep are destined to rise again and torment the ones they love. Sometimes they bring their bodies here for me to deal with."

"And do you?" Wren asked, surprised.

"Of course," Odile said, somewhat defensively. "I am a reapyr. It's my duty."

Technically, Odile's duty was to Lady-Smith Svetlana and the House of Bone, to whom she had sworn fealty, but Wren understood the sentiment. She came to stand next to her, eyeing the map. "Couldn't they just cross? Through one of the gates? Would the king deny them entry?"

Odile sighed. "Unfortunately, many threw their lot in with the House of Iron during the Uprising, so technically, they're traitors to the crown. Plus, where would they go? Live in refugee camps? Most of the wealthy who lived here left in the first wave after the Breach, though some stayed because the *source* of their wealth was here, in lands that had been in their families for generations. Same with the ironsmith families. Their ore is in these hills, and the Iron Citadel in the north is their seat of power, where they train and work. How could they leave it all behind? I'm sure they'd feel differently now, after the Uprising. I don't think they expected to be wiped out."

"You were there, weren't you?" Wren dared to ask. "During the final battle?" Her father always shut her down when she brought it up, but she was intensely curious about it all.

"I was, I'm sorry to say," Odile said, looking away. Her gaze landed on Wren's swords, which she had yet to remove since her return from patrol. "Have you sharpened those since you've been here?"

They'd not been used, so she hadn't bothered. "No."

With a jerk of her chin, Odile indicated that Wren should unsheathe them. Her eyes caught on the empty scabbard Wren wore on her belt—where Ghostbane used to sit—but she made no comment on it.

Digging through the mess on the table, Odile found a pair of whetstones. While she worked on one, Wren worked on the other.

"It was the House of Iron's last and best effort," Odile said after several moments of comfortable silence, save for the steady sweep of stone on bone. "Virtually every ironsmith alive was mustering and preparing to march on the Wall, along with anyone east of the Wall who could hold a weapon. Negotiations had floundered. The king refused to risk foreign trade—which had only just started to pick up again after the Breach—for the sake of the House of Iron. You see, the ironsmiths didn't want rescuing. They wanted help in their war against the Breach. They wanted to reclaim their lands, not leave them to the undead. They wanted *us*—bonesmiths—but the king refused to give us to them. Now they were ready to march in force, to tear the Wall down, to hell with the consequences."

Wren's hand stilled, until she remembered herself and continued her work. She didn't want to draw Odile's attention and end the story. She knew only the very basics of what had happened nearly twenty years ago: There was a battle, virtually everyone died—including her uncle—and the Uprising was finished.

"Your father, Locke, and I were part of an advance scouting unit. We knew they were mustering, but we didn't know where or when they intended to strike. The Wall is long, and there are various vulnerable points. So, along with a contingent of soldiers, we attempted to sneak up on them. The only way to do that, we knew, was by traveling through the Haunted Territory." She swallowed. "So we did. Our forces met there, which meant we were dealing with more than one foe. The ironsmiths, their soldiers . . . the undead. But it was more, even, than that. Something dark lives there. Something evil. What happened was a massacre. Locke, he—" She paused, glancing up before continuing. "He gave it everything he had. Your father and I survived because of him. As you well know, most were not so fortunate."

Wren had heard vague tales of Locke's bravery and heroism. How he had led the charge, mowing down undead to protect their own warriors. They were outnumbered three to one, but the bonesmiths were able to deter the undead, protecting their own forces, while the ironsmiths had no such abilities. Suddenly, the tables had turned, and while many on the Dominions' side did fall to the revenants, they were able to win the battle first.

"It must have been terrible," Wren said, trying to imagine a battle with the undead on such a scale. A battle with the living.

"It was like being torn in two," Odile said, barely above a whisper. "I am a bonesmith, but the town where I was born is on the very edge of the Haunted Territory."

"You were born in the Breachlands?" Wren asked, surprised.

"Well, they weren't the *Breachlands* back then. They were called the Ironlands. But yes."

"Were you born to an ironsmith family?" Smith abilities generally followed bloodlines, but when two smith bloodlines were crossed, one ability became dominant and the other recessive. There was no way to guarantee which would manifest most strongly, and reces-sive traits could pop up generations down the line. It was why most marriages within smith houses were carefully curated to ensure their magic persevered. Lucky Wren had turned out a bonesmith, or her grandmother might not have accepted her at all.

"No, but my father and older brothers worked in the mines."

Wren's stomach plummeted to the floor. "Did they . . . ?"

"Die in the Breach? Yes."

"I'm sorry," Wren said quietly.

Odile waved her off, but her gaze had grown distant. Almost cold. "I'm not sure it mattered, in the end. If they'd not died during the initial incursion, they'd undoubtedly have fought and died in the Uprising afterward. Perhaps it was a mercy that I'd not had to face them while fighting on the other side."

Silence filled the workroom. Odile looked down, then handed Wren her sharpened blade.

Suddenly, Wren's dreams of glory, of making a name and proving herself, felt petty and low.

A messenger arrived then, interrupting the tense quiet. He bore a folded letter marked with the Breachfort's own seal.

"That'll be Commander Duncan," Odile said, taking the letter and dismissing the boy. She broke the seal as she made for her study, and not being told otherwise, Wren followed. As Odile settled behind her desk, Wren sank into her usual seat in front. The fire was burning brightly, banishing some of the chill that lingered in the outer chamber.

Odile's eyes flew across the page. Her expression was grim—or maybe it simply *remained* grim after their conversation about the war. Her eyes fluttered closed for a moment, as if she was steeling or recentering herself, and then she dropped the letter and grinned.

"I think we've found your chance."

"To prove myself?" Wren asked eagerly. "Does this mean you *haven't* been singing my praises on every report?"

As she'd hoped, Odile's smile widened. "The Gravedigger will be nothing compared to the tales I've told of you."

Still grinning, she handed Wren the letter. Wren took it, hastily scanning the page. "A royal visit?"

Odile nodded. "The third prince, Leopold, shall grace us with his presence, drain our meager resources, then continue on his grand tour of the Dominions. There will be meetings. Dinners. *Inspections.*"

"Of the fort?"

"And its defenses."

Wren frowned. "You think I can prove myself to *him*? A prince?"

Odile tilted her head. "Can you think of anyone better?"

Besides her father? No, no, she couldn't.

"How?"

"Leave that to me."

NINE

Over the following days, Odile's mood fluctuated between her normal, wry humor and something detached and forlorn. Wren blamed herself for asking about the Uprising, for bringing up painful memories. Whatever Odile thought of Vance, Locke had been *her* valkyr. They had obviously been close, judging from the way her gaze turned distant and her mouth soft whenever she spoke of Locke, and losing him had to have been difficult. Between him and her family, who knew how many others she mourned.

Despite her less-than-sunny disposition, Odile was true to her word. She kept Wren abreast of the prince's upcoming visit and ensured Wren was properly informed when it came to the royal family history.

"The Gravens of House Bone are the most recent smith bloodline to join the ranks of the nobility—thanks, of course, to the integral role bonesmiths played in defending the Dominions against the Breach. The Iron Uprising continued that relevance, though now that both those threats have waned, we are enjoying less power and influence. It seems the darker the hour for the Dominions, the brighter the light shining upon the House of Bone," she said, wearing her familiar smirk. "Speaking of threats, the Knights of House Iron were the *first* ennobled bloodline."

Wren knew this much. The Valorians, outworld immigrants determined to take control of the Dominions for the rich trade potential, sought out the ironsmiths and paid them handsomely—promising lands, a title, and a wealth of other benefits—if they would swear fealty to their would-be king and help them take over. There was nobody more dangerous on a battlefield than an ironsmith and no weapons as strong as ironsmith metal. As such, few dared to stand against the mighty Valorians and their Iron Legion, the rest of the local lords and petty kings succumbing to their iron blades or bending the knee one by one.

"It was a landmark move," Odile continued, feet up on her desk as she lectured Wren, glass of alka in hand, making her the most unorthodox teacher she'd ever had. "It helped the Valorians secure their throne and the present-day Dominions take shape. House Silver came next. They were elevated after they single-handedly put an end to the cholera epidemic that struck several of the larger coastal cities, including Port Valor. They had saved the capital city from ruin—and the queen's life, if the rumors are true—and soon there were silversmith healers in every town. But the Vanes of House Gold were the first to rise above all others and get a smith bloodline in the royal family. The *ultimate* status symbol."

Wren thought of her father, who had failed to do the same for their own house.

"It was King Augustus's grandfather, King Gaius, who decided to marry his daughter to a goldsmith. Not for their magic, of course, but for their money. House Gold has always been wealthy, thanks to their thriving mints and healthy foreign trade, but none are richer than the Vanes. They could buy anything they wanted, and it was only a matter of time before they set their sights on a throne. The crown had nearly bankrupted itself fighting off a Rhailand invasion, so it seemed an easy solution to the king. He elevated the Vane family to the status of nobility—so there could be no complaints about suitability—then married his daughter and heir, Emmeline, to their eldest son, Henry, a powerful goldsmith. The result is goldsmiths occasionally dotting the royal family line. Two of the king's sisters, and now . . ."

"Prince Leopold," Wren supplied.

"Exactly," Odile said with a nod. "The Gold Prince. By all accounts he is clever, handsome, and bored."

"Just my type," Wren muttered before she could stop herself.

Odile barked a laugh. "Indeed. But he still has influence." She stared down at her now-empty cup, her mood turning somber again. "He may be able to help you."

Wren nodded, though she had a hard time believing it. "If not, at least I've got you."

She smiled, and after a heartbeat, Odile did too. Then Odile got abruptly to her feet.

"Oh, are we done for the night?" Wren asked, standing as well.

"Not quite. Follow me."

As they emerged from the lower-level temple, Wren thought they were heading for the courtyard and gate, but Odile gave a short whistle and steered her in the opposite direction, toward another basement passage on the other side of the keep. It was late, and the fort was quiet, their footsteps echoing softly.

"I've never been down here before," Wren said as they started their descent.

"That's because this passage leads to the dungeons," Odile said, leading the way down the stone stairs, which were sporadically lit by flickering torchlight.

Confusion bloomed in Wren's mind. Why was Odile taking her into the dungeons?

The staircase spiraled down into darkness until they entered the detention levels.

"There are three holding areas," Odile explained. "The top level is for *important* prisoners. Officers, nobility—people with wealth and position. They get braziers and furniture and other creature comforts, while the second level is for more dangerous captives. Enemy soldiers. Raiders. Smiths."

As they came to the next level, the hall was definitely less pleasant looking than the one above, which still held some of the trappings of the upper floors, like carpets and windows. This one was all stone, cold and drafty and dark. It was also empty, as the floor above it had been, without guards or prisoners.

To Wren's surprise, they'd reached the end of the stairs. Hadn't Odile mentioned *three* holding areas?

But the woman only smiled faintly and walked around the bend in the spiral staircase, as if expecting the steps to continue right through the brick wall.

Only, it wasn't a wall. As Wren accompanied her, she spotted a lock embedded in the surface.

And it was made of bone.

Odile produced a matching bone key from a chain inside her robes and fitted it into the hole. There were two clicks before the door opened with a blast of frigid air.

It was a common bit of smith magic, fashioning a key that required two turns—one with your hand, the other inside the lock with your magic.

Bracing herself, Wren followed Odile down another flight of stairs, taking a torch from the bracket next to the door at Odile's instruction. The temperature dropped with every step they took, Wren's torch the only light marking their passage. When they finally emerged from the stairwell, she saw a vast, sprawling cavern, easily three times as large as the dungeons above it.

That's when she understood. They were beneath the Border Wall. She felt it, the oppressive weight—the magic—and that's when she noticed that there were indeed cells down here as well. While they too lay empty, just as the ones above, she didn't need Odile to tell her which prisoners *they* would hold.

"For our undead captives," she said softly, gesturing to the row of bone-barred holding areas, their grotesque shapes producing shadows that danced in the torchlight.

Wren had heard stories about the early years after the Breach, how they had studied and experimented on this new, more powerful breed of undead. How they had sought to understand them. From those early tests came the undead scale and everything they knew about the walking corpses that rose from the Breach.

The cells, however, took up only a small portion of the space.

There were beds lining the far wall, with trays of tools and baskets of linen that put Wren in mind of a hospital. Her eyes lit on some blood-stained rags, and she wondered if they had treated people here during the war . . . and why those people hadn't been brought to the infirmary on the upper levels. Was it simply overflow, or something else?

Beyond the beds were what looked like storage areas. There were casks of wine stamped with the Twin Rivers seal, a famous winery east of the Wall that had been forced to close its doors after the Breach. There were baskets of wool from Highmore's coastal flocks, crates of Adamantine fox furs, and ceramic jars of ironberry preserves.

All highly coveted items that were, allegedly, impossible to get west of the Wall.

There were also items that clearly went in the opposite direction. Silver instruments, golden trinkets, and even some bone talismans meant to ward off undead.

Odile strode into the center of the cavern, and Wren followed, lifting the torch to better take in the size and scope of the place. "I guess it's not just the guards who buy and sell to the Breachsiders?"

"Not just them, no." Odile seemed to be waiting for something. What, condemnation? Considering what Odile had told Wren about her own family living east of the Wall, the fact that Odile would try to help her old friends and neighbors in any way she could made perfect sense. Judging by the items piled around, Odile might be single-handedly supporting their economy as well.

"Does Commander Duncan know about this?"

"I think he prefers *not* to know—about anything that has happened down here in the past or what may continue to happen. He suspects some of my black-market dealings, of course, but he and the majority of the garrison benefit from it. They don't care how I get them ice wine from the Cartesian Valley—only that it's still cheaper than importing it from Maltec or Andolesia. But there are other things that move under the Wall that they might be less pleased with."

Wren looked at the infirmary-style beds again and at the bags of apples, packets of salt fish, and sacks of grain. "People, you mean?"

Odile inclined her head. "People, objects . . . *information*. It's important that we don't entirely lose touch with what's happening east of the Wall, so I make sure to keep on top of rumors and gossip."

"Like what?" Wren asked eagerly.

"Not all of it bears repeating, but with undead roaming freely across their lands, I'm sure you can imagine the sort of thing. Some of it is nonsense, and some of it is intriguing—but some of it is dangerous, too. Until I know fact from fiction, I prefer to keep most of it to myself."

"That makes you, what, some kind of gatekeeper?"

"I guess you could say that. Information is harder to control, but as for everything else . . . I have the only key and am the only person who can manage the lock. Well, myself, and now you."

Wren returned her attention to the woman. "Why are you showing me this?"

Odile shrugged, a determinedly nonchalant gesture, but there was tension in her shoulders. "If anything should ever happen to me, it's important somebody knows their way around. And now you know more than one way out of the fort. Just in case."

Wren frowned, but nodded, getting the distinct impression she was missing something but afraid to pry lest Odile shut down again.

"I'm supposed to be staying *out* of trouble," she said instead, trying to lighten the mood.

Odile's serious expression didn't change. "Sometimes trouble finds us, whether we're looking for it or not."

† † † †

Finally, after weeks of anticipation, His Highness arrived.

Excitement thrummed in Wren's veins as she returned from patrol, the sunset casting dark shadows over them as they passed under the gate.

She had never met a prince before, thanks to her years of intensive valkyr training and the fact that the Valorians rarely deigned to make the trip north to Marrow Hall. The last time they had done so was to honor her uncle Locke after the Uprising, when Wren had been a baby. Typically, her father and grandmother journeyed to their seat in Port Valor instead. The odds of her proving anything to a puffed-up, spoiled royal were long indeed, but it was the most interesting thing to happen since she'd arrived.

"You're late," snapped the steward. They had barely dismounted before he was on them. "Make yourselves presentable. We head for the dining hall at once."

The guards tugged and straightened their uniforms as best they could. Wren hadn't gotten dirty, exactly, but she was still armed and armored, with black smeared around her eyes and on her lips. She *was* a bonesmith, after all; she might as well look the part. If only she had a reapyr's robes, then she'd be everyone's worst idea of the House of Bone.

The steward hustled them toward the servants' entrance to the dining hall, intending for the latecomers to sneak in unnoticed, but when Wren moved to follow them, he halted her progress.

"You'll be sitting at the high table," he informed her, waving a letter in her face. She thought she spotted Odile's spiky signature near the bottom. "The commander requires a representative from each branch of the fort's defenses to demonstrate our full capabilities to the prince, and Odile has fallen ill. As you are the only other bonesmith in residence, you shall take her place."

Fallen ill? She'd looked perfectly fine that morning when she'd informed Wren that the prince should be arriving sometime that day.

Was this her way of giving Wren some face time with the prince? A chance to prove herself?

"Uh . . . right," Wren said, straightening her shoulders slightly. Yes, she could do it—bow and nod and answer questions about the fort's ghostly defenses.

"Ready?" the steward pressed, gesturing for the main double doors to be opened for her.

Before she could answer, he clamped his hand around her arm and guided her, *firmly*, down the main aisle toward the dais at the back of the room.

The tables had been scrubbed, the flagstones mopped, the walls wiped, and the tapestries knocked free of dust.

And there, seated beneath them, was the prince.

He looked every bit the royal, dressed in rich black velvet, with shiny leather boots and a delicate woven circlet atop his head.

But he looked every bit the goldsmith, too.

The thread in his jacket, the rings on his fingers . . . Even his eyes were as golden as a cat's, glinting with amusement as Wren approached.

The steward bowed to the prince before bending to whisper in Commander Duncan's ear.

His face, which was lit with a false, jovial smile, flashed with alarm. He evidently hadn't heard about Odile's absence until now. Seated on either side of him were representatives from the prince's retinue and senior members of the commander's staff, people with at least ten years of experience serving at the fort, including the silversmith who ran the infirmary, the stonesmith who oversaw maintenance, and the captain of the guard.

Then there was Wren, barely a month into her service—and all he had.

Commander Duncan waved the steward away, then sighed, before visibly pulling himself together. "Your Highness, the last of our, uh, representatives, has returned," he announced. "Prince-Smith Leopold Valorian, of the House of Gold, may I present Lady-Smith Wren Graven, of the House of Bone."

Wren knew how to bow—her father had made sure of it, lest she have one more flaw for her grandmother to hate her for—but as she straightened, she saw the prince's eyes lingering on her.

He *was* good-looking, as the reports had claimed, with a halo of caramel-colored curls, full lips, and smooth light-brown skin. He was pristine to the point where she'd fear to touch him in case she wrinkled his clothes or mussed up his hair. Or maybe that would be the *fun* of it . . .

No. Wren was playing by the rules. Following orders, and proving . . . something . . .

"This is Galen Valorian, who has been overseeing the prince's tour," Commander Duncan added, indicating a young man on the prince's other side. He had some of the prince's coloring but none of his charisma, his shoulders rounded and his curls flat.

Wren bowed briefly. Then the commander gestured for her to take a seat in the empty chair reserved for Odile at the end of the high table. Before she could move, however, the prince held up an elegant hand, halting her in her tracks.

"Wren . . . ," he said, his idle gaze roving her from head to toe. "That's an unusual name for a bonesmith."

"It is, Your Highness," Wren admitted, surprised that this shining apparition of a prince knew anything about her house's customs. For a bonesmith, being named after an animal was considered silly and trite. "I was named by my mother before she died."

Wren wanted to kick herself. Three seconds of conversation, and she'd already mentioned the woman her father had spurned the prince's aunt for.

The prince's eyes glittered with suppressed mirth, as if he could see the panic on her face and found it amusing. "I know your father," he said, his voice even and without rebuke. "He often visits the capital. I'm not sure I see the resemblance—except for the eyes, of course." Wren blinked, unsure where this was going. "He's not much fun, despite what the stories claim. . . ." He paused. "Are you? Fun?"

A hint of a smile tugged at her lips. She schooled her features back to seriousness. "I am, Your Highness—or else I wouldn't be here."

He beamed in delight at that, showing dazzling white teeth, though his fine, narrow nose scrunched up, making him look less perfect and more human.

"Likewise," he said, still smirking. Wren sensed in him a kindred spirit.

Commander Duncan was looking between them in confusion, while Galen's lips pursed in disapproval.

Now that Prince Leopold had stopped talking, however, the commander tried to wave Wren off again.

"Your eye black," the prince said before she could be ushered away. "I thought it was only necessary to prevent glare?" He tapped his lips, indicating the fact that Wren's were currently painted black. "What purpose does that serve?"

Wren studied him, studied the way his golden lashes framed his eyes, how his cheekbones seemed to glow from some unseen light and his hair shone like water in the sun. It was elegant, and certainly more subtly done than Wren's, but it was there.

"What purpose does *your* makeup serve, Your Highness?"

He grinned without a hint of embarrassment. He had a dimple. "It makes me look good, of course."

Wren inclined her head. *"Likewise."*

A rush of servants arrived then, with heaping platters of food carried on wide trays, forcing Wren to vacate the space before the dais so the prince could be served. He caught her eye one more time as she took her seat, but then the servants demanded his attention, and the feast began.

Wren found herself alone at the end of the table, smiling.

Perhaps proving herself to a prince wouldn't be so hard after all.

They brought out barrels of wine for the occasion. The best went to the high table, but even the guards and tributes were allowed a single cup of the lesser vintages. Wren hesitated over hers, wondering how far she wanted to push her luck. Openly flirting with the prince in front of the entire fort was one thing, but adding alcohol into the mix was something else. Something dangerous.

As she stared into her cup's rich red contents, she caught the prince watching her from the other end of the table. He lifted his wine in salute, and so Wren lifted hers.

One cup couldn't hurt.

She didn't get a chance to speak to the prince again, but just his presence was a bright spot in the darkness of her life recently—and the ticket to just enough wine to make her cheeks heat and her tongue loosen as she laughed and talked with the other representatives. They seemed surprised by her energy; Wren herself felt as if she'd come alive in the past couple of hours, and she couldn't blame it all on the drink. What she felt for the first time in weeks was *hope*.

Or maybe it was simply the absence of despair.

As the feast wound down, the prince rose, bade them all good night, and was escorted to his rooms.

Wren watched him go, wondering when they'd next get a chance to speak. If Odile continued to play sick, Wren might find herself in his company again soon.

With the prince's departure, the rest of the fort's occupants followed suit, many of the guards having early patrol shifts or late-night duties to attend to.

Wren withdrew with the others up to her room, which she shared with the silversmith Sabina, who had arrived at the Breachfort with her. They didn't have much to do with each other, their various shifts and responsibilities making them cross each other's paths sporadically, like ships in the night.

Even now, as Wren sat on her bottom bunk and started tugging off her boots, Sabina was already asleep in the bed above her. She wasn't the drinking type and had likely slipped out of the dining hall early.

Wren was just kicking her boots aside when a noise drew her to her feet. Something by the window.

"W-was that?" mumbled Sabina, sitting upright, her curtain of black hair covering her face.

Wren threw open the shutters, letting in a blast of frigid air. She stared out across the courtyard and then up, at the battlements before a gasping sound drew her attention immediately downward.

There, hanging from her window ledge, was Prince Leopold.

"*Gravedigger*," Wren swore, taking hold of his wrist to help haul him up. Her room was technically on the first floor, but it was elevated to account for the uneven ground below, making it a good deal higher than a first floor should be. It wouldn't be a *fatal* drop, but it wouldn't be a pleasant one, either. Regardless, it wasn't something she'd want to test after however many cups the prince had imbibed at dinner.

"What the—" Sabina said, before Wren managed to drag the prince over the ledge and onto their cold stone floor.

"Oof, you're quite strong, aren't you?" he mumbled, smiling up at Wren from his heap on the ground. He was a good deal drunker than Wren had initially guessed, withdrawing a golden flask from his breast pocket, proving that he'd kept the party going long after he'd left the dining hall.

"*Healers and helpmates*," Sabina muttered. "Is that the *prince*?" She sent a suspicious, silver-eyed look at Wren. "Did you invite him up here?"

Wren wished she'd thought of that, but she hadn't. "No," she said, at the exact same moment he said, "More or less."

"Excuse me?" Wren said, looking down at him, her arms crossed.

He held up his hands in surrender, spilling some of whatever was in his flask. Wren snatched it. She took a sniff—nearly gagging—then decided to take a swig anyway. The wine from dinner was ages ago.

"I'm not here for that," the prince reassured them, though Wren didn't think he'd be capable of doing anything remotely resembling *that* in his current state anyway. "I'm just looking for a bit of fun, and I knew you'd be the man"—he hiccuped—"*woman*, for the job."

"Just don't kill him," Sabina said, rolling over and putting her pillow over her head.

The prince reached for his flask—rather feebly—before slumping against the wall. "May I please have my drink back please?" he asked with large, puppy-dog eyes. "I'm parched."

Wren took another sip, keeping the container out of reach. "You have half a dozen retainers and a personal guard. . . . How did you ditch them, Your Highness?"

The prince shrugged morosely. "Please, let's dispense with the pleasantries. It's after hours, and I'm in your bedroom. Call me Leo. As for my honor guard, they locked me in my room—standard protocol these days, I'm afraid—and I climbed out the window."

"Very enterprising of you. Now what? Surely someone will be checking on you, and when they don't find you, I'll be the one in trouble."

He sighed, scrubbing a hand across his face, smearing some of the golden paint and mussing up his hair.

"The guards like me well enough—they won't disturb me for the rest of the night. *He,* on the other hand . . ." He turned his head, squinting out the still-open window. Wren followed his gaze, seeing the commander's tower in the distance, the council room glowing brightly in the darkness. "Will check on me once he's finished."

He clearly didn't mean Commander Duncan. "Who?"

"My *handler,* Galen. He is a relentless social climber, distant cousin, and all-around cock."

Wren snorted and handed him the flask. He took it gratefully. As he drank, she peered out the window. "If he's looking for an ass to kiss, Commander Duncan will oblige. The man burns the midnight oil even when he's alone, but with company to impress and the wine flowing . . ." She peered down at him, grinning. "You've got a couple of hours at least."

The prince perked up. "Hours, you say. How shall we fill them?" He waggled his eyebrows.

"Don't even think about it," Sabina said from under her pillow.

Wren reached out a hand and hauled the prince to his feet. He was surprisingly steady, though shorter than she thought he'd be, standing an inch or so beneath her.

"Come on," she said, heading for the door. "I've got an idea."

TEN

With Wren in the lead, they darted between the shadows to avoid the guards, climbing up the ramparts, which themselves offered a wide view of the area, but she had something better in mind. Since he'd already proven he had some aptitude for climbing, Wren took the prince to the Breachfort's highest tower, where they scaled a rickety ladder, climbed over the battlements, and came to stand on the small circular platform next to the flagpoles, the fort's pennant snapping in the breeze.

The crenellated walls protected them from the worst of the cold but still allowed them to take in the stunning view for miles in all directions *and* keep an eye on Commander Duncan's tower.

"Impressive," Leo said, leaning out between a gap in the stones and taking it all in. "Can you see the Breach from here?"

"No," Wren said with a sigh. "Sadly, I haven't seen so much as a wisp of ghostlight since I arrived."

"No sign of the undead—how very sad indeed," the prince said teasingly. The cold air seemed to be sobering him up slightly, cooling his flushed cheeks and making his eyes shine. "Does that make you a zealot, then? Doing the illustrious Gravedigger's good work?"

"What do *you* know about the Gravedigger?" Wren asked dubiously. Even after the Breach and all the House of Bone had done to make the Dominions safe, most regarded bonesmiths with wary superstition.

Leo looked affronted. "I am a prince of the realm," he said. "I know *everything*."

"Really?" Wren said, grinning.

"The Gravedigger is the first recognized smith in Dominion history," Leo spouted, rising to the challenge. "There were likely others before him, but no civilization could truly take root here, in the Land of Magic, before they'd found a way to deal with the rising dead."

"I thought it was the Land of Falling Stars?" she pressed, trying to catch him out. That's where most people believed magic came from—stars falling from the heavens. No other country had it, as far as Wren knew, and certainly not in the same form. She'd heard of Selnori fortune-tellers and Rhai herb witches, but nothing like what they had in the Dominions.

"It depends who you ask," Leo said without a hitch. "The Maltecs called it Majland, and the Andolesians called it Estellaisle. The first settlers called it Smithland, back when everyone who lived here had magic, but now, thanks to my ambitious ancestors, it's called the New Dominions—named for a place that no longer exists."

The Valorians came from a country called the Northern Dominions, but civil war had since seen it splintered into several smaller nations. Their country was officially called the New Dominions, but most dropped the prefix.

"I'm impressed," Wren conceded. History had never been her

favorite subject, but despite his roguish behavior, Leo was obviously more studious than he let on.

He beamed at her praise, tipping his head in gratitude before peering around once more. "How long have you been here?"

"A little over a month."

"And how are you enjoying it?"

"I'm not," Wren said flatly. "I'm bored. Fighting ghosts is all I'm good at, and as previously stated, there aren't any."

"Boredom—now, that is something I completely understand."

Wren turned away from the view to lean her back against the wall, staring at him. "Being a prince not all it's cracked up to be?"

"Oh, it has its charms," he conceded. "But while first and second sons have duties and responsibilities *in addition* to the usual bits—"

"Like money and power?" Wren asked wryly.

"Yes, exactly," he said without skipping a beat. "A *third* son, on the other hand, often finds himself without much to do. You have the heir, the spare, *me*, then the daughter—youngest and favorite, I might add."

"So you're the second spare."

"The spare's spare."

Wren laughed. "But you're the only goldsmith, right? Surely that counts for something?"

"Besides an extra name in my official title that people *rarely* bother to use? Not really. They won't let me actually use my ability. Princes don't *work*, Wren Graven, not even prince-smiths—surely you know that," he said with a smirk. "Once I'd finished my education . . ." He shrugged. "No expectations. No responsibility. Hence the Breachfort visit. It's one of a dozen stops I've made in the past few weeks, tours and inspections all to keep me busy."

"And behaving?" Wren asked.

"*Mostly* behaving," he amended, raising his flask.

"Sounds like an easy life," Wren said, though she suspected that wasn't quite true. She knew what it was to have people expect the worst from you, all the ways you could rebel against or play into those perceptions. Wren herself had only ever done half the stupid things she'd done for the attention. She'd wanted to be caught, to be seen, to be talked about and remembered.

She'd always assumed any attention was better than no attention. Better for people to expect the worst than for them to expect nothing at all.

Then again, that behavior had landed her here.

"An easy life, yes," Leo said, tilting his head back to look up at the stars. "But also an invisible one."

"Could be worse," Wren said bracingly. "You could have failed the test you've been training for your whole life, been banished from your family, and exiled, rather than just popping by for a visit."

Leo's attention dropped back down to her. His expression was serious. "What kind of idiots would exile *you*?"

His tone was incredulous, as if the very idea of it was beyond comprehension. As if, after knowing her for only a few short hours, he saw her value more than her own blood.

"The kind I'm related to," Wren said with a sigh.

Leo nodded. "Ah, yes, the very worst kind of idiots. I know from experience."

Wren laughed, and Leo offered her the flask.

"To the worst kind of idiots," she said, raising the flask before tossing back a burning mouthful.

"And to new friends," he added, taking it back and draining the container in one.

† † † †

The lights in Commander Duncan's council room went dark not long after, forcing Wren and Leo to abandon their perch and hustle back the way they'd come. As it turned out, Leo hadn't climbed out his window as much as fallen, and with the late hour and excess alcohol, he wasn't managing to scale the two-story distance without help.

And help unfortunately came in the form of Wren, standing on the ground beneath his window while he perched painfully on her shoulders, kicking her head and bruising her collarbone as he reached and scrambled and finally, mercifully, got a hold of the window ledge and hauled himself up.

Once inside, Leo poked his head out the open window, tossing her a wink before disappearing back inside.

Smiling, Wren returned to her room—but she took the stairs.

The following day dawned obnoxiously bright, the bell tolling the shift change impossibly loudly—and earlier than usual, Wren was sure—but it didn't matter, as she was already awake.

Suddenly, for the first time in weeks, her life felt like it had purpose. She didn't truly know what Leo could or couldn't do for her, but at least it was *something*, and if she happened to have fun in the process? All the better.

Yes, her head pounded a bit, and her mouth was dry, but a spot of breakfast would surely cure what ailed her.

If Wren was feeling the effects of her late night, Leo was much, much worse. Their eyes met across the dining hall, and though his hair still shone like spun gold and his jacket was pristine, his skin looked pale, his eyes lacking their usual sparkle. Despite being a bit under the weather, he smiled at Wren and nodded in acknowledgment as she entered the room.

She hovered, uncertain. Should she sit at the high table again? Odile was absent once more, and the other representatives were there, but this was definitely a less formal affair than the welcoming feast. Wren was needed to perform Odile's duties, not to warm her seat. When no one called her over, she decided to slide onto a bench and eat with the rest of the tributes.

Still, she watched the high table as breakfast wore on.

Leo sat perfectly straight, not a button or hair out of place, head resting elegantly on his hand—though his eyes were closed. Despite this fact, he managed to flag down a servant for more coffee without needing to open them, his empty mug held aloft until someone had the presence of mind to fill it. The Breachfort did not usually serve coffee, an expensive import from Selnor, but as the prince downed his *third* cup, Wren could only assume Leo had brought the beans himself.

Finally, Commander Duncan stood, and the room fell silent. Leo's eyes opened.

"As a part of his official inspection, Prince Leopold will accompany me and a small party east of the Wall so he may examine our defenses in greater detail and ensure they meet with royal approval."

Leo nodded imperiously, but there was new tension in him that hadn't been there before. Perhaps he was nervous to go beyond the Border? Or maybe he was just anxious to perform his royal duties correctly.

"If you are not assigned to our escort," Commander Duncan continued, "your regular patrols will go on as scheduled."

There was a collective groan and screech of benches against stone as the others got to their feet to report for their usual duties, while Wren waited, hoping . . .

Commander Duncan's searching gaze found her in the tumult, and he waved her over. Her heart leapt.

She joined the group of people milling in front of the high table while the rest of the guards and tributes cleared out. She caught Leo's eye and grinned, hoping her presence might ease his worries somewhat. He smiled tightly and waved for another cup of coffee.

Commander Duncan announced that the patrol party would be made up of a team of Prince Leo's own guards, his cousin and retainer, Galen, the commander himself, and a handful of the Breachfort garrison, in addition to Wren.

When it was time to depart later that afternoon, Wren and the others filed into the courtyard, where horses milled, saddled and ready to be mounted, and the prince's carriage sat, awaiting its royal passenger.

She checked her armor and weapons, knowing they would not be used but wanting to make sure she represented her order proudly. She also ran through everything she knew of the fort's undead defenses. Surely Odile knew more, but she doubted the prince would require a full treatise on the subject. Just a few highlights would do. Besides, she wasn't going to dazzle him with her *knowledge*—her winning personality was her best chance at securing favor. Where it would lead, Wren didn't know, but she allowed herself to envision a letter arriving at Marrow Hall, stamped with the prince's seal, raving about Vance Graven's exiled daughter and her skills at the Breachfort. Maybe he'd even request to take her on himself, have her join his traveling party full-time. It wasn't unheard of and was almost a requirement when traveling to some regions of the Dominions where bonesmiths were less common.

Wren was heading toward one of the horses when Leo hooked her arm. "You'll be riding with me, Graven."

Grinning, Wren turned back around—and walked straight into Commander Duncan. "Mount your horse, tribute. We're preparing to depart."

"You know, Commander Duncan, I'd feel much safer with the bonesmith by my side for the duration of the inspection. We *are* heading east of the Wall."

"Your Highness, we've not had an attack from the undead in seven years! I assure you, it is perfectly safe."

"If it's perfectly safe, I wonder why the crown spends so much gold on the Wall's upkeep?" Leo mused, glancing around. "Perhaps our resources would be better spent elsewhere, if the Breach is no longer a threat. . . ."

"The Breach is still extremely dangerous," Commander Duncan said, changing tack at top speed. "To say nothing of the Breachsiders who linger beyond our borders. I only meant that the specific section of the Wall that you will inspect has not seen action—has been thoroughly tested—rigorous standards—"

"All the same," the prince cut in, "I'd feel safer with someone who is properly armed and trained to deal with such a threat, should it occur. I might be the Twice-Spare-Heir, but I am still a prince of the Dominions."

"Of course, Your Highness, of course—anything to put your mind at ease. Your safety is our top priority, I assure you. Lady-Smith," he barked, flapping his hand at Wren to indicate she should climb up. "You will ride alongside the prince."

Wren climbed up somewhat smugly. It was a strange feeling to be wanted—to be seen as a valued friend rather than a last option or nagging burden.

Better not get too attached to the feeling.

She thought of Odile as they prepared to set out. She hadn't had a chance to check in with her all day, but perhaps it was best, as the woman was feigning an illness. Still, Wren wished she could see the look on her face when she saw how well her plan was turning out.

The carriage was quite snug, with Wren and Leo on one bench and Galen and Commander Duncan opposite, but it was an open-air conveyance, which allowed them to better take in the landscape. While Galen's attention was fixed on the prince, Commander Duncan's beady gaze was trained on Wren.

She smiled. "Ready to have some more fun?" she whispered into Leo's ear. Commander Duncan glared.

"Always."

They passed through the main gate, taking a hard left to ride on the road, allowing the prince to see the breadth and scope of the Border Wall, its full height and impressive length, disappearing over the horizon.

Prince Leo's reaction to the gleaming bonedust bricks was similar to most who laid eyes on such a sight; he tugged at his collar and muttered, "Is that . . . what I think it is?"

Wren smiled and recited some of the information Odile had given her, detailing the keystones and the palisade.

As they continued toward the nearest tower, Commander Duncan pointed out other pertinent details, like how many guards garrisoned each of the forts and towers and how the remnants of the Old Roads provided easier passage across the wild landscape, which was riddled with jagged cliffs, volcanic rock, and steaming geysers. There were deep caves and crevasses gouging the landscape and making travel beyond the roads dangerous and unpredictable. Even the forest that ran alongside the Wall to the north was twisted and dense and impossible to traverse, no matter how much they tried to cut it back. There was some decent farming land to the south, in the Cartesian Valley, but mostly, the wealth of this region had always been in mining.

As the carriage kept up a steady pace, Leo relaxed into the journey, asking questions about patrols and feigning interest at their responses.

Wren did her best to both keep an eye on their surroundings—she was a valkyr-trained bonesmith, after all—and keep Leo company, but he wasn't in the mood to chat. It seemed hangovers were not his forte.

Commander Duncan had just been explaining how the towers operated when the carriage began to slow. Wren and Leo were facing forward, so Commander Duncan and Galen had to crane their necks to see what the holdup was.

"There's some debris on the road," one of the guards said, bringing his horse alongside the carriage.

Wren stood. Several massive stones littered the path, along with a scattering of debris from an apparent rockslide. The road sliced through the rough landscape when it could, as it had done here, resulting in soaring cliffs and jagged outcrops on either side of them. The tower was just out of sight beyond the distant ridge, and coupled with the dense copse of trees that rose to the east, they were left in a bit of a blind spot.

Commander Duncan blustered about patrol routes and assignments—this should have been noticed before their arrival—annoyed that the state of the road made him look inept in front of the prince. Galen, too, was talking loudly, commanding the prince's guards to clear the obstruction at once.

Leo, meanwhile, was tense again, looking around the carriage uneasily.

"Don't worry. You're safe," Wren promised, extending her senses just in case—but the palisade had done its job, and there were no undead to be found. "Come on, why don't we stretch our legs a bit while they sort this out?"

Leo looked at her then, a strange expression in his eyes. Then he darted a glance at Galen. For the first time since they'd left the fort, the prince's retainer was paying him no mind.

Wren saw it as an opportunity. She leapt from the carriage, and with a deep breath, Leo followed. His gaze continued to dart around them as they strolled along the road, soldiers mounted and alert on either side.

"Are you okay?" Wren asked once they'd gotten a bit of distance from the wagon.

"Of course," Leo said abruptly, but he was nothing like the smirking, laughing prince she'd met the night before. Had it all been the alcohol? He eventually did flash her a grin, but it was forced. "I'm always okay."

"Well, maybe we—"

A sudden, strange whistling sound brought Wren up short. She whirled around just in time to see one of the guards standing near the carriage drop to the ground, an arrow shaft protruding from his eye socket.

There was a moment of shocked silence. Then, to the north, a thunder of horses' hooves echoed down the road, followed by another volley of arrows. Several peppered the carriage and landed in the ground, though others found their targets, who dropped the same as the first one.

Galen shouted for the prince, but then his eyes went wide. Wren turned to see more horses coming from the south. These were not Breachfort guards. These were attackers.

They were surrounded.

The debris on the road wasn't from some accidental rockslide. No, it was very much on purpose.

Wren looked at Leo, at the strange mix of fear and resignation on his face.

This was a trap, and they'd walked right into it, delivering Prince Leopold Valorian on a golden platter.

ELEVEN

"Get down!" Wren shouted, throwing herself against Leo and tackling him to the ground.

He looked at her with wide-eyed confusion, wariness etched into every feature. True, Wren was not a properly trained soldier or one of the prince's personal guards, but she was closest to him and surely had more combat training than him—even if it was mostly against the undead.

"Into the trees," she hissed, shoving him bodily, so that they staggered and crawled toward the side of the road.

Shouts went up from the guards, preparing for a fight, while Galen looked around frantically. "To the prince!" he cried. "There, in the trees!"

Wren cursed vehemently, wanting to strangle the man—there was still a chance this was a random Breachsider attack, that they didn't actually know there was a prince of the realm in their midst. Not only was Galen alerting them to that fact, but he was also giving away their position.

Her brain scrambled, but there was nowhere else to go—no place to hide on the open road as their attackers barreled down on them from two sides, and the Breachfort soldiers and royal guard hurried to take up arms. Those on foot ran to the carriage, the only protection available, while those who were mounted prepared a counterstrike.

Then, amid the chaos, the smell of burning wood.

The trees . . . Perhaps they intended to smoke them out.

"We're under attack," Leo said blankly. Wren thought he was in shock.

"Very observant, Your Highness," she muttered. She hesitated, looking back the way they'd come—then forward, into the trees. The *burning* trees.

It didn't matter. It was their only chance. The forest was dense, which provided good cover from the artillery coming their way, and it was their best route for escape. If they could make it through to the other side, they might be able to disappear into the wilderness—find a cave to hide in until they could return safely. Wren could protect them from whatever supernatural threat might be lurking out there, and surely reinforcements would come. Despite the tower being out of view, guards manned the Wall, and eventually someone would see the smoke and raise the alarm.

Whatever happened, she had to protect the prince.

"Let's go," she said, jerking her chin toward the darkness of the trees.

He didn't move. "They're here for me," he said. Around them echoed the clash of metal and the twang of bowstrings and, in the distance, the steadily growing roar of flames.

"You don't know that," Wren countered, though she didn't really believe it. Everything had lined up too perfectly for this to be anything but a premeditated attack.

—113

He continued to stare at her, as if waiting for something, but eventually heeded her order and headed deeper into the forest.

Wren split her focus between their forward progress and the sound of the battle behind them. The horses that came from the south had already passed them, and with the thick tree growth, she and Leo were currently out of sight. She just hoped they could remain so long enough to get out the other side.

As branches snagged against clothes and thorns scraped exposed skin, Wren withdrew one of her swords. Her blades were designed to cut through ghosts, not trees, but she was nothing if not determined, and she hacked and tore and shoved her way through, Leo following close behind. He kept looking over his shoulder, fearful of pursuit, but thus far their passage went unnoticed.

Eventually, each slash of Wren's sword caused flashes of daylight to spill through the shadow of the trees, revealing a patch of grass, a scrap of sky . . .

And a booted foot.

"Fuck," Wren breathed, halting midswing—but it was too late. Another blade met with the trees from the other side, and this one was not made of bone and designed to cut through incorporeal spirits.

It was a sword made of iron, designed to cut through anything.

"Back," Wren said, turning away from the swinging sword and shoving at the prince, but then a gloved hand gripped her shoulder and tore her from the trees.

Her hand, meanwhile, was locked tight around Leo's forearm, so the pair of them went sprawling into the dirt, utterly exposed.

Standing over them was a warrior, dressed head to toe in gleaming plates of metal, face obscured behind a helmet.

The armor was not like that worn by Dominion soldiers. It didn't shine with the familiar, silver-gray gleam of steel. No, it was made of *pure* iron, nearly black in color and molded by magic.

It couldn't be . . .

They'd all died in the Uprising. Their leaders, the Knights, had been defeated, and the rest of them wiped out, like Odile had said.

Or not.

Because standing before Wren was the unmistakable sight of an ironsmith.

Fear lanced through her.

They were the most dangerous warriors in the Dominions, and here one stood, looming over her, black sword drawn.

Every piece of armor fitted him perfectly, shifting and sliding as smoothly as scales. The helmet—with its pronounced cheek guards, long nose piece, and razor-sharp iron plume—gave him a distinctive ironsmith silhouette *and* covered the entirety of his face . . . until pieces started retracting before Wren's very eyes, folding back for better visibility without him having to lift a finger. Ironsmith gear was renowned for its strength, sharpness, and clever design. In short, ironsmith armor and weapons could do things *regular* armor and weapons could not.

While his features remained shadowed, it seemed the ironsmith had seen all he needed to. His attention fixed on Leo, he stepped *over* Wren's prone form, dismissing her in pursuit of the prince—clearly his intended target. Leo might be the spare's spare, but he was still a prince, a son of the king. He was valuable, especially in the wrong hands.

Frozen in fear, Leo stumbled backward, but there would be no running. There would be no escape. Wren glanced around, spotting two mounted riders heading their way. They were dressed like light cavalry, armed with bow and arrow and wearing gleaming black chain mail rather than plate—meaning they weren't ironsmiths, thank the Digger—and riding small, fast horses.

Like the ironsmith, they, too, were focused wholly on the prince, which meant she might be able to get away, if she was quick enough. They might let her go. But the prospect of one more failure laid at her feet was more than Wren could bear.

And Leo had called her a friend. She wouldn't abandon him.

Besides, despite how convenient it might be given the current circumstances, Wren Graven did not like to be ignored.

She got into a crouch and sprang, colliding with the ironsmith and taking him to the ground, his hand still outstretched.

The impact knocked the breath from her lungs, his various iron plates digging into her flesh with enough force to break bones—she just hoped they weren't the ones *inside* her. His sword went flying, joining Wren's in the dirt, but they had barely landed before the ironsmith regained the upper hand, rolling her onto her back and pressing a hand to her throat.

She stared up into his shadowed features, her vision growing dark—until a loud *clang* echoed through the white noise in her mind, and the ironsmith fell to the side, his helmet knocked clean off.

And there stood Leo, with the ironsmith's dropped sword in his hands, his eyes wide.

Idiot. He was the one they wanted, not her! He was supposed to run when Wren tackled the ironsmith, to take the chance that she had not. Now they were both in trouble.

Leo could barely hold the sword upright and was forced to drop it as the ironsmith stirred, the other two riders fast approaching.

Wren needed a distraction, immediately.

"This time," she gasped, withdrawing one of her throwing knives, "you run."

Before Leo could reply, she flung it with all her might. Not at one of the soldiers, whose mail would protect their most vulnerable parts, but at the soft flesh of one of the horses, who were less well protected.

The knife landed true, settling in the nearer horse's foreleg, causing it to shriek and rear up. Wren felt a stab of guilt, quickly stifled. It wasn't a mortal wound, and pain was temporary. Or so her father had always said.

As the horse bucked, the rider struggled to remain seated, and the pair of them nearly collided with the other rider and his mount, slowing them down exponentially.

"Go!" Wren yelled, reaching for another knife, but the next thing she knew, she was on her back again, the ironsmith glaring down at her with eyes black as night, his teeth bared. He was younger than she expected, his cheeks smooth and pale, his dark hair slicked away from his face.

"Get him," he barked, and Wren could only assume that Leo had, in fact, run, and the ironsmith was ordering the others to pursue. On horseback, they'd have him in moments, but Wren had other problems.

Above her, the ironsmith raised a hand, palm open. His sword, which lay several feet away, heeded his magical call and soared into his grip. Then he angled the massive weapon across her neck. There were strange grooves carved into the iron, creating a repeating pattern Wren couldn't identify—and shouldn't bother trying, as her death was imminent.

"Julian!" one of the soldiers shouted. Apparently that was the name of the boy about to slit Wren's throat, because he glanced away impatiently.

The shift in his body freed her right hand—which had been pinned underneath him and still clutched a second throwing knife. With a painful twist of her wrist, she managed to slash the exposed, armorless flesh of the ironsmith's thigh.

He grunted and flinched, and it gave her enough room to free her other hand and plunge it into the pouch at her waist.

A cloud of bonedust filled the space between them—harmless against the living but annoying all the same. Wren held her breath and squinted against the debris, but she'd aimed it all at him. *Forcefully*.

Coughing and choking, the ironsmith stumbled to his feet, wiping angrily at his streaming eyes. The weight that had been crushing Wren's chest eased, and she scrambled away.

Seeking her sword, she copied the ironsmith and raised her hand, calling it to her open palm and sheathing her small dagger.

They faced each other, both breathing hard, his face ashen and streaked with tears. For the first time, he really *looked* at her. At the bone weapons and armor, her black clothing and grease-smeared eyes. Then down at the dust he swiped from his cheek.

"Bonesmith," he said, the word dripping with disdain. It might have been the king's orders that sent bonesmiths and the rest of the Dominion soldiers east of the Wall during the Uprising, but Locke Graven led the final charge, and it appeared that fact had not been forgotten.

Wren inclined her head, poised for the next assault. They'd wound up farther from the Wall than she'd realized, but the palisade was still too distant to be much use to her. The sound of fighting continued to ring out, but it remained on the other side of the trees, which were burning more steadily now. Plumes of smoke drifted in the breeze, blocking out the sun and swirling around the ironsmith, turning all to a gloomy haze.

And Prince Leo . . . Wren's heart sank when she located him, thrown over one of the kidnapper's horses. Their task was complete.

Except for Wren.

Sure enough, one of them was drawing their bow, preparing to nock an arrow. Wren's gaze darted around—could she make it back to the trees?—but then she spotted a dark slash in the ground, a shadowy crevasse near the edge of the copse. If she could just get inside and take cover, maybe they'd simply leave her behind in favor of making a clean getaway with their prize.

Wren sheathed her sword across her back, and the ironsmith's body tensed before he frowned. If she didn't intend to *fight* . . .

He realized it a second later as Wren tore off toward the fissure. Distantly, she heard shouts and knew that while the archer would be aiming for her, it was more difficult to hit a moving target.

Of course, she still had the ironsmith to worry about.

Her goal wasn't far, the crevasse almost within reach, when she tripped over some unseen obstruction, slamming hard into the ground. The wind was knocked out of her, stunning her and making her movements clumsy as she attempted to get to her feet, but there was something tangled around her ankle.

An iron rope?

Looking up, she saw that the ironsmith had followed her, and he no longer held his carved iron sword—or rather, he only held the handle. The blade had seemingly disappeared, the grooves she had seen up close demarcating segments that could be separated, breaking the sword into dozens of pieces that spread along an iron cable that had been hidden within.

It was a whip sword, a legendary ironsmith weapon she'd never thought to see in real life. The rippling iron cord was dotted with pieces of the blade, several of which were digging into her ankle. The only reason she hadn't been sliced to ribbons was because of her bone-armored boot.

As she looked down at it, the ironsmith flicked his wrist, and the whip wrapped itself tighter and tighter, cutting off her circulation.

With a look of satisfaction on his face, he took slow, measured steps toward her. Wren, however, was more concerned with the arrow that was surely moments from sailing her way. She turned her back to him, pulling herself with her arms, the lip of the dark chasm *just* out of reach. . . .

With a hard tug, the ironsmith dragged her backward, and Wren knew she'd need to find a different strategy. She rolled onto her back to look up at him. Hesitantly, she raised her hands. She abhorred the idea of it, but maybe surrender would save her life . . . or maybe she'd forfeited it when she'd thrown herself at this ironsmith in the first place.

A smile tugged at his mouth, but then Wren saw movement out of the corner of her eye.

Apparently uninterested in her surrender, the distant rider let his arrow fly.

It was as if time slowed, the air bending around the oncoming projectile as it barreled straight for her.

No. Not for her . . . the trajectory, the angle, it was all wrong. This arrow was meant for *him*. His back was to the others, and the ironsmith had no idea he was about to be shot. No matter how impressive his armor, there were always gaps—and who would know them better than one of his own?

Though he didn't see it coming, he *did* see her expression. He turned, but he was too slow—the arrow too fast.

It thunked into the top of his chest, and the impact sent his body careening back toward the mouth of the chasm Wren had been desperately seeking. The chasm that, as the ironsmith fell, she was pulled inextricably into, the whip still tightly coiled around her leg.

She struggled—but it was pointless. She had only enough time to gasp in surprise as her body slid after him, dragged into the abyss.

TWELVE

There was nothing to grab hold of, nothing to stop their sudden, desperate fall—until there was.

Wren's heart lurched into her throat, only to slam back down into her stomach as she landed on a hard, rocky surface. The impact rattled her bones, her head ringing, and it took a second for her to understand where she was and who was with her.

The ironsmith had landed first, but his body lay unmoving as she struggled to sit up.

It was dark all around, the smoky gray light from above only just illuminating his prone form, the iron plates glinting dully. Beyond . . . nothing but emptiness.

They'd landed on a ledge, and Wren didn't want to know how deep this crevasse went beneath it, how much farther there might be to fall.

Especially as the ironsmith currently teetered near the edge. Wren shuffled nearer to him, afraid any sudden movement might cause the shelf to give way or his body to slide beyond her reach and drag her down with him.

She needed to *move him*. Fast.

She tugged at the iron coil around her leg, trying to unravel it—but the segments had twisted and locked together. Cursing, she reached for the ironsmith's arm instead, tugging him toward her.

He made a mumbled protestation—proving he was dazed but not wholly unconscious. Or dead. But he was out of it enough not to realize the danger he was in.

The closer he got, the better Wren could see that the arrow had landed in his breastplate, right below his collarbone—but there wasn't any blood. Ironsmith armor was stronger than anything they could make in the Dominions, and whatever that rider used to tip his arrow, it wasn't able to punch all the way through.

The ironsmith would have a wicked bruise, but his heart still beat in his chest, and his blood still pumped through his veins.

As she dragged him toward her and the wall of the crevasse, where she assumed the ledge was more stable, the distant rumble of horse hooves echoed down, and she looked up, realizing how exposed they were. If that archer came to check his work, if he and his companion peered over the edge—which Wren suspected they were about to do—they'd see that she and the ironsmith had survived. Then it would simply be a matter of a couple more well-placed arrows, and they'd finish the job.

But looking over her shoulder, she saw that the wall behind her was steeply angled, providing a substantial recess—and perfect hiding place, if she could get them to it. From above, it would appear as though they'd continued to fall past this stony ledge, down, down, into the dark. The kidnappers would have no choice but to assume the worst—that both Wren and the ironsmith were dead, as they had intended.

Why they had intended it was a mystery she didn't have time to dwell on. The ironsmith weighed a metric shit-ton, technically speaking, his body lax and his iron armor and weapons like weights strapped to his skin. She only managed to move him at all because the ground sloped inward, allowing gravity to help. It was thanks to his own magic that he was able to move and fight under such heavy materials. The law of ratios was never much of an issue with bonesmiths, but ironsmiths monitored the equation with mathematical precision.

Wren pulled with everything she had, gritting her teeth and using her legs for leverage, despite the searing pain lancing through her ankle, jostling the ironsmith roughly as she dragged his body across the ground.

The pounding hooves stopped, and muffled voices reached them. Panic spiked Wren's adrenaline. One more good pull, and she was inside the recess. Another, and he joined her.

She was just grabbing him by his breastplate to ensure his entire body was out of sight when his eyes snapped open, and he shoved her away, his metal clanking.

But the voices were clearer now, their words distinguishable, and Wren did not have time for this.

With one hand she took hold of the arrow shaft and pushed, temporarily robbing the ironsmith of breath as she *helpfully* reminded him of his wound. Then her other hand clapped over his mouth, ensuring that when he could inhale again, he didn't exhale in a shout.

His eyes flashed dangerously, and he struggled against her hold—until the sound of the voices above penetrated his anger.

"...can't see a thing," one of them said.

"Look harder," the second snapped back. "The others are already retreating. The fort's soldiers will be here any minute."

"You got him. What does it matter if we have the body?"

At those words, the ironsmith went motionless.

"I want to make sure the job is done."

"Look how dark it is. The fall is a hundred feet at least—no one's surviving that, especially not with an arrow in their throat."

Wren glanced down at the ironsmith. That slightly missed target—coupled with his powerful armor—had saved his life.

It seemed he knew that too. His expression was unreadable, but he'd stopped resisting her. Still, she didn't dare remove her hand.

"And what about the girl?"

"Even without an arrow, I doubt she's fared any better."

The other man cursed, and Wren thought maybe he kicked something, because a rainfall of pebbles clattered down around them.

"Come on, we'll figure out the rest on the road. Let's move."

There was a whinny, the jangle of a saddle, and then the steady roll of hooves galloping away.

Silence descended.

One breath, two, then the ironsmith batted her hand away.

Even that small movement seemed to cause him pain. He gritted his teeth, sweat dotting his brow as he closed his eyes, collecting himself.

After several panting breaths, he stared down at his chest.

Wren remained crouched beside him, on high alert despite the rough shape he was in. She watched closely, aware of every movement as he reached toward the wound. Wren thought he intended to yank the arrow out, but instead, he rested his hand on his breastplate next to the puncture. Nothing happened, though she could sense he was straining. He kept holding his breath, then releasing it in heavy gusts of frustration before, on his third attempt, the dented metal reshaped and spat the arrow out.

There was no evidence the plate had ever been punctured, yet the arrowhead that landed on the ground next to Wren was flattened at the tip. It was black in color, like all ironsmith metal, but was surely of a lesser grade than what the ironsmiths used for their armor. If she remembered correctly, ironsmiths didn't construct any weapons for sale or wide distribution that could puncture their own plate. The ironsmith warrior must always reign supreme.

That done, the ironsmith attempted to pull himself into a seated position, but his arm caught on the whip sword wrapped around Wren's leg. She was shocked he still held the weapon, even after being unconscious, but perhaps it was more ironsmith magic. After a moment's hesitation, he tugged, and the whip lost its tension. Wren freed her leg from the knot, and then he flicked his wrist, the whip retracting to the hilt, fluid and snakelike, before becoming solid and snapping back into the shape of a blade.

His shoulders sagged before he pushed himself upright, leaving the weapon on the ground. He leaned against the wall, pressing a hand to his chest. He needed to remove the breastplate if he wanted to survey the damage, but Wren knew, somehow, that he wouldn't do it with her there.

The quiet pressed in on them. Moments before, they'd been trying to kill each other, and now they were trapped here on this narrow ledge. Wren's only chance of escape would come in the form of the Breachfort soldiers, but the ironsmith? He'd need to collect his strength and maybe try to extend that whip into something he could climb.

She reached out a tentative hand to the blade, wanting to touch it, to understand—

"Don't," he snapped, but he wasn't looking at her. It seemed he could sense it.

"Why do they want you dead?" she asked. She figured she might as well, as they were currently stuck here together, and it seemed relevant.

He shook his head but didn't speak. He continued to rub at his chest.

"Because they definitely shot that arrow at *you*. I thought it was coming for me, but I was on the ground, and it was way off target. Actually, if it weren't for your stupid whip, I'd still be up there, and—"

"Shut up," he said tiredly, pressing black-gloved fingers to his temples. He sighed. "This doesn't make any sense."

"No shit," Wren said, and he shot her an icy glare, his dark eyes stark against the bonedust on his face.

She ignored him, focusing instead on trying to massage away the pain in her ankle and calf. No doubt she'd have welts on her skin, but for now she wanted to make sure the limb could bear her weight. She got to her feet gingerly, and while her leg hurt, it was usable.

"He must be planning something on his own," the ironsmith muttered, mostly to himself. "Unless he just wants the credit himself. He's an ambitious man. . . ."

"Who?" Wren asked. Standing, she took a chance to survey the rest of her damage, which was primarily surface. She had both her swords, though she'd lost a throwing knife. Her bandolier was stocked, her armor mostly intact, though it had taken a beating.

He hesitated. "Captain Royce."

"Your own captain turned against you?" she asked, surprised. "You're sure the order didn't come from higher up . . . ?"

And who *would* rank higher than an ironsmith soldier as talented as him? He was young, but he wielded his magic with power and finesse, and his whip sword was the kind of weapon she'd only heard fantastical tales about. But how had he been trained? All their masters, all their warriors, were supposed to have been wiped out.

"I'm sure," he snapped, and Wren left it alone.

Craning her neck, she peered out the opening in the crevasse above, which rose nearly twenty feet overhead. It was late in the afternoon, pushing into the evening, but the smoke was thick in the sky, and clouds were rolling in, bringing an unnatural darkness. Distantly, horn calls and alarm bells were ringing from Wall sentries. Breachfort reinforcements were already on the way.

Surely they would find her . . . if the ironsmith didn't kill her first.

When she looked down again, she realized he had been listening as well. His expression hardened, and Wren took a wary step back from the ledge; otherwise she'd be one good push away from a fall into the cavern below. He might be wounded, but he was still an ironsmith—lethal and powerful.

A voice, sudden and near at hand, rang out from somewhere above. "Prince Leopold! Highness! Are you there? Prince Leopold!"

Wren's head snapped up, her lips parted, but then her back was slammed against the crevasse wall and a hand pressed over *her* mouth.

She threw a knee into the ironsmith's groin region, but she suspected she'd aimed high, because while he grunted and cursed, he didn't keel over. Pity. She went for his arms next, meaning to buckle his elbows and twist her face free, when a flash of iron reminded her that he was no ordinary adversary.

She knew the magic cost him when he was in this state, but it didn't stop him. A blade sprang forward from beneath his vambrace, extending past the top of his hand, which he curled into a fist. She had no choice but to cease her squirming or impale herself on it.

"There's no sign of him, Commander," said another voice. It sounded faint, as if he were standing farther away than the prince's captors had. Did they see the cavern's mouth? Would they hear her if she cried out?

"The girl is missing as well," said a third. "The bonesmith." Wren struggled, to hell with the danger, but the ironsmith's grip was firm.

"We must send riders," said the first. "There's a trail heading southeast."

"We can try," said Commander Duncan, his familiar voice grave. "But they know these parts, and they have a head start. We'll be under attack as soon as we reach civilization—they have no love for the Breachfort garrison east of the Wall. There are also raiders and the undead to consider. You must write to the king and see if he will send aid."

"By the time he does, it will be too late." That voice definitely belonged to Galen, whose nasally timbre was as distinct as it was irritating. "Better to wait."

"For what?"

"For their ransom. Surely that is why he was taken and not assassinated on the spot. They want something, these Breachsiders, and the prince's life will ensure that they get it."

Wren couldn't believe her ears. They weren't even going to *try*? The kidnappers had only just taken Leo away. A good horse and a fast rider could make up that time . . . but they didn't know that. They didn't know when he had been taken, or by how many, and even Wren couldn't be sure. Perhaps there were dozens more waiting for a rendezvous.

She didn't know . . . but *he* would. The ironsmith. He would know exactly who had taken Leo and where, and best of all?

They were the very same people who had just tried to kill him.

Wren let her body go slack, trying to tell him without words that she had no intention of fighting him again.

Of course, she could just be baiting him—that's certainly what his suspicious expression suggested he believed—so his hand remained pressed firmly over her mouth, his vambrace blade still inches from her throat.

Above, the talk had turned to logistics and cleanup. They had to put out fires, deal with bodies, and contact the king. She thought again of Odile, who would soon be receiving the news of Wren's disappearance. What would her report to Wren's father say? Would they assume she was dead? Would Commander Duncan and the others say she had fought bravely and tried to save the prince? Or would they say nothing at all?

The murmured conversation and steady hoofbeats slowly faded away.

But the ironsmith continued to hold Wren immobile. He looked . . . lost. He was staring at her, but his attention was turned inward. Wren suspected he was trying to puzzle out some of the same things she had been, including how to get out of this cursed pit, but she didn't have all night.

She had a prince to rescue.

She shifted impatiently, the movement causing the ironsmith to come back to himself. Darkness was slowly descending inside the cavern, obscuring the features of his face. She couldn't see the decision he'd made, but one minute his whole body was pinning her to the wall, his hand over her mouth—and the next, he'd released her and stepped away.

He watched Wren warily as she straightened her clothes and pushed her hair out of her face. No doubt the eye black on her lips was smeared, but she had more pressing concerns.

"We need to get out of here," she said.

"We?" he repeated flatly.

"You think you're getting out of here without me?"

He looked up at the mouth of the cavern, then down at his whip sword. "Yes."

Wren scowled. "Yeah? And how far will you get when you climb out of this place only to walk straight into a Breachfort patrol?"

His lips pulled back from his teeth. "I can handle your patrol."

"Maybe *before* you attacked and kidnapped a prince. But now? They'll be riding double, triple shifts. It won't be a regular patrol. It'll be a small army. And you're wounded."

He clenched his jaw and looked away. This was her chance.

"I know the protocols," she said, taking a cautious step toward him. "I know who they'll send and where. I can get us out of here."

He cocked an eyebrow. "And where will you be going, bonesmith, if not back to your fort?"

She smiled. "After the prince, of course."

THIRTEEN

It was all coming together in Wren's mind.

Prince Leo needed rescuing, but the Breachfort didn't have the resources or the information required to pull it off.

But Wren did.

Not only was she the best valkyr of her generation, failed trial be damned, but she was also standing with the one person who could tell her exactly where Leo was being taken—and probably even what route.

A small, two-person party could pass through the Breachlands unseen, not drawing attention like a mounted force from the fort would. Wren could handle whatever ghosts came their way, and this ironsmith could surely deal with anything living that might cross their path.

He would lead her to Leo, and she would rescue him. If she could do that, if she could save the Gold Prince from their enemies and return him safely to the Breachfort—traversing the dangerous and ghost-plagued Breachlands to do it—no one could deny her talent, her capability, and her right to a position within the House of Bone.

No one could deny that she was worthy.

It was perfect. Genius, even.

She just had to get this ironsmith to agree.

He continued to stare at her, uncomprehending, so Wren elaborated.

"Unless you intended to just roll over and die, you'll want some answers from your comrades who tried to kill you."

His eyes flashed dangerously, but he didn't deny her words.

"And so you intend to follow them. I intend likewise."

"Why?" he asked skeptically.

"That prince is my ticket out of this place," she said, gesturing vaguely in the direction of the fort. "If I rescue him, I'll be able to prove my value and get whatever posting I want. *He* is important, and so by getting him back, *I* will become important."

He didn't need to know that she *liked* Leo. That she had seen the fear in his eyes. That he had raised his flask in honor of their new friendship and that that made him her only one.

Except for Odile, maybe. But that was different. She was Wren's superior. More like a teacher or mentor than a friend. Someone obligated to be around her, even if she'd been more open and honest with Wren than most others in her life. More than her own father.

The ironsmith, meanwhile, curled his lip at her words, as if he was judging her. Let him.

"And so I will get him back," Wren insisted, "and *you* will help me, just like I helped you. You're welcome, by the way."

"You helped me? Was that before or after you sliced open my leg?"

"After," Wren said. "When we fell—your fault—and landed in this

—133

death trap, I dragged your lifeless corpse out of sight and stopped you from giving away our position."

"If you hadn't fallen too, you'd be dead by now. Captain Royce doesn't like loose ends. The fact that you're alive should be thanks enough."

"I'd still like the words, though," she said, unable to help herself. She cleared her throat. "Thank you for *inadvertently* saving my life," she recited with as much earnestness as she could muster. Then she grinned. "See? Easy."

He leaned forward, his words soft and cold when he spoke. "If you want a pat on the back for being a hero, give it to yourself. You're clearly very good at it."

Wren was annoyed. "Yes, I am," she said with a cocky smirk. "Practice makes perfect, after all."

"Is that what you think you are? Perfect?"

Wren opened her mouth to say something along the lines of "if the shoe fits," but before she could, he pressed a gloved hand against her arm, in the gap beneath her pauldron. She reared back—first as a gut reaction to his touch and then, belatedly, because of a stab of pain. His black leather-clad fingers came away shiny with blood. When had that happened?

"Not quite," he said softly.

Wren knocked his hand aside. "I'm not the only one losing blood," she snapped, stalking away. She wiped at her arm, the stinging wound fairly shallow, if annoying.

"No," he agreed, the ghost of a smile on his face. "But I never said I was perfect."

Wren glared at him. "Are we doing this or not?"

His humor dissipated. "Doing what?" he asked.

"Rescuing the prince!"

"You *do* realize I was one of the kidnappers, right?" His tone was arrogant. Superior.

She glared at him. "Yes. And then those kidnappers tried to *kill you*. Maybe this whole thing was a lie—an excuse to target you."

A spasm of anger crossed his face. "No. He wouldn't—" He stopped himself. "They've obviously forsaken our orders. Or Captain Royce has, anyway. Maybe he'll try to turn around and sell the prince to the highest bidder. He has to be stopped."

"Exactly. So we'll stop him. Take the prince for ourselves."

"And then what?" he asked, brows raised.

"We'll figure it out," Wren said confidently. Of course what she *meant* was that she'd return Leo safely to the Breachfort whether the ironsmith liked it or not, but *saying* so would be counterproductive. "Would you rather him in the hands of a betrayer or the fort?"

"I'd rather him in my own hands."

"I'll be sure to tell him that."

He frowned, confused—then rolled his eyes.

"What happens after matters only if we actually *get* him," she said placatingly. "Why don't we cross that bridge when we reach it?"

He surveyed her closely. Wren tried not to squirm. "Fine," he said, agreeing a little too readily in her opinion. The discussion likely wasn't over, but they could pick it up later. "What's the patrol schedule? How long do we have?"

Wren's temporary flare of triumph flickered. She *might* have exaggerated her knowledge of Breachfort protocols post-attack. It made sense that they would increase their patrols, both in frequency and size, but it was hard to know what that would do to the existing schedule, or how it might play out over the following hours. They were still reeling from the attack, and they'd lost people in the fighting. Rosters would need to be adjusted, and new schedules made. There would be a certain degree of chaos as they wrote letters and sent runners north and south, relaying the news and ensuring the entire Wall was prepared in case of further attack—though surely they knew it was doubtful. The kidnappers had gotten what they'd come for.

She joined the ironsmith at the tip of the ledge and peered upward. Smoke was heavy in the dusky twilight, but the black of night wouldn't be far off. They wouldn't be able to see much, but they'd be able to *hear* it. The patrols usually didn't ride beyond the road, but after an attack, they'd be ordered to check everywhere between the Wall and the palisade.

Wren would just have to wait and listen. Once one patrol passed, they'd have the time it took for them to return to the fort—and for a new patrol to ride back this way—to escape.

It was a small window, but it was their best chance.

"Not long," she said, taking a seat along the edge so she could hear any activity above. "There'll be a short gap between patrols."

"How short?"

Wren shrugged. "We'll need to climb quickly, then get past the palisade. Once we do that, we'll be in the clear." He also settled into a sitting position, his movements stiff and awkward as he favored his left side. "You *will* be able to climb, won't you?"

He threw her a cold look. "Will you?"

"As long as that whip is strong enough, I'll be good," she said.

"It will be strong enough."

They sat in silence after that.

Wren didn't have much to do except listen, but the ironsmith took the opportunity to retract his vambrace blade and sheath his sword across his back. He checked the wound on his leg, courtesy of Wren, and rolled his shoulder near the chest wound, grimacing.

She found herself wondering again who this ironsmith was and where he had come from. Evidently, the House of Iron was not wiped out, whatever they believed in the Dominions. And someone in the ranks—or someone this ironsmith served—was making a move against the crown.

A distant, rhythmic noise reached her ears. It echoed around them, distorting the sound, but she was fairly certain . . .

"Hoofbeats," the ironsmith said.

"Hide." Wren hastened away from the edge to take cover in the recessed cave. The ironsmith followed her, silent as the grave, despite all the metal and weapons he wore.

It was harder to hear in their hiding place, but Wren could discern at least two mounted riders as they made their slow progress past the crevasse. She caught random words like "smoke" and "fire," and for a moment the horse hooves paused, and she suspected the riders were peering down into this very space. Was there evidence of a scuffle nearby? Would they probe further?

But then the hooves picked up again, carrying them away.

The ironsmith remained in a crouch, poised for action, but he watched her, waiting for the go-ahead.

Wren itched to start climbing, but there was a chance the patrol was large enough to ride with forward and rear scouts. Sure enough, seconds before she was ready to throw caution to the wind and go for it, a larger group of riders could be heard moving past, followed several minutes later by another pair.

Finally, when those last hooves receded, Wren looked to the ironsmith. She nodded. "Now."

They both rushed to the edge of the cliff, and she had to concede that he moved much better now that there was work to be done.

He withdrew his whip sword and transformed it in a snap, flicking his wrist down so the inner cable extended to the ground, the blade segments sliding out along its length. It coiled at his feet while he stared up at their target.

"Step back," he ordered, and Wren did, watching as he flung it upward in a wide, shining arc. He wielded physical and magical strength, using his muscles to get things moving and relying on his magic to aim and guide the whip. It was a common tactic that Wren herself used, allowing a smith to preserve energy. Doing the same thing with magic alone would be exhausting, and he was in no state to push himself to the brink.

Though the whip reached the sky above and disappeared from view, it quickly slipped back down, failing to grab hold of anything.

The ironsmith's eyes narrowed, and he tried again.

And again.

"There were some roots—" Wren began, but he quickly spoke over her.

"I know." His voice was tight with suppressed frustration, and sweat dotted his temples.

Wren closed her mouth, waiting, until finally, on the fifth attempt, the whip caught and held. The ironsmith gave it a few hard tugs, then glanced over at her.

She stared at him blankly until she realized she should go first in case there were any lingering Breachfort soldiers about. It gave her the upper hand to a certain degree—she could try to push him off or betray him—but as they were climbing an iron-whip-turned-rope, Wren very much doubted she'd be able to do any such thing.

Not that she intended to. She needed him.

For now.

She approached, the ironsmith holding the handle loosely to keep the whip steady. While his hands were gloved, hers were bare, so she had to be extremely careful as she held the cable, avoiding the blades, though they provided handy footholds.

There was no time to hesitate, no time to worry if it could hold her weight. No time to wonder if it would slither around her throat and strangle her.

With both hands gripping just around head height, she nodded to the ironsmith, and he released his hold. She jumped, her arms taking her weight while her feet sought the nearest blade segment below.

She managed it without too much struggle, though it wasn't the same as climbing the librarian's shelves—or even climbing her own swords up that muddy grave in the Bonewood. Now she dangled over the chasm below, nothing holding her up but her own muscles and this strange iron whip.

Her breath started to come in short, sharp gasps, and her hands ached from holding too tight. Muscles she swore she'd never used before began to burn, her arms and chest trembling from the effort. But stubbornness won out, and she gritted her teeth as she climbed, feeling the shift when the ironsmith was on the whip beneath her. It swayed wide, causing her to curse vehemently, and continued to bump and jostle now that there were two of them.

She started to use the blade segments for her hands, too, finding a way to hold the inner seams while avoiding the outer edge. When she finally dared to look up, she realized they had not fallen as far as she'd thought. She was already near the top.

Once she got there, she saw that the whip had indeed been

anchored to a tangle of roots she recalled seeing before they pitched over the edge. She looked around but saw no sign of any riders or torchlight. She tried to look up at the Wall, but the copse of trees blocked her view—which meant it also blocked *their* view of *her*, obscuring whatever the darkness didn't.

They might just pull this off.

With one last burst of strength, motivated by the ironsmith coming up behind her, she crested the ridge, gasping.

He joined her soon after, but with a bit more dignity, resting his hands on his knees to catch his breath before calling the whip up and reshaping it into a sword once more.

Wren got to her feet, peering into the darkness. Behind her, the fires had been put out, and she could just discern the outlines of the bone palisade in front, her magic sensing and filling in what her eyes missed.

Then she looked at the two of them. Her bone armor definitely stood out, paler than skin against the darkness, but it was nothing to all his iron. It reflected the scraps of moonlight that poked through the haze of smoke and cloud like flashes of sunlight on water.

But the time it would take to remove it—not to mention the risk that posed if they were found or pursued—would potentially put them in even greater danger.

Their eyes met, and Wren knew he saw what she saw.

They had only one option: run like hell.

Together they tore off for the bone palisade, stumbling over uneven ground and leaping rocks and debris as they loomed up out of the shadows.

Wren kept her senses sharp, the presence of the bones ahead keeping her on course. She glanced back only once, but everything behind her was darkness save for the lanterns atop the Wall, and they were dim and shrouded in smoke.

The palisade finally reared up before them, and they both slowed their pace, coming to rest behind one of the towering bone sentinels, using it as cover while they caught their breath.

Wren leaned against it, letting the familiarity of the material calm her racing heart. They had made it away unnoticed.

Now they just needed to find the Gold Prince.

FOURTEEN

After they'd both caught their breath, they started walking east, putting distance between themselves and Breachfort territory.

Once the palisade was no longer in sight, Wren looked to the ironsmith for what came next.

As he walked, he sheathed his whip sword and withdrew a staff instead, also strapped to his back. It was unremarkable-looking save for its unique color, which marked it as ironsmith-made.

Wren realized then that they hadn't exactly introduced themselves. They'd gone from fighting each other to hiding together and now . . . whatever this was. A shaky alliance.

With an ironsmith.

Wren's stomach twinged with unease. She would definitely need to fudge *that* detail when she told her father all about her heroic rescue of the prince. Luckily, she was a practiced liar.

Still, they would be allies for the foreseeable future.

"I'm Wren, by the way," she said.

He seemed to have been lost in thought, because he startled when she spoke. His dark eyes flicked in her direction.

"And you are . . . ?" she pressed when he remained silent. "I heard them talking to you—before they tried to kill you, that is. James? *Jules* . . ." His face spasmed at that. "If you don't give me a name, I'll be forced to make one up, and I suspect that will only cause things to further deteriorate between us."

"Julian," he said with exasperation. "My name is Julian."

"Nice to meet you," she said. He shot her a glare. They had met under the worst circumstances imaginable.

With a shrug, she cast her gaze across the darkened landscape. There was less smoke out here, but fog had rolled in from the north, resulting in the same obscuring effect. She turned to Julian. "Now what? I assume you know what direction they traveled?"

"I know what direction they *intended* to travel, but as their plans have changed since then—namely with the attempt on my life—I don't know if anything else has since been . . . adjusted."

"Let's assume their escape plans remain the same. They think you're dead, so they have no reason to change them."

His nostrils flared. "They will have gone south. They can't risk any harm coming to the prince, and the coastal towns are the only places where they can safely stop for food and rest."

"Then we head south," Wren said, turning on her heel.

She had barely taken a step when a noise came from the hazy fog to her left. She froze.

They hadn't been walking long, and Wren feared she had gotten turned around and somehow stumbled upon a patrol, though it made no sense this far from the palisade. There was movement in the darkness, and then a soft clip-clopping sound.

A horse materialized out of the shadows, making its casual way toward them. It was riderless but not dressed in any Breachfort tack.

Wren glanced at the ironsmith. Was it one of theirs? It could have taken off during the fighting, and his people either never saw where it went or didn't bother to reclaim it.

It was exactly what they needed. Their targets were on horseback, and now Wren and Julian could be the same. It was perfect.

Too perfect?

But time was of the essence, and there didn't seem to be anyone else around . . .

Wren stepped toward it, and Julian's hand swiped at the air as he tried to stop her. "Wait. Don't!"

"Why? What's wrong?" she demanded.

He didn't respond. Instead his head swiveled left and right.

"Come on! This is a lucky break, and we need to get moving."

"This isn't luck," he said, before his gaze settled on something Wren couldn't see. "It's a trap."

Wren heard it then—the clank and jangle of weapons.

Then out of the mist came ten, twenty people, lean and mean and raggedly dressed.

"Bandits," Julian muttered, raising his staff in a two-handed grip.

Finally, one of the dangers Wren's father and Odile had promised. She tensed as she withdrew her swords; she had never fought so many people—*living* people, anyway—and most of her fighting experience came from sparring with Inara in the sands.

As the bandits moved to surround them, the mists swirled and parted, and Wren saw an old signpost and what looked like the remains of a village. Beneath her feet the ground was smooth, suggesting this had been a well-traveled area once—likely belonging to the network of Old Roads that crisscrossed this part of the Dominions. Now it was a place for scavengers and thieves.

Upon closer inspection, the horse looked hungry and thin, just like his human counterparts. They must use him as bait, as a means to lure lost or unsuspecting travelers into their clutches.

"Just shut up and let me do the talking," Julian muttered to Wren, lowering his staff and raising a single, gloved hand. "We mean you no harm," he said, turning to the bandits. "Our party is traveling the Coastal Road, and we got separated. If you let us pass, we'll be on our way."

Wren cocked her head at him. Did he think that mention of the fact that they were allegedly part of a larger group would scare them off, or was he actually trying to appeal to their good nature?

"Coastal Road's a long way from here, son," one of them said, a man with what looked like a pirate's tricorn hat over his head of long, matted hair. His voice was mocking, and Wren thought that if she could *see* his mouth through his tangled beard, he'd be grinning.

"Which means we've a lot of ground to cover," Julian continued, voice steady. It had a cultured, imperious edge—the sort of calm assurance that said he was used to being listened to without having to raise his voice—which might have worked on farmers or small-town folk, but not here. "Your horse. I will buy it for twice the market value."

As one, every head swiveled onto Julian's person, looking for a fat coin purse that promised he actually carried such a sum. They'd have it—and the horse—before the night was through, and Wren and Julian would be nothing but corpses come morning.

Perhaps sensing their intentions, Julian adjusted his hold on his staff, and two iron blades sprang from each end, turning it into a deadly weapon.

A collective murmur went through the group—apparently they hadn't yet realized he was an ironsmith. Never mind the coin in his purse. . . . His weapons were worth far more. The only problem was that they'd have to pry them from his cold, dead hands, and as Wren had seen firsthand, Julian was no craftsman. He was a warrior. Even without the element of surprise, he could likely mow down half this group. The fact that he didn't want to was evident to Wren, if not these others, but she didn't have time to puzzle out *why*. The bandits were tightening their circle, pressing closer, and many of their stares fixed on Wren now too. When was the last time they'd seen a bone-smith this side of the Border Wall?

"I don't have the coin on me," Julian said, remaining poised despite the threat, while Wren's gaze darted from side to side as she scrambled for a solution. Something was tugging at her mind, and she tried to steady the distracting pulse of her heart to discern it. It felt like bones, but it was not the pull of the palisade they'd left behind. No, it was something much nearer.

"We can't accept coin that doesn't actually exist," said another of the raiders, and laughter broke out.

Wren gave Julian a look. Whatever his plan was, it wasn't working. "What are you doing?" she whispered, but he ignored her.

"It exists," Julian said, his expression determined as he spoke over their jeers. "And it's in the Iron Citadel's coffers. Perhaps you'd be willing to accept a payment from there?"

The laughter died out. The Iron Citadel was the House of Iron's main holding, their seat of power, and the place they *used* to train ironsmiths.

And it was supposed to be uninhabited. Abandoned during the Uprising. The way Julian spoke . . . Was the Citadel functioning again? And most pressing of all . . . was it ruling over these lands?

Perhaps the ironsmiths were not as defeated as everyone west of the Wall seemed to think.

"He's bluffing," someone said, and those around them nodded their agreement.

The first man with the pirate's hat stepped forward. "Maybe," he said gruffly, peering at Julian closely. "Or maybe we take him with us and find out. See what else the regent might offer us in exchange for his head."

A regent? Living at the Iron Citadel?

Julian darted a look in Wren's direction, and she wondered if he was concerned about his impending kidnapping . . . or what she'd overheard. What she could report back to the Breachfort.

Of course, none of that would matter if they didn't survive this mess, and while Julian might be worth something to the alleged regent, Wren held no such value.

Negotiations had failed.

It was time to act.

"I'm afraid that's not going to work for me," Julian said, his diplomatic tone gone. His words were low and dangerous, the sharpened points of his staff gleaming.

"Good thing there's twenty of us and two of you, then, isn't it?" The pirate man dared to step even closer, and Wren could finally see the smile beneath the beard—and the missing teeth.

Wren caught Julian's eye—she knew they were going to have to fight their way out of this—but he jerked his head slightly, as if telling her to stand down.

To hell with that.

"Good for us," Wren agreed, giving the pirate man her own dark smile. "Bad for you."

She had figured out what was pulling at her senses, a feeling she'd not had since the Bonewood.

There were bodies all around. Bones deep in the soil.

These lands had been a battleground, and Wren suspected that the signpost behind them had once been used as a gallows to warn off bandits such as those that currently surrounded her.

However they had gotten there, half a dozen bodies were beneath her feet or scattered along the side of the road. Hasty burials, rotten corpses picked clean and swallowed by the earth . . . soldiers lost in war.

Which war, it was difficult to say, but while most of their souls had been reaped, she suspected not all of them had. The odds were not in her favor, but she called to them with her magic all the same. She needed a distraction, a way to level the playing field and even the odds . . . and though bones were ultimately harmless to humans, she suspected they'd scare the shit out of them all the same.

It was a risk, like pulling a thread and accidentally unraveling the careful weave of earth and time that had buried these bodies, but it was her best option. She didn't know what Julian was playing at, and she couldn't have his obvious reticence to deal with these bandits resulting in her becoming another body to be buried by the wayside.

"Wait," Julian began in alarm, "what are you—"

But it was too late.

Wren raised her twin swords, but rather than turning them on the nearest bandit, she flipped the blades and pointed them downward. Then she dropped to her knees and plunged them into the earth.

It was a complex mix of muscle and magic, propelling the blades more deeply than would be possible with her arms alone.

Wren's connection was strongest to the bones she carried with her all the time, and by placing them into the ground, she was using them to extend her range and connect with the other bones in the area. They were all linked by the soil, and she was tapping into that matrix.

There was a rumble, causing everyone to look down in alarm, including Julian.

Then Wren stood, wrenching the blades—and every other bone in the area—up with her. It was an exhausting maneuver, pushing her to the very brink of her abilities . . . but it worked.

Bodies burst from the soil in every direction. Not whole skeletons, but fractured skulls and shattered limbs, bits of dust and debris coalescing into a truly haunting sight.

Next to her, Julian cursed, while all around cries of fear and alarm pierced the crunching, cracking sound of shifting earth and bone.

Several people turned tail and ran without a second thought, but the pirate was not one of them. He'd staggered back in alarm, dodging the bones underfoot, but was soon shouting orders and dragging his people bodily into position.

"Get the bone witch!" he said, shoving a pair of bandits toward Wren while the others circled Julian.

"Stay he—" Julian began, but Wren had already started moving. She wasn't trained for this shit, not like Julian, and had to use every trick and tool in her possession—including the ability to move quickly and sense the bones beneath her feet while the others only stumbled blindly.

She put distance between herself and Julian, spreading their attackers and scrambling for her next move. They mostly carried steel knives, though she'd spotted several cudgels and a few short swords. Wren's blades could block a blow or two, but if that metal was even remotely sharp, it would start to chip away at the bone. That was to say nothing of her armor, which was made to protect against the touch of the undead, not the living.

Like she had with Julian, Wren used a few clouds of bonedust to buy herself time, but whenever she opened a bit of space between herself and her pursuers, one of them would cut off her escape and herd her back toward the others.

While she played a strange game of cat and mouse, Julian had started to cut down his foes with brutal efficiency, the blades at the ends of his staff wicked sharp.

All around him his attackers dropped, but he wasn't dealing death blows. Every time one of them fell, they stood up again, however worse for wear. He was still holding back.

Before Wren could yell at him for that, an earsplitting screech rent the night.

Her heart stopped. That was no normal cry of pain or fear. That was a cry from beyond the physical realm.

That was a cry from the undead.

How she knew, she couldn't say—ghosts didn't speak. Didn't cry or moan or shriek their fury. Everything they did was soundless and incorporeal, just as they were. But as surely as she knew the truth of that statement, she knew that the sound she'd heard was not living. Not human.

She spotted the ghost at once, near the signpost. It seemed she had disrupted whatever bones had been keeping the ghost in place, just like she had with the many-elbowed arm in the Bonewood, and now it was free to move.

It slowly coalesced before them, a shining greenish light, reaching such a feverish brightness that many of the raiders covered their eyes or looked away, howling in pain.

Even Julian flinched, leaving only Wren to watch as the figure took shape.

There was something very wrong with it.

Its neck was bent at a horrid, unnatural angle—confirming Wren's suspicion that there was indeed a gallows here once upon a time—making the ghost's figure strange and misshapen. Still, it formed in detailed clarity, including the broken neck and dark, blood-flushed face.

To be able to make sound . . . Following the logic of the undead scale, Wren would classify this as a tier-four geist—able to affect the world around it. Which meant it could do more than just make noise.

Wren tried to spot its body among the mess of bones she had made, but she was no reapyr. She couldn't set this spirit free. Her only chance was to damage it enough that it temporarily vanished.

At the appearance of an actual undead, the bandits immediately scattered, choosing their lives over whatever coin they'd hoped to procure with Julian. Even the horse followed suit.

This was, however, a mistake.

Never turn your back on a ghost.

Never run.

The angry spirit latched on to the movement, lashing out at the nearest living targets. Two of them got away, but the third . . .

Wren stumbled forward, but it had happened in an instant. Looking fearfully over his shoulder, the bandit had run headlong into the ghost as it came to a stuttering halt directly in front of him. He ran clear through, and the result was as swift as it was brutal.

Deathrot.

His screams died in his throat, the deathrot blooming across his chest and up his neck like an ink stain, visible over the collar of his filthy shirt.

He dropped to the ground, twitching. Some deathrot could be reversed, or at least stopped from spreading if it started in a limb or the touch was mild enough. But this ghost had hit his chest first; he didn't stand a chance.

The rest of the bandits were gone, and now it was just Wren and Julian.

The ghost's attention shifted and homed in on the ironsmith. He was the nearer target, and unlike Wren, he was defenseless.

He remained rigidly still, his staff outstretched—though it would prove utterly useless.

Wren had no choice but to utilize a long-range weapon, but her knucklebones would not be enough to stop a tier four, and her throwing knives wouldn't make enough of an impact.

There was only one move that would work. Sheathing one of her swords, she took the other in a two-handed grip and raised it over her head.

She flung it with all her might, blade over handle like a throwing ax. She pushed with every scrap of magic she had left, guiding the blade so that it spun faster and faster before impacting with the ghost's middle, slicing it in two.

There was another cry, trembling and faint. It almost sounded like the creature was trying to speak, its vaporous mouth shaping words, but then the spirit dissipated in a wisp.

Darkness descended, leaving Wren and Julian surrounded by nothing but bones and dead bodies and the sound of their ragged breathing.

FIFTEEN

Wren walked to retrieve her blade, too tired to bother summoning it.

Julian remained immobile, staring at the bandit who'd been taken by deathrot. Or so she thought. As Wren moved closer, she realized there was a second body next to it, pierced through by one of Julian's blades. That was who he was staring at, the man he had killed despite his best efforts not to.

"Is it gone?" he asked hoarsely, his eyes shut in a grimace. Surely he meant the ghost.

It was difficult to know for sure. They were beyond the protections of the Wall, and she didn't understand the rules here. She'd never heard a ghost scream, let alone attempt to actually *speak*. It would need time to gather its strength and re-form, but how much time, she had no idea.

"For now," she said. "But we need to move, quickly."

Something about the words seemed to irk him. His shoulders tightened, and he looked over at her. "You mean to just leave them here, where they can prey on other travelers? Don't you . . . ? Aren't there funeral rites? Things you can do to help?" He waved his hand vaguely in her direction, uncertain what those *things* might be, but asking nonetheless.

"In case you've forgotten, we are on a rescue mission," she said. "There's no time to dig graves and no point when there aren't any reapyrs this side of the Wall to finish the job. The deathrotted one is gone for good, but the other's spirit *will* rise eventually, and there's nothing you or I can do about it."

He looked her up and down, and she realized he might not know the difference between a reapyr and herself, but he didn't question her. "There's such a thing as respect and dignity."

"You want to give the people who tried to kill us *respect and dignity*?" she scoffed.

He rounded on her. "You think they live like that because they *want* to?" he demanded, his words surprisingly sharp. "They wouldn't have tried to kill us if you'd let me negotiate—"

"Negotiate the terms of *your* survival, while I stood there and waited for execution?" She laughed humorlessly. "No one this side of the Wall is going to pay for *my* life, Julian, friend of the so-called regent." Probably no one on the other side, either, but she didn't mention that. "Besides, you were *losing*."

"So you decided to raise the bloody dead?"

"I didn't raise the dead," Wren corrected with exasperation.

"You're telling me those bones burst out of the earth by accident? What kind of bonesmith are you?"

She pointed at the bones. "Most of these bones are not haunted. They are what I reached for—they are all my magic can touch. But when I unearthed them, I accidentally disturbed bones that *are* haunted. And there are probably more, given that signpost was once a gibbet, so we need to get out of here."

"We'll never catch up now," Julian said, heaving a breath as he relaxed his grip on his staff, the blades retracting before he slid it into the holder across his back. He put his hands on his hips, staring off into the distance before sliding Wren an appraising sort of look. "Unless . . ."

The look on his face piqued her interest. "Unless what?"

"Even though this whole thing was your fault," he began, and Wren interjected at once.

"*My* fault? Those bandits—"

"Set a trap that you walked into without a second thought. Then you interrupted my attempts to end this peacefully, and when I asked you to stay put so we could properly defend ourselves, you ran off and summoned a ghost." Wren spluttered, but he just kept talking. "*But*, despite all that, you did dispatch it fairly neatly, and your mastery over bones may have some use. . . ."

Some use? The nerve. "What are you saying?"

"I'm saying that there is one way we could catch up to the prince. One way to put us in a position to head them off and do what we set out to do. Cross through the Haunted Territory."

Wren's heart kicked against her ribs. Everywhere east of the Wall was considered the Breachlands—a den of traitors and undead monsters, the battlefield where wars had been fought against both the living and the undead. The site of the Breach, the greatest calamity the Dominions had ever seen.

Going *anywhere* east of the Wall was a bold and daring move, even for her, but crossing through the Haunted Territory? There was the chasm—the Breach itself, twenty miles long and who knew how deep—and then there was the radius of dangerous land that surrounded it, the place where the undead tended to linger. The Haunted Territory. As Odile had pointed out on her map, the landscape blocked them in on two sides, thanks to the mountains and the river, and it seemed they didn't like to stray far from the deep wound in the ground from which they had risen.

As far as Wren knew, no living people set foot there—or hadn't since Locke and his forces, and only Vance, Odile, and a handful of soldiers had managed to come back again.

What if Wren could do it and survive? More than survive, if she could return alive *and* with the Gold Prince? They'd be forced to give her the respect she deserved and admit she wasn't the screwup everyone thought. Speak of her as they did her uncle Locke, with awe and reverence.

"It would be dangerous," Julian was saying, drawing Wren out of her daydreams of fame and glory. "Finding a way through would be a challenge in and of itself, never mind whatever else crosses our path. There have been a lot of rumors, recently. . . ." He darted an uneasy look her way.

"Rumors?"

He tossed his shoulder in a shrug. "Mostly local gossip. Supposed sightings of a strange woman in a veil. The Corpse Queen."

A *Corpse Queen*? It was a fairly epic name, but what did it actually mean? "It's a walking corpse? Sounds like any tier-five revenant."

He hesitated. "Probably. Most of it sounds like the same ghostsmith stories I grew up on. Evil necromancers enslaving the undead. Bodies going missing. Ghostly specters marching together at midnight, that sort of thing. My grandfather used to always say, 'Get back before dark or the robbers will get you.'"

Wren was fascinated. He'd grown up on ghostsmith stories? When her own house wouldn't even talk about them? "Wait—robbers?"

"Yeah, ghostsmiths. They were graverobbers."

Right, Wren had known that, but she'd never heard it said exactly that way before.

Ghostsmiths were a taboo subject matter in the House of Bone. Naturally, that meant Wren had always been intrigued by them, but all she knew was what she'd cobbled together from servant gossip and bedtime stories from old nursemaids.

And everything she'd cobbled together was deliciously horrifying.

While bonesmiths could sense and control dead bones, ghostsmiths could sense and control the undead *spirit*. The ghost. Once upon a time, the two smiths were a match made in spirit-reaping heaven. The ghostsmith would calm and control the ghost while the bonesmith would locate the anchor bone and sever the ley line. Valkyrs didn't exist back then because they weren't needed.

But eventually the ghostsmiths began to abuse their power. They *used* the undead, forcing their spirits into servitude and denying them their eternal rest. Cook told Wren they'd even started *killing* people in order to get their hands on the freshest corpses, in addition to plundering graves.

The word "graverobber" sounded an awful lot like grave*digger* . . . but she supposed that was why her family had forbidden the subject to begin with. There were too many similarities that could be misconstrued. Because both bonesmith and ghostsmith magics dealt with the dead, many in the Dominions were wary of bonesmiths because of what the ghostsmiths had done, fearing, perhaps, that they were capable of doing the same.

"You think this queen could actually be a ghostsmith?" she asked.

No one had seen or heard of a *living* ghostsmith for centuries. Wren was both thrilled and disturbed by the thought.

He shook his head. "They're just rumors, and it's nothing new. Like I said, this was stuff my grandfather used to say—and his grandfather before him."

Wren tilted her head, considering. "Maybe there have been ghostsmiths here all this time."

He gave her a dubious look. "Forget about the queen. What I know for certain is that undead *will* cross our path. Have you faced real revenants before?"

"Not technically," Wren said. "Revenants can only be found here in the Breachlands. But I've trained to fight them for ten years. I can handle this."

She'd battled countless ghosts in the catacombs at Marrow Hall, where they kept some under careful guard for novitiates to practice against. Plus she'd sparred for hours against Inara, learning the best tricks and maneuvers for facing anything that could walk.

And if that didn't work, she'd remember Odile's advice and trust her gut.

"If we move quickly and quietly, we might be able to make it through unnoticed," Julian said.

Wren was nodding, glad she'd fully armed herself before leaving the fort for Leo's inspection. Wanting to show off for the prince, she had a full stash of weapons and artillery, plus refills.

"I'll lead the way. They were Ironlands, once, and I'll be able to figure out the safest way through. You guard us against the undead."

It was perfect in its simplicity, yet . . . "Are you sure we won't lose them?"

He nodded. "They have no choice but to take the Coastal Road.

We'll take a shortcut and head them off before they reach their destination."

Considering the location of the Haunted Territory and the sweep of the coast, Wren could only assume that destination was the Iron Citadel. The apparently not-abandoned Iron Citadel, which housed a regent—someone who saw themselves as ruler of these lands. Or at least ruler of the House of Iron, if Julian had some sort of loyalty to him.

No matter. Leo wouldn't set foot there if Wren could help it.

"This isn't some graveyard or old execution block," he warned. "This is the Haunted Territory—the doorstep of the Breach."

"I know," Wren said, unable to conceal the eagerness in her voice.

"The only way this is going to work is if you listen to me," he said. "You might fancy yourself a ghost-slayer, but the goal here is to avoid the undead entirely. Understand?"

Wren bristled at the way he commanded her, but she knew arguing would only make him abandon this plan. Besides, while a glorious death in the Breach wasn't the worst fate she could imagine, it would mean nothing if she failed. The recklessness that had served her all her life might well be her undoing if she focused more on *how* to fight the undead than how to *not* fight them. Without a traveling bard in tow, the tales of her epic journey would be *hers* to tell. So maybe she'd embellish a little. What mattered now was surviving the Breach in the first place.

"Fine, yes. No undead are the best undead, as far as you're concerned."

"As far as *anyone* is concerned," he said.

"Not bonesmiths," Wren replied, flashing him her widest grin. "Now, let's loot these corpses before we head out."

"You're joking," Julian said as Wren crouched over the nearest body. She located a jeweled scabbard and held it up, examining the stones—surely only colored glass—when Julian marched over and snatched it away. One of the "diamonds" fell off and cracked in two. "What are you going to do with an empty scabbard?"

"Nothing, now that I know it's garbage," she said. When he continued to glare at her, she sighed. "Trade it, maybe? I don't know about you, but I'd like to eat sometime on this journey. Surely jewels still hold value here in the Breachlands."

"We're headed to the Haunted Territory. There are no inns or peddlers or kind farm folk to trade with for food and a place to sleep. There is *nothing* between here and our destination except death."

"All the more reason to take what we can," Wren insisted, moving on to the next body. The deathrotted one.

"They'll have a cache somewhere nearby," Julian interjected, somewhat loudly. He was plainly uncomfortable with what Wren was doing. "Bandits like them have little safe houses all over the place. We find one, we find supplies."

"Won't they be running there as we speak?"

"It won't be a proper house, just a hole in the ground with provisions. After the stunt you pulled, I doubt they'll stop running until they reach Southbridge."

Wren looked up at him. "Does that mean you don't want this?" she asked, holding up a small black dagger.

He hesitated, then dropped the scabbard and walked over. He plucked it out of her hand, but immediately pulled a face. "Bitter iron," he said, tossing it onto the ground.

"But it's black . . . ," Wren said, picking it up again. Smiths called any variation on their material that they couldn't touch—like alloys for the metalsmiths—bitter. Steel was a popular iron alloy, so they often called steel weapons bitter iron or bitter steel. Wren had heard bronze called "bitter copper" by coppersmiths, and of course, any material not native to their island was resistant to their magic. So gold, silver, iron—even bones—that came from outside the Dominions were called bitter to the local smiths. In fact, after losing several gold mines to the Breach, the king had deemed that only bitter gold—gold mined outside the Dominions and acquired through trade—should be used as currency. The rest was saved for goldsmith artisans to craft into more valuable objects or stockpiled to ensure its value remained high locally and abroad.

"Enamel, most likely," Julian said, nodding at the blade. "Either he got played by someone claiming it was ironsmith-made or he planned to play someone else."

"If you say so." She dusted off her hands and stood. "You know where we can get supplies? Lead the way."

SIXTEEN

Julian insisted on dragging the bodies to the side of the road before they set out.

"Bandits are a major problem in the south," he explained as they searched seemingly random and unremarkable caverns and crevices. "The coastal towns send out local militia in an attempt to keep them in check, and sometimes, when I'm able, I join them. Their movements and patterns are easy to predict. They each have specific territories, and they have to keep mobile, so they can't be bogged down with supplies."

Finally he found what he was looking for, uncovering a stash of barrels and crates in a partially concealed cave.

It was stocked with a decent amount of food—mostly dried fish, but there was some cured red meat, several jars of pickled vegetables, plus water canteens they could refill. There was also traveling gear, including a kettle, blankets, and a flintstone.

"It's cold where we're going, so grab whatever you can," Julian said, stuffing a leather pack.

"It's cold everywhere. It's winter," Wren said, though she did the same.

He shook his head. "Not like this."

Wren considered that. The undead did give the feeling of cold if you came into contact with them—that was why deathrot resembled nothing so much as accelerated frostbite—but she'd never known it to permeate an entire place before. Even the Bonewood was no colder than anywhere else, and it was the most haunted place she'd ever been.

Yet, anyway.

Once they were ready, they stepped out into the night, heading north.

It was the exact opposite direction they'd started traveling, and Wren couldn't help looking back over her shoulder, wondering if she was doing the right thing. Was Leo okay? Had they unbound him and allowed him to ride a horse, or were they still throwing him around like a sack of grain?

Even if they treated Leo well now, with a Gold Prince in their possession, the demands they eventually made could be lofty and unreasonable. They could threaten Leo's life and hold the entire Dominions at their mercy.

She stared at Julian's back, barely visible in the darkness as they climbed over uneven and steadily rising ground.

"There's a narrow gorge up ahead," he called over his shoulder. "It slices through the rock and provides somewhat safe passage to the other side. Then we should have a straight shot into the Haunted Territory."

"It's close," Wren said with an eager grin.

He frowned at her. "There's something wrong with you."

"You're not the first person to tell me that."

"Won't be the last," he muttered under his breath.

It wasn't long before they found the edge of the river—the Serpentine, Odile had called it—which was flat and wide as it bent southeast, but they traveled upstream, where it steadily grew narrower and twistier before slicing through the rising landscape, creating a ravine.

They walked along the stony bank, keeping the water within reach. It was a natural barrier to the undead, so while ghosts could come upon them on its shores, one quick jump into the rush would see them safe from deathrot, even if they risked drowning instead. The river varied between rocky, foaming swells and smooth, gentler currents, but Wren hoped it didn't come to that.

Exhaustion was starting to settle in when Julian came to a stop. He was squinting toward the rising cliffs, and then Wren saw it too—remnants of a broken-down millhouse.

"I say we check it out," Julian said. "Sleep here until dawn, then—"

"We can't stop now! We've barely made any ground, and—"

"*They* will have stopped."

"Which means *this* is our chance to catch up!"

Julian shook his head. "We can't push for three or four days straight, and I'll be damned if I'm entering the Haunted Territory without my right mind. We need sleep."

Wren jutted out her jaw. "We should sleep during the day. The undead are far less active."

He considered that for a moment. Nodded. "We will—but after tonight."

Wren opened her mouth to argue when she caught him shift his shoulders. It was a slight movement, barely noticeable, but as she'd been watching his face, she saw the grimace it caused him. He'd been hurt before the attack by the bandits, and it seemed he was suffering worse than he'd wanted to let on. He'd started to limp, favoring the leg Wren had sliced earlier. Her own cuts and bruises were making themselves known, her ankle throbbing as the adrenaline from the day faded away.

Fine, they could rest, clean themselves up, then hit the ground running the next day.

When she didn't object any more, he moved toward the house, but she held out a hand. "Let me," she said, unhitching her pack and dropping it on the ground.

He opened his mouth as if to protest, but she unsheathed her swords and raised her brows in silent question. He darted a nervous glance at the house, then nodded.

"Stay near the water," she said, before slowly approaching.

Part of the wooden roof was caved in. The place where the wheel had jutted from the stone foundations was cracked, leaving behind a single piece of protruding metal but no sign of the wheel itself.

Wren peered in through the broken shutters on the window, but really it was her magic that was doing most of the searching.

She couldn't sense any bones in the vicinity.

She turned, and nearly leapt out of her skin when the cursed ironsmith appeared directly behind her.

"Clear?" he asked, ignoring her obvious alarm and peering through the shutters himself. "Not just undead we have to be on the lookout for."

"It's clear," she said, and so he did a quick circuit of the house before returning to her side and approaching the door. It was warped and water damaged—easily forced open—and Wren followed him inside to find a small, single-room dwelling, reeking of mildew and rotting leaves that had blown in through the openings, but otherwise completely harmless.

Julian seemed pleased, dropping both their bags on the ground. He had apparently carried Wren's from where she'd left it. "We'll be able to have a fire, I think, if we can find some dry wood."

There was a rusted stove they could use, and next to it, a pile of moldering logs under a tarp. Despite the smell, whatever flooding had caused the damage here had come and gone a long time ago.

Still, most of the lumber was unusable, rotten and crumbling in Julian's hands as he lifted piece after piece. Wren found a rickety old table and four chairs stacked against the wall; she grabbed one of the chairs and snapped off the legs.

Together, they managed enough burnable wood to last for several hours. Julian had the flintstone, so he started the fire.

Soon the place was filled with the scent of smoke and the steadily growing light of the flames.

A strange awkwardness descended. They were basically strangers, technically enemies, and hadn't spent more than a few scattered minutes together when they weren't fighting or running for their lives.

Wren decided to break the silence.

She took a seat on one of the remaining chairs and put her booted feet up on the table. "Why were you trying to kidnap the prince?"

Julian sighed, rubbing a hand distractedly over his chest where the arrow had landed. "Do you ever stop talking?"

Wren smiled. She was just getting started. "Were you trying to barter for something? Gold?"

He didn't look at her when he spoke. "What good is gold when we have no one to trade it with? As soon as that Wall went up, gold as a currency became irrelevant to us."

"Food, then?"

He shook his head and stood, facing her. "Sacks of grain and cattle in exchange for a prince? Are you being deliberately obtuse, or are you actually this stupid?"

Wren took that in stride—she'd been called worse—and instead, she studied him closely. He made the Breachlands sound every bit as wild and untamed as Wren had always thought they were in the wake of the Uprising, except she knew there were towns and cities, thanks to Odile. His clothing was fine, his weaponry new and of the highest quality an ironsmith could produce, and the horses he and his fellow soldiers had ridden were well tacked and healthy.

What if they weren't hungry and poor? What if they were something else entirely?

"You serve that regent, don't you? And he ordered you to kidnap a prince. . . ." She paused. "You want reentry. To become part of the Dominions again." Julian looked away, but a line of tension tightened his jaw. "Forgiveness for the Uprising, and—"

"*Forgiveness* for trying to save our people from the Breach?" Julian snapped. "Forgiveness for storming the Wall that kept us penned in like livestock, like sheep trapped *with* the wolves?"

Wren straightened in her seat. Anger radiated from him, and she feared her attempts at idle conversation might come to more physical blows. But she wasn't going to back down.

"You caused the Breach in the first place!" she said, her voice as calm as she could make it in the face of his fury. "I hardly think—"

"Believe me, I know."

She scowled. "If you hadn't been overmining, none of this would have happened. You'd still be a part of the Dominions, your house noble and powerful."

"And you'd be nothing." Wren glared at him, and he smiled slowly. Viciously. "Isn't that right? Your nobility, your wealth, your revered position in society. The House of Bone has none of that without the Breach."

"You're right," Wren said lightly. "Without the Breach, we'd just be the *only thing* stopping the dead from rising in every corner of the Dominions. There wouldn't even *be* the Dominions without us."

"Ah, yes. Our only defense against the undead. And instead of standing *with us* to fight this threat, your house marched into the Breach, escorting an army onto our lands, and then stood aside, watching as they and the undead mowed us down. How brave. How heroic. You left us here to die, and you begrudge us fighting back? Fighting to survive? We need no forgiveness. We need *justice*."

He stormed out the door without a backward glance.

Wren remained seated, her heart pounding.

At first the bonesmiths *had* fought with the ironsmiths. The Breach was everyone's problem, and so everyone in the Dominions had attempted to stand against the influx of undead pouring into the world.

However, it became obvious fairly quickly that they didn't stand a chance. That's when the palisade was erected. When that proved insufficient, next came the Border Wall and the forts that lined it. Even then the ironsmiths were still considered a part of the Dominions, but when the crown failed to protect them or send aid, they decided to take what they wanted by force. The Uprising was what had truly separated the House of Iron from the rest of the Dominions.

It had been a royal decree, but Wren could see how Julian would blame the bonesmiths. They were the only ones who could protect his people, but they had heeded the word of the king instead of their own calling.

She wished she could talk to Odile about it. Clearly the woman felt terribly conflicted over what had happened. Did Wren's father? And Locke . . . Had he relished his role in the final battle or performed the task with a grim sense of duty?

She got to her feet. She understood Julian was angry, but she hoped he hadn't actually taken off and left her here.

No, his supplies were there, on the floor, which meant he couldn't have gone far. But the whole point of them traveling together and taking this particular route was because Wren could offer him a certain level of protection. If he wandered too far and came across an angry ghost, she would be lost in the middle of the wilderness with no guide and no chance of finding Leo.

A soft splash reached her ears, and she made for the window. She spotted him on the bank of the river, and relief unspooled inside her. She still had her guide, and by sticking close to the water, he would be protected even without her.

It was difficult to see in the darkness, but the fog hadn't followed them into the narrow valley. With the light of the moon dancing on the river, she could make out the ironsmith's silhouette as he crouched by the river, scooping up water in his gloved hands and splashing it over his face and across his neck.

He had removed his armor and weapons, and the effect was to make his body look slimmer and less formidable. In fact, he looked more youthful now, especially with that intimidating helmet he'd worn left somewhere behind.

As Wren watched, his hands dropped, and he seemed to be unbuttoning his shirt. She squinted, wanting to see how bad that chest wound really was—or so she told herself—but he didn't remove the garment entirely. In fact, he seemed to undo it just enough to splash some water across his chest, soaking the dark fabric.

Disappointed, Wren continued to watch as he used his wet fingers to comb back his hair, droplets cascading down his neck and into the collar of his shirt.

He turned away from the river, and Wren drew back from the window, afraid she'd been caught staring.

And why was she staring? Just because he was nice to look at didn't mean she could allow herself to become distracted.

He'd not abandoned their arrangement—that's what mattered—so Wren took the opportunity to see to her own armor, undoing straps and buckles and rolling her stiff shoulders. Her arm wound could use a bit of cleaning, but she'd wait until Julian returned, then wash after.

That done, she turned her attention to the house itself. She extended her senses again, but there were no bones, dead or haunted, in the vicinity. But the way that ghost had moved earlier—nearly fearless in the face of the bones she'd pulled up to obstruct it—told her she needed to take extra precautions.

Like she had in the Bonewood, Wren withdrew a large pouch of bonedust and spilled it in a steady line around the inside perimeter of the house, everywhere except the door, which she'd finish once they'd both settled in for the night.

Wren was seated at the table and chewing on a rather uninspiring piece of dried meat when Julian returned.

He glanced at her briefly, armor and weapons held in his hands, before his gaze fell to the bonedust on the ground. He carefully closed the door behind him so as not to disturb the trail and noticed that the line was incomplete.

"I'll finish after I've washed up."

"I thought you said you didn't sense anything nearby."

"Right now I don't. Doesn't mean it won't change, especially when I'm unconscious. I sleep like the dead," she said with a wicked smile.

He was apparently immune to her charms. He looked confused. "The running water . . ."

"It helps, especially with any attack that might be coming from the opposite shore, but just because they can't cross it doesn't mean they won't approach it at all."

"Will this"—he gestured at the fine white powder—"work like the Wall?"

There was much superstition surrounding all the smiths and their various tricks and talents, but none so much as the bonesmiths. They had been oddballs and outcasts before the Breach made them indispensable not just to burials and funeral rites but to the very survival of the Dominions.

Wren figured it was a good sign that he was trying to understand the magic at play here, and maybe an explanation would put his mind at ease. "More or less. Ghosts hate dead bones, so they avoid them at all costs, and they'll start to dissolve if they make contact with them. My bonedust is made with anchor bones—the bones that held the strongest connection to the soul, which also make them the strongest deterrent against the undead."

"What about a revenant? A walking undead?"

Wren considered for a moment. "They still won't like it, even if they can make themselves cross it. The protections extend beyond the dust itself—above and below—but either way, if one gets near, I should sense it."

Seeming satisfied, he bent to add more wood to the stove.

Wren left him to it, walking to the shore and splashing a bit of water on her hands and face. Her eye black was greasy and difficult to get off without oil or fully submerging her face, so she left it for now, focusing on cleaning her cuts and some of the grime under her fingernails.

Afterward, she returned to the house and closed the door.

Julian had taken her place at the table while Wren used the remaining bonedust to finish the outline of the house and seal them in its protections.

"What if I have to, uh, relieve myself?" Julian asked abruptly, watching Wren make final adjustments.

Relieve himself? How proper. Wren smirked. "Be quick."

He almost smiled at that, and Wren considered it a victory.

Her task done, she dug through her belongings until she found one of the blankets they'd pilfered from the bandits. She laid it out in front of the wood stove. Considering the size of the place and the radius of the fire's warmth, they'd need to sleep side by side.

Julian seemed to realize it as she did, but he didn't make any move to join her.

Looking up at him as she settled onto her makeshift bed, she quirked an eyebrow. "Given what I understand of the Haunted Territory, we're not likely to be as safe as we are here anytime soon. Get your rest. The bonedust will do its job."

"And what if there are more bandits?"

Wren shrugged, wrapping herself in her blanket. "That's *your* job."

SEVENTEEN

All in all, it hadn't been one of Leo's best days of travel. And honestly, that was saying something. He'd once rode in a manure cart for the better part of an afternoon in an attempt to make it back to the palace after an overlong stay at a local fair, and he'd been known to take a pony, donkey—even a large dog, once, though that had been for companionship more than anything else—if a horse was unavailable.

That being said, it also hadn't been one of his best. The saddle had been hard and the ride uncomfortable, but he had endured worse.

Or so he told himself.

In truth, the day had started wrong from the moment he'd opened his eyes, burdened with a vicious hangover *and* the less-than-desirable knowledge that he was going to be kidnapped.

Still, he wasn't going to let a little thing like a hostage situation dampen his spirits. He was hardly the first royal to be held for ransom, and he doubted he would be the last.

They'd forced him to wear a smelly bag over his head for most of the journey—whenever they passed other travelers or identifying landmarks, as if he could do anything about it even if he *did* know where they were or where they were going.

Well, to be fair, he *could* do something, he was quite certain. And intended to, by the way—but *they* didn't know that. And it was thanks to his own dramatics that the bag was ever removed at all. He pretended to lose his balance in the saddle whenever it was on, actually falling once to commit to the bit—and thoroughly bruising his backside in the process—but it meant they let him remove it whenever someone in the party gave the all clear.

Even with the cursed sack, he had a very good guess of their destination, if not the exact route they would take.

It would be nice to get a confirmation, though. "Where are you taking me?" he asked the kidnapper next to him. They'd been riding for hours, and the sun had long since set behind them.

There were always the same two kidnappers nearby: one, grizzled and gruff and prone to speaking in single-word replies. The other was the total opposite: young and green, wide-eyed and handsome.

Leo could use that.

Unfortunately, it was old Gray-Beard who answered. "Quiet."

Leo rolled his eyes, then put them to good use, scanning his surroundings. They had allowed him to ditch the bag after darkness fell, and Leo had watched as everyone in their party grew tense and wary in the coming night. His own shoulders had hunched, especially when the kidnappers started talking among themselves.

"Think we'll see her?" the kidnapper in front of Leo muttered, craning his neck to scan the empty road and barren landscape, painted silver in the moonlight.

"You'd better hope not," said the one riding beside him.

"If you do, it'll be the last thing you ever see," said a third from farther up the line, laughing.

"It's not funny," said the first. "My cousin's friend disappeared three weeks back. Swears he saw her in the trees, right near the path his friend had taken. No one's seen him since."

"Who is this mysterious woman you're all so afraid of?" Leo asked.

"Nobody," came Gray-Beard's predictable response.

Leo pressed his lips together, then noticed the young kidnapper was watching him. "It's a harmless question, isn't it?" Leo asked, keeping his voice low so it wouldn't be heard over the sound of the horses' hooves. "Indulge me, won't you?" He batted his eyelashes. They were no longer golden, unfortunately. They'd stopped earlier in their journey to strip him of every scrap of metal on his body—well, every scrap they could *find*, anyway. "I'm *painfully* bored."

The boy tilted his head, considering. "They call her the Corpse Queen."

Corpse Queen? Leo racked his brain. He'd studied ancient smith lore, and the name rang a bell.

"Isn't she the monster that will eat children who stay up past their bedtime? Surely hardened soldiers like you don't believe such nonsense?"

Leo gave the boy his best grin, and the boy *almost* returned it before he caught Gray-Beard's frown and hastily looked away.

Yes, Leo could *definitely* use that.

The boy didn't respond, but his expression told Leo that he quite plainly *did* believe in such nonsense.

Interesting.

They rode into a riverside town sometime in the middle of the night. It was walled, as all surviving settlements in the Breachlands were, according to his lessons, and they had a garrison, too. Guards greeted them at the gate, as tense as the kidnappers. Mutters of bandits roving the countryside rippled through their ranks, though Leo heard nothing about corpse queens.

The bag was firmly in place again. He could see through the rough weave, though it reduced people to simple silhouettes, a contrast of light and shadow. He'd found a small hole earlier in the day and did his best to peer through it. It narrowed his field of vision to a pinprick, but it helped him make better sense of his surroundings in the darkness.

Bone protections were mounted along the walls of the town, but they appeared old and outdated—a far cry from what he was used to in the Dominions.

"Welcome to Southbridge," came the sentry at the gate, saving Leo from having to pry the information out of someone later.

He pictured the many maps of the region he had seen in his lifetime. They were near the Serpentine River—yes, he could hear it if he ignored the chatter and stomping of hooves—and were on course to continue south toward the Coastal Road, which led all the way to the Iron Citadel. It was the only destination that made sense.

They were quickly admitted, the town a rundown place that had traces of lost grandeur—wide streets and neat stone buildings in organized rows—that had given way to squalor. Empty houses and heaps of garbage, plus gangs of children everywhere, lurking on street corners and peering out from darkened windows. Orphans, he supposed, though they were too young to have lost their parents to the Breach or the Uprising. He thought of the Corpse Queen and missing people, of a land without bonesmiths to properly protect them. He shuddered.

Guards were posted on streetcorners, moving stragglers along with a forceful hand, giving the place a feeling of wartime, though the Uprising had ended years ago.

They were fighting a different kind of war now, and they had the wrong soldiers.

Wren and her bone blades popped into Leo's mind. The way she had defended him without question or hesitation, squaring off with a damned *ironsmith*—completely and totally outmatched—left his stomach tight with guilt.

Especially since she'd been one of his prime suspects.

His entire tour had been an exercise in futility, a means to keep him out of his father's hair. Too many manure cart rides, apparently. Leo had always seen his antics as little more than a humorous annoyance to his family, but apparently his father had disagreed. He'd wanted to put Leo to use, and while Leo had suggested a variety of other occupations—further education, positions on various councils and governing bodies—his father had decided that out of sight was out of mind.

Leo had accepted the task with as much good grace as he could manage and had even allowed himself to be ordered about by his cousin Galen, who was wielding the first scrap of power he'd ever had with a frankly *embarrassing* amount of pleasure—until he'd ended their previous inspection without warning or sufficient explanation. That had caused Leo to go snooping, and then he'd discovered the letters.

As it turned out, Galen was being paid to set Leo up—to hand him over to the very people who now had him in their clutches.

At first Leo had despaired.

He'd wanted to confront the man, to tell his guard captain and raise a self-righteous stink. The problem was, his father had ordered the royal guard to heed Galen's orders over his own—Leo had several years of adolescent mischief to thank for that—and while he could have tried to find help at the Breachfort, he had no idea who else was involved. He might make things infinitely worse for himself if he went to the wrong people, and if he confessed to having seen evidence of Galen's shady dealings, he might find himself not simply a kidnapped prince but a *dead* one.

After that he'd grown angry. That emotion served him for a time and allowed him to hold it together every day while his good-for-nothing cousin smiled and lied directly to his face.

But then? Then he had become *curious*, and that was a far more dangerous thing.

He was just so incredibly *bored* . . . not only with his daily life but with his place in his own family. He was tired of not mattering. Tired of being the spare's spare, no matter how much he joked about it. Maybe he wanted to see if his family cared. Maybe he wanted them to worry, to barter and beg and shell out sacks of coin for him. Maybe he wanted proof not only that he mattered but that he was valued.

And if he happened to be fascinated about the world beyond the Border Wall . . . well, that was *his* business.

So he'd been ready. Resigned, maybe, but ready.

Then the day of the inspection had come, and his carefully held composure had begun to fracture, and he'd started to question all his choices.

Maybe allowing himself to be kidnapped *wasn't* the smartest idea?

Wren Graven certainly hadn't thought so.

There weren't a lot of people in the Dominions who had the gold to pay the price Galen was asking, nor the incentive to do so . . . but the Gravens of Marrow Hall had been at the top of Leo's list. They had risen high in the wake of the Breach, so maybe they wanted some action on the front lines again. Some more relevance after too many years of peace.

Imagine his surprise when one of them was a tribute at the Breachfort—and very recently appointed? It had been suspicious, and so he'd done what he could to get close to her.

He hadn't anticipated liking her so much. He hadn't expected her to fight for him tooth and nail.

Had she survived that dangerous fall?

Leo had *asked* for her. Had sat her next to him. Had put her in the line of fire on *purpose*.

Of course she had survived. She was safe and sound back at the Breachfort. The alternative was too much to bear.

Their party rode through the silent streets, braziers flickering at the major intersections as they made for a large building in the center of town—the inn, no doubt. Their journey seemed to be coming to its end for the day, but Leo's mind refused to settle. He couldn't shake the image of Wren's fall . . . nor the assassination that had preceded it.

While the majority of Leo's less-than-stellar day had admittedly gone as he'd expected—Wren's heroics aside—that stray arrow had torn the entire plot wide open.

Why had they killed one of their own? Ironsmiths were supposed to be extinct, which meant one as young and talented as that should be valued highly, not a target for murder.

It didn't make sense. He needed more information.

Leo guided his horse closer to the young kidnapper. "I never got your name," he said, wishing he could flash his winning smile. He didn't know if he could properly flirt with a sack on his head, but if *anyone* could do it, it was him. "You already know mine, of course. But please, call me Leo."

The guard glanced around before fixing Leo with a somewhat suspicious look. He pondered, and upon deciding his name gave Leo no true upper hand, he shrugged and offered it.

"Jakob."

While Leo often gilded his naturally light-brown hair, Jakob was a true blond, his cheekbones dusted with freckles and his eyes an ethereal, crystal-clear blue. The color was magical enough to make Leo believe in the old tales about watersmiths who lived in the sea, guiding ships safely home . . . or pulling sailors under.

"Nice to meet you," Leo said. "You seem awfully young for a kidnapper. You can't be much older than me."

No response.

Gray-Beard had ridden ahead, and the rest of their party was more concerned with getting to their rooms for the night than with anything he did.

"Is this your first mission?" Leo pressed. "You're surely the youngest member of this, uh, *party*, at any rate."

Jakob shook his head. "No, that'd be Julian, the regent's—"

He paused, catching himself, but too late. He darted an anxious look at Leo, who was glad for the bag over his head for once, which concealed his reaction.

The fact that there was apparently a *regent* east of the Wall was noteworthy enough, but when they'd first set out, the kidnappers had lamented the news of the ironsmith's death by mentioning another man.

"Lord-Smith Francis will be devastated," one of them had said, the others murmuring agreement, the captain among them. He had told them all a bold-faced lie about a Breachfort archer, when in fact *he* had been the one to loose the arrow that had taken the ironsmith down. Leo had seen it right before they'd thrown the bag over his head for the first time, the captain and his accomplice unaware they had an additional witness.

Leo had spent much of the long ride to Southbridge running through every noble name he knew from east of the Wall, which had been the Ironlands not too long ago and a part of his political studies. The problem was, the only lord-*smiths* east of the Wall were the Knights, and even if their bloodline hadn't been wiped out, the name Francis had never appeared on any of their family's birth *or* marriage records. Then again, another ironsmith family might be ruling these days, laying claim to the title of both lord-smith *and* regent.

One with old blood, ties to the Knights . . . and a scion named Francis.

Finally, Leo thought he had a scrap of information he could use.

Especially when, hours later, while he was being shunted down the hall to his room for the night, he caught a glimpse through the hole in his bag of the captain holding the dead ironsmith's helmet.

He was speaking to the other rider who had witnessed the assassination, the one who'd captured Leo and thrown him over his horse.

They spoke quietly but *not* quietly enough. The sack obstructed his sight, not his hearing, and Leo distinctly heard the word "proof."

The helmet was proof. Dented—Leo had done that himself, when he'd hefted that monstrously heavy ironsmith sword in a moment of daring he couldn't quite believe—and therefore, evidence of the fallen warrior. Proof. Proof the ironsmith was dead . . . but proof for whom?

Leo had a guess, if his suspicions about the regent were correct. Even if they weren't, this man was responsible for his kidnapping. For what had happened to Wren.

Who was *fine*. Probably bruised and annoyed but fine.

Still . . . surely it couldn't hurt to spread a few rumors about, even if they were false? That was the point of rumors, wasn't it?

A servant appeared bearing a tray of food soon after he was shoved into his bedroom for the night.

The guards were huddled near the door, murmuring together and leaving Leo alone with the young girl. She glanced at him, wary of this strange, headless figure.

"Hello," Leo said brightly. The girl reminded him of his sister, which helped. "What's your name?"

She glanced over her shoulder at the door, then back to him. She put the tray on the table, then whispered, "Millie."

She darted another nervous look behind her. "Don't worry about them," Leo said easily, knowing that a confident tone could put the most skittish child at ease. "My name's Leo. And I've had quite the adventure today." Her chin tipped up, interest sparking in her eyes. "Would you like to hear about it?"

She nodded eagerly, and he smiled.

EIGHTEEN

As Wren had promised, she did sleep like the dead.

When she awoke hours later to Julian's boot prodding her leg, she lurched upright, hair askew and bone knife clutched in one hand. His lips twitched, and for a second she thought he was going to laugh at her, but instead, he turned away and fiddled with their food supplies.

Judging by the beam of light slicing through the broken shutters, it was still morning but pushing toward the afternoon.

She glanced at Julian, whose hair was perfectly combed back from his face, his armor on and his bags packed. Had he not slept at all?

Wren stretched; she had removed her leather jacket and trousers in the night, sleeping in nothing but a flimsy under-tunic, so she dragged out her movements to see if she could catch the ironsmith's eye.

He didn't notice—in fact, he seemed determined not to look at her.

Annoyed at his lack of interest, she didn't bother putting on anything else as she padded to the table and joined him.

His head was bent over a pair of silver fish, carefully filleted, though he was currently struggling to debone them. He must have also found time to fish this morning, further proving that he'd likely not slept long—if at all.

"Good sleep?" she asked with a raised brow. His dark gaze flicked up at her before returning to his task.

"Fine."

Liar. He wore his gloves, perhaps to keep his hands clean from the messy task, and held a small knife in his right hand.

"There won't always be a river to fish," he said, apparently feeling the need to explain himself. "I figured we should make use of it while we can, save the other supplies for when we're deeper into the Haunted Territory."

Wren nodded. "Need help?" she asked idly, watching him poke and prod but continue to struggle.

He was about to deny her, his mouth open, when he paused and truly looked up at her. He finally noted her clothes—or lack thereof—but spared them only the barest of eye rolls before he sat back. He nodded at the fish, waiting.

Only warm-blooded animals produced a ghost, which meant fish, reptiles, and insects were harmless after death. Even cattle, poultry, and other spirited animals could be safely butchered, as long as it happened immediately after being killed. Since their ties to life weren't as powerful as humans', their ghosts would simply never get a chance to form.

Wren held a hand above each fish, sliced in half and lying open before her, and one by one she drew the bones from the tender flesh, pulling them into the palm of her hand in the blink of an eye, like metal filings to a magnet.

With a satisfied smirk, she dropped the bones onto the table's surface, leaving nothing but perfect, ready-to-cook fish in her wake.

"Impressive," Julian said, somewhat grudgingly, leaning forward to inspect the finished product—the first compliment he'd given her. "You could be a fishmonger."

Maybe it wasn't so complimentary after all.

"Hey, now, don't sell yourself short," Wren said encouragingly. "You caught the fish *and* started the fire—you'd make a fine servant."

Julian shook his head, taking the fish over to the stove, which he must have fed not long ago, the flames burning brightly. "Should've guessed you were noble-born, the way you walk around. Probably grew up in some fine castle with servants to attend you."

That was, Wren had to admit, mostly true. "Wrong," she chirped. "I'm only half-noble, and a bastard, and I behaved so poorly, I did more servant work"—she gestured to the gutted fish—"than they did."

"And you were also sent to serve at the Wall," Julian added, glancing over his shoulder at her. "It's a less-than-desirable assignment, from what I hear."

"What about you?" she shot back. "Ironsmith warriors are famous for their code of honor and their expertise in battle. And here you are, a common kidnapper—no better than those bandits. Are you a true ironsmith or some puffed-up politician's lapdog?"

He turned away from her. "You don't know anything about me."

That was true. But for all his accusations against her, Wren had her own suspicions that Julian must be someone important himself to have been targeted for assassination. He was an ironsmith, so it made sense he would have risen quickly in whatever hierarchy currently ruled in the Breachlands. He might very well be the only one left.

"Tell me, then."

He reared back, suspicion etched across his features. "What—*no.*"

"Until you do, I'll just assume you're out here for personal gain."

"Like you?"

She shifted uncomfortably. "I'm doing the *right thing*, whatever my . . . motivation. You're kidnapping an innocent person."

"He's a Valorian. He was *born* with blood on his hands. That is their legacy."

"One the House of Iron helped them build," she said.

"That's right. And then they turned on us. I'll do whatever I have to do for my people. Here," he said, after putting the fish on a pair of homemade iron skewers. He held one out to her, and Wren joined him crouched before the stove.

Heat washed over her as she huddled next to him. They were very close together, and when she stuck her breakfast into the flames, the open fire spit and sparked as fat dripped onto the burning coals.

"Oh," she muttered, jerking back slightly as some floating sparks singed her tunic.

"Serves you right, dressed like that."

"Like what?"

He cocked his head, turning toward her. This time he didn't shy away—his gaze lingered as he took her in. "Like you want attention."

"I *always* want attention. How I'm dressed has nothing to do with it."

He snorted. "It has everything to do with it, I expect. Surely you don't need that eye black when you sleep."

"You noticed," Wren said, batting her eyelashes as if he had paid her another compliment, and his face tightened in response. Considering that a victory, she shrugged. "I was lazy. I doubt you need those gloves when you wash your face, but here we are."

He stood abruptly, and Wren wondered if his fish was even

cooked. She remained a few moments longer, turning it once or twice more before joining him at the table.

While he took his fish off the skewer and ate it in small, careful bites, Wren bit hers off the stick like a wild animal.

His lip curled in distaste.

Once she finished eating, she wiped her greasy fingers on her shirt and stood to get dressed. She was just lifting her coat from the ground when something clattered to the floor.

It was the ring she'd found in the Bonewood. She had completely forgotten about it.

She lifted it now and recalled the mystery of the dark spike that pierced the bone.

Striding over to the table, she plunked it on the surface right in front of Julian, who was just finishing his meal. He raised his brows at her.

"What's this?" he asked.

"Not sure. I found it back home, in the Bonewood. The ring itself is bone, though we don't usually make rings or jewelry—or carve them with designs." She glanced at him. "The spike . . . is it iron?"

He lifted his head from the ring in surprise. "Iron? No, why would you think that?"

"It's black," she explained, disappointed not to have answered at least one of the questions she had about it, "and it sort of looks like a nail or something. . . ."

Julian reached a tentative hand for the ring, then seemed to decide against touching it. "Definitely not iron."

Frowning, Wren pocketed it and finished dressing, carefully replacing her armor and checking her weapons before collecting the bonedust. She reapplied her eye black, using the reflective surface of Julian's breastplate—much to his annoyance, as he was currently wearing it—to carefully outline her lips.

When they were both ready, they put out the fire and loaded the remaining usable firewood into one of the bags. They'd be unlikely to have another sleep as comfortable as this one—roof and all—but with any luck, they could at least manage a fire in the days to come.

They headed north, crossing a shallow section of the Serpentine before the land around them opened again, flattening out before a dense forest. The river twisted west, following the higher ground, while their path took them east into the trees.

Julian hesitated a moment, staring after the water as if wishing he could remain by its comparatively safe shores.

Wren clapped him on the back. "I'm afraid your only protection from here on out is me."

"How comforting."

It was early evening, the temperature dropping along with the sun. The forest hung in suspended twilight, and Wren's breath puffed in front of her.

"According to the old maps, we should be able to get through the trees by morning," Julian said. "We can camp for a few hours, then proceed into the valley. After that . . . we'll have to figure things out as we go. I know roughly where the settlements were, but things have changed since then. Still, we should avoid them. Whoever we might find there now, they won't be living. Our best chance is to pass through unnoticed."

It was a nice thought, but Wren doubted Julian truly understood how the undead worked, despite living in such close proximity to so many of them. They were drawn to life, and she suspected the ghosts in the Haunted Territory were starved for it. Her and Julian's presence would be like the first drops of rain after a drought, and any undead in the vicinity would ravenously drink them in.

She tried her best to feel if any were nearby, but her range could help them only so far. Besides, her talent lay in fighting the undead, not avoiding them. If any *did* turn up, she'd be ready.

The ground sloped gently as they moved through the trees, which started out fairly sparse but were soon dense enough to make it difficult to see. When night came and the ceaseless darkness pressed in, a part of her longed to spot a ghost, to sense an undead corpse. Anything was better than this held breath, this taut anticipation.

They didn't speak—though Wren had tried several times, much to Julian's annoyance—and instead walked in silence, the only sounds the crunch of boots and their steady, panting breaths.

Julian kept up a relentless pace, and Wren reminded herself to be grateful for it even as her legs ached and her lungs burned. She would rather die than give him the impression she couldn't keep up, and besides, this was all to her benefit—the sooner they rescued Leo, the better.

"How far is—" Wren began, but Julian cut her off.

"Shh," he said, not for the first time.

"You *shh*," she shot back, annoyed. It wasn't *sound* that would bring the undead down upon them—it was their beating hearts.

He rounded on her, ready with an angry retort, but didn't manage to get out a single word. Instead, his eyes bugged out, fixated on something over Wren's shoulder.

She whirled around.

Her senses kicked into overdrive, along with her pulse, as she spotted the unmistakable glow of an undead hovering between the trees. It wasn't near enough to clearly discern—probably twenty feet away and newly risen, but its indistinct edges were becoming brighter with every passing second.

And next to it . . . there was another light, fainter than the first. Farther away, Wren thought, until it started to move. Plodding ever nearer with a slow, lumbering gait.

This was not the movement of a ghost.

This was a revenant.

As it stepped between the trees and into her line of sight, she saw why the ghostlight had seemed faint and distant. The spirit was obstructed by its partially decayed body, the light winking and moving not between bark and leaf, but between flesh and bone.

Wren recalled what Odile had said, something about the way they moved, like a puppet on strings. She thought of everything she'd ever been taught about the walking undead, and somehow it still didn't prepare her.

She returned her attention to the first undead she had seen, and now that it was closer, it became evident that it, too, was a revenant—though its body was in a much worse state of decay, allowing the ghost to more brightly shine through.

Wren swallowed, drawing her twin blades. *Two* tier fives heading their way.

Behind her, Julian shuffled his feet, staggering backward.

"*Stop,*" she snapped, glancing over her shoulder.

This was no different from every reapyr-valkyr training exercise she'd ever done—no different from the Bonewood Trial itself. As creepy as this forest had suddenly become, the milky-green light gilding the trees and casting Wren's and Julian's skin into sickly pallor, it had nothing on the Bonewood.

Except for the tier fives, of course.

The problem was, Julian was not, in fact, a reapyr. He was entirely untrained against this particular adversary, and there was no *defeating* these undead, no distracting them long enough for the scythe's fatal cut.

There was only offense and defense, and Wren knew which *she* preferred.

She met Julian's wide, startled eyes. She shook her head. "Never run."

His muscles tensed, and she knew he wanted to argue. Might even be tempted to remind her that last time they'd fought side by side, he'd asked her to stay . . . and she hadn't. She could only hope that he was a better listener than she was as she turned back to their foe.

Her grip tightened on her swords, and her mind raced through her various options. They *had* covered tier fives in her lessons, but the reality of facing them was far more terrifying than she could have imagined.

Knuckles or bonedust were always a valid stalling tactic, but what good was a few extra seconds of time in the middle of an apparently haunted forest? The undead would only continue their pursuit. Besides, they were *revenants*—they wore bones of their own, which would protect their ghosts and help them keep their form.

Her swords were the best option, giving her range as well as precision. The soul tended to reside in the rib cage or the skull, and while the former would be easy enough to get to, the latter would be far more difficult.

Still, if she could dispatch *one* of them, the other might flee or be hesitant to approach.

Just as she'd decided on that course of action, two more began to materialize in the gloom, nearer than the others and ranged to their left and right. Wren's stomach clenched.

They were closing in.

She raised her swords, and the closest revenants recoiled, but only for a moment before continuing steadily forward.

Except, they weren't actually converging upon her as she'd originally thought. They moved almost in a wave, but not circling or surrounding. Their movements seemed defensive, as if they wanted her and Julian to move in a certain direction.

It was like being herded. Every time Wren stepped to her right, the undead didn't so much as flinch. But even leaning to the left had them bristling within their bones, casting jarring, dancing light across the forest.

They still didn't pursue her—they just crackled with tension and stood their ground.

Sometimes ghosts behaved that way, becoming almost territorial over their corpses and unwilling to venture too far from their anchor bone. But these were tier fives—these were *revenants*—and they brought their bodies with them. What could they be protecting?

Wren took a deliberate step to the left.

"Don't," came Julian's voice from behind her, somehow both breathless and sharp. Wren had almost forgotten him, which was poor behavior for an aspiring valkyr.

"I'm not . . . I'm just . . . ," she replied softly, keeping her eyes on the revenants as she moved, slowly and cautiously. She had been taught to think of them like animals, with simple instincts and predictable behaviors. They were echoes, shadows of their living selves, shackled to their bones and to this world.

They did not think, and they did not work together.

"*Go* . . . ," came a voice, as soft and unpleasant as an icy finger trailing down her spine.

And they certainly did not speak.

Wren halted, tension locking her muscles tight. It *couldn't* be . . .

She searched their rotted faces, seeking moving lips and vocal cords, but if an incorporeal ghost like the one from the bandit attack could shriek and *attempt* to talk, then she supposed these revenants could form words. Obviously the sound didn't come from their bodies at all. It came from their souls, their spirits. It came from beyond.

Wren turned to Julian, but his attention was fixed on something *behind* them.

Another revenant.

This was the one who had spoken, Wren knew instantly, though it stood silent as the grave.

Julian withdrew his staff, releasing the sharpened points and leveling it at the approaching revenant—but he didn't strike.

This undead was small.

Child-small, and it wore the decaying scraps of what had once been a lace-trimmed dress. The fabric rippled in an otherworldly breeze, along with strands of wispy hair, and though the body was little more than mottled bone, the way the ghostlight emanated from its wide, empty eye sockets in focused points gave the impression of keen interest. Of life.

It tilted its head, an uncomfortably innocent gesture, and seemed to stare at the weapon hovering near its face. As if it were curious. Julian's hands shook.

Then it lifted a bony arm and pointed into the trees back the way they had come.

"Go."

The word whispered through the air, raspy with age but retaining the pitch and tone of the child who had spoken it.

Julian didn't move—neither of them did—but then, in a blink, the child's skeletal hand snaked out and took hold of Julian's weapon. He could have dislodged its grip, could have speared it through or struck it hard enough to crack its bones.

But he didn't. He'd gone still as a statue, frozen before the revenant.

As Wren watched, tendrils of the undead's ghost began to lift from its bones like steam. It swirled and eddied and then sharpened, crawling down its arm . . . toward the staff. Toward Julian.

Enough.

Now that the ghost was separating from its body, it was vulnerable. A cloud of bonedust was all it took to have the revenant reeling and screeching in pain. Wren ignored the earsplitting racket and shoved Julian aside. She planted the sole of her boot square into the revenant's now spirit-less chest cavity, cracking the brittle bones and sending the corpse flying to the ground.

In response to this assault to its physical body, the ghost separated even further, rising in a tide that Wren slashed clean through with her bone blades.

The wisps began to dissipate, so she turned back to Julian to make sure he was okay. But she'd barely laid eyes on him when he shouted, "Look out!"

She turned. The ghost's pieces—which should have returned to the ether by now—were swirling and ebbing, reshaping before her very eyes.

Impossible.

Before she could do more than think the word, the ghost dove straight for Wren's face.

Unable to react in time, she felt something hit her shoulder, hard—something living—and the next thing she knew, she and Julian were sprawled on the ground. Above, the ghost had given its final assault; its form disappeared in a cloud of green-tinged smoke.

Wren turned to Julian, her relief at avoiding a collision with the ghost freezing in her lungs when she saw him hunched over his left hand, staring down at the gloved appendage, his face bone-white.

Apparently, they had not *both* gotten away unscathed. The ghost must have hit his hand when he saved Wren. It had been mere vapor. . . . Did that mean the deathrot would be less potent? Wren didn't know.

She didn't know, and the other revenants were coming their way.

"Julian," she said firmly, and he turned an anguished face toward her. "On your feet. Now."

He obeyed at once, clearly in shock, his staff held loosely in his uninjured hand.

"Remember what I told you before?" she asked, sheathing one of her swords and keeping her other blade raised between them and the undead. "Forget it."

"What?" he said distractedly, clutching his hand to his chest.

The row of undead flared brightly, ready to attack at long last.

Wren sheathed her second sword and grabbed Julian's shoulder instead, dragging him with her—turning her back, lowering her guard, and breaking every rule of her training.

"Run!"

NINETEEN

They ran at full tilt between the trees, moving dangerously fast in the darkness, stumbling through the underbrush and narrowly avoiding losing an eye to wildly swinging branches. Wren's ankle throbbed, and she was certain Julian was feeling his own wounds, but they couldn't slow down.

While she kept one hand on him, urging him forward, she dipped her other hand into the bonedust at her belt.

The revenants were behind them, pursuing with a sluggish but steady tread. It was the only reason running was a viable option— their corpses slowed them down.

Fearing what else might decide to pop up, however, she cast handfuls of bonedust in sweeping arcs that painted the trees white and powdered their clothes, but there was no sign of any undead except those that followed them.

If Wren were alone, she'd just run until the sun came up or she cleared the trees—whichever came first—and hope that the undead didn't pursue in the daylight, preferring to remain in the shelter of the forest.

But she wasn't alone. She was with Julian, and not only was he injured from the kidnapping at the fort, but the way he grimaced and clutched his hand told her he had definitely been touched by a ghost, which meant deathrot. He needed to be treated *immediately*. But where? How?

As she continued to run in a panic, the trees began to thin somewhat, and a spindly structure rose before them. It was like a tower on stilts, with a rickety ladder dangling from a trapdoor in the floor above.

It must have been a watchtower—that explained the height at least—and Wren did a cursory scan with her senses before deciding it was safe and shoving Julian ahead of her, up the moldering rope ladder.

The instant Wren reached the top, she peered back down to see the undead ranged below, their necks craned unnaturally to look up at her.

Fear pierced her gut.

Those hollow faces, those empty eyes . . . Wren knew the human skeleton inside and out and had seen it in varying levels of decay since she took her first anatomy lesson at eight years old. But it was one thing to see it on a table for study or to find it buried in the ground, and something else entirely when it walked like the living—but decidedly *unlike* any living person she had ever seen. Everything about them was wrong, and the way their ghost glowed from within . . . It was both like a prisoner desperate to be free and like a supernatural puppeteer pulling strings, and it made her skin crawl.

When one of them put a bony hand on the bottommost rung, the fear in her stomach twisted. Ghosts couldn't leave the ground . . . but maybe ghosts with a *body* could. She withdrew a knife, hacking at the ladder until the rope snapped and fell away.

The undead watched it drop onto the ground before them, then looked up again. Wren glanced around—would they try to climb some other way? She had known the undead to be single-minded and determined when provoked. She had been chased by ghosts before, pursued to the edges of their range or until something easier came along. But she had never known the undead to be capable of problem-solving or strategizing—then again, she had been proven wrong more than once in the past couple of days, so what was one more thing?

When they didn't make a move, just simply stood and stared, Wren expelled a shaky breath. Their ghosts were irritated, but while they could detach from their bodies and pose new and dangerous threats, they couldn't *fly*.

But as she stared down at their unnaturally still bodies, a new worry took hold.

How long could they stand there without moving? Hours, surely— maybe even days?—but before the thought could overwhelm her, the cluster of undead dispersed, all walking in the same direction at the exact same time, as if summoned by an unheard call.

This . . . *group think* . . . it was unnatural. Dangerous. She had not been trained for this.

Wren thought of that rumor Julian had mentioned. A Corpse Queen enslaving the undead. Was it she who called them now?

She quickly shook it aside. She had enough to worry about without scary bedtime stories factoring into the mix.

Whatever might come, she and Julian appeared to be safe—for now.

Turning from the hatch, she found him in the shadows of the small, round tower. He was hunched against the wall, eyes lidded and breath uneven, his staff tossed carelessly onto the floor.

"They're gone," she said, hoping to ease that particular worry as she moved closer to him. Her eyes were adjusting to the gloom after the intensity of the ghostlight, and she could now make out the way his mouth was pulled down in the corners in a grimace.

"Let me—" she began, but he cut her off.

"What the hell were you doing back there?" he demanded.

"I . . . What do you mean?"

"You," he said, gasping, "*attacked* them. You wanted a fight . . . kept edging closer . . ."

"No, that's not—they weren't behaving right. I only wanted to understand—"

"Of course they're not *behaving right*," he said harshly, forcing the words out. "There's nothing *right* about them. They're undead. They're *wrong*, and you . . . you shouldn't have . . ."

He was panting now, clutching at his arm.

"Shouldn't have *what*? That child revenant was seconds away from attacking. I was trying to protect you."

"No," he said, shaking his head forcefully, "you were trying to prove you could. If we had left them alone—they don't *always* chase."

"How do you know that?" Wren demanded.

He sighed, expression bleak as the anger seemed to leech out of him. "That's not the first time I've seen them. Sometimes our patrols . . ." He took a deep, shuddering breath. "Avoiding them is our only hope, and when that fails, we run. Sometimes it works."

Wren faltered. Was he right? Could she have backed down? Could they have simply walked away?

Yes, a voice said in the back of her mind. Yes, they could have if she hadn't been so curious about their behavior. If she hadn't needed to figure it out, to *test* it. But what the undead did and how they acted—it was important to their survival that she understand. She couldn't keep them alive in the Haunted Territory if she didn't know what to expect.

She pressed her hands into her eyes.

"Let me see your arm," she said, ignoring his comment because she was being mature—not because she didn't have a response.

He recoiled. "Don't."

"You have to let me see! If the ghost touched your bare skin . . ."

"It didn't," he said through clenched teeth. "It's just—it's cold. Just cold."

Extreme cold was a precursor to—and often a symptom of—deathrot. Julian's flesh was covered, from his leather gloves to his long-sleeve shirt, coat, and armor, but it wouldn't protect him against a ghost.

"Please," Wren said softly, making her voice as nonconfrontational as she could.

"No," he said back, equally gently.

Something was up with him and those gloves, but she didn't have the time to unpack it right now. The earliest stages of deathrot could be treated, and a person could potentially make a full recovery.

A fire would be ideal, but they didn't have time to waste—plus there was nowhere to safely build it, as the floor was wood.

A fire was not necessary, though. What was necessary was heat.

Trembles had begun to rack Julian's frame, and there was a sheen of incongruous sweat across his brow.

"Get over here," she muttered, though there were scant inches between them. She unbuckled her armor, belt, and bandolier before reaching for his. He stiffened, drawing back. "I'm not—I need to get you warm. If we don't, the cold will only spread, and come morning..."

His eyes, usually cool with disdain, were slightly wild. He nodded warily, watching her every move with bowstring tension.

She hastily removed his armor plate—he helped, using his good hand to unsnap buttons and loosen clasps. The pieces were heavy enough to make her grunt with effort as she did her best not to drop them, laying them aside until his jacket was revealed. She undid the buttons, then pulled the exposed arm out of its sleeve. His under-layers were drenched with icy sweat, and he shivered worse than ever, his chest heaving.

"Trust me," Wren murmured, tugging on his second arm, its sleeve catching on his glove. She worried about the damp sweat trapped within the fabric, but they couldn't afford any more arguing.

"*Trust?*" he repeated faintly.

Wren looked up at him. "I'm all you've got."

His gaze was searching for a moment. Then he nodded, letting her get back to work.

With both arms released, Wren crossed them and pressed his hands against his chest, the left hand—the one that had made contact with the ghost—underneath the other, directly overtop his heart. She could see the way he curled in on it, grateful at the wave of warmth permeating his skin. Wren recalled her first brush with exposure to deathrot, how a ghost had slipped past her guard, and though she had sworn it touched her, there had been no marks on her skin. Still, the cold had lingered, and even after treatment and a hot bath, she'd trembled all night in bed.

She tugged his coat more tightly around his shoulders, securing it—but she didn't fasten the buttons.

Instead, she turned to her own.

Julian's expression was soft with temporary relief, his eyes closed as he leaned against the wall—until he heard the first button on Wren's coat pop.

"What are you doing?" he demanded, standing upright, his eyes wide open once more.

"Do you want to lose your hand?" she snapped. Bending over their bags, she unearthed a blanket and spread it across the cold floor, shoving him down so he was lying on his side, staring up at her as she proceeded to undo her jacket, the cold air creeping in against her shirt.

Rather than protest outright, Julian gave her a weird smile, as if he'd thought of something funny. "No," he murmured, eyes fluttering closed again. "No, I do not."

"Then shut up and count yourself lucky. It usually takes at least a few drinks and some pretty words to get this close to me."

"Somehow I doubt that."

He was not entirely wrong. Wren had tumbled around with boys, with or without the drinks—and with or without the pretty words.

"Are you saying I'm easy?" she asked.

He huffed. "I'm saying you have no interest in pretty words."

For some reason, that statement made Wren's throat tighten. "It's a good thing, too, since I haven't gotten a civil one from you since we met."

"I'm not in the habit of lying."

Wren scowled—not that he saw—and removed her coat. "Good. Then I don't want to hear you complain about this."

"Complain about—" Wren lay down beside him, and he gasped as she slipped inside his open jacket and pressed herself against his crossed arms, enveloping him in what was essentially a hug, her hands sliding under his jacket to meet around his back. Her coat, still clinging to her shoulders, fit under his, creating a barrier to keep the heat in, just as his did for him.

Julian went instantly rigid, spine straightening and pulling away from her.

"Stop it," she murmured, her mouth landing somewhere in the space near his collarbone. She tightened her grip on his back, waiting for the chill of her intrusion to dissipate, for heat to build between them.

It didn't take long. Silent, tense seconds turned into languid ones, each muscle in Julian's back unlocking beneath her hands. She rubbed up and down tentatively, creating more heat, while his hand—which had been cold against Wren's chest—started to steadily warm.

His breathing went from shallow and tight to deep and slow. His cheek lowered, propping itself on the top of Wren's head.

"Sleep," Wren ordered. He needed to gather his strength, and there was no better way.

He muttered something into her hair.

"What?" she asked, tilting her head slightly.

"Thank you."

TWENTY

Wren remained wrapped up in Julian for an hour at least, waiting until every twitch and tremble receded, his muscles heavy and his chest rising and falling in the rhythms of deepest sleep.

He had rolled over slightly, taking Wren with him, so she was essentially sprawled on top of him. She squinted toward the hatch, anxiously looking for the telltale glow of the undead, but all was darkness. Her breath misted before her, but she remained warm in the ironsmith's embrace.

His eyes were closed, his brow furrowed slightly. She drew back carefully, watching his face as she did, but he didn't wake. His skin was dry, with a healthy flush of color—not pale or clammy with cold sweat like it had been before.

She looked at his arms, still crossed against his chest, and pulled one of her hands from behind his back to touch his skin through his shirt. Even though she'd prefer to actually see the lack of deathrot than just assume it, peeking when he was unconscious was a line she didn't intend to cross. Besides, she felt only the warmth of healthy skin beneath her hand, and if the rot had started, he would be in excruciating pain at her touch.

Expelling a relieved breath, she slid her other arm out—it had fallen asleep—shaking it as she extricated herself. His frown deepened at her departure, as if unhappy with the sudden space between them, and the incongruous sight of it wormed its way into Wren's chest. Of course he was sleeping, and how he *actually* felt was the exact opposite. He'd never wanted her so close to him to begin with.

Going to their packs, she unearthed the rest of their blankets and piled them on top of him. She thought again of a fire, but even if she could manage to create something that didn't burn the place down, it would only draw attention to them. There were more than undead threats in the Breachlands, as their run-in with the bandits the day before had proven.

They had gotten extremely lucky finding this place. She didn't know how much farther Julian could have run, and despite how much she liked to brag about her skill, Wren would have had a difficult time protecting them against a handful of tier fives. She could have tried a defensive ring, using bonedust to enclose them in safety, but even at Marrow Hall they had warned that revenants had a certain resistance to its effects. The remnants of their bodies protected their ghost and could allow them to pass through a bonedust ring or at least reach beyond its barriers. Ideally, that's when Julian's iron sword would come in handy, and really, the pair of them might make the perfect team against these walking undead, if they could only find a way to work together properly.

She stared longingly at the nest of blankets, the lingering memory of his warm skin appealing—especially as she had left her jacket somewhere inside. She was exhausted, both from the scant amount of sleep they'd managed early that morning and the series of attacks—before and after it—that had made up the past few days. But as soon as she closed her eyes, she saw those revenants standing below the open hatch, looking up at her. She saw them reach for the ladder, and the vision chased away the possibility of sleep.

Instead, she took up her bone blades and perched next to the trapdoor, watching, waiting . . . just in case.

When Wren next became aware of herself, she was slumped against the wall beside the trapdoor. Golden light filled the tower, and Julian crouched before her, a hand on her shoulder.

"I'm awake," she mumbled, lurching upright. She stared down through the hatch again, stretching her senses, but the revenants had not returned.

Julian sat back on the heap of blankets, scrubbing at his face as if he'd just awoken as well.

"How is your hand?" she asked.

He looked down at it, clenching and unclenching his fist. He nodded. "It's good."

"Good," Wren said. He tugged at the edge of his glove and then smiled—a soft, affectionate expression she'd never seen on his face before. He was fiddling with something . . . a bracelet? "What's that?"

He glanced at her, and apparently he was in a talkative mood, because he actually lifted the bracelet to give her a better view. "It's a good luck charm." It was made of simple iron links, with three roughly hewn beads that slid across the surface. "These are iron ore. Raw and untreated. There's one for each of the House of Iron rankings."

He touched the first bead. "The hammer, which is the artisan—the person who crafts our weapons and armor. Then we have the sword," he said, touching the next, "which is the warrior—the person who uses them. I'm a sword," he added, flicking a look in her direction before he continued to the last bead. "And then the anvil. They are the historians, the protectors of the lore. The foundation."

"We have three, too," Wren murmured. "The reapyr—the person who severs the ghost from its bones. They also handle funeral rites once they age out of active duty. There's the valkyr, the one who defends the reapyr against the undead."

"Let me guess—you're a valkyr?"

She bowed her head in acknowledgment, ignoring the twinge that told her it wasn't technically true, and he smiled smugly. "And then we have the fabricators. They're like your hammers, I suppose, but there are a lot of different specializations. Weapons and armor, yes, but also protections."

"Like the Wall?"

"Right. So they make weapons and armor, plus talismans for roads and towns." He nodded, still toying with the bracelet. "Who wants to keep you safe?" she asked. When he lowered his brows in confusion, she clarified. "The charm. Who gave it to you?"

She knew it was a gift from the way he'd looked at it, like it reminded him of a happy memory. Her guess was maybe Julian had a girl back home, and she felt a bit guilty for the way she'd pranced around him the other day—and a bit disappointed, too, if she was honest.

"Oh," he said, surprised and suddenly uncomfortable. He dropped his hand. "My little sister."

"*Oh,*" Wren echoed, and he looked puzzled at her reaction. She cleared her throat. "Well, I guess it worked, didn't it? You *were* shot by an arrow the day we met."

"My breastplate *worked*," he said dryly, sliding his hand over the place where the armor had saved him. Then he huffed out a laugh. "I tried to tell her. I am literally *covered* in iron—three extra rocks won't do much—but she wouldn't hear of it. She's superstitious. And stubborn."

"I like her already."

He tilted his head. "Yes, I suspect you would."

Wren couldn't figure out what to make of that. "What about last night? That was the hand that almost got exposed. I think she's on to something."

"I think I have *you* to thank for that," he said.

Wren's stomach squirmed at the intense, unguarded look in his eye. "Yeah, well . . . you already have."

His expression flickered, and he glanced down, noticing her jacket amid his blankets and bedding for the first time. She could almost see his tired brain trying to work through it all, recalling how they'd lain in an embrace, and his murmured "thank you" before he'd fallen asleep.

"I thought I dreamed you," he muttered. Then froze. "*It*. I thought I'd dreamed *it*."

Wren stood and picked up her coat, smiling as she pulled it on, delighted at the flush crawling up his face. "I guess today is the day your dreams have come true."

He gave her a flat stare, and she laughed, doing up the buttons.

"You're welcome, by the way," she said. "I knew you had it in you."

He rolled his eyes, but she thought she could see him stifle the smallest of smirks before he cleared his throat and stood. "We need to figure out our next move. Are they . . . ? Are we alone?"

"For now," Wren said, peering down the open hatch again, though she could sense there were no undead in the vicinity. She turned her gaze to the narrow windows that sat at regular intervals along the wall. All she could make out were tree branches. "I just don't know where we've wound up. We ran for a while last night, but in what direction . . ."

Julian, who had been refolding some of the blankets, straightened. His gaze roamed the space before landing on the ceiling, where, much to Wren's surprise, an additional trapdoor sat. It was currently closed, but Julian extended his arm and flicked the latch. "This was a watchtower once," he explained, confirming Wren's suspicion as the door groaned open, revealing a perfect circle of blue sky studded with clouds. Mounted next to it on the ceiling was a rusted metal ladder, which he tugged, and it too screeched and protested before coming loose, the steps perfectly meeting the floor underneath.

"Steel," he muttered with distaste, shaking his head. "We never had to bother with this stuff until the Breach. Suddenly we couldn't afford to waste good iron on anything other than weapons and armor." He actually wiped his gloved hand on his leg, as if the steel left some sort of residue.

Shaking her head in amusement, Wren followed him up the ladder.

The roof slanted away from the hatch on all sides, allowing for proper drainage of rain and snow but making it difficult for them to stand on. Julian pulled himself onto the roof, still moving somewhat gingerly thanks to his chest and hand injuries, and sat down near the top. Wren did the same, and together they took in the view.

The height of the tower helped them see past the treetops in all directions, and the breath whooshed from her lungs as she turned northeast. There was a massive gouge marring the landscape. This was the Breach, the place where the ironsmiths had overmined and caused the land to shake, the ground to split, and whole cities and towns to come crumbling down. And that was to say nothing of what they'd uncovered there, a lost city filled with undead.

It was as jagged as a scar, deep and dark . . . save for a faint, unnatural green glow.

Julian pointed at the vista before them. "There were once three mines here," he said, indicating each spot in turn. One was on the very edge of the Breach, which sat at the base of what Wren assumed was the Adamantine Mountains. "It was apparently Oreton, a newer mine, that caused it," he said. "Not that it mattered. Undead spewed out of every mine within a twenty-mile radius. There was even a gold mine to the north that was overrun, but luckily it collapsed before the revenants could spread. Most of the people escaped, and when they built the Wall, they made sure to close it off with the rest of us."

"Why did they build it underground?" Wren wondered aloud, unable to tear her eyes from the view. Julian shot her a puzzled look, so she clarified. "The ghostsmith city, I mean. It's not like they were mining for dead."

"No," Julian agreed. "They were mining for magic."

Wren turned to him. "What do you mean?"

"Well, magic comes from the earth, right? So the anvils—our scholars," he reminded her, "they think the ghostsmiths were looking for more. They didn't just 'go away' when the rest of the smiths rejected them. They came here and started digging. The anvils think their whole society was built, defended, and maintained by the undead."

Wren gaped. "You think they found it, then? *More* magic?"

"How else do you explain the walking undead? They aren't all

centuries-old corpses roaming the Haunted Territory. New revenants are rising every day. And they only rise here."

Wren was stunned. Like the stories about the Corpse Queen, this
was something she'd never heard before. Unless . . . what had Odile
said? That something dark lived in the Breach? Something evil?
Could she mean this magic?

Wren didn't know if it was what Julian had just told her or the
very real, very visceral sight of the Breach after a life filled with stories about it, but she felt a bit sick as she stared across the landscape.
Even in the daylight, she could see the ghost glow, which added a surreal, sinister tone to the rocks and hillsides. She could only imagine
the view at night. And the undead . . . Would they be visible, wandering to and fro, or did they mostly slumber until the living crossed
their path? Everything looked barren, not a person or animal to be
seen, nor a sound to be heard.

A question rose to the surface of her mind. "Where do we cross?"
The Breach stretched, unbroken, from the mountains in the north to
the dense forest in the south.

A short, sharp laugh. He extended an arm. "We don't. We go
around it, through those trees, which are a part of the Norwood—the
same forest we're in right now—and then turn north on the far side."

Wren followed the path, which required a massive detour.

Julian dropped his hand. "I'd thought that sticking to the outskirts
of the Haunted Territory would keep us mostly safe, but if last night
is any indication . . ." He rubbed at his jaw, then shifted his gaze to
the landscape nearer at hand. "Towers like this were built soon after
the Breach, meant to keep track of any wayward undead that came
anywhere close to civilization, so they could raise the alarm. They
were placed well outside the danger zone. The fact these trees are

apparently crawling with undead means the Haunted Territory has expanded. Exponentially."

"So even your 'safe route' might not be safe at all?"

He sighed but didn't respond. He squinted into the distance again. "I could have sworn the Breach didn't extend quite this far south—as I understood it, it didn't reach the Norwood, but . . ."

"Could it have grown?" Wren asked. The edges were difficult to discern, jagged and crisp in some places but obscured by rock and fallen structures in others. Entire towns had fallen into that gorge when it first cracked open, so it didn't seem beyond the realm of possibility that the ground might give way further.

A visible shudder went down Julian's spine. He hesitated, then shook his head resolutely. "No. It was mining that caused it, and no one would be fool enough to go digging down there anymore. It's going to be a hard journey, but if we stick to the tree line . . ." He trailed off. "It's our best chance."

They climbed back down, Wren going over everything Julian had said. It was logically sound, and before their run-in the previous night, she might have agreed with it. But right now she didn't.

Julian continued to pack up the bedding while Wren dug through their bags for breakfast.

As they sat together on the floor chewing dried meat and sour pickled vegetables, Wren asked about something she'd seen spanning the gaping maw of the Breach.

A bridge.

It had looked spindly and unfinished, a skeletal scrap of metal.

"Has anyone ever crossed it?"

Julian's hand stilled as he reached for another piece of meat. He darted a glance up at her before focusing on his meal. "My father did," he said shortly. "During the Uprising. It was built to sneak troops to the Wall."

Oh. So *that* was how they'd tried to outsmart the Dominion soldiers. Instead of traveling miles to avoid the Haunted Territory, making it easy to predict their strikes, they'd decided to cut through, hoping to catch the Dominion soldiers and the garrisons at the Wall unprepared. Unfortunately for them, Locke's scouting unit had found them first.

Looking to Julian, an unasked question hovered on the tip of her tongue: *Was Julian's father lucky enough to walk away, or had he died not long after crossing that bridge?*

"Has anyone crossed it since?" she asked delicately.

"Why?"

"Because I think we should."

"You want to cross over the *actual* Breach when we barely survived crossing the border into the Haunted Territory that surrounds it? You're mad. This is last night all over again—you don't think."

"This *is* me thinking," Wren protested. "We need to get to the prince, and this route you've proposed will waste too much time. I can't afford to fail."

"That's all this prince is to you, isn't he? A trophy to be won? A balm against your wounded pride? A chance to prove how tough you are, how many ghosts you can take on by yourself?"

He may have hit closer to the mark than Wren wanted to admit, but he didn't understand. In the Bonewood, she had *tried* to do things the right way, the honorable way—and look what had happened. How else was she to regain her place? How else was she to prove herself to her father?

She crossed her arms over her chest. "And what is he to you? An object to bargain with? A pawn in a game?"

"My life, and the lives of my people, are no game," he practically growled. "You see them out there, don't you? You see what we're up against? Every day we're trapped in here is a day closer to all of us winding up like that. Do you know what we do with our dead? Have you ever even thought of it?" Wren didn't respond, but it seemed he didn't need her to. "We used to burn them." Her stomach twisted, knowing what he would say next. "It didn't work."

Without severing the soul from the bones first, that spirit would be doomed to wander the living world for eternity, their bones too damaged for their soul to be properly reaped.

"Now we toss them into the ocean in cages. They sink to the bottom, undead but unable to hurt the living. Trapped there until we find a way to free ourselves from this waking nightmare."

"I know it's not a game," Wren said, once she found her voice. "He's a friend, okay? The prince is a friend."

Julian's anger seemed to have subsided somewhat. He slumped against the wall opposite, staring down at his food once more.

"And even though he's a prince . . . they left him, didn't they? Everyone at the fort, they discussed his life like he was . . . like he's nothing but—"

"A pawn?" Julian supplied dryly.

Wren rolled her eyes but nodded. "I suppose being a pawn is better than being nothing at all." He continued to stare at her, and she wished she'd never opened her mouth, but she plowed on. "I mean, I was missing too. Not that I'd fetch any sort of price—I'm no royal— but, well . . . Suspecting that no one will care if you're gone and then knowing it for certain are two different things. The fact of the matter is, I care that Leo was taken, and I'm in a position to do something about it. So I will."

Julian straightened a bit at her words, and his cool gaze roved her face, searching. Then his lips quirked. "Leo?"

Wren felt her cheeks flush, though she didn't know why. "He told me to call him that."

An eyebrow shot up. "I bet he did."

"He wishes," Wren muttered. "Look, I know it's risky," she said, referencing her original proposal. "And I know I've acted without thinking things through before. . . ." She swallowed. "I've been doing that long before I met you. But this time I *have* thought this through, and given what I've seen so far, *nowhere* is safe. And these undead . . . They're nothing like what I've studied or been told about. They're intelligent and seem to have some means of communicating or connecting with one another. They have unified goals, some joint purpose, and I worry that the longer we take, the greater the chances they could bring the entire undead population of the Haunted Territory down upon us. The sooner we get through, the better."

She met Julian's gaze. He didn't speak, his expression unreadable.

"I know it's the reckless thing to do—" she continued, but he cut her off.

"But that doesn't mean it's not the right thing."

Wren could only stare at him, stunned. "I thought you said I was mad."

He shrugged. "You are. I also think you're brave."

TWENTY-ONE

They set out soon after. They needed to make the most of the daylight, and Julian figured they could make that bridge crossing before darkness fell. What they'd find on the other side, they couldn't be sure, but they'd have to deal with the threats as they came.

The silence between them felt . . . less charged than usual. Less tense. Wren doubted they'd had their last argument, but she felt that perhaps they were starting to understand each other. They each had reasons for being here, and it extended beyond simple, selfish gain for both of them. Julian had a protective streak when it came to the people east of the Wall, a sense of responsibility that Wren suspected had something to do with the little sister he'd mentioned. He also had loyalty to whoever was calling the shots in the kidnapping—likely the regent—and believed that person wasn't to blame for the attempted assassination. He wanted to get Leo away from the kidnappers who currently held him, so for now their goals aligned.

Of course, once they actually had Leo in their possession, things might change. Quickly. But focusing on that now was a waste of effort. They might never make it there, but they stood a better chance of surviving if they trusted each other in the interim.

As they left the cover of the trees, the ground sloped away from the forest, leading into a swath of low fields dotted with dead grass and patches of snow. Beyond were massive boulders and soaring bits of rock, obscuring the view of their destination. They had to cut through that landscape to make it to the bridge, which meant that the undead could be around every corner.

And Wren had thought the forest was bad.

At least they had daylight on their side, though the swell of dark clouds to the east told her not to remain too optimistic.

They took a break around midday at what was once a village, though the buildings were little more than foundations and rotted beams of wood poking out of the ground. This had surely been abandoned even before the Breach, and while Wren *did* find bones as she checked the area thoroughly, they were dead ones.

"It's a mausoleum," she announced, crouching before the marble structure. It was roughly the size of a wagon, heavily overgrown with creeping vines, its surface so dirty that it blended into the surrounding scenery. Mausoleums were a foreign concept brought to the island and made popular by the Valorians, a custom from their homeland. Traditionally, all bodies on the island had been buried. Since magic came from the earth, so did all life, and so that was where they were meant to return, giving their magic to future generations. It's part of why the ghostsmiths' necromancy was seen as so terrible. They were not only denying a dead soul rest, but they were denying future generations of their magic.

"What are you doing?" Julian asked as she tugged at the ensnaring greenery, searching for the handle.

"Don't worry, these are properly reaped. Nothing but the dead in here." She pulled, the door resisting but eventually opening enough to reveal the pure darkness within.

"Then why are you disturbing them?"

Wren had to give him credit; he'd have yelled at her the day before, but while his voice was tight with frustration, he kept his anger in check.

"Weapons," she said shortly, glancing over her shoulder. "Not," she said, cutting him off before he could speak, "the kind you're thinking of."

She wasn't here looking for old iron swords. She was here for bones.

"All of these repel the undead?" Julian asked, looking uneasily over her shoulder.

"Well, the bone with the most power is the anchor bone—the one that holds the spirit. It's the payment we take for performing funeral rites. They get to bury their dead without fear of haunting, and we get the material we need to make weapons and defend lives. Only the rich can afford to pay coin instead and keep the anchor bone, preferring to bury their loved ones intact. So, unless these people were very wealthy . . ." She leaned forward, peering at the neatly stacked bodies on three levels of shelves, then drew back and shook her head. "There are no anchor bones in here."

"Doesn't that make them no good?" Julian asked, watching as she reached inside.

"They're not perfect, but they'll do," Wren said, sweeping her hand across the shelves. Her bonedust was most in need of replenishment, but she'd settle for some knucklebones in the meantime. They were the least useful of her weapons, but they still did damage.

Julian wore a thoughtful expression as he helped her close the door after she'd finished. "Did you ever consider being a reapyr?" he asked.

"No way," Wren said at once. "I always wanted to fight."

"Unsurprising," he said dryly. "Are all valkyrs as reckless and fool-hardy as you?"

"I mean . . . they *try*," Wren said, and he actually smiled. A full-blown, teeth-bearing smile, and fuck if it didn't make her smile in return. She was suddenly desperate to change the subject. "I *did* take some introductory reaping courses—we all have to. Learning about anchor bones and ley lines. I hardly paid attention. I just wanted a sword. Or two. My father is a valkyr, so it seemed the only path for me."

"I know the feeling," Julian said softly, staring in the direction of the bridge. "Honestly, I wasn't really interested in fighting. But I guess you could say it was a family tradition."

"Your father," Wren began, choosing her words carefully, "he's a sword, too?"

"He was," Julian said, not looking at her. His hand was resting against his chest over the arrow wound again. She'd have thought he was in pain from the way he kept touching it, but he never winced or grimaced, and she suspected it was more of a nervous gesture than anything else. "Until he fought during the Uprising. He never came back."

Their path toward the bridge was an indirect one.

They had to move around the landscape, climbing every now and again to make sure they were on course. They'd gone farther north than they should have, but eventually they found the remnants of an Old Road, and it was a clear shot from where they stood to the bridge.

The iron structure pierced the gray clouds above, the glow of the Breach painting everything in shades of eerie ghostlight.

It was a foreboding sight, causing tension to tighten Wren's shoulders.

She turned to Julian to gauge his reaction, but he was staring in the exact opposite direction.

Behind them the road continued, cutting through a rocky hillside before dipping into some sort of valley. And rising from that sunken landscape was another wash of familiar, otherworldly green. The daylight coupled with the rising hills must have blocked it from their earlier view, and Wren's magic struggled in their heavily haunted surroundings. But with the amount of ghostlight emanating from that direction, there was certainly *something* undead nearby. Most likely several somethings.

A part of her wanted to investigate, but her curiosity had already gotten them into trouble, and she'd promised to avoid the undead.

Julian, however, seemed to have forgotten that promise *and* the logic behind it. He strode toward the valley without a backward glance.

"Hey, what are you doing? We need to make that bridge before—" Wren followed him, but as soon as they crested the ridge, the words died in her throat.

What lay before them was the remnants of a battlefield. Churned-up earth, rusted wagons, and broken weapons, sun-bleached and grown over with grass and wildlife.

And there were bodies. Countless corpses strewn across the road, human and horse, decomposed and picked over by whatever scavengers dared to venture here, leaving nothing but dented bits of armor and moldering leather behind.

Nothing.

Not even bones.

Or rather, there *were* bones, but they were so severely damaged, they were little more than dust blowing in the wind. And their ghosts? They were less than tier ones; they existed in a haze of green ghostlight, their bodies broken beyond repair—beyond reaping—the spirits of these poor undead souls suspended in this state of not-being forever.

How had this happened?

She had seen damaged bones before—those that had been burned by people who didn't know any better, or a body crushed in some horrific accident, the ley lines destroyed beyond recognition.

But this was a battlefield. These people died together this way, yet there was no evidence of fire, no reasonable explanation for this.

"What . . . *is* this?" Wren asked, stunned.

Julian turned to her, eyes darker than she'd ever seen them. "The end."

"Of what?"

"The Uprising. The House of Iron. Everything."

But that meant . . . How had Locke and her father, Odile, and the Dominion soldiers done *this*?

Julian laughed at Wren's silence, the hollow sound echoing across the ghostly field. "Figures. What sort of story did they tell west of the Wall? Heroic battle? Good persevering over evil?"

"I . . ."

Julian shook his head. "Some say it was the undead."

"No," Wren said, shaking her head. "With deathrot . . . there's no ghost, no haunting. And the bodies, they wouldn't—couldn't—look like this. . . ."

"No," Julian said softly, as if he agreed. "Others say it was the Graven heir."

Locke. Wren averted her gaze, desperately glad she'd never given Julian her family name.

"They say he had limitless power. That he was able to control the bones of the living as well as the dead. That he was able to bend and break and *shatter* them. He turned it on *everyone*, even some of his own people, before the abuse of power killed him."

"But that's not possible," Wren argued despite seeing the evidence right in front of her. Julian's gaze was intent, and she felt the need to explain—to defend. "Bonesmiths can't touch the bones of the living. They can't touch revenants, either. Any bone with a spirit still attached is beyond our reach."

"Yours, maybe. Not his."

"But it's not . . ." She trailed off, thinking. Limitless power . . . Could that have anything to do with the magic the ghostsmiths dug so deep for? Julian said new undead continued to rise as revenants. Did that mean whatever magic they found emanated from the Breach? Could it have touched Locke somehow? *Changed* him? But no one had ever told her anything like that. . . . Of course, her father never told her anything, full stop. It was Odile who had told Wren the most about the Uprising, but she hadn't mentioned anything about Locke, though she did mention something dark and *evil* living there. . . .

But if it was true, if her uncle Locke *was* to blame for . . . for *this* . . . Wren suddenly understood why her father never wanted to discuss it. Why they had chosen to paint him a hero rather than tell the truth.

All she could see was death. But even that wasn't true. This was worse than death. This was not-death. This was eternal damnation.

Julian wandered toward the edges of the battlefield, staring intently at the iron-armored corpses there, as if he wanted to go near but feared the haze of undead swirling about.

Wren took her sword and swiped it carefully through the mist. It swirled, parted . . . but there was no reaction.

"They won't attack," she said softly, coming up behind him. "They can't. They're too . . . disconnected from their bodies, from their lives. They just . . . are."

He glanced her way, then knelt over the nearest body.

It wore iron armor, like most of them did, its condition pristine despite the years and elements that had attempted to weather it.

Given Julian's reaction to Wren wanting to loot the corpses of the bandits, she was unsurprised that he made no move to take anything.

But what had he said? That since the Breach, they couldn't afford to waste iron on anything but weapons and armor? It made sense given that they'd had to close the mines and were forbidden from reopening them.

And yet here was a field of it, just waiting to be taken and reused. . . .

He glanced up, and somehow he seemed to know what she was thinking.

"Once an ironsmith wears their armor in battle, it's considered 'blooded,' and a bond forms between the smith and the armor. They say it strengthens the magic, and the more battles fought, the stronger that bond. It's familiarity, basically—the cornerstone of all smith magic."

Wren nodded. The more time a smith spent with their material, the stronger their power became. Both specifically—as in the case of personal armor and weapons like Julian was describing—and generally, with years of training encouraging magical talent to grow over time.

In fact, the very first smiths in existence developed their abilities based on where they lived. The first woodsmiths had lived in the forested regions to the north, the first stonesmiths, in the western highlands and rocky shores. All the metalsmiths found themselves conveniently living near large deposits of iron or veins of gold, and the first bonesmith had been one in a long line of gravediggers, toiling in the dirt. The first ghostsmith had apparently owned a cemetery.

"But it's more than that," Julian continued, frowning as he struggled to find the words. "It represents *struggle*, I think. Like, nothing good should come easy, and power should be earned."

Wren tilted her head, considering. She liked the idea. That a person was rewarded for their hard work, even if magic—like power—was something some people were born with.

"When an ironsmith dies," Julian continued, getting to his feet, "they are buried with their armor. Weapons can be repurposed, especially in families. The bonds can pass through bloodlines to create powerful magical connections. But armor? It's made especially for the wearer. It's . . . personal."

"I suppose this is why you didn't appreciate my corpse-looting before?" Wren asked, feeling a twinge of shame.

"No," he said hastily, apparently wanting to make her feel better for some reason. "It was . . . You were just being pragmatic."

"I think, sometimes, it's hard for me to see bones and bodies as sacred. They're a part of my everyday life."

Peering out across the field, she spotted several bodies in Dominion colors, too, their steel rusted red and damaged. Whoever had done this had indeed attacked both sides, though whether that was on purpose or not . . .

Julian soon moved on to the next ironsmith body, and the next, carefully avoiding the pockets of greenish haze, though their spirits were so weak, they'd be unlikely to give him a head cold, never mind deathrot.

It was clear he wasn't paying respects or taking in the sad sight. He was *looking* for something. Or someone.

"Julian," Wren said, following him into the wreckage. She saw flashes of bone armor and broken bone swords but didn't stop to investigate.

Julian didn't respond to his name, but when he stood to make for the next body, Wren grabbed his arm.

He looked at her, but his gaze was distant, and his expression lacked its usual sharpness. His brows were high, not lowered in a scowl, and his mouth was a thin line, his lips trembling ever so slightly.

"We need to get moving," Wren said, as gently as she could. "We don't have time for this."

He blinked as if coming back to himself. "I thought," he began, his voice slightly hoarse. "I hoped . . ." He looked over his shoulder at the seemingly endless mass of bodies.

He was obviously searching for his father, for answers, but he would not find any he liked here.

"You could look for years, and you might never find him," Wren said. "Even if you did . . . you wouldn't know him. He's dead, Julian. Your father is dead."

Some people, in their grief, didn't hire bonesmiths for death rites. They *wanted* their dead loved ones to rise again. Unable to say goodbye and hoping, maybe, that the ones they lost could remain in their lives in some way. It never ended well. While ghosts might remember something of their former lives, they could never truly reclaim them. They suffered in their half state—not alive, not dead— and eventually they lashed out, hurting the very people they'd once loved. Their melancholy was able to infect the living almost as surely as deathrot. That was why people often described ghosts as cold. It was the effect the presence of the undead had on the living spirit.

Besides, ghosts made for poor company. They couldn't talk, think, or communicate. . . . But even as Wren thought it, she amended the statement. Normally. *Normally* they couldn't talk, think, or communicate. But like everything else so far, that had been different here in the Breachlands.

"No," Julian said, his voice hard once more. "He's *undead*, doomed to wander, to exist here in this—this *hell*—forever."

"If we don't get out of here soon, you'll be joining him."

"I need to know—"

"You *can't*," Wren snapped, her patience fraying. The clouds were moving in their direction, bringing early night with them, and the bridge was a long walk away. "That's death. You can't always know. You think I don't wish, that I don't wonder—" She cut herself off. She had a dead parent of her own, after all. But now wasn't the time.

He gave her a curious look before clenching his hands and turning away.

She sighed, the frustration leaving her as swiftly as it had come. "We can make a marker, if you'd like."

He kept his back to her, but his head turned—the only sign he'd heard her.

"I know marble is the preferred material," she said, casting her gaze wide. "But I think granite will do nicely. It's what the southern kings used."

Still he didn't move, so Wren took the task upon herself. She found a good-size stone, turning it on its side so it jutted from the earth. She considered her weapons, wondering if she could spare a blade to leave here, embedded into the ground in front of the marker, but then Julian was there, offering one of his own. It was short and simple, withdrawn from one of several sheaths on his belt.

Wren wondered if it was a family heirloom. If it was, Julian would surely never gamble it like she had with Ghostbane.

Once the blade was deep in the earth, Wren knelt before it.

Julian, meanwhile, stood next to her, hovering uncertainly. He didn't seem to know what to do with his hands. First he wiped them on his legs, as if trying to remove nonexistent dirt. Then he fidgeted with his armor before clenching them into fists at his sides.

With an impatient—but not wholly unaffectionate—eye roll, Wren reached up and took hold of his right hand, yanking him down onto his knees next to her. He stumbled and shuffled into position, but when he tried to pull his hand back, Wren gripped it tighter, meeting his gaze. Sometimes people did this—held hands as they attended burials and funeral rites. She could only assume it was a way to feel less alone, and being here on the edge of such a brutal battlefield, Wren figured he could use it.

Maybe they both could.

He looked down at their joined hands, surprise quickly shifting into desperate, aching gratitude, and suddenly Wren had to look away.

She took a deep breath, then spoke the ritual words. She'd never performed death rites herself before, but she'd borne witness countless times.

"Death is as certain as the dawn, and just as a new day will come, so too will the new dead rise. And we will be there. To find. To fight. To free. So the living may thrive . . ." She glanced at Julian, and he joined her in the last few, which would be more familiar to him. "And the dead may rest in peace."

TWENTY-TWO

Despite Julian's stance on the matter, Wren had taken some bonedust from several of the bonesmith corpses before they left. She had not relished it, but she needed to replenish. Besides, the House of Bone didn't have the same conventions as the ironsmiths did. Wren would welcome any bonesmith who needed to loot her corpse should she happen to die on this mission. It was only pragmatic, like Julian had said.

The bridge loomed in the distance as they left the battlefield behind, tantalizingly close but also too far. They had at least an hour until they reached the crossing, and glancing up at the sky, Wren thought they had even less time until darkness fell. The clouds above hung heavy and low in the sky, bringing early night and threatening rain, stealing what little protection sunlight might have given them.

They were just making their final approach when her senses started to prickle. Squinting into the growing darkness, she came to an abrupt halt, throwing out an arm to stop Julian as well.

Revenants blocked their path.

There were three of them in varying states of decay, maybe twenty paces from where Wren and Julian stood. Beyond, just visible over the rise, was the bridge.

Wren's hands went for her swords.

"*Go,*" they said, all three of them in unison. Just like those from the forest, speaking without lips or lungs and making the same simple request.

Fear lanced through her, quickly followed by anger. Her hands, resting idly on the hilts of her swords, tightened. This was the world of the living, and she was a bonesmith, a *valkyr*, here to protect the living from the undead. She would not allow herself to be afraid of them, and she'd be damned if she started taking orders from them.

"No," she replied firmly. Julian's head whipped around, as if he thought she'd been talking to him.

"*Go. Now.*"

"No," Wren said again, grip tightening on her swords. "Why should we?"

"*Go. Because she wills it. And he commands it.*"

She wills it? Maybe that meant the Corpse Queen . . . but then who was this *he* they were referring to?

"What are you doing?" Julian asked, expression bewildered.

"I'm talking to them?" she said, assuming that answer was obvious. But no, Julian was wide-eyed with confusion.

"And they're talking back?" he asked.

Could he—did he not hear it?

"They . . . ," she said breathlessly. "They're telling us to go. Like last night?"

He shook his head, uncomprehending, and Wren swallowed thickly. She looked away from him, staring down the revenants instead.

Three she could handle. Three she could deal with.

But then she remembered what Julian had said. It didn't matter that she *could* take them. What mattered was that she shouldn't. They had a better shot of getting away if she didn't engage them.

So, as much as she wanted a fight, she dropped her hands from her weapons and reached for him instead.

"Come on," she said, diving between a cluster of rocks along the side of the road.

If they moved quickly, they might be able to lose them—or lure them into following behind, opening a path to the bridge.

"Here," she said, tossing Julian one of her swords. Her senses were ratcheted up, and she had the feeling there might be more undead to worry about.

He caught it deftly but stared down at it like it was some strange, foreign object. "I don't . . . ," he began uneasily.

"A sword is a sword," she said shortly. "Aim for the heart—the soul's most likely hiding place—but any contact with the ghost will cause them pain and buy you time."

Julian's eyes were wide as he adjusted his grip. He nodded.

"Come on," she urged, continuing a path between boulders and scrub brush, away from the road but still heading in the direction of the bridge. She didn't know if the revenants had pursued, but they had to keep moving forward regardless.

They were rounding a large thrust of rock when Wren's magic flared up in warning.

A soft green mist preceded the arrival of a ghost, so subtle that Wren almost missed it and Julian absolutely did, nearly running headlong into it.

Wren cried out, swiping for his shoulder and missing.

Then she remembered he carried one of her swords. She pulled on it, the feel as familiar as her own hands, and it thumped into his chest with enough force to halt his progress. The rest of the ghost exploded from the stone to their left, appearing exactly where Julian had been, its bones either near enough to provide easy movement or its tether weak enough that it did not matter.

The ghost solidified, and Wren could see the impression of its face, its features . . . its rage. It was more a sensation than a visual marker, a feeling—the way the spirit bunched and gathered, preparing for a sudden strike.

"Get down!" she bellowed, the instant before it happened.

Julian dropped to the ground like a sack of potatoes, leaving Wren alone to face it.

The ghost streaked toward her, and she had only one choice, one maneuver that would work—though she'd never dared it outside lessons, which was saying something, as Wren would dare a great many things.

It involved holding her sword out, blade forward to meet the coming attack. The idea was to split the ghost in two, to cut through the spirit like the prow of a ship through waves. The problem wasn't in the initial strike but in the runoff. If the ghost was moving too slowly when the blade cut through, the scraps of the spirit that were meant to slip to either side of her might in fact come to a stop, ebb and flow and swirl against her flesh.

It worked only if the attack was fast and strong, the ghost's momentum taking it clean past her and ensuring there could be no sudden redirections.

Wren, who always fought with two swords when she could help it, preferred to hack and slash her opponents, but with the ghost barreling down upon her, this maneuver was the only thing that would save her.

She raised her sword with two hands, narrowed her stance, and braced for impact.

The ghost slammed into her blade, the flare of light causing her eyes to water and Julian to throw up an arm against the glare.

But Wren could afford no such reaction. Eyes streaming, muscles straining, she held her ground as the ghost split in two, streaking past on either side of her in an explosion of sickly green light. A rush of cold threatened to sear her skin—but never made contact.

The ghost dissolved, reduced to wisps of icy vapor. Then nothing.

Julian stared up at her in the sudden darkness, awe etched into his features. "That was . . . You are . . ." He swallowed. Shook his head. "Amazing."

Wren was panting as if she'd run a mile, but it was his words that momentarily robbed her of breath. Had he just called her amazing?

Heart hammering against her ribs, she finally lowered her blade, glancing down at her arms to make sure she hadn't been harmed, but she was safe.

Julian got to his feet, looking to her for direction.

She gathered her wits. "Let's keep moving."

They encountered no further undead, and when they circled back toward the bridge, they came at it from the side.

Unfortunately, the undead that had blocked their path had not pursued. Worse, they had been joined by at least ten more. They were clustered there, unmoving, *waiting*. Working together, like those revenants in the forest.

Again, the wrongness of it hit Wren in the chest. The undead should be wandering after them, drawn as always by the flame of the living. Instead, they patiently awaited their foe, as if they knew where Wren and Julian intended to go. They were thinking, problem-solving, and *taking orders*, if what they had said to her before was true.

As if a land overrun by the undead wasn't bad enough, these undead were unlike anything Wren had ever seen.

Now that they were nearer, it became evident that the bridge was damaged—bent and rusted in places, while in others, the iron had given way entirely. The structure had been built in a rush, meant for a hasty crossing, and did not represent the ironsmith's best or most enduring work.

Beyond it, beneath it, was the wide chasm of the Breach itself. It glowed brightly now, coloring the landscape and revealing swirling tendrils of mist. Could those be ghosts, floating so high in the air? It shouldn't be possible, but Wren wouldn't take anything for granted.

Her mouth went dry. Maybe this wasn't such a good idea after all.

Julian sidled nearer to the bridge, which was about twenty feet away, his movement drawing the attention of the revenants standing on the road. They turned to face them in a single, unnatural movement but did not pursue. Yet.

"Do you trust me?" Julian asked.

Wren turned to him. "Seriously?" she asked, waiting for him to elaborate.

"I'm all you've got," he said, parroting the same words she'd given him inside the watchtower.

She blew out a breath. "I guess so."

He shrugged. "Good enough."

He looped an arm around her back, pulling her to his chest. Wren staggered against him, suddenly awash in the scent of worn leather and cold iron.

"Hang on," he said, drawing his sword and flicking it downward, transforming it back into a whip with a snap. He cocked his arm and tossed it out, across the abyss and toward the struts that rose over the bridge's deck.

It was an impossible throw—by anyone other than an ironsmith. In his hands, it landed exactly where he intended, wrapping easily around a joint, the segments of blade interlocking securely.

Wren's heart stuttered when she realized what he was about to do. "You've gotta be fucking kidd—" she began, but she never finished, her breath leaving her lungs in a rush as Julian leapt from the edge and they went plummeting to their deaths.

Or, at least, that's what Wren expected to happen. Instead, they dropped several stomach-tightening feet before the whip took their weight. There was a lurch—Wren clung to Julian with every ounce of strength she had—and an abrupt change in trajectory. Then they were no longer dropping but swinging across the open space, soaring toward the bridge.

They collided against the outer railing, clinging to one of the vertical beams as the metal shook with their impact. They remained motionless, ensuring their perch was steady, before Wren dared to open her eyes.

Unfortunately, she was looking down when she did and could see nothing but swirling green mist in the seemingly bottomless chasm below. How deep was it? And were there countless undead staring back at her?

"Eyes up here," Julian said sharply. Wren's attention snapped to him. "Do not look down."

"Got it," she croaked.

But looking up meant looking back at the bridge, and while they had landed safely, they were not actually safe.

The railing they clung to rattled loosely, and the undead hadn't missed their little trick. They turned together, starting their slow, staggering plod toward the bridge. At least they insisted on bringing their bodies with them. If they left their corpses behind, their ghosts could cover the distance between them in seconds.

"Up and over," Julian said, as the two of them climbed the railing and landed with a clatter on the wide deck of the bridge.

Wren took a moment to rest her hands on her knees and revel in the somewhat stable ground beneath her feet before gathering herself once more and facing their approaching enemy. They were starting to cross, causing the entire bridge to shake, but with her and Julian's head start, she was confident they could win a footrace.

Until she looked the other way.

While the western side of the bridge appeared relatively stable, the eastern side was barely standing upright. Whole beams of metal were gone, or rusted through, or dangling from missing bolts and damaged struts.

They couldn't run across this bridge. They'd be lucky if they could crawl . . . slowly.

"Shit," Wren said, reaching for a pouch of bonedust. Crouching along the walkway, she poured a thick stream from one side of the bridge to the other.

"Genius," Julian said, and Wren refused to be flattered by that.

"It should buy us time, I hope," she said, returning to the problem that lay before them. "Can you swing us across?"

Julian glanced down at his whip, which he had tugged free from the strut. "I can try."

He whipped it through the air again, securing it to an upper beam and tugging to make sure it was secure. Wren stepped against him, and he wrapped an arm around her once more.

"One . . . two . . ."

"Three," Wren said, and they jumped, swinging smoothly along the bridge. At this rate, they'd cross it in no time.

They were just extending their feet to land when the beam above them snapped, shrieking loudly and dropping them in midair.

They landed hard, skittering across the pocked and unsteady deck, the broken metal swinging dangerously above. The iron plank beneath them groaned ominously, and Julian hurried them both off of it and onto one of the crossbeams.

"Well, this bridge was clearly not built to code," he said, somewhat indignantly.

Wren laughed despite herself. "No shit."

He recoiled his whip and sheathed his remade sword before kicking at the plank beneath him, then craned his neck to look at the broken beam above. "This iron was never properly treated, and obviously no one's been maintaining it. I don't think we should try that again."

The steady rumble of the approaching revenants came to a sudden halt.

They had reached the bonedust.

Wren held her breath, then expelled it in a gust as the revenants recoiled, angry hissing noises emanating from their mouths—though no flesh moved to make the sound.

A surge of triumph rose in her chest, only to be quickly stifled. A fat raindrop landed on her nose. Then her forehead. More followed, pattering against the metal and creating a tinny, echoing song.

Never mind the soon-to-be-slippery bridge planks. Never mind the diminishing visibility as the drizzle slowly turned into a downpour.

The bonedust—any minute now, their only defense against the encroaching undead would be washed away.

"Do you have any other ideas?" Julian asked.

"Keep moving."

They darted from plank to plank, leaping over gaps and holes or sidling along the railing to cross when whole pieces were missing. Julian used his whip to carefully tie them together, and every time his foot slipped or balance wavered, Wren's own body felt the jolt. The reverse was also true, of course, and when her boot went clean through a rusted plank, Wren's descent was halted by the tether.

They constantly looked over their shoulders, watching as the undead pushed against the bonedust barrier, which was growing flimsier by the second, until, with a triumphant screech, one of the undead broke through.

Julian tried to make a barrier of his own, reaching for the iron behind them with his magic, bending and warping where he could, making the surface uneven and causing the bars and beams to snap loose. It worked, causing several pursuing bodies to fall, but the undead were fearless, and when their way was blocked, they simply found another—or plunged into the misty nothingness below, their descent followed by a distant, echoing sound of impact.

With a growl of frustration, Julian stopped moving and turned, planting both hands against the deck. He wrenched up the entire plank, tossing it roughly aside and leaving the revenants no way to cross. Wren gaped, temporarily distracted by his sudden, ferocious strength.

But, after two more revenants dropped, the remaining half dozen undead finally did the one thing Wren feared.

They left their bodies behind.

The process took time. First they released their corpse, drifting into the air like steam in the hot sun. In this case, the rain actually worked in Wren and Julian's favor, making it more difficult for the ghost to coalesce and re-form. Difficult, but not impossible.

Julian turned, fear flashing in his eyes, but then his face went as white as bone.

Wren, who had paused in her progress to watch him work, whipped around to find a revenant crossing the bridge from the other side. She had been so distracted by their pursuers that she'd forgotten to be on guard for what lay ahead.

She cursed. Bonedust would be useless in the rain, and knuckle-bones wouldn't do much against a revenant with its rotting body for protection.

Raising her single sword—Julian had her other one, currently tucked into his belt—she took her battle stance.

This revenant was fresher than the others; it looked almost alive, save for the pallor of its skin and the way a sickly green glow emanated from the wound in its chest. But while its remaining flesh and muscle made it stronger, it also made it heavier.

As it took a step toward Wren, the iron plank beneath it bowed slightly under its weight. Another step, and then the plank gave way.

It would have been a lucky break . . . if Wren had not been standing on the same plank.

Her breath caught, and once again she expected to plummet to her death—but then her body came to an abrupt, painful stop, the wind knocked out of her as the iron whip dug into her stomach. Distantly, she heard Julian shout in surprise as he slammed onto the ground, her body dragging him down with her.

He managed to cling on to something, because Wren stopped falling.

She dangled, gasping for air, but the panic was not entirely for herself. The bridge was crawling with revenants, and rather than being his defender or his shield, Wren was now deadweight, pinning Julian to the bridge and making it impossible for him to fight.

They were both trapped, unable to help themselves or each other.

There was only one thing to do.

She twisted in midair. "Julian!" she cried, swaying back and forth as she tried to look up and see his face, blinking through the rain. His head was visible in the space where the plank had once been, but the board he balanced on shrieked and groaned in protest. He slid forward a bit, arms scrambling, trying to find the strength, the leverage to haul her back up again. "You have to let me go."

"What?" he said, gritting his teeth and straining against the pull of gravity. Wren felt the whip around her middle tug, raising her slightly, before she slumped down again. She could try to climb it, to swing it toward the bridge supports below. But every pull in her direction, every movement to save her life could cost Julian his. He still had her bone sword. He could defend himself—if he let her go.

Wren looked down into the nothingness of the strange green mist. "There's water," she said. She had heard it—before, when the other revenants fell and again when the one who'd broken their shared plank plummeted from the bridge. She'd been too distracted to truly register the sound until now.

It was hard to gauge the drop, to know how wide or deep the water. . . . But there was only one way to find out.

She was reckless, after all. Foolhardy.

And for all her family's accusations of selfishness and arrogant pride, Wren was no coward, and she wasn't about to start being one now.

Julian had called her brave, and she would prove it.

"You have to drop me, or we both go down. There's water. I'll be okay."

He stared at her, shaking his head, even as the ghosts continued to detach from their bodies, preparing to strike, and the metal plank he was pressed against creaked. All he had to do was let go—Wren had told him to, so he could do so free of guilt or shame—but the stubborn asshole did no such thing.

"I won't," he said, focusing on her with renewed determination. His hands, which had been bracing against something she couldn't see, released their grip and sought the whip instead. His body slid forward precariously, and Wren cried out in alarm.

The whip was tied around his waist, the same as Wren's, but rather than try to draw his whole body back from the brink, he decided to only pull hers.

His hands took hold of the cable, gloves slipping and muscles straining as he pulled. With each slide of his hand, Wren's body lifted. She grasped the whip, climbing with him. If she could just get high enough, if she could reach his hand . . .

With so little iron to pull on, Wren suspected Julian's arms and back were doing the brunt of the work. The whip around her midsection slipped and slid, the knot keeping it secure made mostly of magic . . . and Julian's magic was failing him.

She was close now, barely an arm span away from him, and she could see the strain now, the sweat across his brow, the way his hands shook.

One more pull. One more—

A ripple went through the whip. It was so subtle that Wren would never have noticed the difference between that and the other swings and jostles that had been happening, except for Julian's reaction. Her gaze had been fixed on him, on his lowered brow and fierce, determined movements, but at the flash of true, visceral fear that colored his features, Wren followed his line of sight.

The knot at her stomach was unraveling, Wren's weight pulling the whip one way while Julian pulled it the other.

"Julian," Wren gasped, knowing it was too late.

The whip gave way, and she dropped.

Down into the darkness.

TWENTY-THREE

Leo had kept his chatter up throughout the journey.

He already knew the careful balance required after a lifetime of practice. It was important to talk about nothing as much as you talked about something, so that people stopped being able to tell the difference.

He continued to question Gray-Beard—whose name was Ivan—and Jakob, who were his constant companions, but it didn't stop there. He talked to the other kidnappers, to the villagers and town garrisons and traveling merchants.

They told him to shut up at first. Sometimes cuffing him on the back of the head or demanding he replace his head bag.

Unfortunately for them, he talked just as easily with it on as without, and they couldn't do any real damage to him because he belonged to someone else.

The regent.

And so Leo talked and talked, and before long they stopped

trying to shut him up. They stopped trying to listen. They stopped paying attention . . . which was exactly what Leo intended.

Now he could ask the real questions and spread the real rumors.

Yes, Leo was feeling quite pleased with himself.

He'd learned more about the Corpse Queen, though the stories the townsfolk told him held less appeal than the reaction of his kidnappers did whenever she was mentioned. He'd have expected worldly, battle-hardened travelers such as them to be a bit more circumspect, a bit more skeptical, but they seemed more certain than anyone that she existed.

What if it wasn't the stuff of children's nightmares, but a mantle, a persona adopted by someone wanting to make themselves feared and respected?

What if it was both?

When he wasn't stirring that particular pot, Leo was trying to learn more about his kidnapping.

It had taken longer than it should have, but when they'd left Southbridge that second morning, Leo had registered for the first time that they had two riderless horses with them.

One, surely, had belonged to the ironsmith. But what of the other? He'd heard nothing of any additional casualties, and while it wasn't uncommon for traveling parties to switch out their horses for maximum speed, one would hardly be enough to accommodate such a large group, and besides, they were stopping daily, with plenty of opportunity for rest.

It didn't add up.

"Did we forget somebody?" Leo asked Ivan and Jakob, nodding in the direction of the two additional horses that rode at the back of their party.

"The bag," came Ivan's blunt reply.

Leo released a long-suffering sigh; he'd known that speaking would be a risk, since it would draw attention to himself. He said goodbye to the fresh air and rocky countryside and withdrew the smelly sack, pulling it on again and breathing through his mouth to avoid the stench.

"I was only trying to help," Leo explained, his voice nasally. "I'd absolutely *hate* to leave one of our companions behind."

There was soft laughter. Was that Jakob? Leo found the hole in the fabric and turned in his direction, but if it had been him, he was too late—the boy's face was impassive.

"Calm yourself, Your Highness," said Jakob's quiet voice, though Leo thought he could sense lingering amusement there. "We haven't forgotten anyone."

Which suggested . . . "Oh dear, now you've gone and made me self-conscious, Jakob," Leo said. The boy craned his neck, confused. "It seems I was not meant to be your only guest of honor on this trip."

To that, Jakob had no response.

Leo chewed on that for the rest of the day, coming to the conclusion that this wasn't an average, run-of-the-mill kidnapping and hostage exchange, as he'd initially thought. It had not only been used as an opportunity to stage an assassination, but apparently Prince Leopold Valorian had not been the only person of value to be found at the Breachfort.

The question was, who was the second?

Despite circumstances, Leo felt he had everything in hand—or he *had*, until they'd set out the morning of the third day.

Prior to that point, all was as it should have been. Kidnapping aside. He was using his charm and his wit to collect seeds of information, to spread rumors—true or false—and was generally doing the best he could with what he had. He was certain that any day now he'd get to the bottom of this plot. Ideally before they reached the Iron Citadel.

But then, after taking the Coastal Road ever since they'd left Southbridge, it seemed their party was poised to diverge. They had passed various crossroads and offshoots throughout the journey but had always stayed the course.

Until now.

"Doesn't the Coastal Road lead to the Iron Citadel?" he'd asked, looking right, while the riders in front of him steered their horses left.

Ivan turned his way.

"I know, I know. The bag." Leo put it on but still waited with hope that his question might be answered.

"It does," replied Jakob. Good, reliable Jakob.

Except . . . they were turning left, west, *away* from the Coastal Road.

The realization hit Leo like an arrow from someone who was *supposed* to be on his side.

They weren't going to the Iron Citadel.

And if they weren't going to the Iron Citadel, maybe everything he thought he knew, everything he was certain he'd discovered . . .

Maybe he wasn't as smart as he'd thought.

Above, rain clouds rumbled, dark and ominous.

A storm, which they were riding directly into. And if his bearings were correct, he was headed for more trouble than his mouth could talk him out of.

But he would damn well try all the same.

TWENTY-FOUR

Wren was accustomed to the dark.

Death was her trade, and ghosts were her bread and butter. She thought she had known what it felt like to blink into the shadows, to gasp for breath—to not know what horror might lurk around the next corner. She thought she knew fear.

But this . . .

This was beyond anything she had ever felt before. Falling, endlessly, into the unknown. Julian's terrified face receding from view and the nothing below rushing up to meet her. Green mist whipped past, tugging at her clothes and hair. Were they ghosts? Was she already dead?

The sudden impact robbed the breath from her lungs and hit her body like a brick wall.

But it wasn't a wall at all—or anything solid. Wren attempted to suck in a breath and took in a mouthful of water instead. The delayed sensation of plunging into wetness hit her, and she flailed, completely disoriented.

The undead had fallen down here. They could be anywhere below, sinking in the deep, unable to swim or leave their watery graves.

She kicked, sending her to the surface, and her head shot out into open air. Coughing and spluttering, she struggled to properly draw breaths. Her entire body ached, her legs kicking and hands working on instinct alone. She started to sink again, the water too deep to stand, and panic seized her.

The shore—she needed to find the shore.

The straps from her satchel dug into her shoulders, the weight of her supplies dragging her down. After a moment's struggle, she managed to remove one strap, then the other.

That weight gone, her chin cleared the water again, but she had no idea which direction to swim or where the shoreline was.

Miraculously, she still held her bone sword. She cocked her arm back and tossed it as far as she could.

It clattered against *something*, either a rock in the middle of this body of water or, if she was lucky, the shoreline—but it didn't matter. Focusing with all her might, Wren reached for the sword and pulled. She was more likely to drag it to her than her to it, but all she needed was a sense of where it was so it gave her a firm direction to swim.

Energy failing fast, Wren pumped her legs and paddled, fighting to keep her head above water. The bone drew nearer and nearer in her mind's eye, and when her foot kicked out and met with solid ground, she wanted to weep with relief.

She did cry, and laugh, and hiccup as she stumbled out of the water and threw herself onto the shore. Her breath came ragged, her lungs aching, but she was alive.

Somehow, she was alive.

Blinking into the darkness, she tried to discern her surroundings. She squinted up, toward the bridge, but the eerie mist obscured her view.

She hoped Julian made it safely across the rest of the way. Though it pained her to have lost a sword, she was relieved that he had some manner of proper protection.

She supposed they'd be on their own from here on out. Maybe that was better. It saved her from having to ditch him or fight him later when it came to getting Leo to safety. They might have been working together, but they both wanted different things in the end. They were on opposite sides in more ways than one.

Yes, this was definitely better.

Wren was, however, a little worse for wear. She had lost her satchel of supplies as well as her only remaining sword, had scraped her hands on the shoreline, and her head pounded from the initial impact.

She was just picking gravel from her bleeding palms when she noticed the steam.

Her entire body was releasing it, and her foggy brain remembered that the water she'd plunged into wasn't icy and frigid as it should have been, but warm. Now, meeting with the cooler air, her damp clothes and skin were steaming.

This must be a hot spring. They were all over the Dominions, but Wren had never been to one. She'd spent so much of her life focusing on her valkyr training, she'd never done a lot of things.

It explained the mist, though it didn't explain the color. The water, the rocky shoreline . . . Everything was tinged with that same sickly green, very clearly ghostlight, though she couldn't detect a source. She'd also fallen through it without deathrot, so it couldn't be made of undead spirits . . . could it? Then again, this was the Breach. Maybe some of the undead here were so old, so ancient, they were no harm to the living—like those poor souls on that battlefield or like the center of the Bonewood, which had had its own soft green haze.

Leaning forward, she swirled a hand into the water, marveling at the warmth it brought to her already cold fingers. If it had been a regular river or lake, even if Wren did manage to combat the lung-restricting cold and make it to the shoreline, she'd probably die here of hypothermia.

As it was, she knew she needed to get out of her wet clothes. But she had nothing dry to wear, and she was tired.

Keeping her feet partially submerged, Wren lay there for a while, catching her breath, a leaden exhaustion settling into her body. She couldn't sleep here like this, no matter how tempting, but her eyes drifted closed all the same.

A shiver slipped over her. Everything was dark, and wet, and cold . . .

Her eyes flew open, and a skull loomed before her.

Her heart seized in her chest.

It was a revenant, bent over her prone form, barely inches from her face. . . .

Wren gasped and scrambled back into the water with a splash. The undead, little more than a skeleton, stared with sightless eyes and smiled with a lipless mouth. Ghostlight spilled between its ribs and seemed to wrap itself around its every bone, creating a glowing head-to-toe apparition.

Her sword—where was her sword? But the revenant didn't pursue her. That was when her senses caught up with her, and she remembered that she was in the water. It protected her.

Her thundering pulse steadied somewhat, but it continued at an unnatural rhythm as the revenant remained there, barely three feet away, head tilted.

Wren knew it was going to happen before it did, a premonition deep in her stomach.

"*Alive*," it said. The voice was raspy like the others, and the way it echoed off the cavern walls sent chills across Wren's skin. "*Shouldn't be here. Alive. So alive.*"

Wren was fully shaking now, even though the revenant wasn't threatening or ordering her to go. It sounded more like advice . . . or a warning.

Another revenant lumbered toward them. This one was even more skeletal, its bones dark and thin and broken in places, but the ghost was solid and strong, keeping it all standing upright.

"*So alive,*" it said, repeating the last words of the other revenant. "*For now.*"

More undead sprang to life all around, winking into existence like fireflies, drawn to the presence of the living. They lined the shore in both directions, while behind her, ghostlight danced across the water, reflecting more undead specters from across the spring.

They were in various states of decay, the glow of their souls alternating from pure, brilliant light to flickering and dim.

Would all of them speak, like some sort of haunted chorus?

Or, Wren thought as she pushed herself to her feet and waded along the shore, would they follow?

As long as she stayed in the water, she should be safe—she knew that—but it didn't stop her from splashing and stumbling through the knee-high current, going as deep as she could while still being able to move. She cast her senses in all directions, looking over her shoulder again and again, expecting one of them to lunge and drag her to the shore or pull her under.

Thanks to their light, she could see that the soaring cliffs on either side were pocked with caves and crevices. If she could find one, if she could get herself inside and ride out the night . . .

There was a soft, scraping sound behind her, then a splash. Wren spun around—

Only to find herself face-to-face with *Julian*.

His gloved hands were raised, weaponless, and Wren's thoughts stuttered. In fact, her whole body started to shake and tremble, shock and cold and exhaustion seizing every limb.

"What the fuck?" she said, legs giving out beneath her.

Julian leapt forward to catch her. He was warm and dryer than her—above the knees anyway, which were currently submerged— his upper body speckled with rain but otherwise untouched by the spring . . . until Wren dripped all over him. He didn't seem to mind.

Remembering that the undead were ranged all around, she threw a wary look over her shoulder.

"They didn't follow," Julian said softly, gaze roving the shoreline. "They can't."

He said the words as if he needed to hear them himself, as if he needed the reminder. There were so many now, lining both sides of the hot spring, like a hundred flickering candles.

"But you did." Wren didn't mean to sound accusatory, but it seemed every conversation between them brought out that challenging tone in her.

"I . . . yes."

"You didn't fall." It was a statement, not a question. She pulled back to give him a proper once-over. His hair was still perfectly combed back from his forehead, and as she'd already noted, his armor and clothes were mostly dry.

"No," Julian said. "I swung myself across as fast as I dared and found an old mining shaft. It got me down here in a hurry."

Laughter bubbled out of Wren's throat as she imagined the state of the mining shaft and the dark, sightless descent he must have taken. "I bet it did."

Rather than coaxing a smile out of him, as she'd hoped, Wren's words caused Julian's expression to become troubled. Was she talking nonsense? She didn't think so. Then again, he didn't know her that well. . . . Wren often talked nonsense. Another shiver racked her body, and her teeth chattered.

"Did you hit your head?" he asked, reaching a tentative hand to her temple. Wren closed her eyes, and when she opened them, there was blood glistening on his gloved fingertips. It brought her back to the last time she had fallen, in the crevasse near the Wall. He had accused her of thinking herself perfect, then presented the blood as proof that was untrue. Why did she think of the memory with fondness?

She had followed *him* that time, but it had not been on purpose. But here . . . now . . . he had come back for her. Chosen to, when he could have kept walking.

Why?

"Come on," he murmured, slipping an arm around her shoulders, the other drawing her bone sword from his belt and holding it out before them. Wren recalled she had yet to recover her own and tried to look back for it, but Julian urged her forward.

The farther they moved through the water, the more the world around them began to change. The spring narrowed, bringing the shore nearer on both sides . . . but it was no longer rocky beaches backed by soaring cliffs.

There were *buildings*—or the wreckage of them, anyway—and other signs of civilization, like crumbling staircases and broken pieces of pottery. The structures rose from the spring on high foundations, as if designed around the flow of the water, though some were almost entirely submerged, suggesting the water levels had changed over time.

These weren't Dominion ruins—towns that had succumbed to the Breach. No, these were much, much older, their style like nothing Wren had ever seen before, and she knew immediately what they must be.

Ghostsmith ruins.

This was the lost necropolis, the *source* of all the revenants roaming their lands. The source of the deep-rooted magic that reanimated them.

Magic that apparently continued to spill forth to this day, reanimating fresh corpses and potentially giving them the new abilities Wren had witnessed, like speech. Potentially giving *Locke* new abilities.

To actually lay eyes upon the city . . . to see it before her . . . Wren was overwhelmed.

And confused.

She recalled the view from the watchtower, when Julian had pointed out the mines. The Oreton mine had looked so close to the Breach, it had seemed obvious that mining there had caused the problem. But now, from within the Breach itself, she could see no evidence of it.

She looked back the way they had come.

"You said you came down here through the mine?"

"Not exactly. Oreton is on the eastern side of the Breach, and since it was supposed to have caused all this, I assumed there'd be a way down and through. There was, but it was a path that splintered off the main shaft, heading in this direction. It was narrow and steep . . . *meandering* almost . . ." He trailed off. Frowned. "It looked stonesmith made, like most mining shafts, but this definitely wasn't for mining. It was like someone was trying to find a way here. To this."

"You think someone was *looking* for this lost city? That they *meant* to disturb all these undead and cause the Breach?"

"I don't know. Surely whoever did died with everyone else, so what would be the point?" Still, he looked troubled.

Wren couldn't blame him. It was shocking to consider that the Breach hadn't been an accident. That it might not have been from overmining at all. That it might have happened on purpose.

But who would do that? And *why*?

As they continued toward the ruined buildings, the undead that clustered around its edges petered off, unable to cross the water.

Despite this, the ever-present mist lingered. Some of it *was* green, or tinged that color when the undead were around, but most of it was not. Without them, it was as pale as moonlight, growing brighter the closer they got to the ruins. Was it . . . ? Could it be magic? Visible when they were so deep underground and close to the source? She thought of Odile's words, but nothing about it seemed evil or sinister. Wren passed a hand through it but felt no different.

Julian released her to approach a mostly intact structure. It was made of native stone, like all the others, seemingly carved directly from the ground. This wasn't stonesmith work, however. It had undoubtedly been chiseled and carved by hand.

Undead hands? That's what the ironsmith historians had believed, according to Julian. She examined the soaring buildings and darkened tunnels, disappearing in all directions like an ant colony. She tried to imagine revenant builders. Revenant servants and guards.

She'd always been taught that the undead didn't create. They didn't use weapons or instruments or tools.

But maybe they *could*, if someone ordered them to.

Before coming to the Haunted Territory, she'd never have thought such a thing was possible, but after the past few days ... it seemed not only possible but entirely likely.

Julian glanced over his shoulder, waiting for her to give him the go-ahead. Despite her mind being a bit foggy, her senses felt sharp.

"It's clear," she told him, and he nodded, accepting her words as he ducked beneath the low doorway.

The entrance was deeply submerged, causing the water to rise to Julian's chest as he passed through. He lifted his satchel to keep it dry, and Wren thought longingly of her own, somewhere deep in the spring.

She followed, finding that only half the room beyond was filled with water. There was a second-floor garret, open to them and high enough to be untouched by the spring, with a set of steps emerging from the water, giving them fairly easy access. The walls were solid, the roof intact, and with water lapping on all sides, they'd be safe from the undead.

Julian mounted the stairs, then turned to help Wren. Her shaky legs were evident again as she climbed from the water, but she forced them to cooperate. She would be damned if he had to carry her.

Once she reached the top, Wren slumped against the wall, her head pounding again and making it hard to keep her balance.

Julian, meanwhile, was digging around inside his satchel. He withdrew some of the dry firewood they'd been carrying, as well as the flint.

It was so damp in here, even above the touch of the water, that Wren worried it was a lost cause, but the sounds of him stacking the wood, muttering to himself and striking the flint, were almost as soothing as the flames would be.

"Wren," Julian said sharply, drawing her back to herself. Her eyes were closed, though she didn't remember shutting them. "Stay awake, okay? Can you stay awake a little longer?"

She nodded, lifting her head and straightening her posture. The scent of smoke reached her, and she looked to see a fledgling fire started in the corner, bits of broken stones ranged in a makeshift pit. There was a small window set high in the wall above, providing ventilation.

"We'll need more, before the night is through," he murmured, mostly to himself, before shifting and adjusting the logs. He reached with his gloved hands, apparently unconcerned about the heat. That was one benefit to the fact that he never seemed to take them off, though Wren was dying to know the *real* reason.

"N-not sure we'll find any d-down here," Wren said, struggling to get the words out through her chattering teeth. Maybe she should get back into the water, which was warm, even if it was wet.

"Come here," he said, reaching for her hand, "closer to the fire. It'll help warm you up." He turned to stare at the struggling flames. "Eventually."

Wren released his hand in favor of crawling rather than attempting to stand again, but when she reached the edge of the fire, the cold stayed with her.

It was her clothes—she needed to get them off.

Deciding there was nothing else for it, Wren stood. Julian, who had been poking at the flames, watched her warily, perhaps afraid she might keel over.

She fumbled with her belt, then her bandolier, and the straps for her back sheaths. She dropped the items carelessly, but Julian stooped to gather them one by one and place them by his pack.

Wren felt strangely exposed as her armor gave way—her last protections. Against the undead, of course, but also against him. She was a bonesmith, he an ironsmith. It was how they related to and understood each other. Without their separate identities between them, they were just two people alone in the dark.

Julian took his time stacking her armor, as if delaying on purpose—or giving Wren time.

She looked at her drenched clothes, heavy with water and clinging to her skin, her muscles like jelly. Defeat slumped her shoulders.

"I can help, if you want," Julian said stiffly, standing before her. "I'll close my eyes."

Wren rolled hers. "That won't make you m-much use to me," she said, clenching her muscles against the trembling. "Can you just hurry up? Please?"

He nodded, closing the distance between them. He undid the buttons on her jacket, peeling it down her arms and tossing it to the ground. While he'd treated her weapons and armor with the utmost care, it was clear he was going for speed now, determined to get this task done as quickly as possible.

In another time, with another kind of boy, Wren might have thought he was in a rush to see her naked, fumbling with clumsy hands out of eagerness. But with Julian, she suspected the opposite was true, that he dreaded every moment of this. He pushed on out of necessity, for Wren's sake, and to complete the task at hand. Not out of any desire or lust.

That was its own kind of disappointment, though it made things easier. The entire thing became clinical and detached as he peeled back layer after layer.

When his gloved knuckles skimmed across her bare chest as he undid the shirt buttons, Wren settled a hand on his wrist.

He froze, and his gaze—until then focused intently on his hands and his hands alone—rose hesitantly to meet hers. His face was inches away, his usually smoothed-back hair coming undone, a single forelock dangling across his brow.

She met his eyes and nodded. He understood. He withdrew with almost comical speed, though Wren didn't feel much like laughing. She pulled off her shirt and tugged down her pants, all while Julian's back faced her. He was bent over, messing with the fire again—surely he was doing more harm than good at this point—and he stayed that way until the sound of Wren's sodden pants slapping onto the ground announced that she was fully naked.

He straightened, turning his head a fraction of an inch.

"Finished," Wren said, stepping toward him—barefoot after kicking off her boots—and putting a hand on his shoulder. As usual, he tensed under her touch.

"Here," he said, barely above a whisper—and without turning around. He held up one of the blankets from his pack, rough but dry and large enough to wrap her from head to toe.

She flung it around her shoulders and relished the wave of warmth that enveloped her. She just stood there, swaying on her feet, her eyes drifting closed again. . . .

"Can you eat?" Julian said, his voice very far away. "We have—*Wren*."

She jolted awake to find him watching her with an expression she would have described as fond if it weren't on him. As it was, she thought maybe he was amused at her falling asleep standing, like a horse.

She decided to blow out her lips in imitation of one, and it seemed to alarm him more than her giddy laughter had out in the cavern. He pulled a scrap of cloth from somewhere and dabbed at the spot near her temple where he'd found blood before.

"Not too deep," he muttered. "Come sit—here, on this other blanket, so I can see to it."

Wren obeyed, sitting patiently as he dipped the rag in the spring water and proceeded to clean the cut. It was unnerving to have Julian's complete and total focus. His face was so close, his eyes so bright and intent, that it made her stomach clench.

It seemed the cut had stopped bleeding, and once he'd dabbed away the worst of it, he left the wound uncovered.

"They talk to me, you know," she said. He met her gaze, brow furrowed in confusion. "The revenants. They talk to me. . . . They've *been* talking to me. Ever since we got here."

He turned away, squeezing out the blood-soaked rag. "I've never . . . I didn't know that was possible."

"Neither did I," she admitted. It made her think, uneasily, of the battlefield, of the "Graven heir" story Julian had told her. Nothing made sense anymore, and it seemed the rules no longer applied—to bonesmiths or to the undead. Or maybe Wren wasn't as well informed as she'd always believed. There was magic here—more magic than in the world above. It made things that shouldn't be possible, possible.

She thought she'd been sitting, but the next thing she knew, she was on her side, face pressed into the cold stone floor of the cave, and Julian was shaking her gently.

She attempted to lurch upright, forgetting for a moment where she was, her brain scrambling through the bridge, the fall—the *revenants*—but Julian pushed her back down.

"Easy," he said. "You're safe."

Wren blinked at him for several frantic moments, then nodded. Strange to think that being alone with *him*, an ironsmith, in the *Breach*, was as safe as Wren had been in days . . . but it was true.

The fire was crackling merrily now, bathing the room in a warm, welcoming glow. Her clothes were laid out, her boots propped up next to the flames, drying under its steady heat. Julian's armor was also removed and leaning against the wall.

"I just wanted to make sure you were okay," he explained, pointing at her head, and she realized that he feared she was badly concussed . . . that if she slept too long, she might never wake up.

Wren really looked at him then and saw that despite removing his iron plate, he still wore his damp clothes and had been sitting on the ground. Wren had stolen all their blankets—at least, those that weren't currently sitting soggy and submerged at the bottom of the spring.

His boots were off, though, piled next to hers, and Wren caught a glimpse of his bare feet. They were pale, well formed—ordinary— but the sight of them sent an illicit thrill down her spine, especially extended as they were toward the fire, his posture more casual than usual. Maybe it was the lowering of his guard she found so appealing, but whatever it was, she wanted more of it.

She carefully stood—waving away Julian's offer of help—then gathered the blanket from beneath her and held it out.

"It's a little wet, but dryer than what you're wearing," she said.

"I'm fine," he insisted, and Wren glared at him.

"Humor me," she said, tossing the blanket at him. He caught it, then after a pointed look, wrapped it around himself—even his feet.

Satisfied, Wren settled down next to him again.

A log cracked in the fire sometime later, and she blinked awake. She was close to the warmth of the flames, and Julian was beside her—wrapped tightly in his blanket. Across the floor, his jacket was lying out to dry along with his pants.

She smirked at him, then closed her eyes once more.

TWENTY-FIVE

Julian stared at Wren.

He had been doing that a lot. She was something to look at, in his defense. More so when she was awake, of course.

Those eyes.

That armor.

After spending his entire life hating bonesmiths, it was utterly surreal to walk around with one. To fight alongside one.

To laugh with one, even.

And just when he thought he'd had her figured out, she had shown a level of kindness on that battlefield he hadn't believed her capable of. Finding a way to honor the fallen when he could not. When all he could do was stumble around, searching and searching and *terrified* to find what he was looking for.

But she had taken control and taken his hand, and everything had been a little easier.

Placing that marker and walking away had been a soul-deep relief, though his search remained incomplete. Maybe he would never know, like Wren had said.

Maybe the question of what had happened to his father would haunt him, literally, forever.

Wren shifted in her sleep, drawing his attention without his consent, like a moth pulled inescapably to a flame.

He wouldn't soon forget the look on her face as she'd fallen from that bridge, expression entirely devoid of its usual brazen sarcasm and arrogance. Her fear had been plain, her defenses stripped away, but somehow it was Julian who felt raw. Even now, knowing she was safe—seeing the proof of it before his eyes—was not enough to banish the feeling.

There had been no question of going on without her. No question of leaving her behind.

He knew, distantly, that there *should* have been.

Maybe if he'd given himself a second to *think*, he'd have reconsidered chasing after her—or realized what he was risking by doing so. But all he'd been able to focus on was that look on her face and the way he'd feel, every day for the rest of his life, if he didn't at least try.

How he'd always wonder. How she'd become one more search he couldn't complete.

How she might die with his name on her lips, thinking that he had done it on purpose. That he had killed her. Or worse, that she'd *survive* and carry that conviction with her, seeing him as a coward and would-be murderer.

Of course, what she thought of him *shouldn't* matter.

But it did.

Wren was everything that was wrong with his world, but she was also the only thing that was right. The only thing that made sense.

Which was why it was so dangerous. He *had* to stop staring at her. Stop thinking about her.

He couldn't afford to get caught up, to weaken himself with feelings he couldn't control, with a *wanting* he couldn't shake.

With a trust that might be misplaced.

He pressed a hand against his chest, where Captain Royce's arrow had landed. His iron had protected his body, but his mind . . . It was a betrayal he still couldn't wrap his brain around. The lines that had defined his life were now irrevocably blurred.

The Border Wall demarcated more than just the barrier between his home and the rest of the Dominions. It separated friend from foe.

Or so he'd thought.

Now his supposed enemy was his only friend, and his supposed friends were the ones who had tried to kill him.

Wren rolled over, her spill of pale hair gleaming in the flickering firelight. The flames added warmth to her otherwise ghostly complexion, turning her ivory skin flush, her icy hair warm and golden.

With her eye black mostly gone thanks to the spring, it all served to make her look more *human*. More . . . normal.

Strange, then, that he found it so off-putting. That it unsettled him worse than her bone armor and colorless eyes ever had.

He'd actually come to find those attributes a welcome sight. A comforting one. He wanted her fierceness, not this softness on display right now.

But he kept staring all the same.

It was either that or let his mind wander in less pleasant directions. He rubbed at his chest again. The soreness had receded to a dull ache, but he couldn't allow himself to forget. He pressed harder, awakening the nerves and causing pain to radiate outward.

It was sobering.

And after that wave of clarity came the question, the one he hadn't been able to answer.

Why?

Everything he'd said to Wren could easily be true. Jealousy was common where Julian was concerned; he was one of only a few remaining ironsmiths alive, powerful and important. To someone ambitious and wanting to climb the ranks, like Captain Royce, Julian could definitely be seen as in the way. The kidnapping mission itself was a perfect example. Julian was sent to "ensure things went smoothly," undercutting the man's competence and insinuating he needed the help.

So yes, it made sense that Captain Royce might seize the opportunity to get rid of Julian . . . and yet it felt a bit too simple. A bit too neat.

But the alternative? Impossible.

Julian wasn't in the regent's way.

He'd done everything the man had asked him to do. Everything, all his life.

Things he hated. Things he regretted every waking moment.

He fidgeted with his glove, his skin damp and clammy underneath, but he refused to remove it—despite Wren being asleep.

It was an unwelcome sight even to his own eyes.

At least she had touched his good hand, his right hand, on that battlefield. Otherwise he'd have pulled away and ruined the moment.

He sighed, securing his glove and dropping his hand.

No, it couldn't be the regent.

Because if it were, the threads that held Julian's life together would start to come undone, and he was already wound too tight. One loose strand, and everything would fall apart.

So he did what he had always done. He straightened his spine and tightened his resolve. He found his strength.

But then he looked at Wren, and suddenly, he didn't want to be strong.

He wanted to surrender. To let go. To unravel.

Even just for a moment.

Which was exactly why he couldn't.

TWENTY-SIX

When Wren awoke again, the fire was sputtering and tendrils of misty moisture filled the small space. A chill slipped in with it, making her shiver.

Julian loomed before her, fully dressed once more. "I'm going to look for more firewood."

"Where?" she rasped as she sat up. She felt like death, though her headache had receded to a distant, dull pain, and she no longer felt woozy.

He hesitated. "I saw some old driftwood on our way here. I could easily break it down and—"

"You're not going that far without me."

"Wren, you're wounded."

"Excuse me, but you took an arrow to the chest and were up and moving again hours later. We can't afford to waste any time."

"Actually . . . we can. It's raining pretty heavily out there."

She sat up, adjusting her blanket before picking her way to the edge of the water. She crouched, peering out the door, where a relentless downpour turned the world beyond into a curtain of silver.

"It's been going all night," Julian said, watching her. "A lucky break."

"How so?" Wren asked. As far as she could tell, it meant a miserable day of travel.

"They won't ride in this," he said, and she knew he meant the kidnappers who had Leo. "They can't risk any harm coming to their prize, and the roads are . . . less than ideal in good weather, never mind torrential rain. Plus there'll be flooding."

"So we're stuck here?"

Julian shrugged. "Could be worse. That water is warm, and it protects us from the revenants. We also have shelter from the rain. Besides, you need to rest."

"I'm fine."

"Humor me," he said dryly. Wren's eyes narrowed.

Smiling, he turned to go.

"Okay," she said, halting him before he could walk past her. "We rest here another day—but I'm coming with you now. We'll need more wood than you can carry on your own, plus I left my sword and my satchel out there."

He opened his mouth to argue, but seeing her stubborn expression, he faltered. Sighed.

"Fine. Let's go."

Another good thing about the rain was that the undead apparently did not care for it. Either that or it obscured their senses, because Wren and Julian walked through the shallow waters in near darkness, their passing unmarked by the sight of glowing revenants.

However, the cover was so good, the downpour so relentless, that it became clear fairly quickly that their own senses were equally obscured. They tried but couldn't seem to find their way back to the mining shaft passage or the place Wren fell from the bridge. She reached with her magic but couldn't feel her sword at all, and they were soon forced to give up.

They did find the driftwood though, a definite necessity given how soaked they had gotten in the pursuit, and luckily it had stayed mostly dry thanks to the rock outcrop above it. *Keeping* it dry would be the real challenge, but they found some partially sunken canoes tethered along the shore near a cluster of buildings, one of them undamaged.

The boat looked too new to be from the same era as the ghost-smiths, and Wren wondered if other people had come and gone in recent years. The craftsmanship was crude, which either meant it was constructed in haste or by people lacking skill.

Julian ran a hand along the side of the boat, his expression dark. "I wonder . . ."

"Who made them?" Wren asked, and he nodded. "Do you think—" she began, but cut herself off.

"What?"

"I just . . ." She swallowed. "They're capable of following orders— at least, according to what they said to me. The undead. And your anvils seem to think revenants built this city. Making boats isn't too far a stretch."

"Yes, but they built this city centuries ago on ghostsmith orders. These boats can't be more than a few years old."

"Which means they've gotten *new* orders recently. . . ."

Julian tossed his head in a half shake, like he wanted to argue, but didn't. Maybe he just didn't want it to be true, despite the evidence.

There was more going on in the Haunted Territory than either of them knew, but with a kidnapped prince and an assassination plot, they had enough to be worrying about already.

They bailed out what water they could, then loaded the boat with the driftwood before covering it with one of the blankets they'd brought with them and pulling it back to their temporary camp.

The pair of them were drenched by the time they returned, and while they had managed to keep the wood dryer than themselves, it would take a while to get the damp kindling to burn.

"Maybe we should have stayed dry and cold instead of wet and cold," Wren mused as they attempted to rebuild their fire.

Julian gave her a flat look, as if to suggest her comments were not helpful—which she supposed they weren't—and returned his attention to the flickering flames. He had already removed his armor and jacket, but even his undershirt was soaked through and clinging to his back.

They were both filthy, their hands covered in mud and muck, and while most of Wren's eye black had been washed away in the spring, she still had old blood in her hair.

The fire caught, and though the damp wood smoked, the old embers smoldered hotly, and Wren knew the rest would burn.

Julian sat back on his heels, pleased, and looked at her.

"Why did you come back?" she asked abruptly. "That fall . . . those revenants . . . I was a goner."

"But you weren't, were you?" She looked at him, brows raised, and he turned away. "I had to know."

She thought of his father, of the hundreds of other people he might have known and loved and lost to the Breach, never completely dead, never fully at peace. If he had found her dead body, what would he have done?

"It was an accident," he said, and Wren frowned in confusion. "The whip."

His expression was strained, and she realized he'd been dying to say this—probably since the moment he'd found her.

"I know," she said, somewhat incredulously, though she supposed if something similar had happened at the start of their journey, she might have wondered. The fact was, the idea had never crossed her mind. Whatever she might think about the House of Iron and their plans east of the Wall, she didn't believe Julian capable of looking her straight in the eye and dropping her deliberately to her death.

But his words caused something heavy to settle in Wren's chest. "Is that why you're here? To prove you didn't try to kill me? To clear the air?"

"No," he said carefully, not meeting her eye. "Not entirely."

"Then why?"

Wren wasn't certain what she was hoping for, but as the seconds passed without a response, she decided she didn't want whatever evasion he was contriving.

"I'm going to clean up," she announced, standing. "And I need to dry my clothes again."

Understanding dawned, and Julian glanced down at himself, at his sodden clothes and grimy gloves. There was a smear of dirt on his face that Wren had been staring at since they'd returned, the filth marring his otherwise perfect, pale skin.

"I'll take my time so you can clean up too, if you want."

Wren didn't know why she offered him that kindness, not when he was currently annoying her for reasons she couldn't explain. But while his reaction—or lack thereof—to *her* nakedness was one thing, his reaction to his own was something else. He never removed his gloves or his shirt, not even when threatened with deathrot, so there was something going on, though she couldn't imagine what it was. Wren had plastered herself against him on several occasions now, and he definitely had no cause for concern regarding his physique. Whatever his issues, he wasn't averse to bathing, so Wren would give him the privacy he needed.

"Right," he said, standing too. Then Wren started undoing her shirt, and he turned away. "Right."

She tugged down her pants and kicked off her boots, willing him to look at her like he had the night before when he'd turned all his attention and focus on cleaning her wound.

But he didn't.

She struggled less with the heavy, wet fabric than before and did her best to lay them out rather than leave them in a sodden heap. All the while, Julian stared fixedly at the far wall, as distant and untouchable as ever.

Wren waded into the water, walking down the slippery steps until she was covered to her chest. She turned, but Julian hadn't moved.

Disappointed, she was about to fully submerge herself when he spoke.

"I need you."

Wren startled at the words, unable to help a suspicious furrow of her brow. He watched her from the corner of his eye. Seeing that she was covered by the water, he fully faced her.

"You have my sword, and you've faced more revenants than any bonesmith born in the last two decades," Wren argued. "You don't *need* me."

He didn't answer immediately. Instead, he looked at her—*really* looked at her, like he had the night before. Staring first at her eyes and her lips and then lower, down, into the water. The spring was milky and translucent, thanks to the rich mineral content and the darkness, which meant he couldn't see much. But he *was* looking.

His eyes were hooded, irises as black as his pupils, the expression in them making her stomach tighten.

"Want, then," he said softly.

Wren's lips parted, but she had no response.

He walked toward her, gaze never wavering. When his boots reached the edge, he crouched, his gloved hand planting between them for balance. He took a breath.

"I don't *want* to finish this crossing without you," he continued, voice low. "We—you and I—we're good together."

Wren swallowed. He was saying things Wren never expected anyone to say to her, to be honest, and least of all him. It seemed to be costing him something to say it, and as much as Wren wanted to gloat or throw it in his face to embarrass him, what she *really* wanted was for it to be true. She had never been chosen before, and certainly not by someone who had seen all her faults and shortcomings firsthand.

Leo had pegged her as a good time—which she absolutely was—and had wanted to associate with her based on that factor alone. In truth, she and Leo were similar, like reflections of each other. But Julian . . . he and Wren were more like opposites. She was rash and bold, where he was thoughtful and strategic. She liked to laugh, to find the humor in situations, no matter how dark. He took things seriously, treating even those who meant him harm with respect.

They didn't reflect one another, but rather, seemed to round each other out. Like puzzle pieces fitting together.

Julian's expression was shuttering, his emotions closing off, and Wren realized she had yet to respond. He had bared something to her, bared himself and his desires, and she had not reciprocated. She was naked, but it was not the same thing.

He was so close, she could see the way his pulse jumped in his throat, and she would bet Ghostbane twice over that he was desperate to unsay his words, to take it all back—it's what she would have wanted to do. But he didn't. He stood by them, even if it was killing him to do so.

"Can you swim?" she whispered.

"What?" he asked, taken aback. "Yes."

Before she could think better of it, she took hold of his wrist and pulled.

His eyes bugged out before he came diving, headfirst, into the water.

Wren shoved herself backward, waiting until he emerged, shocked and spluttering. He tossed his head to get his hair out of his eyes, turning in place until he located her. The surprise on his face shifted—not into anger but into something fierce and competitive.

He lunged for her, and Wren cried out, kicking off the side to push herself out of reach and diving under. She made for the open door, swimming out into the wider spring. She came up for air, Julian surfacing behind her a second later. The rain was still coming down in sheets, trickling off the rocks above and dousing them like they were under a waterfall.

He shook away his hair again and pushed forward to cut off her retreat.

Wren shrieked, spinning around, but she was trapped against the rocky shore. He approached slowly now, knowing he had her, smiling triumphantly. The sight of it made her already tight stomach constrict even further.

"You're going to pay for that," he said, planting his hands on either side of her, caging her in.

It was hard to swim without kicking him, and Wren struggled with warring emotions. She wanted to fight, to laugh, to demand that he *make her* in one breath, then *beg him* if he didn't in the next.

They were close now, so close, and the intense, mischievous glint in Julian's eye turned wary. Uncertain.

"I don't want to finish this without you either," Wren said quietly, feeling like she was flayed open.

His expression softened at her words, and his attention fell to Wren's mouth again. His gaze was heated, intense, and then he reached out with a tentative hand. His thumb landed on the edge of her bottom lip, dragging against the skin. Did some of the eye black remain, or had he wanted to touch her skin, bared to him at last?

She wondered if she looked more appealing to him this way, without the obvious markings of a bonesmith. Or less? Was the draw between them the thrill of the enemy? Of the unknown? Or was it something else? Something . . . more?

In response to his touch, Wren's tongue shot out, following the path his thumb had traced. He watched it, his expression hungry, and she couldn't hold back any longer.

She pushed off the rock behind her, crashing into him, legs wrapping around his middle and fingers raking through his hair.

Her lips met his, soft and smooth and the tiniest bit salty with spring water.

Though she had made the first move, he met her with enthusiasm, and when their mouths opened, it was *his* tongue sliding into her mouth, deepening the kiss. Warmth suffused her skin, spreading from the point of contact, making her face flush.

His hands splayed on her back, unmoving at first, then with a soft growl sliding lower. He clutched her, dragged her against him, resisting the ebb and flow of the water and creating a rhythm entirely their own. Wren's lips burned, glittering heat sweeping her body. And his mouth . . . Wren wanted to devour him. She dove into the kiss, biting and teasing and drawing him closer, closer, closer.

Though she had wanted to touch Julian's hair ever since she'd first met him, to thoroughly mess it up—which she did—her hands began to stray . . . down his neck and across his shoulders, his heart thudding beneath her fingertips as she slid her palms against his chest. She was careful to avoid the place where the arrow had almost killed him, assuming there was a painful bruise, and instead trailed her fingers down his arms. Through the dampened fabric of his shirt, she felt a raised ridge, like a scar. . . .

Julian jerked away from her, removing his hands from her body and using them to push against the rocky shore, putting space between them. His pupils were blown wide, his hair standing on end, his chest rising and falling rapidly.

"I—I'm sorry," Wren managed, though her brain was foggy and she couldn't quite put her finger on what she was apologizing for. Everything, most likely. She was usually at fault when things went awry.

"No, I . . ." He looked away, throat working as he swallowed. The rain was still falling, though it was more of a mist now, collecting in droplets on his skin and sticking his eyelashes together. "This was a bad idea."

Wren nodded. Though it seemed she'd been naked more often than not in the past twelve hours, she felt exposed for the first time. Vulnerable.

Rejected.

She allowed herself to sink into the warmth of the spring, submerging her chin and letting the water lap against her lips as she spoke. "I'll be—I'm going to stay out here a little longer."

Julian stared at her mouth again, then nodded before turning and swimming back, through the doorway and out of sight.

TWENTY-SEVEN

Wren floated there for a while, mind oddly blank in the swirling steam. The rain had finally let up, allowing her to better see her surroundings. Maybe she should go looking for her sword and satchel again. Her eyes had adjusted to the strange, hazy light of the Breach, and besides, Julian clearly wouldn't object to being alone for a while.

This was a bad idea.

Dipping low again and blowing some exasperated bubbles, Wren glanced at the door, where the warm glow of the fire was visible through the darkened frame.

Yes, she would go searching—but she should probably get dressed first.

She was about to dive under when another flash of light caught her eye. Not a warm glow but a cool green shimmer.

Ghostlight.

Now that the rain was little more than a drizzle, Wren suspected more undead would make an appearance on the banks of the spring. Likely they'd just retreated into the caves or some of the ruined structures that remained untouched by the water.

Squinting, Wren saw that indeed, the undead that had drawn her attention was emerging from a massive arched doorway across the spring—deeper into the ruins than she and Julian had dared to venture. But strangely, the glow seemed to come from behind the revenant rather than the revenant itself. It was silhouetted against the light, and it looked full-bodied—almost alive—except for . . .

What was that on its head? Was it a *crown*? Her mind jumped to the rumors of that Corpse Queen again, but then the figure shifted, and she realized it wasn't a crown; it was *horns*. Part of some helmet or headdress, maybe?

More undead appeared, emerging from their hiding places and dotting the far shore, heading toward the horned figure. The longer Wren watched, the more certain she became that whatever it was, it wasn't actually undead. The ghostlight of the approaching revenants *illuminated* the figure rather than emanated from it.

She thought it might actually be a boy, something in its musculature slim and lanky but not emaciated. Not decomposing. The figure turned their head, and Wren saw vivid green eyes staring out from the darkened face. *Ghost*-green eyes, visible even at this distance.

Hadn't those revenants also mentioned a he?

Because she wills it. And he commands it.

Wren was desperate to see more, but she didn't dare swim closer— the Breach was unnaturally silent save for the gentle pitter-patter of the rain and the soft, shuffling sound of the revenant corpses. She didn't want to disturb whatever was happening or draw attention to herself, naked and unarmed as she was.

In fact, it was so quiet that when the boy spoke, Wren heard it as clearly as if he were five feet away, not fifty.

"Come," he said softly. His voice was scratchy, as if from lack of use, and surprisingly deep. The undead stood before him, five in total, and he seemed to be surveying them closely. "You." He indicated the least decomposed of the figures, though Wren could see its ribs, powerful ghostlight shining through. "With me. The rest of you, go."

And they *listened*.

"Go," they echoed, over and over as they wandered away.

Then the boy and his chosen revenant turned and walked through the archway.

"Julian!" Wren spluttered when she burst from the water inside their camp.

He whirled at the sound of his name but turned away at once when Wren began to climb from the water.

Things were awkward between them—they *had* just kissed, and he *had* called it a bad idea—but frankly, Wren didn't have time for that. She found her abandoned blanket on the ground and snatched it up, using it as a towel and a buffer so Julian would face her again.

"Get your gear on," she ordered, moving around the fire to gather her own clothes. They were dry*ish*, which was the best she could do.

"What? Why?" he asked, looking at her now that she was covered, though his expression was wary. His clothes, on the other hand, were still very wet—and still on his body—though it was clear he'd been standing near the fire, so they didn't drip, at any rate. Not that it mattered; they'd be heading back into the water shortly.

"I saw . . . something," she said, pausing. She'd been tugging on her pants—or trying to, anyway, with the blanket about her shoulders and the fabric sticking to her damp skin.

"You'll have to do better than that."

When Wren failed to elaborate as she struggled to get dressed, he rolled his eyes and approached.

"Here, let me," he said, prying Wren's fingers from the edges of the blanket.

Surprised into obedience, she released her grip. He spread the fabric wide, holding it away from his body and turning his head, creating a small changing screen for her to hide behind.

She was oddly touched by the gesture, though it was more for *his* benefit than hers. She'd gladly have dressed right in front of him, but at least this helped to move things along.

"I think we should talk—" he began, his tone apologetic, and Wren knew he was going to discuss the kiss. To tell her *why* it was a bad idea, as if she didn't already know, and say a bunch of other boring, responsible, placating shit that she did not want to hear.

"There's someone else down here," she cut in, finishing with her pants and adjusting her shirt. "Someone *alive*. I think he was a ghostsmith."

He reared back, throwing a startled look in her direction before he remembered that he wasn't supposed to be looking, and turned away again. She was mostly covered anyway, except for the open buttons on her shirt, so she tugged the blanket down and turned her back to him to fasten them.

"What makes you say that?"

"He had eyes the color of a ghost, for a start," she said. "Plus, he was talking to them. The undead. There were five of them, and they didn't attack him. He actually called them to his side, and when he spoke . . . they listened."

"Wren," Julian said uneasily. "I'm not sure . . ."

"Come on," Wren said forcefully, pulling on her boots and coming to stand before him. "This could be where those Corpse Queen rumors came from! These revenants have been acting strange ever since we arrived. Moving in packs, working together, guarding—"

"And they talk to you, too."

Wren's gaze darted away. Yes, that was definitely a large part of her curiosity, but it went beyond that. "I know you think I just go blundering into things, but if there are people here, inside the Breach, *controlling* the undead . . . It's relevant to *everyone*, no matter what side of the Wall you live on."

And maybe they could find something to explain what Locke had done. What Wren was doing.

"Please?" she whispered.

He lifted his chin, considering. "Okay."

They took the boat. They had only one oar, so Julian used it to paddle them deeper into the ruins while Wren remained on high alert, her single bone sword across her back and the rest of the artillery she had left tucked in her belt and bandolier. She had taken a moment to hastily reapply her eye black, aware of Julian's attention on her, but it had felt empowering to rebuild that smallest of barriers between them—her lips cold, dark, and untouched, her eyes shadowed and unreadable.

As they moved through the cavern, she kept her senses stretched wide and was certain the only undead nearby were those few that had rematerialized along the shore and the solitary figure that had joined the boy inside the distant building.

This was the Breach, however, and she knew better than to assume. Dozens could be lurking just out of her range, so they had to be extremely cautious. They'd sneak into the building and peek around, but stealth and safety were their top priority, and the water gave them an easy escape route.

What she'd seen . . . She couldn't just forget it. The boy *must* be a ghostsmith—there was no other explanation—but they had long since been considered extinct. All of them buried along with their undead city.

Suddenly, the impossible was possible—all thanks, apparently, to the Breach. She thought of her uncle Locke, of the crushed bodies, of all the things she didn't understand.

Beyond her curiosity, if Wren could return with Leo *and* information that could save the Dominions, she'd be even more valuable to her father and her family. But she needed something concrete, not snatches of words and wild claims that her father probably wouldn't believe. This boy could be useful to them. And if he didn't want to be useful, then he was an enemy they had to keep track of.

Their boat bumped against the shore of the building Wren had seen, the structure bigger and more impressive than it had appeared at a distance. And more disturbing.

It was little more than a facade, a portico, while the rest of the building went deep into the rock behind it, carved from the natural stone.

The columns on either side of the arched entryway—easily twice Wren's height, if not more—were revealed to be carved figures with their hands raised, as if they held the roof upright. Only they weren't like the other sculptures Wren had seen in her lifetime, beautiful and idealized, with perfect musculature and faces frozen in eternal dignity. These were unmistakably meant to be undead . . . their texture mottled and uneven, sculpted bones protruding from rotted flesh, and their faces fixed in expressions of pain and agony.

There were other examples of similar embellishments, including a frieze atop the entryway depicting ghostlike figures, their shapeless bodies writhing and their mouths forever opened in silent screams.

These were monuments not to the undead but to the ghostsmith power over them. Everywhere Wren looked, she saw ghosts and revenants in subservience. It made her stomach twist, especially because of the incongruous familiarity.

The House of Bone aesthetic could certainly be considered gruesome. They had a forest made of bones, after all, and Marrow Hall had walls of skulls and catacombs stocked with skeletons. But while the House of Bone dealt with the dead, they did so from a place of mercy and reverence.

Though valkyrs might "fight" ghosts, it was only so that a reapyr could perform their sacred duty to save the dead from their fleshly prisons. Wren felt a stab of guilt at the idea of how much she had always enjoyed her work, but if the goal had been to dominate and control the poor souls, she was certain the task would have quickly lost its appeal.

Yes, the House of Bone might be dark, but this House of Ghost was far more sinister . . . exultant in its darkness and proud of its power. They bent the undead to their will, to serve their own ends. They commanded them.

Like the boy.

Julian was crouched before some runes on the stairs, tracing his finger over the deep grooves. The writing didn't use any alphabet Wren knew, but as she stared, she was hit with a sudden jolt of recognition.

Her hand flew to her pocket, to the ring. She withdrew it, and her heart stopped. Some of the glyphs matched, though the full message was different. Julian stared, making the connection as well.

Shock rooted her to the spot.

The ring was a *ghostsmith* ring. Made of bone, engraved with ghostsmith writing . . . and somehow, it had found its way to the Bonewood. Recently, too, if it indeed belonged to the corpse Wren had discovered during her trial.

Heart hammering, Wren stared fixedly at the open archway. There would be answers inside; she knew it. Green light spilled out, illuminating the swirling steam that clung to the ground in wisps, making it seem alive . . . reaching. . . .

She swung her bone sword through it, but of course it was not a ghost, and there was no reaction.

"Now what?" Julian asked, getting to his feet.

"We go in," Wren said with more confidence than she felt. But that, she had learned, was the way confidence worked.

The door revealed nothing of what lay beyond.

Sword raised, Wren led the way, blinking through the haze. Several steps into the building and the mist started to clear, revealing that she stood upon a gallery that wrapped around a long, cavernous space. A grand staircase descended from the point of entry down to the lower level, and the balcony, enclosed by simple columns, disappeared into the shadows on either side.

While the upper level was dark, more light came from whatever lay below. She was about to descend the stairs when footsteps echoed up to her. She and Julian ducked to the side and crouched behind a column, seeking an angle to view what was happening on the lower level. The place appeared all but empty, but then the boy and the revenant appeared, making their slow way down the length of the room.

In the middle of the space was a rectangular depression, a pit or pool from where the pale, misty light emanated. Liquid reflections danced across the floor and pillars, putting Wren in mind of the spring outside, though whatever was within the basin was oddly silent. No splashes or gurgles. No sound at all.

Julian nudged her, pointing to something beside the pit. At first she thought it was another person—but then she recognized the sheen of metal. It was a suit of armor, but an empty one, resting upon a rack as if proudly displayed. It looked brand-new, not broken or salvaged, pristine and well made and patiently awaiting its wearer.

As she watched, the boy and the revenant approached the suit. Wren's spine tingled with foreboding. She met Julian's eyes in the dark.

Loud clanking echoed up to them as the boy struggled to remove the heavy pieces of gleaming iron. He didn't put them on himself, though.

He put them on the revenant.

TWENTY-EIGHT

The boy ordered the revenant to be still, and it obeyed, just as before, standing unflinching as he carefully placed the armor on its corpse.

Now it was no ordinary revenant. It was an *iron* revenant.

Then the boy—the *ghostsmith*, for now there could be no doubt that was what he was—was *touching* the revenant with his bare hands, as if there were no threat of deathrot, even though the revenant's ghost pulsed from within its body, weaving through muscle and bone and shining brightly out of sunken eyes.

Despite looking brand new, the armor was old-fashioned in style, like the illustrations of the Iron Legion Wren had seen in history books, and quite different from what Julian wore. It was rigid and boxy, leaving no gaps or weak points, and once every piece was in place save for the helmet, the boy turned toward the recessed pit. There were steps leading inside, like a soaking pool in a bathhouse, meant to be traversed from one end to the other.

He didn't walk into it, however. Instead, he crouched by the edge, reaching forward with his hands alone.

There seemed to be some kind of resistance, an invisible barrier that slowed his movements. But eventually he pierced the hidden veil, and his hands plunged into the pit.

There was a sudden, blinding surge of molten white light. The boy flinched, but only to brace himself against the onslaught.

The pool swirled and rippled, growing impossibly brighter as it illuminated the entire space. Wren saw a throne carved into the far wall, a high seat with two smaller ones on either side, plus other details like broken columns and scattered debris. There were deep cracks emanating from the pool, and they too began to fill with light, the entire thing pulsing like a heartbeat, the glow traveling from the source outward like veins.

Soon the stones that surrounded the pit also began to shine with some inner radiance, and beneath her feet, Wren felt a bone-deep vibration. The air itself was charged, like a storm, and her hair started to stand on end.

She looked to Julian, who clearly felt it too, and then placed her palm flat on the ground. Her skin tingled, then a burst of magic shot up her arm. She took a breath, the power crackling in her lungs and surging through her body.

Limitless power.

Dark power.

Fear quivered inside her.

This, surely, was the magic that created the revenants in the first place. The reason the ghostsmiths had built their kingdom so deep.

The power that may very well have destroyed the ironsmith army, the Dominion army, and Locke Graven himself. The "something evil" Odile talked about.

Had the ghostsmiths discovered this well of power or had they built it themselves, somehow finding a way to trap the magic of the earth? It felt wrong to Wren, the idea of containing magic. No one person was meant to draw so much, but the ghostsmiths had created an entire *society* around doing so. As she tried to pull away, Wren noticed for the first time that the ground was shaking, the entire building groaning with tremors. Bits of rock fell from the ceiling, distant cracks and crumbles telling her other, larger items were being shaken free.

Was *this* how their necropolis was buried in the first place? Not by some natural disaster but by constantly pulling on this source of magic and drawing it up from the depths of the earth, destabilizing the world around them? It was no wonder the Breach happened after this place was accidentally rediscovered. It was obviously unstable.

Again Wren tried to detach her hand, but she couldn't. Staring down in alarm, she saw tendrils of white light had seeped up from the stone and wrapped themselves around her wrist, steadily climbing.

Seeing her struggle, Julian took hold of her arm and, with difficulty, pried it away from the ground, breaking the contact. The reaching strands of light evaporated, and Wren blinked, still feeling the effects, but she shook them off and returned her attention to the boy below.

Like what had happened to Wren—but with far more potency—tendrils of light were crawling up his arms, swirling over his skin, then sinking deeper. He glowed, the light coming from his very bones, each standing out in stark clarity as the magic filled him from within. His skeleton must be holding the power his body drank in, acting as storage containers, as reserves, and after each bone had taken its fill, the magic spilled over, flooding the next and the next.

His face was frozen in something like pain, jaw clenched and muscles straining. The light reached his skull . . . but it didn't stop there. The magic kept going, traveling from the tip of his head and into the horns, illuminating what appeared to be a partial ram's skull worn over the top of his face like a mask. It must aid him somehow, enhancing his magic or his ability to store it. The light pooled there, around the horns, as well as in his right hand.

There was a final burst of light before he withdrew and staggered away.

He breathed deeply, and the magic glittered and swirled within him, becoming even brighter, while the pool softened and settled, the glowing cracks and stones surrounding it dimming. The building grew darker, and the tremors ceased, the boy's illuminated skeleton and glowing flesh standing out all the more as he turned back to the suited revenant.

All that remained to put on the revenant was the helmet, but he didn't lift it.

That's when Wren noticed for the first time that he held something in his hand. A long, narrow object, dark against his faintly glowing skin . . . and pointed at the end, like a spike.

Before she could react, he lifted it in one hand and a small hammer, withdrawn from his belt, in the other. He lined it up with the center of the skull's forehead, then struck it home with one precise hit, the brittle crack of bone ringing out. Wren's knowledge of reapyr lore had always been patchy, but she was quite certain it had pierced the revenant's ley line.

An otherworldly wail filled the silence, reverberating off the walls in a painful cascade.

Wren clapped her hands to her ears, though again Julian appeared unaffected. He stared at her with concern, but she gritted her teeth, determined to watch what was happening below.

Apparently in pain, the revenant reached for the spike with gauntleted hands, tugging and scraping, but the boy paid it little mind.

"Stop," he ordered, almost distractedly, and the revenant stilled.

Then, carefully leaning forward, he examined what he had done. Wren got the impression something had gone wrong.

Indeed, wisps of ghostlight emerged, and the boy muttered under his breath. If the spike had traversed the ley line, then the ghost should lose its tether to its body. But apparently, that was not what the boy had intended.

As the spirit began to release before their very eyes, swirling through the suit of armor like steam, the boy raised his hammer again. Heedless of the ghost, he carefully lined it up with the spike, then tapped it with a single, ringing impact, embedding it half an inch deeper. Wren suspected too much force would rent the skull in half, but that didn't happen.

The screeching ceased, and the boy's shoulders slumped in apparent relief.

The ghost, which had been steadily dissipating, froze in midair, tremulous.

Then it *retracted*. Sucked into the suit of armor like water swirling down a drain.

Somehow, the boy had brought it *back*, remaking the tether. Binding the ghost to its body through its anchor bone.

A surge of light exploded from the revenant, spilling *through* the iron the way the magic spilled through the boy's body, and then all the light—save for the ghost glow—went out. Even the boy's inner light was gone, his magic apparently used up.

Panting, he took up the final piece of armor—the helmet—and slid it over the obedient revenant's pierced skull, the iron ringing when it settled against the neck piece. It had no eye holes, no slots for breathing, because of course, the revenant didn't need them. All was darkness.

"Go," the boy rasped, head hanging, not bothering to look at the thing he had just made. "To the others. To Caston. Find her. Obey her."

Others? How many others?

The iron revenant moved at once, armor clanking with every footstep, out through a door somewhere in the back of the throne room.

"We should follow it," Wren said, though a part of her was desperate to speak to this boy, to *understand*, and he was currently all alone. . . .

"Come on," Julian said, getting to his feet. "We need to—"

As Wren moved to stand, her boot connected with a piece of rubble. The pebble went flying, skittering across the ground before cascading down the wide staircase, echoing loudly on every step.

She froze, but too late. The boy was on his feet, squinting up at the gallery. Their eyes met—hers bone-white, his ghost-green—and then he spoke, his voice booming with residual power.

"Trespassers," he said, and Wren thought he was talking *to* her and Julian until he added, "Stop them."

The words ended, ringing in the silence . . . until new sounds filled the hall. Scraping, scuttling, hollow rattling . . . Spots of light flickered into existence below, and higher, along the gallery, emerging from the shadows, from hallways and rooms, from entire wings of this building shrouded in darkness. Wren's magic was alive with their presence, their appearance bursting to life in her senses like fireworks.

She and Julian made for the door, but several undead had beaten them to it, and not all of them had bones to carry. Some were ghosts, their bodies out of sight, tethers stretched to unknowable lengths in this magic-rich place, while others were surely geists, setting up winds and sending dust and pebbles scattering.

Julian lifted his staff on instinct but knew better than to swing. The undead didn't attack—the ghostsmith's orders had been to *stop them,* not harm them—instead circling around them like wolves on a hunt.

Wren raised her bone sword. All she needed to do was clear a path to the water, but as she swung left and right, other undead swarmed in behind her, cutting her off from Julian.

She thought of her lessons. She had been taught to protect, to fight in a pair, and she had allowed herself to be separated from her charge.

Expression frantic, Julian raised his staff again.

"Don't," Wren warned, afraid any sudden movement might goad the undead into an attack. *She* was usually the reckless one—which Julian had pointed out several times—but the terror was plain on his face, and he wasn't thinking straight.

Despite his fear, he heeded her warning and halted his staff mid-swing, but apparently it was too late.

One of the revenants snapped its head in his direction, sensing his violent intention. Then it detached from its corpse right before their eyes, the rotten body tumbling to the ground while the ghost surged directly at him. It retained its body's shape, a human figure, face contorted as it barreled toward Julian with outstretched hands.

It would kill him, here and now. A single touch and the deathrot would set in.

And he was out of Wren's reach.

Panic seized her, and she did the only thing she could think to do.

"Stop!" she shouted at the ghost, dredging the word up from deep within.

And it did.

The ghost halted in midair, as if it met with some invisible barrier. It crackled and hissed, brimming with pent-up energy, but it did not move again.

It remained suspended mere inches from Julian, who had flinched away. He looked at it now, then at Wren, open shock on his face. Then his gaze shifted, spotting something behind her, and before Wren could turn, a hand landed on her shoulder.

She jumped, whirling around, heart galloping in her chest. She expected to find a revenant, to feel the telltale cold of deathrot sweep up her arm.

Instead, she was face-to-face with the ghostsmith boy.

The sight of that horned skull looming before her caused her stomach to clench painfully with a deep, primal fear that robbed her of breath and rooted her to the spot.

Realizing how badly he'd frightened her, maybe, or just wanting to see better, the boy's other hand reached for the mask, pushing it off his face to rest atop his head, allowing Wren to truly see his features for the first time.

He was starkly pale—paler even than Wren—with matching hair and a delicate nose under stern brows. There were dark shadows beneath his eyes, which were wide and uncertain, and his mouth was pinched—he looked exhausted, confused . . . *scared*. His expression tugged at her, and the mystery of who he was and what he had done made her take a hesitant step forward.

Seeing this, his wariness faded and his demeanor turned thoughtful, his green-eyed gaze unnerving as it took her in.

He had seen, of course.

Wren had commanded the undead, just as he—a ghostsmith—had done, and he had seen it.

She tugged at his grip, her chest heaving, her breath ragged, but he didn't let go. Looking down, she saw that he wore a ring on one of his long ivory fingers.

Her heart, which had been thundering against her rib cage, seemed to stop.

The ring. It was bone-white, with a black spike . . . and birds engraved on either side.

Her other hand flew to her pocket. The boy stilled—maybe he thought she'd been going for a weapon. Perhaps she should have. Instead, she withdrew the ring she had found in the Bonewood. The exact twin of his.

She held it out in her palm, and the boy stared at it, then up at her face again. His features shifted rapidly from suspicion to confusion to dawning comprehension.

"Wren!" Julian cried out, trying to go to her, but every time he moved, the undead shifted and crackled in warning.

Wren looked back at him, then at the ghostsmith boy. His gaze, meanwhile, never left her. He was drinking her in, she thought. Memorizing her.

Finally, he released her arm, but only so he could raise his hand, the ring gleaming in the ghostlight.

He pointed at one of the birds—the larger of the two, the bird of prey—then at his own chest.

Wren, breathless, followed his every movement. Her body was

wound tight, her muscles poised to flee in the face of information she didn't want but desperately needed. He seemed to sense her struggle, his actions slow and cautious, like she was a deer in the woods he didn't want to startle.

When his finger pointed at the smaller bird, the songbird, Wren started to shake. Knowing, even before it happened, what he would do.

Raising his hand, he pointed squarely at Wren.

She shook her head. Slowly at first, then more forcefully.

Her fingers closed around the ring, hard, her hand curled into a fist. She turned.

"Move!" she bellowed at the revenants that stood between her and Julian—between them and their escape.

And they did, parting for her like a ghost for a bone blade. She looked once over her shoulder, but the boy didn't attempt to follow her.

He let her go.

"Move," she said again as she came to Julian's side, putting as much force into it as she could, though her voice shook. Their eyes met, and Wren saw a different kind of fear in them.

Fear of *her*.

All around, the undead obeyed, stepping aside with varying levels of grace and coordination. Sword held high, Wren grabbed Julian by the arm and dragged him with her, out the door and into the cavern.

More revenants dotted the shore, but as Wren and Julian made their way to the water, they shuffled and ambled and floated aside.

"Move," Wren whispered, whenever one lingered too long. "*Move.*"

They reached the boat. Julian was staring at her like she'd grown an extra limb, but she couldn't smile or laugh or shake her head. She still held the ring in her fist, the shape imprinting itself into her palm.

Julian paddled them into the center of the spring, deciding without words that they wouldn't return to their makeshift camp. He had brought his satchel with them and left it in the boat, and now there was nothing to do but make for the mine shaft passage that had delivered him here.

The silence was deafening, and more revenants winked to life along the shore as they passed, silent specters in the darkness. Wren didn't dare command any more of them, afraid this newfound power would run out at any moment. Because surely it would—it was temporary, connected to whatever was in that pool, whatever she had absorbed when she pressed her hand to the ground.

The ring in her hand called her a liar, its sharp edges cutting into her palm.

Her senses tugged suddenly, and she poked her head over the side of the boat. She didn't know how she knew—or how she could possibly sense it—but she was certain her satchel was directly below them. There *was* bonedust inside, though the amount was small and the water should have obscured her senses. *Should have* but didn't.

After she pocketed the ring, a determined yank with her magic was all it took to drag the bag up from the depths into her outstretched hand.

How deep had the water been? How much farther was her range?

Swallowing, Wren hauled the sodden bag into the boat. Several moments later, she sensed her sword on the far shore. She suspected that, right now, she could have called it into her palm—no matter the distance—but she didn't, instead waiting until the boat headed in that direction. There were revenants standing nearby, but as Wren leapt from the boat and splashed closer to shore, they remained immobile.

The entrance to the mining passage, too, was surrounded by revenants, and Wren gathered her strength as they approached.

Disembarking in the shallows and sloshing toward the shore, Wren found her voice again.

"Move," she said, feeling as she had before that the word came from deep within her. That it was laced with power. With magic. "Step aside."

They did, clearing a path but not leaving entirely. Their presence chilled Wren to the bone, her instincts to fight rearing up, but she didn't want to test the limits of their obedience.

Once they were inside the passage, darkness closed in, and the lack of ghostlight—along with the misty atmosphere of the spring—eased the tension in Wren's shoulders, though she didn't dare relax. The way was steep and slippery, winding and bending in odd places, just as Julian had described.

Finally, they reached the mine itself.

Julian led the way, up some old stone stairs and around a bend until they arrived at a lift. It operated with a crank, though Julian didn't use it, instead pulling on the metal chain with his magic, speeding them to the top.

Away from the boy with the matching ring, the Breach, and the countless undead who obeyed her command.

TWENTY-NINE

Once they reached the surface, Wren's eyes needed a moment to adjust. Everything looked startlingly clear, the lack of mist and ghost-light casting the world into simple black and white—sky and stars, mountains and rocky ground. The bridge was visible behind them, silhouetted against the spangled backdrop, and the far side was dark once more, no undead ranging there unchecked.

And if there had been . . . could Wren *check* them? Could she banish them with a word?

Everything that had just happened felt miles away, a part of that hazy, surreal landscape—impossible in the stark light of the moon.

"Come on," Julian said, leading them away from the mine shaft. They cut between several buildings that were scattered nearby, mostly ruined or fallen down, until they arrived at one that was still standing. Ducking behind it, they stopped to catch their breath.

Wren's ears were ringing, her blood pounding so hard and fast she could barely think straight.

"Well?" Julian said, staring at her.

"What?" she asked, dazed.

"Are they following us?" While she leaned against the wall, he stood facing her, peering around the edge toward the mine shaft.

Closing her eyes, Wren steadied her breathing and extended her senses. "No," she said, with unnerving certainty. It wasn't that she couldn't sense anything—she could, but the undead she could sense were at the bottom of the Breach. *Well* outside her normal range.

At least they weren't in immediate danger.

Had the boy called them off? Or had Wren's order, "step aside," superseded his? She suspected his magic was thoroughly depleted after creating that iron revenant, so maybe his commands were similarly weakened.

Opening her eyes, she found Julian staring at her intently. "What did he say to you?"

"Nothing," she said, which was true. He hadn't spoken a word, but he *had* told her things . . . things she didn't understand. Julian pulled a skeptical expression, and Wren reached into her pocket, withdrawing the ring. "He was wearing the same one."

She couldn't bring herself to explain about the birds. She didn't know what they meant, not truly, and she didn't want to speculate.

Julian ran his hand through his hair, thinking. "How long have you known you could do that?"

No need to ask what he meant. "I didn't."

He looked unconvinced. "You're telling me one touch of your bare hand to that glowing stone, and suddenly you can command the undead? Suddenly you're a—"

"*Don't,*" she said, her voice ragged. She swallowed several times,

—301

trying to get herself under control. "It was that well. It must be more than just magic. It must somehow give a person abilities beyond, give them . . ." *Limitless power. Dark power.*

"Can you do anything else?" The words were pointed, and she knew he was thinking of Locke, the same as her.

She forced thoughts of obedient revenants and crushed bones from her mind. "My range feels wider. My senses . . . sharper. Beyond that . . ." *I don't know.* "And you? You were right next to me—"

He held up his hands, showing the leather gloves. "I didn't touch anything."

"Still," Wren prodded, needing him to be affected too. Needing to be less . . . different. "You felt it, didn't you? In the air?"

He shrugged, though the casualness was undercut by the tension in his neck. "I don't know what I felt. I just know what I saw, and that—that *boy* was doing more than commanding them."

Yes, he was. He had plunged a strange spike through a piece of bone, just like on the ring they both bore. And somehow that had stopped the ghost from separating from its body. Made it impossible, Wren guessed, so that it would remain inside that armor.

She frowned at Julian. "Where did he get it? The armor?"

He reared back. "How am I supposed to know?"

"Where else would he get a full suit of ironsmith armor than the House of Iron?" Wren demanded, glad to be on the offensive. "That was custom work. No eye holes. No ventilation or gaps."

Julian shook his head. "Every scrap of iron we have is under close guard, and every hammer who survived the Uprising is in service to the regent." He paused, seeming to realize what he had just said. "But there's no *way* he'd . . ." He trailed off, his gaze growing distant. Even if the ghostsmith had salvaged iron from a battlefield—House of Iron traditions be damned—he'd still need a hammer to create that custom suit. He'd still need an ironsmith.

Perhaps there was finally a crack in Julian's ironclad faith in this regent and their cause.

"Whatever that boy is doing, he's *not* doing it alone," Wren said pointedly. They needed to find out more, but she had no idea where that armored undead had gone. She craned her neck in both directions, then cursed. "We need to follow that iron revenant, but we lost it."

Julian cocked a brow. "Iron revenant?" he repeated. Wren shrugged—it seemed an accurate name to her—and he shook his head before continuing. "We didn't lose it. That boy told it to go to Caston. I know where that is. Or rather, where it *used* to be." Wren had forgotten that he'd given a destination, the place unfamiliar to her. "It's supposed to be in ruins, overrun like everywhere else," Julian continued. "But maybe that's just where he's storing these things."

"Let's go, then."

He hesitated. "Caston is on the southeastern border of the original Haunted Territory."

"Meaning?"

"Meaning, it's the exact opposite direction we were traveling. If we follow that iron revenant, there's a good chance we lose the prince."

"Oh," Wren said. Right, the prince. Emotions warred within her. She had set out to save Leo and prove her worth. But along the way, she had seen and heard things she could not forget, things that were, if possible, even more dire than a prince of the realm being held as a hostage and a prisoner. Her curiosity pulled her to the iron revenants, to the ghostsmith boy, wanting—no, *needing*—to understand it all, if only to understand herself. But there were larger ramifications to what was happening here, something much bigger than a single prince. Or her personal pride. This boy wasn't just making curiosities. . . . He was controlling the undead and fitting them with armor. He was turning them into weapons.

She thought of the coldness in her grandmother's voice when she'd proclaimed Wren a failure, the disappointment in her father's eyes when she'd been forced to hand over Ghostbane.

She thought of Leo, the look of fear he'd worn as the kidnappers descended on him.

They were her family. He was her friend.

But this was bigger, even, than that.

"Do you think Leo will be safe? If the exchange happens, your people . . . They won't hurt him, will they?"

"No," Julian said with certainty. "Whatever Captain Royce is cooking up, the prince will be safe because he's valuable. Plain and simple."

Wren wasn't as convinced, but she knew she didn't have a choice.

"I say we pursue the iron revenant. We can't pretend we didn't see it, can't turn our backs and continue with the mission as if nothing has changed. It has. Whoever that boy is working for, both sides of the Wall stand to suffer for it."

"Agreed," Julian said, and they shared a strange smile, as if both of them were expecting an argument.

"You do realize that you might miss out on your chance, too," Wren said. "To confront the captain and learn the truth."

Julian's smile turned sharp. "Oh, I'll have my chance."

A chill slipped down Wren's spine, and she was glad that they were currently on the same side.

† † † †

They consolidated their supplies first. Wren's pack was sodden, and with the cold night wind whipping across the landscape, it would remain that way for the foreseeable future. She ditched the extra blankets she'd stuffed inside, along with the firewood they'd have no time to dry. The remaining food stores went into Julian's pack, the extra bonedust attached to her belt, and the empty bag was left behind.

They stopped twice to take turns resting. Wren let Julian sleep for as long as she could, but when it was her turn, she only lay there, her mind racing.

Rather than try to sleep, she stared at the ring, fingertips running over the ridges in the smooth bone, over the glyphs and the birds. A bird of prey for him. A songbird . . . a *wren* . . . for her.

"I wonder if it's an amplifier," Julian said, making her jump. It was sometime in the middle of the night, and she'd been so absorbed she'd forgotten he was there.

Wren looked down at the ring. "Amplifier?"

"They store extra power. It takes magical familiarity—like ironsmith armor bonding—and increases it exponentially."

"But this is *bone* . . . That would make him a bonesmith, when his abilities . . ." She trailed off. When his abilities were clearly *ghostsmith* abilities, she was about to say, but *she* was a bonesmith and had wielded the same powers as him. Or some of them, anyway. The ring *had* glowed brightly when he'd drawn up the well's power, just like the horned skull mask had, suggesting they did indeed hold magic. And though she hadn't seen it, she would bet the mask had one of those dark spikes through it, the same as the ring. So maybe it wasn't about the bone at all but the spike. The same kind of spike that had bound that revenant to its corpse.

Did that mean these rings, that skull mask . . . Were they haunted? Was *that* the material a ghostsmith needed to be close to . . . the spirit?

"It's just a theory," Julian said quietly. "But amplifiers are common among metalsmiths. You saw how much gold that prince wore."

"I thought he was just vain," Wren mused, though at the mention of Leo, she felt a pang of guilt for abandoning him.

Julian grinned. "That too, maybe, but I'd bet one or two of them were amplifiers. They're usually jewelry—family heirlooms, if they can get them, so they hold decades of shared contact between the material and the user's bloodline. In fact"—he cleared his throat—"sometimes they even mix them with blood—or other living matter—to increase the bond, or implant amplifiers inside their bodies. Permanently combining magic and blood."

Living matter? Magic and blood?

She stared at the ring again, made of *someone's* bone—though she didn't know whose. She ran her finger over the songbird, then put it back inside her pocket. "I heard silversmiths actually *eat* silver," she said, needing to divert the conversation. "Is that the same sort of thing?"

Julian laughed, the sound low and rich. He seemed less wary of her now that she'd stopped commanding the undead, which was a relief.

Wren started to smile in return, but then she remembered the kiss. The rejection. *This was a bad idea.* They were slipping back into the easy rhythm that had landed them in that spring together, which made it difficult not to think about . . . not to *want* . . .

The warm glow in her stomach turned cold, and she looked away.

They were here together because they made a good team. Not for anything else.

"They do that because silver has healing properties, so they use it as a treatment," Julian replied, oblivious to her thoughts. "They've definitely *tried* to do implants, from what I've heard, with varied success. It's generally considered too risky, whatever the benefits. The procedure is painful, the implanted object often rejected by the body, and the amount of additional power it actually provides is debatable. It comes down to the quality of the material and its compatibility with the host. It's long since fallen out of practice."

Wren narrowed her eyes. "How do you know so much about it?"

He laughed again, though it sounded a bit forced this time. "I—unlike you, I can only assume—was actually a good student."

Wren snorted, but she sensed he hadn't given her the whole truth. He wasn't wrong, though.

"I thought that's what the well might be," she admitted. "Some sort of amplifier."

"I think it was closer to raw magic. It doesn't just increase power. . . . It *is* power."

They continued on after that, making their way through the steadily lightening dark. More undead rose and flickered to life as they passed, clusters of ghosts and the odd revenant, but none pursued.

Wren didn't speak to them again, but she held her last command—"step aside"—in her mind whenever she saw any, and perhaps that was enough to extend the magic. Maybe by repeating it internally, she gave it new power—or maybe she was just imagining things. She also continued to fiddle with the ring in her pocket, unable to resist running her finger along the well-worn grooves and that strange, dark spike.

They moved through the Haunted Territory unscathed, and when the sun rose, it highlighted the rooftops of Caston in the distance.

Julian stopped in his tracks, and a second later, Wren did too.

Smoke rose from several chimneys, along with the faint but unmistakable sounds of life—the clatter of movement, the murmur of voices, and something else, ringing in a steady, echoing rhythm.

Caston wasn't an abandoned ruin. It was filled with people, living and working in the Haunted Territory.

And an iron revenant was heading this way.

THIRTY

They approached Caston warily, finding a high vantage point to perch themselves and observe before they strolled through the town gates, which were tall and well fortified, in addition to the river that wrapped around it. There were bone protections too, but they were poorly placed and in desperate need of repair. Whoever had done them had not been a bonesmith, but the river made up for their failings.

Wren was amazed by the geography, until Julian pointed out that the water had been diverted and directed to encircle the town—via several dams and an aqueduct, visible in the distance—and had *not* been an original feature.

He looked grim, and Wren couldn't blame him. That kind of work did not come easily or cheaply. Whoever was running this operation was well connected and well funded, and who would fit that bill more than the regent of the Iron Citadel? Julian believed their people were struggling to survive, and surely many of them were—but not *all* of them. And the Haunted Territory wasn't just a wasteland threatening their very existence. . . . It was also apparently a smokescreen, a way to conceal certain activities. Whether what they'd witnessed in the Breach was connected to what was happening here remained to be seen, but Wren suspected they'd soon find out.

The question of why someone would put so much money into keeping such a dangerously positioned town alive was soon answered.

Mining.

That was the source of the rhythmic sound they could hear, emanating from an apparently active mine situated on the northern border of the town.

"This must be where all that shiny armor for the iron revenant came from. I thought mining was illegal." As far as she knew, it had been ever since overmining had been determined to be the cause of the Breach in the first place—whether or not it was true.

"Who's going to enforce it? We aren't a part of the Dominions anymore—still," he added, before she could protest, "I didn't know about this, and I don't support it. Things are bad enough already; we don't need them to get worse. We don't need a second Breach."

"But maybe whoever is behind this *wants* things to get worse," Wren murmured. "Think about it. That boy can control them. Suddenly, the revenants aren't a blight on your lands. They're an army."

"What good are they if they can't get past the Border Wall?" Julian asked. "They're undead. They may be a threat east of the Wall, and maybe they can build, but they aren't strong enough to tear down . . ." He trailed off, seeming to come to the same realization Wren already had.

"I suspect those suits of ironsmith armor might solve that problem," she said softly.

It made sense. The Breachsiders didn't have the numbers to muster a force that could take down the Wall—not since Locke Graven—and even if they did, they'd lose too many lives in the effort. But with the undead, they could set them on the Border and its defenders, let the revenants do the dirty work, and then they could stroll through afterward.

Those iron suits would protect the revenants *and* their ghosts, making them nearly impossible to stop by bonesmith methods. The metal would allow them to touch the Wall and protect them from bone blades that might pierce their spirit, and reapyrs would struggle to make a clean cut with their scythes. Even regular weapons couldn't pierce ironsmith metal. They were warriors the Dominions couldn't defeat.

"Do you see them anywhere?" Wren asked.

"Who?"

"The iron revenants. According to that boy, there were others here. But the people seem . . ."

"Fine," Julian agreed, nodding thoughtfully. "Either they know about the iron revenants and don't fear them, or the revenants are stationed somewhere nearby but out of sight. . . . Do you think they could actually get into the town? With the water?"

"There's a drawbridge," Wren said, pointing it out. "You have to assume at some distance, the water doesn't affect them. Think about the spring in the Breach, and the revenants crossed the bridge over it. And there are underground rivers and wells all over the place. Maybe they found a height that works?"

"Or maybe the iron suits offer some manner of protection?" Julian said. "Like a body?"

Wren tilted her head, considering. "Could be. We'll need to get inside and look around."

"How? I doubt they get many visitors," he said dryly. "You and I will stick out like sore thumbs."

"Not necessarily," Wren said, peering into the town's center. "Look, there. It's a market, and there are wagons equipped for long-distance travel. There aren't any farms around, obviously, so they must get traders coming here, even if they're infrequent. They aren't completely isolated."

"What are you suggesting?"

"We blend in, see what we can overhear—now, while the sun is high and the streets are busy. We'll try to poke around, too, see if we can find where the iron revenants are kept, if they're inside the town walls. Come nightfall, we'll have to figure out our next move."

"Blend in?" Julian asked with a raised brow, his gaze raking her up and down. "Good luck."

His attention made heat sweep her face, and she forced herself not to look away. "I'll take it off," she said, gesturing to her bone armor.

"Still," he muttered, and Wren couldn't figure out if it was meant to be a compliment or not.

Their plan decided on, she reluctantly removed every piece of armor, save what could be hidden under her clothes. Her swords remained on her back, their sheaths concealing all but the hilt—which was inconspicuous and wrapped in leather—but her bandolier and throwing knives joined the armor inside Julian's pack, and her pouches of bonedust got tucked into pockets. She was just reordering her belt when she spotted Ghostbane's empty dagger sheath. She hadn't been able to bring herself to remove it before, but there was no time like the present.

Julian eyed it curiously. "You never had anything there, did you?"

"Not since I came to the fort," she replied shortly. Then, because she was feeling morose and wanted pity, "I used to have a family dagger, but it was tak—I *lost* it, before I was shipped to the Wall." Svetlana may have demanded it after Wren's disastrous trial, but *she* had gambled it mere hours before, had chosen to risk it all to defeat her cousin and come out on top. Much as she'd tried to deny it until now, it was her own fault, and she knew it.

Julian, who had been removing his own armor—he was too recognizable in it—reached into his belt and withdrew one of his. "Here. I know it's iron, but . . ."

Wren gaped at it. Leave it to her to find the gift of a used weapon the height of romance, but there it was. She took it, examining the details. It was beautifully made, particularly the swirling designs along the hilt.

"It's called Ironheart," he said quietly, then cleared his throat. "It belonged to my mother. Most of my first weapons did. When I was a child, they were the perfect size for me to train with. After I outgrew them, well . . . they were all I had left of her."

"Thank you," Wren said sincerely, the value of the gift taking on new meaning. She hadn't known that Julian's *mother* was dead too. He was even more alone than her, it seemed. At least she still had her father. "I lost my mother too. I mean, she died when I was born, so I never knew her."

Julian nodded. "I was a baby when my mother died, so I never really knew her either. But . . ." He trailed off.

"But what?" Wren pressed.

He gave her a self-conscious shrug. "I've heard stories." Wren waited patiently, so he continued. "She was always helping people. She used to visit all the local towns, bringing them extra food or supplies if it was a hard year. She was a sword too, and after the Breach, she did everything she could to protect the miners and their families. To get them out of the Haunted Territory and relocate them somewhere safe. She was trying to evacuate one of the mines when it collapsed. This was before we abandoned the area entirely." Wren frowned slightly, attempting to puzzle out the timeline. He had a *little* sister, didn't he? "My father remarried," he said by way of explanation, his expression stiff. Wren suspected he didn't like his stepmother much, but the stories of his mother explained why he was so protective over the people east of the Wall. He was trying to live up to her legacy.

"And you got a little sister out of it," Wren offered, wanting to make him feel better. "A superstitious and stubborn one?"

His mouth quirked up in the corner, and he seemed pleased that she remembered what he'd said about her. He fiddled with his bracelet again. "Rebecca—*Becca*. She prefers Becca."

Wren was strangely gratified that he had told her his sister's name. That he trusted her with something so simple yet so personal. They stood in silence a moment. Then, all at once, they both seemed to remember what they had been doing. Wren carefully slid Ironheart into Ghostbane's empty sheath.

When Julian looked at her again, it was with a critical eye, and it didn't take long for him to spot a problem. "You should probably, uh, clean your face."

Wren scowled. They'd been traveling for days; it wasn't like *his* face was pristine and—well, actually, it pretty much was. How did he do that?

"The makeup," he clarified, gesturing vaguely at her. His expression was strange, almost anticipatory, and Wren remembered the last time he'd seen her without it.

"Oh, right." She swiped ineffectually at her face with the back of her hand, but all she managed to do was make things worse, if Julian's hastily stifled smirk was anything to go by. The eye black was greasy and mostly waterproof, making it difficult to take off. "I use oil at home . . . ," she muttered.

"Try this," he said, reaching into his breast pocket to produce what looked suspiciously like an embroidered silk handkerchief. Wren had no idea ironsmiths were so proper.

"Wow, *elegant*," she said, taking the pristine scrap of fabric in her dirty hand.

"It's a handkerchief, not a ball gown," he said dryly, handing over a small flask. "This is mineral oil. I use it for my blades, but I think it should do the trick."

Wren held the bottle over the fine silk, hesitating. Shaking his head, Julian took both from her, soaking the handkerchief before giving it back.

"It's so white . . . ," Wren argued, though she brought the corner to her eyes and swiped underneath. Julian watched her intently.

After cleaning around her eyes with the edges, she pressed her lips against the center of the cloth. She let the oil soak against her mouth for a moment, then dragged the silk across her face. The result was a black, lip-shaped smear on the fabric.

"That okay?" she asked uneasily, wishing for a mirror. He had already removed his breastplate, which she had used to see her reflection before.

Julian's gloved hand came up to her face, hovering there for a moment, before it dropped.

"Fine," he muttered, taking the used cloth and turning away.

Wren started fussing with her belt again, anything to break the tension, though she watched him from under her eyelashes.

His back to her, he stared down at the handkerchief, at the

imprint of her mouth visible there. Then he carefully folded the silk and tucked it safely back into his breast pocket. Wren expelled a shaky breath.

"You'll have to keep your hood up," he said over his shoulder. "There's no changing your eye color, but hopefully without direct sunlight on your face, no one will notice."

"Right," Wren said, drawing up her hood and composing herself.

Julian hefted the bag, which would be impossibly heavy for Wren, given all the iron armor inside, and they set out.

Getting across the moat was easier than Wren had expected. The water was shallow, meant to deter undead attackers—not living ones—and they scaled the walls using Julian's whip sword, avoiding the north-facing gate and the guards posted there.

They climbed near a cluster of grain silos, which gave them good cover as they dropped down into the town.

Sticking to shadowy streets and back alleys, they only passed through the main thoroughfare when absolutely necessary. They poked their heads into doorways and paused outside open windows, listening for any sign of the iron revenants. Wren knew Julian's senses were also on high alert for large amounts of iron, but given that there was an active mine within the walls of the city, she doubted he'd be able to get an accurate reading.

All the while, Wren kept an easy pace, her chin high, elbowing Julian when he walked too fast or looked anxiously around.

"Clearly this is your first time sneaking into someplace you shouldn't be," Wren said under her breath with some exasperation. "Skulking around trying *not* to draw notice is a surefire way to be noticed. Walk like you belong here."

He scowled at her before sighing and raising his head, throwing back his shoulders and putting some of his usual grace and confidence back in place. Wren stared at him, worried she'd made a mistake. With his elegant features and aloof expression, he was bound to draw a different kind of notice now.

They were just sidling around the edges of the crowded market when a shout went up.

Wren froze—they'd been seen!—but then she realized the sound had actually come from the far side of town. There was a second gate situated there, this one facing south, and as she turned, the doors were slowly cranked open. The thunder of horses' hooves shook the ground and kicked up a cloud of dust in the afternoon light.

It was late in the day for traders or farmers, and as the riders drew near, she saw they were soldiers. It wasn't a massive force by any means, around twenty by Wren's count, but next to her, Julian's face blanched.

A waving pennant caught her attention, borne by a rider near the front. It was a black field with a red tower, the sigil of the House of Iron.

Next to the flag bearer rode a man in black iron armor, ornate and extravagant, with red enamel accents and a spiked plume on his helmet twice the height of the one Julian had worn.

It was another ironsmith.

Riding alongside him were soldiers with more flashes of red, though they wore iron chain mail rather than plate, meaning they were not smiths.

The whispers that had begun from the moment the gate opened finally reached Wren's ears.

"The Red Guard is coming . . . the regent of the Iron Citadel . . . the regent is here. . . ."

Wren ducked into the narrow space between two buildings, dragging Julian with her, and both of them watched through the gap as the procession entered town.

There was no way they were riding *through*, and sure enough, soon after passing their hiding place, the riders had slowed their pace and were moving toward one of the buildings on the main road, which appeared to be a public house or inn.

They were greeted, their horses tended to—their arrival clearly expected.

Wren leaned back.

"He's meant to be at the Citadel," Julian said faintly. Wren turned to face him. He still looked shocked. "That's where the exchange was supposed to take place. He can't . . ." He ran a hand through his hair distractedly.

"Well, he's here now. Apparently he has other business to attend to."

Julian's hand froze. "You don't mean—"

Wren shrugged. "It seems strange he'd turn up here the same day an iron revenant was meant to do likewise. Not to mention there are allegedly others here. And this mining, it must be happening with his permission, and likely his financial support as well. Why else would he push iron production in such a dangerous place? He needs it. Unless you're mustering an *ironsmith* army . . ." She trailed off, but he just shook his head. She'd figured as much. "Then the regent's here to build an army of his own."

"We don't know that," Julian said, though he didn't seem quite as certain as he had before. He had been a staunch supporter of the man from the start, but now, in the face of so much evidence, there was a sliver of doubt in his dark eyes.

"Who is he, Julian? Who is the regent?"

"He's head of the House of Iron," Julian said.

"Yes, but who *is* he?" Wren pressed. "The Knights were wiped out in the Uprising, so by what right does he rule your house?"

"He is strong and the house is weak," Julian said dully, the words sounding like a phrase he had long since memorized. "It's thanks to him we even have a house, after everything. He rebuilt us from the ground up, and now—"

"And now he might be making a bigger play."

"For all we know, he could be here to shut it down," Julian persisted stubbornly.

Wren didn't believe that, and deep down, she didn't think Julian believed it either. "There's only one way to know for certain. Come on, we need to get inside that inn."

THIRTY-ONE

"Looks like they'll be here awhile—the horses are being brought to the stables," Wren said, peering intently around the corner. "I have a hard time believing those iron revenants are holed up inside an *inn*, but maybe whoever makes them is."

"You mean the ghostsmith boy?" Julian asked. He sounded like he was only half listening to her, his thoughts likely still on the regent.

"No, I mean whatever ironsmith constructs those suits. Or whoever is pulling that boy's strings," Wren said over her shoulder. "You heard him. He didn't just tell that iron revenant to come to Caston. He told it to 'obey her.' Maybe we'll finally meet this Corpse Queen everyone is talking about." She turned her attention back onto the street. "We *have* to get in there. . . ."

"I can't," Julian said, and Wren moved back into the alley. "They all know me. And they'll wonder why I'm not with Captain Royce and the others."

"Or they'll wonder why you're not dead, like you're supposed to be."

His jaw clenched. "He didn't—"

"Why are you so sure?"

"Because he wouldn't—it doesn't make any—"

"Why, Julian?" she asked again. She was tired of dancing around the subject. "Give me the real answer."

He expelled a breath, then closed his eyes in defeat. "Because he's my uncle, okay? The regent. He basically raised me."

Well, *that* explained why he couldn't believe the man was responsible for the assassination attempt or had anything to do with Caston's mining or the iron revenants.

"A regent usually governs because the rightful ruler is absent, unfit . . . or underage." She stared at him. "Which is it?"

Julian swallowed. "I'll be twenty in six weeks."

"Which means . . ."

"My name is Julian Knight. I'm heir to the House of Iron."

The handkerchief he'd given her outside the village flashed before her mind's eye, the memory of vague embroidery sharpening into the distinct and obvious initials "JK." He had put the truth of who he was *right* into her hands, and she hadn't spotted it.

Frustration at herself reared up, but she was irritated with him for keeping this from her, too. Not because it mattered to her—not really, though she suspected who *she* was would matter to *him*—but because it pointed the finger of blame squarely at his uncle. The man who ruled in his stead and who would stand to lose that position in six weeks.

And Wren had just allowed Leo to be delivered to him. Except, if the regent was here, where did that leave Leo?

"It's a closely guarded secret. I don't tell strangers, or . . ."

"Enemies?" Wren asked somewhat coldly, his rejection still stinging.

"I probably should have guessed, *Lord-Smith* Julian. Your weapons and armor. The way you talk—and that posh accent."

"What do you mean?"

"You sound prissier than the prince."

"No, that's not—" He shook his head, evidently taking issue with the adjective, before continuing. "What do you mean, 'the way I talk'?"

She shrugged, slightly uncomfortable now. "The way you always said 'my people.' How protective you are over them, including bandits who wanted to kill you. How you reacted to that battlefield. Even the stories about your mother were about admiring the way she had cared for others. You're like her—you feel a responsibility to those under your care."

Why did that statement make her feel like she'd revealed something? Yes, she'd felt a taste of it when he'd found her in that spring and watched over her, checking her wound and building up the fire.

And yes, maybe she had liked it.

"Oh," he said softly. His cheeks flushed, like he was embarrassed. Or pleased. "Right. Well, I guess it was about time. I think it's safe to say we're not strangers anymore."

"Or enemies?" she asked, trying to sound indifferent, but she feared she'd come across as self-conscious instead.

He was serious when he replied. "No."

Something in his expression made the fact that she hadn't told him who *she* was weigh heavily on her. "Well, speaking of—"

"Look," he said, cutting her off, his attention back on the main street. "They've gone inside. Now what?"

Wren looked out of the alley once more, thinking hard. "They must get camp followers and hangers-on—bored locals throwing themselves at those soldiers every time they visit." Sure enough, several villagers milled around the stables already, chatting up their favorites or perhaps hoping to meet new ones. "I could slip in among them, see if I can extricate one of the soldiers. Maybe the flag bearer—he looks young and gullible."

"Extricate?" Julian said with a frown. "You can't just march over and drag him out of there—the others will see."

Wren crossed her arms. "You think that's the only way I can get a boy alone? By dragging him?"

He raised his brows at her, and she recalled that she had technically dragged *him* into the spring before they'd kissed, but that was different. It certainly wasn't the *only* tactic at her disposal, at any rate.

"I am capable of subtlety," she said, with as much dignity as she could muster.

Was it doubt that tightened his mouth and darkened his expression—or was it something else?

"What are you going to do, then?" he asked stiffly.

Wren shrugged, lowering her hood and removing her swords. "Try to find out who the regent is meeting. Where." She pulled off her coat next and undid her shirt buttons, loosening them one after the other until her cleavage was exposed. Then she tied the jacket around her waist, accentuating her hips and removing some of the militaristic air of her outfit. "They might sit in the main room, or maybe he demands some sort of private parlor. Either way, there'll be windows, servant corridors, empty closets. . . ."

Julian had been watching her, but now that she met his gaze, he looked away. "Why do I get the feeling you've done this before?"

"Because I have." She didn't have a reputation as the worst instigator and rulebreaker in her house by accident. "How do I look?" she asked, fussing with her shirt and smoothing her hair. She pulled some strands across her forehead, hoping they would help obscure her eyes and soften her appearance.

Julian surveyed her closely. "Like trouble," he said, almost reluctantly.

"The right kind?" she asked. She didn't want to look like a thief or vagabond. She wanted to look like innocent mischief.

He hesitated. "Yes," he said. Then— "I almost feel sorry for him."

Wren flashed a smile, warmth spreading in her chest. "Stay here. I'll come back as soon as I can."

He nodded, but as she turned to go, he called out, "Wait."

Turning, she cocked her head. "Are you going to tell me to be careful?" she asked teasingly.

Expression serious, he stepped toward her and reached out, unfolding the neckline of her shirt to further expose her collarbone. He bent slightly to whisper into her ear, "Be *convincing*."

As it turned out, she was.

She strolled into the stable yard like she belonged there, and her calm, carefree attitude ensured that the stableboys only watched her idly, not suspiciously. She smiled, casually turning her head when any of the locals glanced her way, and found herself next to her target: the flag bearer. She made sure to arrange herself in the shadows of the building, hoping that the fading sunlight along with her hairstyle would keep her smith identity concealed.

While the other soldiers enjoyed the attention of a handful of young men and women, the flag bearer was very much on the outskirts. He was tall but thin, his face covered in preadolescent spots, and he turned endearingly red when she leaned against the fence next to him, smiling.

All Wren had to do was hint, heavily, that she wanted to "see his room" before he was spilling their secrets.

"Oh, we don't get a room. We'll be sleeping outside."

"Is the inn so very full?" she asked, tilting her head shyly and tucking a wayward strand of hair behind her ear. It felt like she was being a little too obvious, but he didn't seem to notice—or mind.

"Full? No. Booked? Yes."

"What does that mean?" she asked in polite confusion.

The flag bearer glanced around. Wren leaned closer, as if rapt, as he spoke. "The regent is conducting *business*," he said ominously. "That means he gets his fancy suite, and the rest of the rooms besides. He doesn't want people on either side, able to overhear his conversations, so he insists on having the *entire floor* to himself. Any traders in town will be sleeping in their carts tonight."

Wren glanced up at the inn, at the series of second-story windows. She suspected his suite was in the middle, with the double-doored balcony. Which meant the rest of the windows led to empty rooms, perfect for eavesdropping. They just had to get inside.

She made her excuses to the crestfallen flag bearer, promising to come back around later, before darting away from the inn. She was just about to duck into the alley with Julian when another shout echoed down the street, similar to before.

Again, the southern gate groaned open, but this time the riders that piled into Caston wore no distinguishing colors and carried no banners.

They were, however, familiar.

Riding at the front of the column was the captain that had tried to take Julian's life. And next to him, tied to his horse and with a dark hood over his head, was undoubtedly Prince Leopold. She'd recognize his elegant posture anywhere, and she was relieved to see that days of captivity hadn't changed it.

The sight of him caused her heart to kick against her ribs. She was happy he was here, within reach, even though they'd gone off course, and that he appeared unharmed.

But this meant the regent was *surely* involved in the attempt on Julian's life. And it also complicated what they were trying to do here exponentially. How would they ever extricate him from a contingent of the regent's private guard?

"He's here," Wren gasped as she stumbled into the alleyway.

"Who?" Julian said, emerging from the shadows. It had grown darker in their time apart, the narrow gap between buildings sitting in early twilight.

"The prince. They brought him here, which means—"

"This was the plan all along," he said, stunned. "To betray me."

Wren privately agreed, but the look on his face made her want to ease the blow. "Maybe, maybe not. The only way we'll know for sure is if we somehow get eyes or ears on the exchange that's about to go down."

He nodded, staring off into space for a moment. He looked lost, but as she watched, he visibly pulled himself together. He was toying with the bracelet his sister had given him, and it seemed to help ground him. Bring him back to himself.

"Did you manage to get any information?"

"I did. The regent has the 'fancy suite' on the second floor but demands the rest of the rooms remain empty. He doesn't want his *business* to be overheard."

"He can definitely be overcautious, bordering on paranoid," Julian admitted. "We need to get into one of those empty rooms."

"Agreed," Wren said. "But I'm not sure how. The street is too busy to climb through a window, and we can't very well walk in the front door. Even the servant entrance would be too risky."

"We could wait until nightfall . . . ," Julian mused, peering up at the sky. But they had an hour at least until they could count on the cover of darkness, and who knew what important information they'd miss in that time? As it was, the kidnapping party had already passed their alleyway and were now starting to dismount and deal with their horses. The meeting with the regent could happen in mere minutes.

"It must be quieter around back?" Julian asked.

"Well, yes, but that's where the stables are, which means servants, and some of the regent's guards are there as well."

"For now," Julian said. "Come on, I have an idea."

They took the long way around, coming up on the stables from behind. While Wren kept a lookout, Julian slipped into the hayloft and got to work with their flint and striker. The idea of starting a fire made Wren extremely nervous, but he insisted there were too many people—and too much water nearby—for the flames to rage out of hand. What they really wanted anyway was smoke, so he used some damp kindling and ensured the conflagration burned near a window.

He'd only just rejoined her on the sloping roof of the storage shed when the scent reached her, and before long, plumes of smoke followed.

One of the regent's guards was the first to notice—actually the flag bearer, with no one to distract him now that Wren had disappeared. The stableboys shouted, the guards abandoned their hangers-on, and soon everyone in the courtyard was either staring, moving to protect the animals, or hauling buckets of water.

Now was their best shot.

Releasing his whip, Julian threw it across the space between the shed and the inn, wrapping it around a drainage pipe, the blade segments locking together securely. He tugged twice before wedging his end behind a lantern sconce. Then he did something he'd yet to do: He called the blade segments to the base of the handle. The result was a taut cable between them and their target, which was actually slightly lower than they were, meaning they could take hold of the segments, let gravity do the work, and zip across.

"Here," Julian said, handing Wren a spare pair of gloves from his jacket pocket. They were soft and well worn—and far too big—but they would help to protect her hands as she slid along the cable.

Julian went first, slowing himself by holding tighter to the iron to control his pace and avoid making any noise. Once he got to the other side, he withdrew a paper-thin dagger, sliding it under the frame and hooking the latch, unlocking the window.

Wren remained crouched on the rooftop, her attention split between Julian climbing quietly into the darkness of the room and the commotion below, which was—as promised—quickly coming to an end. Night was falling, but not fast enough. If she didn't get into that room in a hurry, she'd be caught.

After ditching his bag, Julian reappeared in the open window, gesturing for her to make the leap. She did, throwing herself onto the rope with as much force as she could. She sailed through the air at an alarming speed, and as the window and Julian quickly approached, she realized she had no means to slow herself down.

He seemed to realize the same thing, his eyes bugging out a second before he stepped back. The smart thing would have been to step aside entirely, but that would mean Wren hurtling through the window and landing on the ground. No doubt the regent or his men stationed next door would hear the commotion, and their plan to eavesdrop would be over before it had even begun.

So instead, he braced himself and held his arms wide. She collided with him, hitting his chest hard enough to elicit a muffled grunt. He staggered backward, but rather than release Wren to alleviate the weight—and momentum—he held her tight against his chest, refusing to let her hit the ground.

His determination impressed her, as did the tight bands of his arms pressed against her back. She reminded herself that he clutched her this way to avoid making a sound, *not* for any other reason.

Still, it was nice to be held by him.

They remained like that, gasping, until he regained his balance. At last he drew back, their faces inches apart. His gaze flicked down to her mouth, and Wren's heart stopped.

"You okay?" he said, dragging his attention away from her lips.

She nodded, and he released his grip, allowing her body to slide slowly, gently, down to the floor. Afterward, her cheeks felt hotter than the sun, but luckily, the second he deposited her onto the floor, he rushed to the open window. With a quick tug, he released the whip from its mooring on the storage shed and drew it back into a sword, sheathing it. Then he shut the window, blocking out some of the sounds from below.

Now that her heart had stopped racing and the noise from the courtyard was cut off, Wren could hear movement and murmuring through the wall to her right.

Together they edged closer, pressing their ears against the paneling, but then Wren spotted a closet and wrenched it open, ducking inside the tight space, which was only made tighter when Julian joined her.

The voices grew louder, and when Wren pressed her ear against the back wall, she could hear the words through the cracks in the warped pieces of wood that made up the rather flimsy barrier between the rooms. No wonder the regent insisted on emptying the entire floor.

Getting an idea, Wren reached back to close the closet door, shutting them in total darkness. As her eyes adjusted, she saw narrow beams of golden light spilling through the gaps. Several of them might even be large enough to see through.

She glanced at Julian, and they bent their heads, squinting into the room beyond.

THIRTY-TWO

Leo entered the room via a shove between the shoulder blades. It was wholly unnecessary—he was walking just fine, thank you very much, despite his sore muscles from days in the saddle—but it certainly added to the whole "your life is in mortal peril" atmosphere they were attempting to cultivate.

Before him was a large suite, fitted with the kind of furniture and decor that was meant to be elegant and refined but read to him as nothing so much as quaint and outdated.

Still, it was the nicest space he'd been in for weeks, the rugs beneath his feet well made, if worn, and the furniture covered in rich fabrics. The bed was a massive four-poster, visible in the adjoining chamber, and the wood-paneled walls were recently painted and free from dust and soot. A fire blazed merrily in the hearth—the gilt detailing on the mantel too low in quality for his magic to register it—and seated in front of the flames in a cozy sitting room was surely the man he was here to meet. The other side of the bargain that had landed him here, miles from home, from safety, in the lawless wilds of the Haunted Territory.

The man was decked out in House of Iron colors, his armor gaudy with bloodred accents and spiked embellishments. The shade matched his personal soldiers—the Red Guard according to the locals Leo had overheard on their way in—who were ranged around the room, and he sat comfortably in a high-backed leather chair, his helmet propped on the nearest table.

This could only be the regent of the Iron Citadel.

For now. His ambitions extended beyond the Wall, and Leo was at the heart of them. But he was not there alone. There was the assassination at the fort. The extra horse. Not to mention this town in the middle of the Haunted Territory. This was one tangled plot, and Leo was determined to unravel it.

He had been at it for days, and while he didn't have the whole picture, he thought he was getting close.

It was the captain who had shoved him into the room, and it was he who spoke now. "Stay there and stay quiet," he muttered under his breath, indicating that Leo should remain standing next to the hearth. He yearned, suddenly, for the quiet contempt of Ivan or the sincere honesty of Jakob. But they had been told to remain outside. They weren't privy to the darker details of their mission, which were about to come to the forefront.

At least they'd removed his bag. From the way the regent's dark gaze raked over him, he suspected it was so the man could properly see his face.

"Lord-Smith Francis," the captain said, going down to one knee on the faded carpet, gaze averted.

A small flicker of triumph lit in Leo's breast. He'd suspected that the Lord-Smith Francis who would be "devastated" when he learned of Julian's death and the regent of the Iron Citadel were one and the same. And if that was true, that meant . . .

"We came as quickly as we could," Captain Royce continued. "The prince, as you requested." He gestured to Leo, who had the urge to smile. Or spit. Or drop into a curtsy.

He did none of those things, however. He still had his dignity.

More or less.

The regent's gaze slid over him, past him, and Leo knew *this* was where things would get interesting.

"The Breachfort fought back well enough," the captain continued, swallowing audibly. "But they were too slow to muster a pursuit. Likely they knew a ransom would be forthcoming."

Still, the regent didn't speak.

"As for the other targets," the captain continued, speaking faster now, "we had a slight hiccup."

"A hiccup?"

The captain dared a glance up before looking at the ground again. "Everything went according to plan, until your—"

The regent cleared his throat, cutting off the words, his eyes flicking around the room. Too many ears, too many witnesses.

"Excuse me, my lord. The second target was taken care of, as per your instructions. However, the landscape and the defenders made it difficult to . . ."

"Spit it out, Captain."

"The target went down with an arrow in the neck. Unfortunately, we were unable to recover the body. He fell into some sort of crevasse— a hundred feet deep, at least. And the third target went down with him."

"Dead but with no proof," the regent said, voice flat.

"We have proof, Lord-Smith," Captain Royce said hurriedly. He waved at his co-conspirator, the only other member of the kidnapping team to accompany him to this room, who produced the dented iron-smith helmet.

The regent looked at it, brows raised, but did not take it from the man's outstretched hand. One of his personal guard did instead.

Tension was heavy in the room. It was plain that the helmet was not *sufficient* evidence according to the regent, and furthermore, that the third target was meant to be kidnapped—a prisoner, tied and delivered alongside Leo.

The captain had failed twice over. In fact, he should be kissing Leo's ass for being successfully captured in the first place so the man didn't arrive completely empty-handed. Ungrateful, really.

"I see," the regent said at last. He sighed. "Then it appears our business here is done."

A subtle nod, and then the nearest Red Guard slid a knife across the captain's throat.

Blood spurted across the carpet right before Leo's eyes, while sounds of a further scuffle could be heard behind him, where another Red Guard had descended upon the captain's other man. Leo managed to tear away his gaze from the spreading bloodstain only by closing his eyes, fear tightening his stomach.

The danger he was in truly hit home for the first time. Thus far, it had all seemed an exciting adventure, a puzzle to solve. Suddenly boredom didn't seem so bad.

Silence descended, and the regent's attention fell on Leo once more. "It seems my plans are coming undone," he said, his tone musing. He was clearly a ruthless man—what he had just done had certainly proved that—but also, Leo suspected, a vain one. His choice of armor spoke volumes, as did his flashy guard. He didn't just want power—he wanted to project it. To have others believe it.

Perhaps Leo could use that.

"I don't see it that way," he said, his voice strained. The smell of blood was thick in the air.

The regent's brows shot up—of course he hadn't been talking *to* Leo. He'd merely been talking *at* him, around him, as if he were little more than a piece of furniture that no longer fit inside his room.

Leo was valuable only as long as he was useful. He was useful only as long as he played a part in the regent's plans. He scrambled for an idea.

"Please, Lord-Smith Francis, let me ride back to Port Valor and deliver your terms myself. We can present this entire affair not as a kidnapping but rather as a diplomatic negotiation."

The regent's mouth twisted at the corners, his eyes crinkling in amusement. Leo recognized the look. It was the face his father wore when he found Leo on the entertaining side of ridiculous. Like a dog performing a trick. Fun to watch, perhaps, but not to be taken seriously.

"A diplomatic negotiation, you say?" the regent said easily. "No, I suspect you'd paint a different picture entirely."

"Not if you let me go."

"That would rather defeat the purpose of having taken you in the first place," the regent drawled.

"But at least your requests will be heard."

"Oh, they'll be heard," the regent said softly.

"And," Leo said insistently, panic searing his chest, "I'll be able to help with damage control."

The regent pulled a skeptical face. "Damage control?"

Leo smiled. "As far as I understand it, the Breachsiders are a loyal people. Devoted. I've met quite a few of them on my, uh, *journey*. And to none have they been more devoted than to the Knights. How do you think they'll respond when they learn you ordered their beloved heir *murdered* in order to advance your own ambitions and take what is rightfully his?"

The man's face went abruptly, almost comically blank.

"He was your nephew, I believe?" Leo prompted. It had taken some time, but he had placed the name the other kidnappers mentioned. Lord-Smith Francis was the only son of an old ironsmith family that had ascended in the wake of the Breach, thanks to his sister's marriage. She had borne a daughter to Jonathan Knight, the heir of the House of Iron, before he died and had become stepmother to his son, Julian.

"That won't look good, will it? Weaseled your way into power through your *sister*, then robbed the poor boy of his birthright after his father was brutally murdered fighting for your people during the Uprising. No, you won't come off well, my lord, if you don't mind my saying so. Not well at all."

For the first time, he thought he truly had the regent's attention. The man's expression was dark, a thundercloud, but Leo had managed to surprise him, too. That was information he was not meant to be privy to.

At this point, Leo figured he had nothing to lose.

"You see, your captain failed to mention that I *love* to talk. I figured out your assassination plan days ago, and I've been telling every barmaid, servant, and stableboy who was within earshot ever since. We did do a rather *thorough* tour of the coastal towns, didn't we? They make up, what, ninety percent of the Breachside population? Already that gossip is spreading like the undead across your lands. You may have sought to solidify your rule of this house, but I think you've likely lost it instead."

The regent tilted his head, considering. He stood, taking several lazy steps forward—then cracked Leo across the face with the back of his hand. He wore iron gauntlets, and the blow was enough to knock Leo off his feet. Or it would have been if one of the Red Guard hadn't caught him.

Staggering upright, his ears ringing, Leo wiped a hand across his split lip, his mouth filled with blood. That was going to leave a scar, the bastard.

"You're smarter than you look," the regent said. "I'll give you that."

Leo waited, unsure if he should be offended or not. Unsure if his life was in danger or not.

"As the son of a king, you know the influence of words," the regent continued, moving to stand before the fire, staring into the flames. "Of stories and reputation. But there's something people respond to beyond all that, something that cannot be faked or misconstrued, and it's *power*. Strength. That is how I will solidify my rule, boy, and the House of Iron is only the beginning." He turned to retake his seat but paused. "As for your rumors . . . well, that's all they are, aren't they? I will deny everything, of course, and mourn my nephew deeply—just as I did his father before him."

THIRTY-THREE

Wren had long since stopped trying to see through the gap in the wood. Instead, her attention was fixed wholly and completely on Julian. He sat there, still as a statue, his face illuminated by a single stripe of golden firelight from the room beyond.

There was a lot spinning through her mind, including the idea of *multiple* targets—hadn't the captain said one of them went *down* with the other, like Wren had gone down with Julian?—but the regent's most recent words had caused all the air to leave the cramped closet space.

He made it sound like Julian's father was killed not with his fellow ironsmiths during the Uprising, at the hand of Locke Graven and the Dominion army, but by assassination. That the regent had done the same thing to him as he had done to Julian. Sending him off to fight in order to mask a murder. Only, in the case of Julian, he had failed.

This regent, Julian's own *uncle*—the man who had raised him in the wake of his father's death—was now trying to usurp him. Trying to take away what little he had left. In fact, the man had already taken from him, if Wren was understanding things correctly.

The conversation continued on the other side of the wall, but Julian had started to shake, his entire body trembling with barely checked rage. She had never seen him like this. Never seen him lose control.

It was his face, though, that Wren couldn't look away from.

His eyes were wild, his mouth working, his jaw clenched.

She reached out to him, laying a gentle hand on his arm. She meant to calm him, to remind him that they couldn't be overheard—that he couldn't explode here and now, unless he wanted to give his uncle the chance to finish what he'd started.

But she was too late.

Her fingers had barely brushed the fabric of his coat when a resounding *crack* echoed inside the darkened closet. There was a wooden shelf behind Julian, which he had apparently been clutching in an attempt to get himself under control.

And which he had snapped clean off, reducing the shelf into shards of wood and dust in his hand.

Wren gaped at the surprising show of strength, but there was no time for a proper reaction. The voices on the other side of the wall had gone abruptly silent, then—

"What was that?"

"That wall, over there."

"Next door—"

Julian burst from the closet, striding to the door and sliding the lock into place right before a body slammed into the wood, rattling the knob several times before more shouts echoed down the hall. The wooden door was banded, giving Julian iron to press against in an attempt to hold them off.

Stepping back from the door with his hand still outstretched, he looked over his shoulder at Wren. "Go. Now."

"What?" she said. "I can't leave you here—with him!" She pointed at the room next door, where Julian's would-be murderer held court, surrounded by allies.

"You have to," he said, just as the door rattled on its hinges again. No matter how firm his hold on the iron banding or how strong the lock, if they wanted to get in badly enough, they'd just break through the wood.

"No, I don't," Wren said, her throat tight. "We'll both go. We'll—"

"They'll chase us," he cut in. "If they find me, they'll think I'm alone—you're safe. Please. I want to face him. Take the window and climb up on the roof."

"But what about Leo? The iron revenants?"

Sadness touched his eyes, even as he extended both hands toward the door, fighting against the continued bangs and shouts from the opposite side. His feet were actually starting to slide against the floor, the force of his magic was so strong.

"There's time for *both* of us to get out of here," she insisted. "You didn't leave me in the Breach"—she crossed her arms, planting herself next to him—"so I'm not leaving you."

The look he gave her was one of surprised gratitude, and Wren tried not to let it shake her—both in its sincerity and its suggestion that he *expected* her to cut and run.

He considered her a moment, then seemed to come to a decision. "Okay, open the window," he said, grabbing their bag from the floor and following her, all the while keeping his attention and his magic fixed on the door.

Wren ran to the window, wrenching it open with a blast of frigid air, then climbing onto the sill. Julian reached around her to toss the bag onto the roof, the impact of his armor loud against the tiles.

The door was splintering now, and she was just making room for him on the ledge when Julian reached for the open window. "This is for your own good," he said, and before her brain could catch up, he'd slammed it closed, trapping her outside and him in.

They stared at each other through the pane, Wren's startled breath fogging the glass.

"I'm sorry," he said, sliding the lock in place before turning his back on her and striding toward the door. He withdrew his sword, preparing for a fight, but he wasn't wearing his armor. He was vulnerable.

Frustration climbed up Wren's throat. He was *right there*, but she couldn't reach him. She wanted to scream, to shatter the glass and stand by his side—but how could she, when he was essentially sacrificing himself in order to save her? She couldn't just throw it back in his face. She also couldn't stay here, perched on the windowsill, just waiting to be caught and captured.

Cursing, she hoisted herself onto the drainpipe and out of sight, tears stinging her eyes—tears that had nothing to do with the cold.

She had just landed on the roof tiles when the sound of the door bursting open and slamming against the wall reverberated from below.

She crouched, utterly still, but could hear very little besides shouts and ringing metallic impacts. She lifted her gaze to take in her surroundings—night had fallen, her presence atop the inn unmarked and unnoticeable from anyone below.

She was a ghost, a shadow . . . but she had no idea where to go or what to do.

Julian meant for her to leave—to get out while she could.

It was the smart thing. The logical thing.

But since when had Wren Graven ever done that?

THIRTY-FOUR

Julian was ready to fight. To hurt. To bleed—no, to make *them* bleed, anyone who stood in his way.

Anyone who stood between him and that man.

But when the door burst open, kicked in so hard the wood split, Julian found himself face-to-face with a foe that *couldn't* bleed.

Standing there amid the dust and splintered wood was an iron revenant.

The sight sent a shock wave through him.

Another sin to lay at his uncle's feet.

The figure might have been the one Julian had just seen created, though he couldn't be sure. The iron was plain and unadorned, the style decades out of date. While modern swords like Julian still wore full plate, the armor was fitted and streamlined and didn't technically cover him head to toe, allowing for freer movement. He currently felt naked without it, but there hadn't been time.

He raised his hand on instinct, intending to use his magic to halt the creature's approach, but he knew it would be futile. The size of the suit, the density of the iron . . . It must easily weigh twice what Julian did, which meant he had no chance at slowing it down, never mind stopping it.

He didn't care.

Logic, it seemed, had fled him.

Fuck magic, fuck *logic*—he'd tear the creature apart with his bare hands.

And he tried.

He hacked and slashed, his sword thrusts ruthless and without technique, but no matter where he struck or how hard he swung, his sword ricocheted off the ironsmith plate, leaving little more than a scratch. The armor was thick, thicker than any living person could bear. . . . But that was the *point*, wasn't it? The undead didn't follow the rules of the natural world, and the magic well that powered these iron revenants certainly didn't.

The undead before him took whatever punishment Julian dished out, either knowing that he wouldn't succeed or forced to take it whether it wanted to or not, bound to the orders of others. He suspected it felt no pain, no fear, and even if Julian could pierce its dense iron armor, his sword would be useless against its undead body.

Panting with exertion, Julian finally relented. His rage was in danger of fading in the face of this obstruction, and the result was unwanted clarity. Maybe he *should* have left with Wren when he'd had the chance.

Maybe he was a fool.

Mind racing, he took a step backward, deeper into the room, his gaze darting around the small space. If he could lure it away from the door, he might be able to use his speed to get around it and—

His thoughts—along with his strategies—sputtered out as the revenant moved into the room to pursue him, and a second one filled the empty frame.

Julian's back was against the wall, literally and figuratively.

But this was what he wanted, wasn't it? He didn't want to escape. He wanted to look his uncle in the eye. He wanted to demand answers. But as talented as Julian was, there was no way he could defeat two iron revenants and a full squad of his uncle's personal guard.

If he wanted to face him, he would have to do so as a prisoner.

Heart hammering, Julian lowered his sword in surrender.

The cowards that made up his uncle's Red Guard waited until Julian was subdued by the revenants before they entered the room. Prudent, maybe, but also pathetic. He thought of what Wren would say if she were here. The insults she'd spit. The way she'd throw them a challenging smile, even in defeat.

His stomach twisted. Better that she wasn't here.

His uncle wanted her, for some bizarre reason, and Julian felt nothing but deep satisfaction in denying him that.

His uncle. His *uncle.*

The reality of it finally hit home. This was the man who had raised him, saved him, built him up only to break him back down. The man was a monolith, the foundation upon which Julian's life was built.

The man he thought he'd known. The man he thought he'd *understood,* flaws and all.

Julian understood him, all right. Understood he never should have trusted him in the first place.

The revenants each took one of his arms, holding him in a grip strong enough to bruise. Then one of the Red Guard hastened to disarm him, avoiding his eye. Julian knew these people, had trained with them, walked the same halls as them, had served alongside them.

Did they know what his uncle's orders had been? Even now, did they know the full picture? Or had Francis cooked up some story to justify the action? It wouldn't be the first time.

The revenants increased the pressure on his arms, pulling him forward, and Julian wondered idly whose orders they were actually following. He'd thought only that ghostsmith boy—and Wren, apparently—could command the undead. But maybe the Corpse Queen was real. Maybe Francis wasn't actually calling the shots. Maybe he, too, was a puppet in someone else's game.

Julian thought he was ready to confront his uncle, but as he entered the next room, a cold sweat broke out over his brow, despite the warmth of the fire. Warring emotions battled inside him. He had always feared this man—but he had trusted him, too. Looked up to him. Taken his lessons about strength and sacrifice to heart. Believed him when he said everything he did was for the good of their house.

But Julian was a *part* of that house. Born to be its leader.

And so was his father.

If this man could so easily use them for what they offered and then casually order their deaths, that meant his uncle was less concerned with what was best for their house and more interested in what was best for him.

"Julian," his uncle said, tone incredulous as Julian was pushed to his knees before him. "Thank hammer and sword, you're alive. I—"

"Save it," Julian snapped.

"I don't know what you think you've heard, son, but—"

"Don't call me that," Julian said, voice barely above a whisper. The worst part about all this was that he'd *let* it happen. Welcomed it, even. He'd been young and scared, and so he'd let this man take from him over and over again. Had been grateful for it.

Thank you, Uncle, for taking over the House of Iron.

Thank you, Uncle, for forcing me to be strong.

Thank you, Uncle, for turning me into a weapon . . . whether I wanted to be one or not.

He clenched his fists.

His uncle noticed but made no comment as he turned to one of his guard. "Did you check the room? And the rest on the floor?"

"I came alone," Julian said.

Francis ignored him, keeping his attention on the guard, who confirmed it with a sharp nod. "We're just checking the last of the rooms, Lord-Smith, but no sign of anyone else."

Julian allowed himself a small moment of relief. If Wren got away, it meant not only that she was safe but that she could ensure that the truth of what was happening here didn't remain inside this room. Julian was dubious that anyone from the Dominions gave a damn about him or his house, but they cared about Prince Leopold and the danger he might be in. And if they were smart, they'd see the bigger picture and send aid. Quickly.

His business taken care of, Francis reclaimed his seat in the high-backed chair by the fire.

He was a shrewd man, and like his Red Guard, he'd not bothered himself to get involved with the discovery of a spy in their midst, even though he was an ironsmith and more dangerous than all of them put together—except for the iron revenants. Julian didn't know what they were truly capable of, but judging by the smashed door and their bruising grip, it would be fearsome to behold.

No, Francis was more than happy to let others do his dirty work. Julian had never seen that more plainly than he did now.

"So," his uncle said, fingertips steepled together and all pretense at affection and concern gone. "You tricked Captain Royce and somehow got away unscathed. What of the girl?"

Julian lowered his brow. "Girl?"

He noticed the prince in the room for the first time—he was being held in the corner by two of the Red Guard but had shifted at the mention of Wren. His golden gaze flickered, and Julian knew the prince was listening closely for the answer.

"The bonesmith," his uncle said impatiently. "The one Captain Royce said fell *with* you into some crevasse."

"I expect she's *still* there," Julian said indifferently, "wherever her body landed."

His uncle's eyes fluttered closed, a spasm of anger flashing across his face.

Julian relished the sight. Let the man's disappointment fuel his own emotions.

That's right. All your planning, all your plotting, and you failed.

At least when it came to the present.

"Tell me why," Julian said into the silence. His voice quivered with suppressed emotion.

"Come now, Julian, don't be a fool. Don't be like him."

Don't be like him.

All Julian's life, his uncle had belittled his father. Called him kind but weak. Good but lost. He was a man to be pitied. Honored but never emulated.

Julian was *lucky* that his uncle had been there to pick up the slack. Fortunate that there had been *someone* competent to take the reins.

Julian had never questioned the story. His father, grief-stricken in the wake of his mother's death and the catastrophe of the Breach, had allowed their house to fall into ruin. Even a marriage into a good ironsmith family and a second child had not been enough to save him. He'd marched bravely but recklessly on the front lines during the Uprising. And tragically, but not surprisingly, he'd never come home.

Julian had believed every word and sought to do better. To be better. To be smarter and braver and stronger. Always, it was about strength.

Little did he know, the weakest thing he'd ever done was listen to the man seated before him.

"Jonathan Knight was unfit to rule. He was a blight on our house and had to be removed. We were all but defeated when I stepped in, and now? We're poised for a resurgence."

"On the backs of undead monsters."

"A bit poetic, don't you think? The creatures that were meant to be our undoing bent to our will instead."

"*Her* will, you mean. You certainly don't command them on your own, do you, Uncle?"

"Like every good politician before me, I have cut deals, made plans, and built myself a network of allies. But in the end, I will reign supreme. Which is why, I'm sure you understand, you had to be removed as well. There can only be one head of the House of Iron, and it will be me."

The words caused an icy drop of fear to cut through Julian's burning anger. Because he wasn't the sole heir to his house. He had a sister.

"And what of Becca? Your sister's daughter? Do you intend to kill her, too?"

"Come now, boy. I'm not completely heartless. Rebecca's future will be secured, as will mine. You'll see. Or, well, I suppose you won't."

Julian wanted to believe him when he said Becca wouldn't be harmed, but how could he trust anything the man said? And while his brain puzzled over what he meant when he said her "future will be secured," all those worries fell by the wayside at the final words his uncle had spoken.

He attempted to wrench his arms free from the unforgiving hold of the iron revenants, but they held fast. "So you'll kill me here and now, in cold blood?"

His uncle, who had stiffened at Julian's abrupt movement, settled back in his chair and sighed. "I can tell you've not done much murder in your life, Julian, to use such a phrase. If I killed you in hot-blooded anger, would that make things better? Or worse? Your death will not be without *meaning*. Just because I have purpose does not make me cold. Quite the opposite. I kill because I must."

Julian clenched his jaw in frustration, but before he could figure out what to say or how to reason with the man, one of his guards rushed in.

"Forgive me, my lord, but she's here. Now. Waiting outside."

"She's what?" his uncle snapped, all arrogant superiority gone in an instant, his face pale.

Julian looked between them in shock, then laughed darkly, his nerves frayed beyond caring. "Speak of the devil," he said, smiling savagely. He had long abhorred the idea of this Corpse Queen and the way she haunted his people, but if she was powerful enough to make his uncle sweat, he couldn't help but be glad for her existence.

"What was that you said about reigning supreme? Your master beckons. Better not keep her waiting."

His uncle's mouth tightened in anger. "Gag him. Both of them," he said, speaking to one of his guards before turning to the one who had delivered the message. "Tell her I'll be down at once."

While Julian was gagged and bound and dragged over to the corner with the prince, his uncle ran his hands through his slightly disheveled hair and reached for his helmet.

The Red Guard did the same, preparing to depart. All of them.

Julian looked around, not daring to get excited—and sure enough, while the human soldiers departed and closed the door behind them, the two iron revenants that had hauled him in here remained. They positioned themselves in front of the locked door, still as statues.

Julian turned to Leopold, getting a good look at him for the first time. There were bags under his eyes that certainly hadn't been there before, and his hair was flat and lacking the golden luster he remembered at the Wall. His lip was split from the blow his uncle had delivered, but his gaze was sharp as he took in their situation, his attention lingering on the iron revenants.

Then he started to wiggle, struggling obviously against his binds. Julian glanced at the iron revenants, but they didn't react or make a move to stop him.

The prince noticed. Frowned. He clearly had no idea what they were dealing with. Julian tried to catch his eye, to shake his head in warning, but all at once Leopold seemed to lose interest. His shoulders slumped and his eyes hooded as if in resignation or boredom.

Julian, meanwhile, shifted his focus to his weapons, which were held by one of the revenants. If he could just free his hand, maybe he could summon them. . . .

Before he could do more than twist his wrist fruitlessly, Julian became aware of the prince again. He was moving his jaw around. Julian thought it was just discomfort—his own jaw was starting to throb from the thick gag tied tightly behind his head and stretched between his teeth—but the movement was constant and almost rhythmic.

Then, right before Julian's eyes, the fabric tore in half and Leopold spit the ends out. Seeing Julian's shocked reaction, the prince smiled, wide and brilliant—revealing golden *fangs* as sharp as daggers capped over his teeth.

Leopold glanced over his shoulder, in the direction of the iron revenants, but they remained oblivious.

He turned back to Julian. "Hold still, won't you?" he said casually. Then he *lunged*, clamping his teeth around the edge of Julian's gag near his jaw.

It would appear to the casual observer that Leopold was trying to tear out his throat or, perhaps, drink his blood. But before Julian could react with anything more than stunned shock, he began *to feel* it, the seesawing motion and the way that, fiber after fiber, the gag started to sever.

One last pull and the fabric tore. Julian twisted his head, and the gag fell away.

They stared at each other. "Clever trick," Julian said faintly, more than a little impressed.

"Thanks," the prince panted, leaning against the wall to catch his breath. "Gold's softer than iron. More malleable. I hid these pieces on my back teeth, and when they searched me—rather thoroughly, I might add—they never thought to look there. Then I just had to reshape them. I'm very good with my tongue." He smiled wickedly, and Julian thought of Wren. No wonder these two were friends.

"Unfortunately, it'll be no use against these." He lifted his hands, which were bound in thick rope, knotted tight. "I just can't believe they let me do it," he added, glancing at the iron revenants, who hadn't so much as moved an inch.

"I'm not sure they can see," Julian said, studying them, "or if they have a will of their own."

"What do you mean?" Leopold asked.

Julian gave him a bleak look. "They're undead, encased in iron, and ordered to do another's bidding."

The prince's eyebrows shot up into his hairline. He looked over his shoulder at them again, then turned back to Julian. "Indeed," he said.

"Even untied, we'd have no chance against them," Julian said, feeling desperation seep in. "At least, not by ourselves."

Then, right on cue, the door banged open, and *Wren* stood before them, armored in bones, with black lips and eyes.

"Stop!" she shouted before the iron revenants could do more than turn her way.

And, just as they had in the Breach, they did.

As she moved into the room, Julian swore he saw a flicker of green in her eyes. He thought he'd seen the same thing in the Breach, but just as quickly as it had been there, it was gone again, and he was certain he'd imagined it.

A swell of emotion rose inside his chest. The fear that pierced him whenever Wren used her strange new power paled in comparison to the odd thrill he felt at seeing her there in all her glory, fearless and dangerous and *on his side.*

In an instant she was crouched before them, using Ironheart to cut through their ropes.

She started with his.

"You're here," Julian said blankly.

Wren smirked. "I've never been very good at following instructions." He smiled back, and she turned to Leopold. "Apologies for the delay, Your Highness."

He looked flabbergasted. "You're alive! And you came here . . . for me?"

"And made a right mess of things along the way," she said, tossing a conspiratorial look at Julian as he disentangled himself from his ropes and got to his feet. "We need to get out of here, now."

"But how did you—"

"I'll explain everything once we're free of this place."

Julian reached down to help Leopold to his feet. "The regent's men'll be downstairs," the prince protested, rubbing his sore wrists. "We can't risk going that way."

"We won't," Wren said, sheathing the dagger. "We'll be taking the roof."

"My weapons," Julian said, and Wren spotted them in the iron revenant's grasp. Squaring her shoulders, she walked over. "Give those to me." The words had a strange feeling to them, different from her regular speech—some subtle pitch or tone that Julian couldn't quite put his finger on. There was a pause, and then the revenant held out the weapons. Wren grabbed the bundle and heaved it across the room, to Julian's open arms. Relief swept through him at their familiar weight and feel. As he moved to follow Wren, he spotted his dented helmet sitting on a side table. He snatched it up.

Wren had reached the balcony doors and was flinging them wide, just in time for Julian to stride through. It felt good to be working together again. It felt right.

"Come on," Wren called over her shoulder, as Julian put a foot on the balcony railing for leverage and leapt onto the roof. When he looked down, Wren was offering the prince a foothold while Julian reached down for him. He hefted Leopold onto the tiles next to him before turning back to help Wren.

"Stay here," she said into the room, giving the revenants a final order before closing the doors and gripping Julian's hand. He stood as he lifted her, drawing her all the way up to her feet. "Oof," she gasped, somewhat surprised, and Julian had never wanted to kiss her more. But that was a bad idea. He'd told her as much.

It was a bad idea because he'd lose himself to it. To *her*. Like his father had done.

But that was his uncle talking, wasn't it?

Maybe the only way he would *lose* was if he let her go.

"Where to?" Leopold asked, cutting into the moment.

Wren released Julian's hand, looking flustered. "We can cross over the alley to the next building," she said, pointing to the other side of the sloping roof.

"Hang on," Julian muttered, digging into their bag and hastily donning his armor. He added his dented helmet, making a mental note to repair the damage as soon as possible.

When he was ready, Wren led the way, up the peak of the roof and back down again. The building next door was level to this one— a quick jump was all it would take to get them across.

Julian was already taking several steps backward, preparing for a running leap, when voices echoed up from the street below. He skittered to a halt.

"Your Majesty," came the unmistakable sound of his uncle's voice.

He looked to the others. Then all three of them threw themselves down onto the tiles, creeping to the edge of the roof on their stomachs.

His uncle stood at the mouth of the alleyway, his Red Guard ranged around him, while opposite stood a woman, tall and veiled, surrounded by gleaming iron revenants.

THIRTY-FIVE

Wren sensed them before she saw them—the presence of the undead. Ever since the Breach, her magic was powerful, *vivid*, and her new-found abilities continued to linger. She feared they'd disappear at any moment while secretly hoping they *would*, that she could go back to being a regular smith and an excellent valkyr.

With Leo and Julian on either side of her, she took in the scene below.

The regent and his guards. A woman, draped in a black veil and surrounded by at least a dozen iron revenants.

The rumors, however limited, didn't do her justice.

Yes, she wore a veil, but it was no maidenly shroud. The fabric was jagged and uneven, trailing to the ground and nearly opaque, giving only the vaguest sense of a face, a person, beneath. And atop her head? There was a crown, made of twisted, broken bones—a sick parody of the champion's wreath Inara had won during the Bonewood Trial—punctured at irregular intervals with the same dark spikes that pierced Wren's ring, creating a haunting halo. When she moved, she sounded like a revenant—bones shifting and clacking together—but they weren't her own. Bright in Wren's senses but barely visible through the veil were bracelets and necklaces, pieces of pale bone flashing like scraps of moonlight on inky black waters.

"It's her . . . ," Wren whispered, mostly to herself.

"The Corpse Queen," said Leo, his expression intent.

"Forgive me," the regent continued, though his voice held no contrition, "but I thought we had agreed to meet *outside* the walls?" He glanced around, at the street behind him, where people huddled together or poked their heads out windows and doorways, watching and whispering.

"We agreed on many things, Regent." Her voice . . . it reminded Wren of the boy's—low and rasping—but there was an edge to it, a sort of rawness that grated against her skin, making it tingle. "Where is my prize? I will not grant you continued use of my iron revenants without it."

What prize? She couldn't mean Leo, could she?

The regent's expression turned cold. "They wouldn't be *iron* revenants without me, my lady."

"I'm not a lady. I'm a queen."

"Rule you may, but not over me."

There was a note of amusement in her voice when she replied. "Nor you over me, Regent. You know why I am here. It's time for you to uphold your end of the bargain. We cannot proceed without her."

Her? Both Leo and Julian turned to look at Wren, and she was reminded of the conversation between the regent and the captain. The third target.

Wren didn't know what "proceed" meant, but she could only

assume it had something to do with that boy, the legions of undead . . . and the fact that Wren could command them, the same as him.

"I'm afraid we'll have to. I don't have her. You'll need to find another way—"

"*She* is the only way."

"She's dead," he snapped back. "Somewhere near the fort. It's over."

The woman took a slow step forward, bones rattling. The regent's men tensed but didn't act—the iron revenants loomed large and threatening without moving a single rotted muscle.

"Death is not the end."

A collective shiver went through the entire group, as if an icy breeze had blown down the alleyway, though there wasn't a hint of a wind. Even Wren felt it.

"We'll find you another bonesmith," the regent said reasonably. "There are hundreds west of the Wall."

"It is her, or it is no one," the queen said, complete and utter conviction in her voice. Wren thought again of that messenger in the Bonewood, the ring in her pocket. . . . What if this was not the first time the queen had come calling for her?

One of the Red Guard moved from the back of the group to the regent's side and whispered in his ear. Wren feared their escape had been detected, but the regent nodded and turned to the queen.

"I've requested a private parlor at the inn. It's ready. Why don't we step inside and discuss a solution that suits us both?"

"Why don't you step inside *alone*, Regent, and think of a solution yourself. I'll be taking my revenants with me, and you'll have no further use of them until I am satisfied."

She turned on her heel, walking away from the regent—whose

expression tightened with frustrated rage—into the shadows of the alley and away from the main street.

Thus far Wren had only been able to see the side of the queen's head, but now she caught a glimpse of the face—or rather, the impression of a face behind the veil. Wren kept telling herself that the woman wasn't *actually* a corpse; she just commanded them. But she couldn't shake the uneasy feeling that the sight of the woman gave her.

Especially when her gaze flicked up to the rooftop and landed squarely on Wren. Her eyes were visible through the fabric, shining an even more shocking shade of green than the ghostsmith boy's, and they bored into her.

Fear pierced Wren's gut, rooting her to the spot.

She expected the woman to stop, to point or cry out . . . but she kept moving. When at last she looked away, it was to turn her head slightly and speak to one of the iron revenants. It halted in its tracks, while the rest continued. It didn't crane its head or look her way, but it didn't need to. When it spoke, the words echoed as loudly and clearly as if they'd come from inside Wren's own mind. And they might as well have, because no one else could hear them.

"*Come to me when you are ready to know more. Come to us. I know you feel it. Blood calls to blood and like to like.*"

And then it walked away.

Wren stared, unseeing, at where it had stood until Julian touched her arm.

"You ready?" he asked, and she blinked, realizing the iron revenant had gone and the alleyway was empty. The regent had returned to the inn—he'd discover their disappearance in no time. They had to move.

They leapt the gap between buildings, climbed down a trellis, and made for the exterior wall.

"We should take horses," Leo panted, trying to keep up with them as they ducked between buildings and ran past the glow of lantern lights.

"Even if we managed to steal them, how do you propose we get out of here?" Julian asked. "If we reveal ourselves at the gate, we're finished."

Leo cursed. "They'll find us. We'll never outrun them."

"Maybe we won't need to . . . ," Wren said, glancing back toward the inn. "When do you suppose they'll discover our absence?"

"Imminently," Julian said.

"And then what?"

He considered. "Well, they won't know which way we've gone, which means they'll have to check everywhere. They'll search the inn, the rest of the town, plus send riders out both gates. He won't want to risk his men in the Haunted Territory at night, but he won't have much of a choice."

"That's a lot of ground to cover," Wren said thoughtfully. "He'll have to split them up."

Julian's face changed—he saw where she was going with this. She'd known he would. "He has, what, twenty Red Guard with him? And ten extra soldiers from the kidnapping party. Without the iron revenants at his disposal, he'll keep six, minimum, to protect himself. Of the rest, he'll need . . . at least twenty to properly search this place, even if the locals help. There are too many buildings, streets, and dark corners. Plus the walls themselves will need to be checked."

"So that leaves four?" Leo said.

Julian nodded. "He'll divide them, send two riders out each gate."

"Three against two," Wren said with a smirk. "I like those odds."

"Are we counting on me in a fight?" Leo asked delicately, brows raised. He pressed his fingers to his lip, which was starting to scab over. "I'm not much by way of a warrior."

"I think Julian's helmet might disagree," Wren said.

Leo beamed, but Julian narrowed his eyes, annoyed at the reminder. "You might not be a fighter," he said, "but you'll make excellent bait."

Leaving the way they had come, they were scaling the outer wall of town when a commotion outside the inn told them their time had run out. The Red Guard could be seen spilling out onto the streets, orders barked and soldiers sent this way and that. It would take time to saddle horses, but it wouldn't be long until the gates opened and they were searching the roads.

Hurrying toward the southern gate, Wren cast her senses wide, but she couldn't detect the iron revenants or any other undead in the vicinity. Still, their presence, along with the Red Guard, could lure any number of ghosts or revenants, so she drew her swords and kept herself alert.

Julian, meanwhile, scanned the landscape for a likely location for an ambush.

He eventually found a bend in the road where the ground dipped on either side, giving them darkened ditches to hide in—Julian on one side of the road, Wren and Leo on the other.

A part of her realized that a few short days ago, she'd have taken the prince and run, to hell with Julian and the Red Guard.

It might have worked, for a time, though they'd struggle to survive on their own and their pace would be laughable. She'd have seen it as a challenge, a chance to prove something.

But after everything she'd been through, she realized that would have been shortsighted, rash, and just plain stupid. Horses were their best shot at making it back to the fort . . . and having Julian by her side would only speed things along.

They had actually done it. They had rescued the Gold Prince. They had *also* discovered a larger plot that made her petty goals and Julian's personal vendetta pale in comparison, but they had done what they'd set out to do.

The question of what would happen now was far harder to grapple with. Julian wasn't just an ironsmith—he was Julian Knight, *heir* to their house. They couldn't show up at the fort with him—the commander would have him in a cell in the blink of an eye. Even if they kept his identity a secret . . . he'd been seen during the kidnapping. He was guilty, regardless of what had happened afterward. And when Wren told them about the regent's plot and the iron revenants, it would put Julian in *greater* danger. But she *had* to tell them, right?

"So, bonesmiths and ironsmiths, working together to save a goldsmith prince?" Leo said conversationally, as if they weren't huddled in the haunted dark, waiting to ambush a pair of highly trained warriors. "Last time I saw you two, you were—"

"Trying to kill each other, yes."

"And now? You're . . . friends?"

"Allies," Wren corrected shortly.

"Kissed and made up, have you?" Leo asked with a quirk of his lips. Wren opened her mouth, then shut it—which was surely damning enough. His smirk split into a full-faced grin. "*Really?* I get it, truly, but . . . *wow.*"

Wren closed her eyes. "Shut up, idiot. Our lives are on the line here."

"Yes, of course," he said, and she looked at him in time to see his expression turn gravely serious. "Dangerous. *Thrilling*, even." His eyebrows waggled.

"If we make it through this night, I'm going to murder you myself."

"I missed you too."

Across the road, Julian waved a hand, then pointed in the direction of the gate. It was creaking open, and the silhouettes of two riders could be seen exiting the glow of the town beyond. The gate shut, and they disappeared, save for the steady clatter of horses' hooves.

The plan was simple.

They'd wait until the riders were within sight, and then Leo would stumble out onto the road, flagging them down. Wren and Julian would take care of the rest.

When the time came, Leo performed his part well—almost too well, as far as Wren was concerned. He staggered into the path of the horses, crying out helplessly and waving his arms like a true damsel in distress.

The nearer rider halted and leapt from the saddle, and that was when Wren and Julian struck.

While he targeted the still-mounted rider, she tackled the guard who was on his feet, colliding with him from behind.

A handful of bonedust had him choking and stumbling, and then between her and Leo, they held his arms from his weapons long enough for Wren to pull Julian's knife on him and press it to his throat.

Julian handled the other guard by himself, the man sprawled and unconscious in the dirt, before chasing down the startled horse. After a glance at Wren, Leo did the same, soothing the other and guiding it back to their side.

They tied the soldiers together, leaving them to stumble back to

Caston and admit their defeat. By the time they arrived and were let in, Wren and the others would have a good head start—plus, they didn't intend to take any roads, which meant finding them again would be nearly impossible.

As they checked the horses and ditched any unnecessary items, Wren registered the fact that there were only two mounts and three riders. *Someone* would always have to ride double, and she would be damned if it was only her. The image of Leo and Julian riding together flitted into her mind, and she was determined to make it so.

That being said, they needed to get a jump on things, and as Julian was leading the way, she offered to ride with the prince for the first leg of their trek.

"Are you sure *you two* don't want to ride together?" Leo asked innocently, and Julian cast a curious—maybe even suspicious—look over his shoulder. "Since you're, ah, *better acquainted* and all?"

Julian flushed.

Leo grinned.

Wren punched him on the shoulder, and he laughed.

THIRTY-SIX

Their journey *away* from Caston went much faster than their journey toward it, thanks to the horses, of course, but also the lack of detours like being set upon in the woods or falling into the Breach.

Leo *did* have a moment of panic when he realized what route they were taking, however.

"Wait—we're cutting *through* the Haunted Territory?" he'd demanded before leveling Wren a curious, appraising sort of look. He didn't fully understand her apparent control over the undead, though he had witnessed it with those iron revenants.

"It'll be fine," Wren had promised, and he'd taken her at her word, though his shrewd expression told her she'd have to explain herself eventually.

When hours passed without any undead crossing their path, he relaxed a little, though their absence actually made Wren feel *more* tense. Had the queen summoned them to her side? Were they gathering to mount some sort of attack? Or was it something to do with

Wren herself? Did she repel them, or did they sense her desire to be left alone and obeyed her even without words?

Julian had pushed them hard to the tree line, and now they traveled along its edges. He looked at Wren. "Is it safe, do you think?"

He obviously wanted to disappear into the forest before the sun rose in case any Red Guard managed to follow their trail. He seemed okay, despite everything that had just happened and all he had discovered. He *looked* different, though, with his helmet back on. More like the enemy she had fought *against*, not the ally she'd come to fight *with*. She focused on the dent, on the proof of passing time and shifting allegiances.

She hadn't been able to overhear the conversation between him and his uncle in that room, but maybe Leo would tell her about it. Or maybe she should let Julian share, if he wanted to. Whatever the case, he appeared more determined than ever to get the prince away from the man.

"As safe as anywhere," she said, looking around. "I don't sense anything, which either means there's nothing nearby or I've lost whatever boost of power that well gave me."

"Boost of power?" came Leo's voice, slightly slurred and reverberating into Wren's back. He'd fallen asleep hours ago.

She jumped, startled. "I'll explain later," she muttered.

Brow furrowed in thought, Julian edged his horse closer. He leaned forward in the saddle, reaching for Wren—or rather, for one of the throwing blades she kept in her bandolier. After testing the weight—bone was lighter than iron—he turned and flung it end over end somewhere into the trees. It landed with an echoing *thump*.

He tilted his head at her. "Can you find it?"

He was trying to test her range, and it was as good an idea as any.

She would normally lose track of a bone weapon if it was farther than ten feet or so.

But not only could she sense the knife—easily *twenty* feet away—but with her hand outstretched, she summoned it back, yanking it from the wood and catching it deftly as it whipped through the air.

"Impressive," Julian said. "I think we're good to stop here for now."

Rather than seek out another watchtower, which would keep them protected but also *trap* them should any Red Guard or undead descend—to say nothing of the danger the horses would be in—they camped in a hollow ditch beneath a massive fallen tree, the roots providing cover for themselves and the horses.

Julian got the fire going while Wren cobbled together a meal with whatever rations she could find in the saddlebags. Leo, meanwhile, wrapped himself in a blanket and curled up next to the flames.

Julian raised his brows. "Don't strain yourself, Your Highness."

Leo cracked a single eyelid. "I don't intend to."

"Clearly not. We're all tired; the least you could do is help."

"While you two were *chumming around* for the past week," Leo drawled, eyes closed again, "I was *alone*. There was no one to watch my back, so I didn't sleep. I didn't rest."

Julian caught Wren's gaze over the fire, and she had to admit that while their travel was far from uneventful, they'd had each other. She'd hardly call it "chumming around," but she saw his point. Especially when you took the kissing into consideration.

"So, excuse me for taking advantage of the current circumstances.

And believe me," Leo added, shifting into a more comfortable position, "I'll be plenty helpful when we arrive at the Breachfort—if you want to keep your head, that is."

Wren rolled her eyes, but he wasn't wrong. They'd need Leo's testimony to keep Julian from a prison cell. Or worse.

As Leo nodded off, she and Julian ate together in silence.

"Speaking of the Breachfort," he said after a while, using a stick to poke the flames.

"You won't lose your head," Wren said with more certainty than she felt. She was staring at his helmet, which he'd removed and rested against their packs.

"No—it's not that." He frowned, expression thoughtful. "We can't take him to the Breachfort, Wren."

She'd been expecting this from the moment they'd set out together. But after the regent had been exposed, she'd thought he might see reason.

"We need to report"—she waved a hand—"all this. We can't fight them by ourselves."

Julian tilted his head at her. "What happened to the girl who was convinced we could cross the Breach and rescue a kidnapped prince all on our own?"

"This is different," she said defensively. He sounded disappointed in her, and she hated how much she cared about that.

"How?" he demanded.

"Back then I thought I knew everything there was to know about the undead. I have since been proven wrong—repeatedly. We're in over our heads. The Breachfort will help us."

Julian stared broodingly into the fire. "I'm not so sure they will."

"What's that supposed to mean?"

"Not only are they the same people who have refused to help us Breachsiders for the past *two decades*, but I think you're forgetting how this all started."

"I believe it started when you attacked the Wall and kidnapped a prince?"

"It started before that, Wren. We were tipped off. Didn't you ever wonder how we turned up out of nowhere, perfectly positioned to kidnap him? We were told exactly where to be and when."

Wren *did* recall some strange details from that day—the blockage on the road, for starters, and the way she had so easily gotten the prince alone. "You're saying there's an informant?"

Julian nodded. "Inside the prince's own retinue. He won't be safe there."

Wren looked down at Leo, then back up at Julian. "What would you suggest, then?" she asked warily.

"I say we circle back north," he replied, speaking carefully. "They'll assume we're riding to the Breachfort, won't they? So heading in the *opposite* direction will be the last thing they'll expect."

"North," Wren said flatly. "You mean, toward the Iron Citadel?"

"No," he said hurriedly. "Just somewhere we can lie low and stay safe until the regent stops his search."

"And where would that be?"

"We could use my mother's family estate. It's currently unoccupied except for a few servants. We could regroup, rest, and figure out our next move."

"A *family* estate? Surely they'll look for you there."

"My people will protect us."

"Your people? Wasn't *the regent* one of 'your people' up until yesterday? And what about Captain Royce before that? You're asking me to put trust in the people who caused this mess in the first place."

He tugged at his breastplate in agitation. "No, I'm asking you to put trust in me. You've done it before."

"It's not the same thing," Wren said, ignoring the twinge in her stomach at the memory of their time at the Breach. "No way am I taking Leo anywhere near 'your people.'"

His nostrils flared. "Is this still about you and your golden prize? Your stupid mission to prove yourself? You already have, Wren! If they don't see that, that's on them."

Wren looked down, struggling to hide the emotion she felt at his words. He made it sound so easy. Like what others thought of her didn't matter. And she wanted it to be true . . . but it wasn't. It *did* matter. It was how she'd lost Ghostbane and wound up banished from her home.

But it was also how she'd wound up here, with him.

"Look," he continued, "all I'm saying is, if we hand the prince over to the Breachfort, then we did all this for nothing. You said you care about him. But if you bring him back there, you plainly only care about yourself."

"Fuck you," Wren spat.

Julian bit down on a retort, glowering into the flames. Wren did the same.

She *did* care about Leo. She wanted him safe, and surely the Breachfort was safer than *anywhere* east of the Wall, even with a spy in their midst? Wren would just stick close to Leo's side until . . . until he was shipped off somewhere else and she was forced to remain behind? And Julian . . . Who knew what would become of Julian at the fort.

But Wren would have pulled off the impossible. She would be praised. Rewarded. What that would mean, she couldn't know for certain, but she had to try, didn't she?

"It's more than that," Julian said, his voice quiet but fervent. "We're not finished here. Those iron revenants, the undead . . . There's more work to do in the Haunted Territory. We make a good team."

"A good team?" Wren repeated, arching an eyebrow. "I thought you said *we* were a 'bad idea'?"

"Aren't we?" he said, meeting her gaze.

Wren shrugged, going for indifference. "Maybe I like bad ideas."

He looked away. He appeared frustrated, like he was fighting some internal battle with himself. "It's not—this can't end well. For either of us."

There it was, another rejection. Wren didn't reply because she didn't know how. She wanted to argue—it was what they were best at—but to do so would be to reveal how much it mattered to her. How much she cared.

So she said nothing.

He stood, scooping up his helmet. "I'll take the first watch."

He stalked through the trees, and Wren threw herself down next to Leo. As she did so, she glanced at his face—his eyes open and reflecting the firelight.

They headed out again in the afternoon. They'd reached a stalemate regarding their destination, but their path would be the same over the next day or so, regardless of where they went. They couldn't head east—the Coastal Road and populated towns would be crawling with the regent's men—so they had to backtrack west, skirting the

Haunted Territory in order to either head south again toward the fort or north toward Julian's proposed hideout.

Wren had been itching to talk to Leo ever since she'd awoken, but when they left camp, Julian offered to walk—depriving Wren both of the sight of him and Leo pressed together in the saddle *and* the chance to speak to the prince in private.

The ground was sloping and uneven, slowing their progress, but it would also slow their pursuers if any picked up their trail.

Since they were avoiding the deep forest, they found themselves walking along the banks of a familiar river. Julian proposed they should camp at the old mill again, and after they made the crossing and it came into view, the sight of it was strangely off-putting. They'd been here mere days ago, but it felt like a lifetime. So much had changed.

Wren did a cursory look around for any undead while Julian gathered wood and Leo tended the horses.

With Julian crouched in front of the stove, working on starting the fire, Wren saw her chance.

"I need to get cleaned up," she announced, making her way to the river. The sun had disappeared beyond the western hills, but the narrow valley still clung to some vestiges of sunlight.

"Agreed," Leo said, leaving the horses tied up and moving toward the house. "And a comb through that hair wouldn't go awry, either."

Wren didn't break her stride as she took hold of his arm and pulled him with her. "You're coming too."

The water was icy as she crouched in the shallows and splashed it on her face. She looked back at the house, and while Julian was nowhere in sight—and certainly out of earshot—it didn't mean they had long.

"Look, I don't know what you heard earlier, but—"

"Are you going to break my heart and tell me I'm *not* a golden prize?" he asked. "I thought it was a rather endearing way of putting it. Better than 'bargaining chip' or 'hostage,' don't you think?"

Wren sighed. "That's not—"

"It's okay," Leo said, his expression earnest for once. "Regardless of your motives, you've saved my life. Both of you—though he didn't come around until someone tried to kill *him*. So, I mean, between the two of you . . . you're definitely the more altruistic."

Wren laughed. "Low bar."

Leo shrugged. "Keep the bar low enough, and you're never disappointed."

Wren's laughter faded, and she glanced over her shoulder again. "He wants to keep you here, east of the Wall. He said there was an informant at the Breachfort, but I don't know who."

"I do."

Wren straightened. "What?"

He gave her a strange look. "Julian's not the only one who knew I was going to be kidnapped."

Wren gaped. "*You* knew?"

He stared out across the river. "I found letters in Galen's pack."

"Galen, your cousin?"

"Indeed. He was paid—quite handsomely, I might add—to keep certain parties apprised of my whereabouts and to deliver me defenseless east of the Wall." He paused, looking contemplative. "I didn't know who would be doing the kidnapping, though I could guess, considering where we were. I also didn't know who was paying him, but I've been trying to figure it out ever since."

"Who would have something to gain by it?" Wren asked. "Commander Duncan, maybe?"

"Not sure his family is wealthy enough to buy Galen, and besides, being kidnapped on his watch only hurts him, even if he thought he might make the Breachfort relevant again."

"Maybe someone else at the fort?" Wren mused.

Leo hesitated. "I did consider the other bonesmith in residence— what was her name?"

"Odile," Wren said, and apprehension landed in her gut. "But why . . . ?" Even as she said it, reasons flitted through her mind. She was *from* east of the Wall and had hated what the Dominions did during the Uprising. Maybe she thought she could finally bring the conflict to an end. But handing over a prince to traitors and rebels could easily mean *more* death—she had to know that. It also meant that, since there was meant to be a second kidnapping, she had set up *Wren*, too. . . .

Had it all been fake? Every kind word and piece of advice? Or had their bond been real, despite what the woman had felt compelled to do? Wren didn't know which was worse, that Odile might have played at being a friend and mentor from the start or that her feelings had been true . . . and she had betrayed Wren anyway.

There was also the matter of Locke Graven and the well. That *must* be how he got the magic to do what he did on that battlefield. Which meant Odile had *been* there—Wren's father, too—and they had decided to bury the truth. What other information had they kept hidden from the world?

From Wren?

"Any conflict east of the Wall would certainly move her up the ranks," Leo continued, unaware of Wren's spiraling thoughts. "But the question then becomes: How much did this person know? It's one thing to facilitate an exchange of lands or dispensation to settle in the Dominions for a political hostage and quite another to support whatever the regent and that queen are up to. I doubt they've gone through all the work of making those iron revenants for an empty threat alone."

"So you think they want a war, no matter what might have happened with you?"

"We don't know for sure if I was meant to be a hostage at all. . . . There are other ways to use a prince."

They were both lost in their own thoughts for a moment, until Leo spoke again.

"I must admit, I thought *you* might be a part of it too," he said, darting a wary, apologetic glance her way. "Your family certainly has the funds, and the timing makes sense. . . . But then we spoke together, and drank together, and, well, when those kidnappers descended—*you* were there defending me." Wren tried to muster a smile, but she couldn't shake his earlier words about Odile. His tone grew more serious as he continued. "And then you actually chased me down, risking your life to save mine. It means more to me than I can possibly say."

"You're welcome," Wren said, though her mood was still dark. If someone at the Breachfort—Odile or otherwise—*was* to blame, then was Julian right that they shouldn't return?

"And there is, of course, the fact that you were apparently a kidnapping target too. So I'm fairly confident that exonerates you, if not Odile."

Wren's heart was heavy. "She *did* manipulate things to ensure I was the one on your patrol." In fact, she had pushed Wren onto Leo from the start—allegedly for Wren's benefit, but clearly there had been other forces at work.

"I see," Leo said softly.

"But she couldn't have known," Wren protested. "The whole reason this queen wants me . . ." She hesitated. "Remember that boost of power I mentioned? When Julian and I were in the Breach, there was this well there. A font of magic. We saw a boy draw upon it— his whole body glowed with it—and *he* made those iron revenants. I don't know how long he'd been drawing on it, because he could control the revenants before we saw him at the well. I got a brief exposure to it, but . . ."

"You can do the same," Leo finished, having seen it firsthand.

"But I've never done anything like that before," Wren said quickly.

"Maybe the queen just needed a bonesmith, and there you were," he said, though his expression was skeptical. They had both heard what the queen had said when the regent proposed a replacement: *It is her, or it is no one.* Then, later, she had spoken to Wren alone via the iron revenant next to her. *Blood calls to blood and like to like.*

"Maybe," Wren hedged uneasily, kicking at some stones and sending them splashing into the river. She had the urge to touch the ring again but didn't want to have to explain it to Leo. Or to think about it herself.

Leo laughed darkly. "So it seems that, by returning to the fort, we're putting ourselves at the mercy of our betrayers once more?"

"Or," Wren said, whirling around to face him, "putting *them* at our mercy instead."

Leo frowned, arms crossed. "Elaborate."

"They don't know that *we* know," Wren said, thinking out loud. "And even though we *do* know—or have a good guess—we don't really know *why*. We don't know the endgame. But maybe we could. So we show up, tired and grateful to be back, to be 'safe,' and meanwhile we dig and question and forage for answers. You with Galen, me with Odile. By the time we're through, we'll have what we need to make a better decision." And maybe enough for Wren to understand who she was and where she fit into all this.

"I'll need Galen's letters," Leo said, nodding. "I can't prove anything without them. If he has any sense, he'll have destroyed them by now—but there might be fresh correspondence. New leads." He looked at her. Shrugged. "I'm willing to let this whole charade play out a little longer."

Despite the adrenaline pumping through her veins, Wren had to ask. "Are you *sure*?" She may have been a target, too, but Leo was the one who was *actually* kidnapped. His betrayer had succeeded where Wren's had failed. They might just be pushing Galen and Odile to more drastic measures.

Leo cast his gaze out over the water. "I suspect I am in danger no matter where I go. At least my dear cousin will have to pretend relief at my rescue and play nice for a while—until he can come up with a new scheme. That will buy us some time."

"You wouldn't rather stay east of the Wall? With Julian?"

"What? Of course not," he scoffed, turning away from the water, and relief washed through her. "I'd rather be alone among the wolves I know than alone among those I don't."

"You won't be alone. You'll have me."

He smiled then, wide and true, before glancing toward the house. "What about him?"

Julian. Maybe she was every bit as selfish as Julian had suggested, wanting to drag him there when there was no benefit for him at all. More than that, it was dangerous.

"I'll speak up for him if I can," Leo said, "but he attacked the Wall.

His people killed ours. I don't think he'll walk away from this. Just being an ironsmith will be enough to condemn him, never mind the fact that he's Julian *Knight*, heir to their house."

Wren knew he was right. Julian would certainly be imprisoned. Questioned. Punished, maybe. And then what? Wren *and* Leo could argue for him all they wanted, but while the prince's word would certainly carry weight, Wren's was decidedly less important. Depending on who you asked, her support might just make things worse for Julian.

She couldn't subject him to that.

But things were equally dangerous for him here, weren't they? His own uncle had ordered his death. Julian might think his mother's estate was safe . . . but was it? And what could he really do? Hole up there alone, indefinitely?

But he didn't *want* to go alone, did he? He wanted Wren and Leo to go with him.

Wren had her uses, especially with her newfound abilities, and Leo was Julian's only scrap of leverage. He needed to wrest control from his uncle, and even if he didn't intend to ransom Leo himself, it was in his best interest to ensure that the regent didn't do so, either.

She suspected Julian would fight tooth and nail to keep Leo away from his uncle or those who were in cahoots with him—like Galen and possibly Odile.

The way she saw it, her options were to either insist upon the Breachfort, all the while waiting for Julian to make a move and betray her . . . or to betray him first. At least, that's the way *he'd* see it. In actuality, she'd be *protecting* him. But she knew he wouldn't thank her for it.

The idea of deceiving him made her stomach twist, but it was for the best. Wren and Leo would get their answers at the fort, and Julian would retreat to the safety of his mother's estate.

She didn't have to hurt him or turn him over to his murderous uncle.

This can't end well. For either of us.

She just had to leave him behind.

THIRTY-SEVEN

After they returned to the mill house, they ate in silence and settled in for a few hours of sleep.

This time Wren offered to take the first watch. She couldn't sleep even if she wanted to.

As Julian lay down, his back facing the room, Wren and Leo stared at each other. Were they really going to do this? They had to, didn't they? Not just for their own sakes, but for Julian's too. He needed to get to safety, and he would find none at the fort.

Really, she was helping him—making the decision *for* him so he didn't risk his life trying to keep his grip on Leo at the expense of his own well-being.

And despite what had happened between them the past few days, they were not friends. Not really. They were each other's only life raft in a storm, but the storm was over, and they were back on solid ground. For now.

No, they weren't friends. They weren't anything.

So why was this one of the hardest things Wren had ever faced? As she waited for sleep to claim him, her mind refused to settle.

Strangely, it wasn't Julian that she found herself dwelling on, though. It was the idea of going back to the Breachfort.

It had been her goal from the start, the destination for her triumphant return—and here she was, on the brink of delivering the prince, yet the victory felt flat and hollow.

Her vision of the future—praised by her father and her house and lauded as a talented valkyr—was hazy, the image dull and lifeless compared to the thrill and danger of her recent days spent east of the Wall. Every moment here was seared into her skin, vivid and visceral.

The fact was, she was not the same person she had been when she'd left. She reached into her pocket, intending to touch the ring— but stopped herself.

Yes, she was changed magically. But also mentally.

She had been out in the real world for the first time in her life. That was why she'd wanted to be a valkyr so desperately—to actually *leave* Marrow Hall and travel the Dominions. To battle the undead. To challenge herself and to *win*.

Never in her life had she imagined a challenge quite like the Breach, and a part of her hated the idea of leaving it all behind. Unfinished, like Julian had said. There were questions that needed answering, but surely some of those answers waited for her at the fort? From Odile, certainly, and maybe, eventually, her own father.

The problem was, things were more complicated than they had ever been. When she'd left, she'd just wanted to be a valkyr, to make her family proud. To belong.

Now she feared the truth would make that impossible.

What she had to decide was if the truth was worth giving that up . . . and if that was something she still wanted anyway.

Wren added a new log to the fire, the stove's door screeching in response to being opened, but Julian didn't move.

She looked at Leo again, and he nodded.

Quietly, he stood and slipped out the door.

Wren, meanwhile, unearthed the length of rope she'd found in one of the horse's saddlebags. She closed her eyes for a moment, bracing herself.

She'd only get one shot at this.

Moving carefully, she stepped around Julian's sleeping body, searching for his hands. They weren't conveniently together, laid out before her and ready to be bound.

One was above his head, the other under his cheek. He continued to wear his gloves, a mystery she had yet to solve.

Wren blew out a breath. This would be harder than she'd thought.

First she wrapped the rope around one of the load-bearing beams that ran down the center of the room.

Next she went for his outstretched hand, slipping it through the loosened knot she had already made in the rope. A sharp pull would tighten it. She caught sight of his good luck bracelet and had to look away, the guilt like bile in her belly.

The other hand was where the real challenge would begin. In order to tie it up, she'd have to slide it out from under his face. She crouched before him, then, seeing an opportunity, she threw a leg over his body, thinking she could nudge him slightly, onto his back, releasing the hand.

She'd only just managed to get into position, her body suspended over his, their faces inches apart, when his eyes snapped open.

He startled, his gaze foggy with sleep, until he blinked away his confusion and truly saw her.

Straddling him.

His expression changed, his body shifting subtly from rigid surprise to tension of a different sort. Something anticipatory.

Wren did the only thing she could do. She kissed him.

His mouth opened for her, eager, like last time—but there was an underlying darkness, a desperation that Wren was certain hadn't been there before. Was it coming from her, knowing this was the beginning of the end, or did he, too, sense that this would be the last time?

As she pressed herself against him, Wren fumbled with the rope, managing to slip his slackened hand through the knot just in time. He reached for her face—or tried, his hand coming up against the restraint, tightening it with his own movement.

His eyes bugged out, and he broke the kiss just as Wren leapt back from him. She tugged on the other end of the rope as she went, securing his second hand. He struggled, but in a stunned sort of way, disbelief etched across his features.

Leo spoke from the doorway. "Ready."

Julian craned his neck to look at him, then at Wren. He pulled again, harder this time, before his gaze darted around the room.

"They're outside," Wren explained, knowing he was looking for his weapons. Leo had already gathered everything and put it safely out of reach. She had no doubt he'd break free soon enough—she hadn't tied him flush to the support beam, which meant he'd figure out a way to loosen the binds or call his weapons. She suspected he might even have other bits of iron concealed on his body that she didn't know about, but that was okay. She didn't intend for him to *die* out here. She just needed a head start.

He shook his head, a humorless smile on his face. Then it fell.

"Leaving?" he asked conversationally.

"Yes," Wren said, jaw set. "I can't stay. *We* can't stay."

"No," he said thoughtfully, head tilted. "I suppose not. Still, I never pegged you for a coward."

"I'm not—" Wren began hotly, but Julian cut her off.

"I mean, I know if it were *me*, I'd want to know why I could speak to the undead—and why the undead *listened*. I'd want to know if I was a ghostsmith." Wren bared her teeth, but he kept speaking. "But I think you'd rather a kind lie than a hard truth, wouldn't you? Because the hard truths are *here*, in the Breachlands—not there, in the Dominions. There, they'll tell you whatever they have to, to shut you up and keep you under control. Just like they did when they kept what really happened during the Uprising a secret. When they labeled your Locke Graven a war hero instead of the war criminal he ought to have been. When they put the good of your house over the truth. But you don't want to face that, do you, Wren? The fact that your whole life is built upon lie after lie?" He smiled, but it was a cold, cruel thing. "Or are you afraid of what you'll find out about yourself if you stay?"

"I'm not afraid," Wren snapped, her entire body tingling with repressed emotions. Anger. Frustration. And something very close to shame. She clenched her fists, fighting to keep herself under control. "I'm doing the right thing. I'm reporting what we discovered to the fort. I *will* learn the truth, and I *will* come back—but when I return, it'll be with an army."

He lunged forward suddenly, the rope creaking against the wood as it strained—but held.

Wren leapt back, though she was well out of reach. He laughed darkly. "You still don't get it, do you? They aren't planning an *uprising. . . .* They're planning an invasion. Those iron revenants were built to take down the Wall. By the time you and your politicians decide what to do, it'll be too late. He'll"—he jerked his chin at Leo—"be tucked away somewhere until my uncle can get his hands on him again, and *you'll* be right back where you started, exiled at the fort because your family doesn't want you—"

Wren didn't remember moving, didn't remember *touching* Julian at all, but the next thing she knew, she'd flung him against the pillar, his head cracking hard against the wood. She didn't know where she'd gotten the strength, but the force of the impact stunned Julian into silence.

He was looking at her like he'd never seen her before, but all Wren could see was that vision of herself—the picture his words painted—and she hated it.

She took a deep breath as they stared at each other, several feet of charged space between them. The shock was still evident on his face, though some of the tension had left him. He slumped against the beam.

Wren looked to Leo, who was also staring at her in surprise at what she had done.

"Let's go," she said. Leo left, but Wren paused in the doorway, looking back. "It's better this way. If you came with us . . . I don't know what would happen. Trust me. Just stay until daybreak. Then you can make your way to your family estate."

"*Trust?*" he repeated, in exactly the same way he had in the watchtower. While then it had seemed almost a joke—what other choice did they have, when it was just the two of them?—now it seemed like a dirty word.

"You'll be safer here," Wren whispered.

"Is that what all this has been about?" he asked. "Safety?" Wren didn't answer. "You think you'll be safe there in your fort when the iron revenants march? Or will you return to your house in a blaze of glory, only to spend your life fighting undead farmers and poor folk who couldn't afford proper burials, knowing you were meant for more?"

Her heart clenched at those last words. *Meant for more.* "It's not about being safe. It's—"

"It's what?"

"It's about where I belong."

"Right. You belong there, with them. Not here." And, unspoken: *with me.*

"I'm sorry," she said, turning to go.

"No, you're not," Julian said, so quietly Wren wasn't sure she hadn't imagined it.

Wren and Leo followed the river south until dawn. It took them several hours off course, but not only did it keep them safe from the undead; it was the only way she knew to get to the fort. As soon as they reached the Old Roads, they'd head west until the Wall came into view.

There was probably a faster way, but she didn't know it, and unfortunately, her guide was currently tied up in the mill house.

"Here," Leo said at one point when they'd stopped to quickly water the horses. He tossed her a small iron dagger—it was Ironheart, the weapon Julian had given her. She gave him a questioning look, and he shrugged. "Call me sentimental, but I thought you might want a souvenir."

Wren hesitated but returned the knife to Ghostbane's empty sheath before glancing over her shoulder again. She kept expecting

Julian to appear on their tail at any moment, but all was darkness and silence.

By the time sunlight crested the horizon and their shadows grew long on the ground before them, they were moving at a steady clip, veering west on one of the Old Roads in what Wren hoped was a straight shot for the Breachfort.

They rode all day, stopping several more times to feed and water the horses, but never for very long. Their mounts were tired, but they'd be well treated once they got to the fort.

She and Leo didn't speak much, but as the road stretched out longer and longer—their destination feeling farther and farther away—she couldn't help but ask, "Are you sure you're ready for this?"

"As ready as I'll ever be," Leo said, expression thoughtful. "I *want* to face him. My cousin. I want to understand what he's after. I want to unravel the mystery."

"It'll be risky. Dangerous."

"I think you mean *thrilling*," he said, using the same intonation he had before when referring to her time with Julian. Wren scowled at him, and he laughed. "Okay, okay—maybe not *that* thrilling, but a man can dream." He winked, and Wren rolled her eyes, though she was smiling.

"I'd have thought the past few days were exciting enough for you," Wren said. "What with being kidnapped and all."

"I didn't much care for being a prisoner," he conceded, "but I'm not entirely sure it's all that different from my life in the Dominions— though the clothes and food are generally much better."

"Is it so bad? Being a prince?"

"If you asked my brothers, I think they'd tell you it's a grand old time. But if you were the *third* prince to a father who has no use for you and a mother who has no use for anyone, I think you'd find it's rather . . . lonely. And dull. But not since I met you. Things have been decidedly *exciting* since then."

Wren smirked. "Not sure I can take all the credit."

"I should hope not," he said. He cocked his head at her, squinting into the sunlight. "You might be my only friend, Wren Graven. So I'm in this with you, for better or worse."

Wren's throat tightened. She cleared it. "You're definitely mine." He beamed. "And it'll probably be for *worse*, by the way," she added, and he laughed.

As they rounded yet another bend in the road with no sign of the fort or the Wall, Wren started to worry they'd gotten lost. Then, out of nowhere, a band of riders bore down on them.

"Kidnappers!" Leo shouted, just as Wren said, "Bandits!"

They were *both* wrong, as it turned out.

A second after Wren drew her swords, she recognized the familiar uniforms of the Breachfort guard.

It was a patrol.

She slumped in her saddle. They'd made it.

Once Wren was recognized—and then Prince Leo—the patrol circled them like an honor guard, preparing to escort them back to the fort. They'd yet to pass the palisade, which meant the fort was patrolling beyond their usual route for the first time in years.

Wren supposed they had Leo's kidnapping to thank for that.

Before they set out, a handful of guards detached from the main group and rode past, scouring the nearby landscape for pursuit.

Wren opened her mouth, prepared to say there hadn't been any, when two of them dragged a figure out from behind a cluster of rocks.

Her stomach dropped.

Julian.

THIRTY-EIGHT

They forced him to his knees and quickly disarmed him.

Wren couldn't figure out why Julian was *letting* two Breachfort guards overpower him—she had seen him take on worse odds against the bandits—when she spotted a third guard with a bow, an arrow nocked and ready to fire. Julian wore his helmet, but unlike those on the iron revenants, it had eye holes, and the archer was close enough that he would not miss.

He definitely looked the worse for wear, and Wren's mind scrambled to understand how he could *possibly* have caught up. Then she looked past him, at the soaring rocks that separated them from the river canyon where she'd left him. Rather than journey for hours *around* the landscape, Julian must have cut through. Wren would bet anything his whip sword had come in handy, allowing him to scale sheer cliffs and choose paths revenants simply could not follow.

Still, it had been shockingly reckless. Then when this patrol had arrived out of nowhere, his only choice had been to hide.

Heart in her throat, she watched numbly as the guards led him forward on foot between their two horses, one of them holding a rope connected to his hands. She darted a glance at Leo, and his expression of mingled shock and alarm surely matched hers.

Wren squeezed her eyes shut in exasperation. She had forced herself to betray Julian in order to save him from this, and yet here he was, in a worse position than he would have been if he'd come with Wren and Leo in the first place. He must have thought he'd be able to catch up to them, and it had been a very near thing. If this patrol hadn't been riding beyond the palisade, he'd have managed it.

Fear flickered in her stomach. What would have happened if he *had* caught up to them? Would he have fought Wren for Leo? Or simply taken him and forced her to follow or return to the fort in shame?

It seemed to take forever for their party to mount the rise before them, but as soon as the ground sloped downward again, the fort came into view.

Bells tolled as they approached the bone palisade, one of their number riding ahead to alert the fort of their arrival. The distant gate opened to emit two additional columns of riders.

Wren expected Commander Duncan in the lead, or perhaps Galen—the last person she wanted anywhere near Leo—but the person riding at the front of the lines was none other than Vance Graven, her father.

Wren gaped.

What was *he* doing here?

It was true that she'd gone missing, along with the prince—so they'd have notified him. And he'd come. Of course he would.

He loved her.

Even if he *had* sent her to this hellhole in the first place. Or rather, allowed his mother to do so without much resistance.

A mix of emotions reared up then. She was relieved to be here at last and glad to see him—but angry at him too. If he'd had a little more faith in her, none of this would have happened.

And wasn't it strange to realize *that* thought produced melancholy of its own?

As he drew up his horse before them, Wren smiled weakly, stunned.

"*Wren*," her father breathed, his expression oddly blank for a moment before he leapt from his saddle. He was dressed in full armor, something Wren didn't see very often. He was mostly retired from the field, though he'd seen fit to wear full Bone House regalia today, save for the eye black. He'd likely gotten dressed in a hurry.

The rest of the riders arrived, swirling around them in a rush of hoofbeats and horseflesh. Most of them descended upon Leo, and Wren wanted to keep him in her eyeline, but the next thing she knew, her father was pulling her down with him and enveloping her in a hug. He pressed his lips to her forehead, holding her close, and Wren let herself enjoy it.

"I came here as soon as they told me you were missing," he said, releasing her, his eyes bright. His soft brown hair was wind-tossed and his olive skin flushed from the ride. "With the details of the attack, I feared the worst. But now here you are—and *with* the prince," he added, bowing to Leo. He shook his head as if in disbelief. "You had me worried, little bird."

Wren looked away, swallowing thickly. That nickname, once treasured, now made her feel sick. She had to ask him about it. About the ring, about the well and Locke and herself. Julian was wrong. Wren wanted the hard truths, whatever they cost her. She *needed* them.

Speaking of Julian . . .

The guards who were escorting him stopped before Commander Duncan, who had dismounted beside her and her father.

"He was one of the kidnappers, Commander," one of the guards said. "I recognize him."

"And he's an ironsmith," said another, disdain in every word. While Julian had been disarmed, he still wore his armor, though his helmet had been removed.

"What are you waiting for?" Vance said, looking between the commander and the guards. "Kill him." Then he wrapped an arm around Wren's shoulders, preparing to walk her back to the gate.

Commander Duncan held up a hand, staying the guards, and frowned at Vance's turning back. "We should question him, should we not, Lord-Smith Vance?"

There was tension in his voice—he clearly did not like being ordered around on his own turf, but Wren's father was the highest-ranking person here. He was not only nobility, but he was also heir to his house. Even Leo couldn't claim that same status, despite being royal.

Julian, on the other hand, could.

"He'll just spew lies and misinformation," her father drawled, and Wren was surprised at his apparent lack of interest. It was almost like he didn't *want* Julian to talk. Did he suspect Wren's involvement with him somehow?

"All the same, given what has happened here, we should at least hold him until—"

"I'd rather take the word of my daughter and a prince of the realm over some traitor's brat."

Julian's attention had been fixed on the ground during this entire conversation, sparing Wren the decision of whether or not to meet his eye. . . . But he raised his head at Vance's words, specifically "my daughter."

He stared between them, lips pulled back in a sneer. All this time they'd discussed Locke Graven and the House of Bone, and she'd never told him her connection. That she, too, was theoretically in line to rule her own house.

"Better to kill him here and now and put his head on a spike. Send a message to those who would target us. Their assault on the fort was an act of war, and we will treat it as such. There is only one way to deal with treason."

Commander Duncan appeared like he wanted to argue but didn't. The guards around them looked ready for blood, given that they'd lost several people to Julian's original attack. Galen was there, too, and his face was pale—shocked, no doubt, to have the prince he'd betrayed back in his midst.

"He's not just some ironsmith," Wren blurted. Julian's gaze snapped to hers, his eyes wide. Pleading. He had protected his identity the entire time she'd known him because he was heir to his house and there were people who would use that against him. His own uncle had turned on him, and Wren was about to reveal it to the entire fort. But what other choice did she have? Stand aside and let him die? "His name is Julian Knight. He's heir to the House of Iron."

Julian looked down again, but there was tension visible in his corded neck muscles. He wasn't disappointed or hurt. He was livid.

Let him be.

She'd take the rage of the living over the silence of the dead any day.

"How do you know that?" her father asked sharply, and Wren was forced to look him in the eye.

"H-he and I, we rescued the prince together. He was my guide. And then"—she swallowed, hating herself for what she said next—"once we'd gotten Prince Leopold to safety, I tied him up and left him behind. He must have gotten free and followed us."

Her father's expression was unreadable, but she saw a barrage of emotions flicker through—surprise, distaste, and then something almost like fear. Wren knew he'd have questions for her. Many questions.

"Lock him up," he said. "No one is to speak to him until I do." Then his arm tightened like a vise around Wren's shoulders as he led the way to the fort.

Julian was dragged off to a cell without a backward glance, and though Galen insisted that Leo needed rest, Wren's father demanded Leo and Wren speak with him *immediately*.

"My rooms will work just fine," Vance insisted, steering Wren toward the stairs. "Have some food and drink sent up, won't you, Galen?"

The man looked unhappy at being reduced to the level of a servant, but then he glanced at Leo, who looked dirty and exhausted, and straightened his spine. "I shall bring it up myself."

"That won't be necessary," Wren's father cut in with gracious equanimity. "A servant will do just fine."

And just like that, a line was drawn in the sand—and Galen was on the wrong side of it. Wren couldn't help but feel smug. It was what the traitor deserved.

Galen turned on his heel and made for the kitchens, waving at a pair of servants as he passed, who followed behind.

"I won't be so easily dismissed, Lord-Smith," said Commander Duncan, coming up on their other side, a shrewd look on his face.

"Of course not," Vance said easily. "However," he continued, releasing his hold on Wren to step nearer the fort's commander, "given there is almost certainly a spy in your midst, I think it's best if I take over the preliminary investigation. If you were to sit in and rumors were spread . . . It may come out bad for you, Commander. Let me handle things for now. See if we can't suss out the perpetrator. Then you will have full command once more."

Like Galen, Commander Duncan did not look pleased. But rather than bluster and shuffle away on Vance's orders, he stood there, hands clasped behind his back, and watched them disappear up the stairs.

Servants had preceded them to her father's room—which was actually a series of rooms, meant for visiting nobility—lighting the fire and setting out a pitcher of water and cups.

They had barely settled into the chairs by the hearth when an additional wave of servants arrived. Leo's water was soon replaced with wine, and he was given a thick woolen blanket, produced out of nowhere.

Leo shrugged and spread his hands wide as if to say "see, told you so," as pillows were stuffed into his already soft chair and a plate of various meats and cheeses was assembled for him.

Wren, on the other hand, had to reach for her food—though reach she did. She was starving.

"Enough fussing," Vance said, sounding bored despite his stiff posture, his hands steepled together before him.

The servants retreated, leaving the three of them alone.

"Tell me," her father said without preamble. "Everything."

The beginning of the story was easy enough, though the middle was where things got disjointed as Wren and Leo recalled their different experiences. While Vance didn't react to Wren's account of the surprising behavior of the revenants she and Julian encountered, he went unnaturally still as she got to the part about the Breach. She glossed over certain parts, *obviously*, but she did tell him about the boy and the suit of iron armor. About the well and the strange power it granted him.

"Have you ever heard of anything like that before?" she asked, watching her father closely.

"Iron revenants? Certainly not."

"No, I meant the well of magic. I thought maybe . . . during the Uprising . . ." She trailed off, waiting for him to react. To interject. He didn't move a muscle. "That you might have seen it. You or Locke. That maybe it was part of how we'd won when we were so outnumbered."

She was treading dangerous territory with this subject, she knew. If her father was aware, there was a reason he'd concealed it. And to admit she was taking the word of an ironsmith would undercut her argument, even if she had seen the evidence with her own eyes. But she wanted to give her father a chance. Maybe he truly didn't know. Maybe Locke had separated from the rest of them, and only her uncle knew what had happened that day.

"We were at war, Wren, not exploring ruins." It was not, exactly, an answer.

"It affected me," Wren revealed. "Even at a distance. I was able to do things I'd never done before."

"Such as?"

She swallowed. "The undead . . . I told them what to do, and they listened."

"Anything else?" he asked idly, as if the question were of no real importance to him—but the tightness around his eyes betrayed him.

She should tell him about the ring. About the queen's words. About the pull she felt. The confusion.

"Nothing."

Leo cut in then, explaining how during his travels, he'd heard rumors of what was happening in the Breach. Of *who* ruled there. The tale culminated with their paths crossing in Caston, the regent and his alliance with the Corpse Queen.

Vance scrubbed his hands over his face. It was clear some of this, at least, was news to him—but how much?

Eventually he had questions, but they were primarily about the lead-up to the kidnapping and so directed at Leo.

He and Wren had agreed on their journey here not to point the finger at Galen—or anyone—until they had proof to back it up. Leo mentioned his travels before arriving at the Breachfort, including the fact that his previous inspection had been suspiciously cut short and that the tour beyond the Wall was orchestrated by several members of his entourage, Galen among them, and the Breachfort's own administrators, including Commander Duncan and Odile.

"Wren was chosen for the party, being the only *active* bonesmith in residence, though traditionally it should be the highest-ranking," Leo added as if it were an afterthought.

"Odile was sick," Wren explained, hating the thought that the whole thing had been a lie . . . *not* to get her face time with Leo, as Odile had insinuated, but to get her on that patrol so she could be kidnapped.

"Which could be a timely coincidence . . . or something more," Vance said gravely. He straightened in his chair. "You've both been through a terrible ordeal, and I commend you on your bravery, fortitude, and quick thinking. You've earned some rest. As we still do not know for certain who was involved in all this, I will post some of my men outside your door for the night, if that is agreeable to you, Your Highness?"

Leo nodded.

Getting to his feet, Wren's father opened his chamber door and spoke to his personal guards, who were stationed in the hall. Galen was there, as well, hovering nearby.

"You and I will speak later," Vance said, interrupting anything Galen might say. He turned to his guard. "I want a full escort to accompany the prince at all times. He should remain in his rooms for the time being."

"But Lord-Smith Vance, Prince Leopold already has an entire complement of—"

"And no one goes in or out, save for me," Vance finished, cutting Galen off. "Understood?"

His guard captain nodded, then barked orders.

Leo's expression was grim—a prisoner again, it seemed—and their eyes met over his shoulder before he was ushered away, the door slamming shut.

"You look pale," Vance said, passing a critical gaze over his daughter in the sudden silence. While Wren was used to the feeling of him measuring her, there was something distinctly *doting* about it now that was wholly new.

He poked his head out the door again. "Send for the kitchens to get Wren some proper food. Something hot. And a hearty drink. Mulled wine? Be quick about it."

Wren blinked at her father. She'd asked him for mulled wine once during her grandmother's birthday feast. He'd said something along the lines of "You can hardly make it through a meal without embarrassing yourself even when alcohol *isn't* involved." Of course, she had always managed to get alcohol on feast days—it just wasn't from him—so he was wrong in his assessment.

Still, apparently things were different now.

Her heart squeezed at the thought, and it wasn't an entirely pleasant experience. She was gratified to have possibly earned his respect, but a part of her grated at the idea that she'd had to in the first place. He was her *father*. He should have respected her before she was useful, should have loved and cared for her before she had proven she deserved it.

While they waited for the food, Vance poured himself a large measure of alka from a decanter on a side table. He took a long swig before settling back in his chair, smirking at her.

"I'm impressed, Wren. And you know I do not use such a word lightly."

That she most certainly did know. She fidgeted under his stare, so he cast his gaze into the fire instead, taking another drink before continuing.

"I'm impressed by your initiative, your apparent rapport with the prince, and your ability to see him and yourself safely through these wastelands. Truly. There are bonesmiths twice your age who could not have done the same."

Wren glowed at his praise.

"I have something for you," he said, pale eyes twinkling. He put his drink down on the table and headed toward the bedchamber.

"When I heard you'd been taken, I feared the worst. But somehow I knew you'd find your way home. So I wanted to be ready when you did."

Wren gaped. There in his hands lay a familiar weapon, Ghostbane.

"It should never have been taken from you," he said quietly, crouching before her. "You are my daughter, and it belongs to you. I'll never let anyone take it again."

Tears pricked at Wren's vision. It was everything she'd wanted, all she had lost—and some things she'd never dreamed she'd have—placed before her, ready and waiting.

She hesitated. "Does Grandmother know?"

He quirked her a smile. "Leave her to me."

Wren took the dagger in trembling hands. She felt truly seen by her father for the first time in her life. Like he was looking at her not as a bundle of mistakes and poor choices—some of which were his own—but as a capable human being.

And yet . . .

He still wasn't seeing *all* of her, was he?

He didn't know that she had feelings for Julian, their alleged enemy, and that betraying him was tearing her up inside.

He didn't know about the ring, about its connection to the boy. *Her* connection to him.

Wren had been lied to, and now she was doing the same thing, withholding information because it suited her, because she was— as Julian had rightly pointed out—*afraid* of the truth. Afraid of the repercussions of it.

Afraid that somehow the truth would change her . . . but she was already changed, wasn't she?

"Dad, there's . . . there's something else."

"Hm?"

"I found a ring," she burst out.

"In the Breach?"

"No—well, *yes*, but . . ." She reached into her pocket and placed the ring on the table. "I found it in the Bonewood during my trial. It was next to that . . . that fresh body I told you about?"

"I don't recall you mentioning a ring," Vance commented, his tone even—but Wren heard accusation in it all the same.

"I forgot."

"I see," he said, though they both knew she was lying. He picked it up and examined it closely. "These are ghostsmith runes," he said, which Wren had already pieced together.

"I saw similar glyphs in the ruins in the Breach," she said, watching him as he studied it.

"It *was* a ghostsmith city, after all," he mused, his gaze snagging on the birds carved into its surface.

"I also saw an exact duplicate of this ring there. On the boy's finger."

Vance leaned back in his chair. "What is it you're trying to say, Wren?"

"That he . . . that he and I . . . You never talk about my mother."

He blew out a breath. "Honestly, Wren, I hardly knew her. It was wartime. And then she died giving birth. There isn't much to tell."

"But what if she . . . ? What if I'm . . . ?"

"Wren, you are my daughter. Whatever this is, whatever you're thinking, it doesn't change anything. Do you understand?"

She nodded, her throat constricted.

He reached for her shoulder, mouth open to speak, just as a servant arrived.

While her father directed the food to be placed on the table, Wren stared at Ghostbane. The ring was gone—still in her father's hand, she assumed—so she focused on the knife instead. She lifted it, feeling the familiar weight and heft of the weapon in her hand, before taking a deep, steadying breath.

She moved to slide the weapon into her belt sheath—and found Julian's mother's blade there instead. She darted an anxious glance at her father, but he was distracted with the food, his back to her. He hadn't yet noticed that she carried an iron weapon, of all things.

She hastily removed Ironheart and stuck it into her boot, replacing it with Ghostbane.

By the time he turned around, she was sitting motionless once more, and a steaming platter of stew and fresh bread was laid out before her, the scent of gravy and onions and the rich, spicy notes from the wine driving all else from her thoughts.

She ate ravenously, her father throwing her indulgent looks as he sat opposite, drinking his liquor and going over papers with an air of comfortable self-satisfaction.

Though she had a room in the fort, her father insisted she take his bed and asked for extra blankets to see her comfortably settled.

But as she fell asleep, Ghostbane tucked under her pillow, her mind wandered helplessly to the knife in her boot, the ironsmith imprisoned several floors below . . . and the answers she still hadn't gotten.

THIRTY-NINE

Despite falling unconscious almost instantly, Wren's sleep was restless.

She was both comforted and agitated by her father's presence in the next room. Every movement, every rumble of his voice, sent shock waves through her sleeping brain, like horn calls or ringing bells.

Like warnings.

The door in the next room closed, and she lurched upright, drenched in sweat.

This wasn't right. None of it was right, though she wasn't exactly sure why.

Her father had said what she'd wanted to hear, given her comfort and praise—*kind lies*—but he hadn't actually given her the answers she sought. He had *reassured* her, but that was not the same thing. She remembered Julian's remarks before she'd left him in that mill house: *They'll tell you whatever they have to, to shut you up and keep you under control.*

He was right. But there was someone else here who might be able to give her those answers.

Climbing out of bed, she dressed quickly and padded out into the hall.

Her father's guards were there, startling her. "You must remain inside, Lady-Smith. Your father's orders."

Another alarm sounded in her mind. Another warning.

"Do you know where he's gone?" she asked, though she suspected that even if they did know, they wouldn't tell her.

"No, my lady."

She retreated inside, thinking fast. There was no telling where her father was or how long he would be, but she wasn't about to sit here waiting to find out.

Prowling the rooms, she sought a servant's passage or a window with a likely escape route. Unfortunately, her father's accommodations were higher up than Prince Leo's, meaning a dangerous drop should she attempt to climb down. Plus his windows faced the main court-yard, which could lead to witnesses.

There was, however, a balcony. It was on the opposite side of the room, with nothing but a distant view of the Wall and rocky, unkempt grounds below. It was still too far to climb without a rope—she thought of Julian and his whip sword with a pang—and had no easy way back in, but there *was* another balcony adjacent to it. She didn't know what room it was connected to, but she'd worry about that after she made the jump.

It went smoothly enough, though her stomach slammed into the railing of the next balcony with enough force to knock the wind from her lungs. She recovered, throwing her legs over the balustrade and landing on her knees, crouching there for a moment to catch her breath.

Still struggling, she reached up for the handle and found the door mercifully unlocked. Wren swung it open and found herself face-to-face—or rather, face-to-*knees*—with Inara Fell.

"Knew it," Inara said, arms crossed as she smirked down at Wren. Inara looked as she always did: bone armor polished and pristine, her dark braids combined into a single no-nonsense coil that draped down her back. Even her boots were recently waxed and scuff-free.

Wren scrambled to her feet. "Knew what?" she gasped, ignoring the lingering ache in her stomach.

"That guarding the front door would not be enough to keep you in."

Wren supposed it was vaguely flattering that Inara thought so highly of her skills, though it came on the heels of realizing that her father thought so little of them.

"Is that why you're here, then? To guard me?" Wren asked with a quirked brow. She was the better fighter between them, and Inara knew it.

Inara rolled her eyes, her eye black neat and perfectly symmetrical, stepping around Wren and strolling idly about the room, her ease belying the fact that she'd backed away from the confrontation.

"I'm no sentry," she scoffed. "I just enjoy being right. You wouldn't understand."

Now it was Wren's turn to roll her eyes. "What are you doing here, Inara?" Her presence provided a complication Wren really didn't need right now.

Inara spread her hands. "I'm a valkyr, Graven. I go where the work is."

"You're working with my father?"

"Technically, I'm working *for* your father," she said. "They placed me with Sonya." Wren wondered if their pairing was part of the deal the reapyr had struck with Inara in order to double-cross Wren during the trial. Whatever the case, the two of them were living the life Wren had always wanted.

Why did it not appeal the way it once had?

"Well, I hope you enjoy the empty room. I've got to go."

"Where? To visit your Gold Prince?" She waggled her eyebrows. "Or is it the ironsmith you're missing?" Wren didn't answer, but Inara only smirked. "It's the ironsmith. I knew it."

"You don't know shit," Wren snapped, heading for the door, though her angry retort only proved Inara right.

"I'm actually impressed, you know," Inara called to her retreating back.

Wren turned on the spot. Frowned.

"I always knew you were ambitious, but this? This was *smart*. Strategic. I didn't know you had it in you."

"What are you talking about?"

"The *prince*. Gaining his favor will get you far, I think."

Wren hated the fact that Inara *did* know her well, better than most, in fact, and that those had initially been Wren's exact thoughts. "He's my friend," she argued, but Inara was already speaking over her.

"I mean, after everything they did to get you here, it didn't break your spirit."

"*They?*" Wren repeated incredulously. "*You're* the one who landed me here."

"Keep telling yourself that," Inara said, shaking her head, a superior, condescending look on her face. "It still had some of your old flair, I'll admit. Clearly you had no plan, no exit strategy. You just tore off after a prince, into unknown—and highly dangerous—territory and teamed up with a bloody ironsmith to do it. Classic you. Messy. Dangerous." She paused. "Free. Or, at least, you were."

"What's that supposed to mean?" Wren asked, trying to keep up with Inara's startling—though not without its barbs—praise.

"You've always been free. Honestly, when we were younger, I wanted to be you." Her jaw clenched in embarrassment at the admission. "Not for the reasons you think—you are *not*, for the record, the most talented valkyr of our generation." Wren barely registered Inara's familiar dissent, still fixated on her initial statement. She had wanted to *be* Wren? "I was jealous of the way you always did what you wanted. Followed your own rules and fuck everyone else." Her gaze landed on Ghostbane, returned to Wren's belt. "But I guess even the great Wren Graven can be broken eventually."

"I am not broken—"

"I mean, a cage is all the prince knows, and while you might have forced that ironsmith into his, you flew willingly into your own, *little bird*."

Wren's mouth fell open. She turned on her heel and strode from the room, but not before she caught Inara's last words.

"I hope that knife was worth it to you."

Out in the hall, Wren struggled to catch her breath. It was the aftermath of winding herself earlier, surely. It was late, she was tired, and . . . Inara's words meant nothing.

Wren mentally sifted through all her cousin had said, focusing on the beginning of their conversation. Those guards had been posted outside Wren's door not to keep her safe but to keep her *in*.

Which meant whatever her father was doing, he didn't want her to know about it. Maybe she should forget Odile and see what he was up to instead?

She'd lost precious minutes talking to Inara, but she could catch up.

She knew this place better than Vance. Too bad she didn't know where he was going. . . .

Out into the main hall, Wren looked in both directions, but the corridor was deserted. She closed her eyes, trying to think of where he might go. To question Julian, maybe? To speak to Galen—or Leo?

She was on her way to check the dungeons when she caught sight of Vance disappearing down the stairs that led to the bonesmith temple.

He was going to see Odile.

To question her, maybe? To accuse? Wren had to know.

Desperate to hear their conversation but knowing that even her father's recent goodwill toward her would not allow her to be present, Wren slipped out from her hiding place.

There were two entrances to Odile's domain—one through the temple, which was where Vance was heading, and another that led to the storage rooms via the cellar.

Wren made her way to the cellar. She hadn't seen Odile since she'd been back, and she wondered how the woman would react to this late-night visit. Would it be a pleasant surprise or an unwelcome intrusion?

As Wren drew near, the low rumble of voices reached her—coming from the back hall that connected to the storage room. Quickening her pace, she slipped from the cellar and into the storage room attached to Odile's chambers. The voices grew louder, but she still couldn't make them out. It wasn't until she crouched behind the door itself and, with a held breath, turned the knob.

It opened barely a sliver, but it was enough to hear Odile's words ring out, clear as day.

"... know what we have to do."

"And what is that?" came her father's reply. The door where Wren currently hid was behind Odile's chair, in the shadows of the corner of the room. There was little light save for the lantern on her desk, but it was enough to see Vance's face and Odile's profile, her copper hair shining.

"Destroy it. Bad enough what happened to Locke, but these iron revenants, this queen . . . We must march on those ruins in force, bring the full might of the House of Bone to bear, and be rid of that well once and for all."

Wren held her breath. So they *did* know about the well and the power within it.

"Don't be ridiculous," he said in that dismissive, slightly condescending way that Wren knew far too well. He was sitting very much at his ease, a cup of alka held loosely in his hand, but his gaze was sharp. "In order to do that, we'd have to reveal the fact that we've been lying about the Uprising for nearly two decades. We'd destroy our house, not to mention—"

"There is more at stake here than your bloody house, Vance." Odile, on the other hand, gripped her cup tightly. For the first time since Wren had met her, the contents appeared untouched.

"It was *our* house, last I checked," he said. "And I'm pretty sure we both agreed to tell the story we told."

Odile looked away. "I was afraid. Now I think there are bigger things to fear than the truth."

"We didn't lie, Odile. We omitted. There is a difference, and what we did saved lives."

"The only lives we saved were our own. You might be able to fool yourself, Vance, but you can't fool me. I was there, the same as you. And I told Locke not to do it. But that *woman* . . . She had her claws in him from the start. She saw his hero complex, his *need* to do whatever it took to protect the Dominions, and she exploited it. He couldn't resist it, the power she promised. So he took it without a second thought."

There was a strange, bitter expression on Vance's face. There was jealousy, too, the kind she always saw there when people talked about Locke.

"The way he glowed with it," Odile continued, and Wren knew exactly what she meant. "I thought he truly was a hero, some figure from legend. But then, when he mowed down those people—*our* people—I knew he'd become something else. That power . . . it was too much for him. I'll never forget the look in his eyes, the fear, as it took control of him. As he lost himself to it. We can call him a hero all we want, Vance, but it doesn't change the fact that he was a mass murderer. We cannot allow the same thing to happen again. We cannot omit the true threat here, and it isn't the regent, or the queen, or the iron revenants. . . . It's that well of power. Without it, the others are nothing."

Vance stared into the contents of his cup. "Funny you should have such strong feelings about omission, given how in the dark you have kept me."

"I don't know what you're talking about."

"Don't you?" he asked, glancing up at her.

Odile leaned forward. "I tried to tell you the truth once, and you *buried* it, along with the body of my messenger and the package he delivered."

"Part of the truth," Vance corrected lightly. "And this package, do you mean?" he said, placing Wren's ring on the table between them. "Wren found it."

So that messenger Wren found in the Bonewood had not come from the Corpse Queen but from *Odile*?

"I guess you didn't bury it as well as you'd thought," Odile said, smirking.

"Apparently it's part of a set," Vance said idly, and the smile slipped off Odile's face. "But you wouldn't know anything about that, would you?" When Odile didn't respond, he slammed his hand on the table. "First you send some anonymous messenger across the entirety of the Dominions carrying information that could have ruined me, my house, and my daughter, and then you have the audacity to keep *this* from me?"

"I still don't—"

"Come now, Odile. Wren has just told me everything. There is a Corpse Queen, and there is a boy. You seemed quite certain about who the former was, according to your messenger. What about the latter?"

There was a long silence. "I was trying to protect you."

Wren's heart plummeted. Did that mean . . . ?

"Excuse me?" Vance said, bristling at the suggestion that he needed such care. "I am not a child to be coddled. I want the truth."

"Because you responded so well the last time," Odile snapped, putting down her cup. "We have more important matters to—"

"The truth, Odile. All of it."

They stared at each other for a long moment, then—

"Fine," she said with exasperation. "*Fine.*" She took a heavy breath, then straightened in her chair. "If you'll recall, after Ravenna came here, fit to burst, you wouldn't see her." Her tone made it perfectly clear what she thought of that. Wren, meanwhile, was hung up on the name. *Ravenna.* Her father had never given her one. "Lady-Smith Svetlana was here, the war was almost over, and with Locke gone, you were all your mother had. Her shining war hero. Her brand-new heir. You didn't want to give that up, did you? Didn't want to show her the ugly side of what happened during that campaign. No, instead you pushed that little problem onto me."

Vance rolled his eyes, then waved his hand impatiently, telling her to get on with it.

"She gave birth in the dungeons, with only me and the old healer for company. Ravenna was *different* from when we'd met her in the Haunted Territory, when she was pretending to be the sole survivor from some attack, alone and afraid. I had always known her poor damsel routine was an act, but I couldn't figure out what she really wanted. Well, besides attention from both of you."

Both of you? Did she mean Locke? From the way Vance's jaw clenched, Wren would say yes.

"Now I could ask her. Why had she led us to the well in the first place? How had she known of it? And where had she gone when things went . . . wrong . . . with Locke?"

Wren had suspected the well was the source of Locke's power . . . and that things must have gone awry for him to do what he had done. The confirmation did not comfort her.

"She was delirious with pain—and the drugs the healer had given her—so much of what she'd said made little sense. But she made a few noteworthy confessions. She said she wasn't just a fair-haired, green-eyed girl of Andolesian ancestry, trapped in the Breachlands after her family had died. She was Ravenna Nekros, a smith—and not just any smith, but according to her, the last ghostsmith. Her people had been living in secrecy for decades, and she had known of the well because it was her birthright, stories of its power and location passed down generation by generation. She said *they* were the ones who'd caused the Breach, taking their chance by diverting an ironsmith mining tunnel and seeking out their lost city. She intended to reclaim her house's fallen glory and insisted that this was just the beginning. I didn't get much more out of her . . . until the child was born. A girl, and she had bonesmith eyes, which was a relief . . . until the second set of contractions started."

Wren looked at her father then. He was perched on the edge of his seat, appearing ravenous for every scrap of detail . . . but also slightly sick. Like each word was causing him pain, yet he wanted them all the same. Wren understood. This story was tearing her world apart the same as his.

"By then Ravenna was moving in and out of consciousness. At one point she'd bitten her lip so hard it bled. But she only smiled at me as I held her daughter, her teeth red. 'I know you loved him,' she said, smiling wider as she clenched her jaw through the pain. 'So I want you to know they're his.'"

His . . . ? Wren was confused. Odile had loved her father? But Vance's expression had shuttered, and suddenly Wren understood. Odile had loved Locke . . . and Locke had loved Ravenna. Or had had sex with her anyway. And these children, this bonesmith daughter . . .

"Maybe she wanted to wound me," Odile said with an unconvincing shrug. "Maybe she sensed she was fading and said whatever she needed to say to guarantee I took care of them." She darted a look at Vance, but his gaze was distant. He had asked for the truth, the unvarnished facts, and here they were. Wren's stomach twisted with the thought that maybe he wasn't hers . . . that she wasn't his. . . .

In a flash, she saw a very different life. Daughter of the beloved Locke Graven, adored by her grandmother and favorite of her house.

"Then came the son," Odile continued, her voice slightly hoarse.

The vision shifted. Wren and her brother, hand in hand. They would make mischief *together*, neither of them ever truly alone because they had each other, their loving parents looking on. She wanted it, she yearned for it, and yet . . . Locke wasn't a hero; he was a murderer. And Vance . . . he *was* her father, no matter her true parentage, while her mother was something else entirely. Was she evil? Did she want Wren because Wren was her daughter or because she carried ghostsmith blood?

The images, equal parts tantalizing and taunting, were little more than soap bubbles—beautiful and fragile and not meant to last.

"Only . . . he was not well. Sickly, whereas the daughter was strong. She had come out screaming, lungs heaving, while he was mewling and weak. Silent as the grave, and he never opened his eyes. The healer shook her head. He would not be long for the world. And Ravenna herself was losing too much blood. Despite that, her instructions were clear. Give the daughter to the House of Bone. Call her Wren. Birds were sacred to the ghostsmiths, representative of the soul. Finally, give her the ring so that she might know her heritage. Then we strapped that dying baby to her chest while she continued to bleed out and got her on a horse. She rode for the Haunted Territory—for the well, I assumed—and never looked back."

Wren sniffled softly. She couldn't take her eyes off her father—off *Vance*—but he was staring down at the floor.

"Should I have told you all that? Every bloody, gruesome detail?

Or should I have cleaned it up, made it shine . . . just as we had done with Locke? I . . ." Odile swallowed audibly. "I wanted the child to be raised with love, so I didn't tell you about Locke or the ghostsmith heritage. Wren was a bonesmith, so no one ever needed to know. I suspected the son would not survive, so I didn't tell you about him, either. Honestly, Vance? I thought to spare you the pain. Years passed, and it seemed I had made the right decisions . . . until rumors reached me of a Corpse Queen ruling in the Haunted Territory. So I sent a messenger with the news, the ring, and what Ravenna had told me of her bloodline. I'd heard nothing of the boy, so I left him out. I left Locke out too. His name hurts us both, you know. And maybe what she said was a lie. That's what I kept telling myself, anyway. Maybe it was a lie."

Vance's fingers were speared through his hair. Wren had never seen him look so shaken. *Regret.* That was what she saw on his face. Seventeen years' worth of regret.

"Would it have changed things?" Odile asked softly. She sounded sincere, like she was genuinely curious. "Even without knowing all this, look how you've allowed your mother to treat her. How *you* have treated her. What if you had suspected she wasn't truly yours?"

"A part of me did wonder, sometimes. . . ." He lifted his head, his voice hoarse. "She looks so like Locke when she's angry. Or excited. Something in her eyes . . ." He cleared his throat. "And I'll thank you not to turn your judgment on me, Odile. Your hands are dirty, the same as mine."

"I did what you ordered me to," Odile said, outraged. "That is all I have ever done. When Locke murdered hundreds, you ordered me to keep my mouth shut and follow your lead, so I did. When that woman turned up here, pregnant, I handled it, just as you ordered me to. And seventeen years later, when you sent that child to me like a lamb to the slaughter, I delivered her east of the Wall, *just as you ordered me to.*"

"No." Wren breathed, the word soft and silent and heavy with pain. Everything she'd heard up until now, all of it seemed to coalesce in this one final, terrible truth.

"And what of it?" he snapped, the words shattering what little faith Wren had left. "I was doing my part to ensure the future of my house—something you would *both* benefit from. Without an enemy east of the Wall, without the undead on our doorstep, our position in the Dominions is precarious. Rather than fade back into obscurity, we are simply giving our enemies the tools they need to dig their own graves."

"They rise up, and in swoops the House of Bone, coming to the rescue once again?" Odile said, lip curled in disdain.

"It worked before, didn't it? I just wish I'd thought of it myself. Wren was only ever meant to be a temporary hostage to ensure the House of Bone followed through with its end of the bargain and didn't reveal the regent's activities to the king. I knew she'd be fine. She's been in scrapes before. She's tough. Resilient."

"She's your *child*, your responsibility, whatever her blood."

"And she's been raised as such. She knows how important it is to honor our house. To ensure its future. And she will *be* its future— *whatever her blood.*"

Those words should have comforted her, but Wren felt sick. Was it better to be the daughter of a murderer or the daughter of a coward?

"And what price will you make her pay next? What else will she have to give?"

He looked away. "Perhaps it's time she met her mother."

"You can't be serious."

"Deadly, in fact. I had no idea Ravenna was involved in all this. From what Wren has told me, *she* was the one to push for Wren's kidnapping, and the regent simply complied in order to seal their own side bargain. She *wants* Wren. I can use that. I think that together, Wren and I could dissuade her from this course. Make her see reason. I can offer her a home and a position."

"You want to make her your *wife*?" Odile asked incredulously. "You sound like a damned fool. Not everyone can be bought with a title."

"So you say," Vance said, unaffected by her words.

"You don't want a bride. . . . You want that power for yourself, don't you?" Odile asked, and Vance lifted a shoulder indifferently. "You want to do what your brother did, but better. It's just like when you were kids, always trying to be faster, stronger, *more* than him. It's how you were with Ravenna. . . . You didn't want her until you saw that Locke did. Don't deny it." He didn't. Odile laughed humorlessly. "You thought standing in his shadow was cold while he was alive, but standing in the shadow of his martyrdom is colder, isn't it?"

Vance's eyes flashed dangerously. "You have no idea what it's like to be in my position. To do *everything* you can your entire life and still constantly come up short, measured against a standard that is impossible to meet—because it doesn't exist."

"You're right, I don't . . . but I suspect Wren does."

His face was wiped temporarily blank. Had he truly never seen it? Seen that exactly what his mother did to him, he did to Wren?

"So let's be done with the false narrative. Let's *finish this*."

Vance wavered—then shook his head. "We're smarter now. More prepared. It's a *tool*—"

"*You* will be the tool, Vance, and Ravenna will use you as she sees fit. It will *ruin* you, that magic, just as it ruined Locke. This is exactly what she wanted to happen during the Uprising. She wanted us to destroy ourselves, and you're only too eager to oblige. Except this time, instead of sacrificing your brother, you'll endanger your daughter. She has already drawn upon it and somehow come away unscathed. Do not risk it again."

"I will do what I must. For the good of my house."

Odile sighed heavily. "I thought as much. It's a good thing I already contacted Lady-Smith Svetlana."

He stilled. "You've spoken to my mother?"

"She's on her way. When she arrives, we can decide together what is best for *our* house."

"What did you tell her?" he demanded, getting to his feet. "What did you say about Ravenna? About Wren?"

"Nothing . . . yet, but I will. She has to know about Locke and the Uprising, about the iron revenants . . . even your deal with the regent, Vance. She has to know what we're up against. That well must be destroyed."

He pinched the bridge of his nose. "I really wish you hadn't done that, Odile," he said, his voice weary. "Now you leave me no choice."

There was a flash as her father withdrew a dagger from the inside of his jacket, gleaming and bright. Not made of bone, as Wren would have expected, but made of steel with a gold filigree handle.

"It seems I must be the one to clean up the mess—again," he continued, staring down at the blade. "It will be a pity to lose a war hero." Odile's entire body tensed, and dread coiled in Wren's gut. "Then again, as you've pointed out—if my brother is anything to go by, you'll be remembered as a martyr instead."

Odile leapt to her feet, but Vance was faster. He was a trained valkyr, after all. She'd only just made it out of her chair before he crossed the space between them and plunged the dagger into her chest.

FORTY

Wren watched in horror as Odile struggled, fruitless, before slumping back into her chair.

Leaving the knife embedded, Vance hastily wiped any sign of blood from his appearance, scrubbing at his hands until they were raw. He took a deep, shuddering breath, collecting himself. Then he drained the contents of his cup, placed it on the sideboard, and pocketed Wren's ring, hiding the evidence that he'd ever been here.

Wren caught his expression as he moved for the door, a grim resolve settling on his features. Had he looked the same, she wondered, when he'd murdered that messenger in the Bonewood? And when he'd turned his back on her mother? He hadn't loved Ravenna. He'd loved the idea of *having* her when his brother wanted her. It was beyond pathetic.

As soon as his footsteps had faded away, Wren shoved the door open and rushed to Odile's side.

Wren thought she was already gone, but the woman flinched at

Wren's wary touch on her shoulder. She took a wet, rattling breath and tried to speak around the knife in her chest.

Her lips moved, but no sound came out. Her eyes widened in panic and she scrabbled at her neck. Wren thought she was trying to lower the collar of her robes—to better breathe, maybe?—but then her trembling fingers latched on to a thin chain hanging around her throat. She tugged fitfully, and Wren helped, withdrawing the necklace until a key appeared dangling at the bottom.

A bone key—the same one she'd used to take Wren into the lowermost dungeons of the Breachfort.

She pushed it onto Wren, who stared down at it. What had Odile said before?

If anything should ever happen to me . . . now you know more than one way out of the fort. Just in case.

When Wren looked up again, Odile's gaze was clouding over, distant and unfocused.

She was gone.

A cloak of grief settled over Wren . . . for the loss of a mentor—someone she'd liked and respected—and the one person who seemed willing to tell her the truth. Now she was dead, and whatever other secrets she had known had died with her. Why had Locke never loved Odile as she had loved him? Had he loved Ravenna, or was their twisted, tangled love affair toxic on all sides?

And if it was, what did that make Wren as the spawn of it?

Footsteps sounded from the staircase beyond—had her father returned?

She darted back to her hiding place just as the door to Odile's chamber creaked open.

"It's rather late for a—" came a voice that did not belong to Vance

Graven. Peering through the gap, Wren spotted Galen standing there, mouth agape at the sight of Odile, murdered, in her chair.

Before he could do more than peer around in confusion, a second wave of footsteps echoed down to them. Now Wren heard her father's voice, but he wasn't alone.

"Haven't the faintest notion why she called this clandestine meeting, Commander, but—"

The door swung wide, revealing Vance and Commander Duncan.

"What is the meaning of this?" Commander Duncan demanded. He took in the scene, and Wren saw it through his eyes—Galen alone with Odile, who had been recently murdered . . . the weapon, golden handle reflecting the lantern light, protruding from her chest. The look on Galen's face told Wren that the knife was definitely his—as did his hasty check of his belt and jacket pockets, but she already knew what he'd find: an empty sheath.

Apparently Vance had gotten better at hiding his tracks. Wren had no idea when he'd stolen that golden knife or when he'd known he might have to remove Odile, but now he'd ensured that only *his* version of events was relayed to the fort and the Dominions as a whole. Galen was a liability, since Vance had obviously been the one to pay him to assist in the kidnapping, and now the only people in the fort who could prove Vance's story wrong were Wren and Leo and, to a lesser degree, Julian.

They were all in grave danger.

"Guards!" Commander Duncan shouted into the hall, and while they rushed in to apprehend Galen—who was wide-eyed with shock— Vance hurried to Odile's side. With his back to the others, he would appear frantic and concerned, checking for a pulse, but Wren could see his face. His wide, anxious eyes and lips downturned with disgust, proving that he didn't necessarily have the stomach for these games, though he played them all the same.

Wren had seen enough.

Disappearing down the dark hallway, she climbed the stairs from the cellar in a daze.

It was too much. All of it. But while her mother's identity—past and present—was shocking enough, it was her father's various betrayals that hurt worst of all. If he even *was* her father.

She had built a life, an identity, out of wanting to please him. Of trying—and failing—to be good enough for him. Without that, Wren didn't know who she was. Where she belonged. She'd told Julian she belonged *here*, but nothing had ever felt less true.

And considering what her father wanted to do next . . . Wren was firmly with Odile. That well contained a power she wanted *nothing* to do with. It should be destroyed, not *used*, no matter how much her father deluded himself that he wanted to use it for good. She had seen what it could do, even in the hands of someone with noble intentions like Locke. And she had seen it turned to something twisted and sinister with the iron revenants. The magic itself might not be evil, but the power was more than any one person should have.

Before she knew it, her feet had taken her back the way she had come, to the room that was a balcony hop across from her father's chambers.

Inara was still there.

"You look like you've seen a ghost," she said, smiling at her own stupid joke.

Wren put both hands on Inara's chest and shoved, slamming her up against the wall. Inara looked stunned, and though she struggled, Wren's hold was too strong.

"What the fuck, Graven?" she demanded.

"He put you up to it, didn't he?" she asked, watching her cousin closely. "During the trial?"

She didn't know why it mattered. He had done worse, hadn't he? But it made a difference, somehow, to know whether her father had taken advantage of a situation that presented itself or deliberately set out to ruin the most important day of her life. That he had played into her desires, using her love for him against her.

Inara's gaze skittered away, something like shame flashing in her eyes. Then she shrugged—or tried to, with Wren's hands pressed against her chest. "He offered me a deal I couldn't refuse."

"Which was?"

Inara laughed, but there was no humor in it. "He told me to do it or else. He's the heir of our house, Wren. I didn't have much of a choice."

"So . . . the bet? The stakes? Everything?"

Inara lifted her chin. "He even dug the hole. Or made someone else do it, more like."

Wren nodded, releasing her. It hurt, but distantly. In reality, this last bit of truth made things clearer in her mind. Easier.

"What's happened?" Inara asked into the silence. "What is he up to?"

"Currently?" Wren asked, running a hand through her hair. "Covering his tracks."

After that? She had thoroughly messed up his original plans by failing to get kidnapped, but now that he'd heard everything about the Corpse Queen and . . . the boy . . . it seemed he had new plans involving the well. Of course, his mother knew nothing about it, and he intended to keep it that way for now. She'd be furious at him for striking a deal with their enemies and potentially further embroiling the House of Bone in scandal, never mind the decades of lies about Locke and the truth of Wren's parentage.

Wren suspected Vance would keep Svetlana busy and distracted with the political angle, as they had both rescued a prince *and* wound up with a high-value prisoner of their own in Julian. Meanwhile, he'd plan a journey east of the Wall. A journey that would likely include Wren.

Too bad she intended to make a journey of her own.

She had no idea what his ultimate goal was—to be a greater hero than Locke? To reclaim the royal bride he'd lost? Or did he actually intend to marry Ravenna, like he'd claimed to Odile, even knowing what she was? Surely not. His mother would never allow it. Regardless, she knew he intended to get to the well and the power within, so she'd have to beat him to it.

She left Inara behind and crossed the room, swinging the doors to the balcony wide. She leapt across, heedless of the danger, and was back in her father's chambers in seconds.

The familiar smell of him, clinging to his clothes strewn about the place, turned her stomach, but she couldn't afford to be queasy.

She doubted she had much time.

Recalling what Leo had said about Galen's letters, Wren wondered if her father might not have some of his own. They could be enough to incriminate him, or at the very least, direct suspicion his way and trap him here for a time. But whatever papers he had been reviewing at the table earlier were gone, and what remained were benign letters and scraps of incoherent notes.

She wasn't surprised—he was not a careless man—but it had been worth a shot. She hesitated over a couple of the remnants, one of which held his signature and the other a botched glob of wax with his seal.

Back on the opposite balcony, Inara was waiting for her.

"What do you mean?" her cousin said without preamble. "Covering what tracks?"

Wren wavered over what to tell Inara. It wasn't just the lifelong animosity between them but the fact that Wren didn't want to drag her any further into her father's schemes.

"Just stay out of it for once, okay?" Wren said. "And pretend you never saw me. If he asks, say you found this."

She withdrew Ghostbane. It truly was a beautiful weapon, but all she could see when she looked at it was her father.

She held it out to her cousin.

Inara blinked. "What're you . . . ?" She trailed off, taking Ghostbane. Her gaze was searching, but Wren avoided her eye.

"I owed you an ancestral blade, remember?"

"Since when do you pay your debts?" Inara asked, staring down at the weapon. Then realization dawned on her face. "You're about to do something stupid, aren't you?"

"By your standards, everything I do is stupid."

"Not everything," Inara admitted, and that meant something to Wren. It occurred to her how much more fun she would have had in her life if she and Inara had been on the same side from the start. But that was a dangerous line of thinking, one she'd been tempted to follow all night. What if she'd grown up with a mother *and* a brother? What if her father wasn't who she'd always thought?

What if, what if.

As before, the images wouldn't stick, like water on wings.

"I guess this is goodbye," Wren said. "For now, anyway."

Inara frowned, then nodded. "For now."

Then she turned her back on the life she'd always known, leaving Ghostbane, her father, and her family behind.

Perhaps Wren should have waited until the following night—given herself a chance to pack and prepare—but that really wasn't her style. It had worked out before, hadn't it?

Besides, look what her father had managed to do in a *single* night. She didn't want to give him even another minute to wreak more havoc on herself, Leo, or Julian.

The halls were quiet as she moved through the fort—no doubt her father and the commander were holed up together right now, discussing the night's events—but the places she needed to go would be well guarded. Her father's men would be posted outside Leo's door, and she knew from experience they couldn't be cajoled or reasoned with. Wren wouldn't be surprised if her father had shoehorned some of his men into the dungeons as well, ensuring everything was within his control, but she'd worry about that later. First she had to save a prince.

Again.

Good thing he'd already shown her how to do it.

The last time they'd been at the fort together, Leo had managed to give his guards the slip by using his window. His rooms were on the second floor, the windows facing the small courtyard off the kitchens, which was busy during the day but quiet and deserted at night.

The problem was, Leo had only managed to return to his rooms with Wren's help. The wall was ill suited to climbing, with little in the way of ledges or handholds. In short: It was an easy trip down, *not* an easy trip up.

But maybe she was looking at things from the wrong angle.

Leaving the courtyard, Wren decided to take a page out of Inara's book. She found an empty room that was ideally positioned directly *above* Leo's, and then, using a rope she stole from the stables, she prepared to rappel down to his window.

Again she found herself thinking of Julian's iron whip, his sure grip and reassuring strength, but she pushed the thoughts aside. She could do this.

She'd bolted the door and fastened the rope around the heavy latch, double- and triple-checking the knot before scanning for any wandering eyes, but she had no control over the wind as she carefully descended, her body buffeted this way and that.

Still, Wren was nothing if not stubborn, and she shimmied down the wall with determination, if not grace.

When at last she reached Leo's window, she tapped gently against the pane—not wanting to startle him or rouse any of his guards. Being a prince with some manner of his own authority, she suspected he would be alone inside his room, but she pushed herself to the side and tensed in case someone else came looking.

The latch flipped and the window slid open, revealing a golden head of tousled hair. He looked at her without so much as a raised eyebrow. "Evening," he said, as if he'd spotted her walking down the street and not hanging, midair, outside his window.

Wren *attempted* to look at him—the wind was combining with the rope to twist her around backward—and when she finally managed it, he was grinning. "Well?" she said. "Are you coming?"

It appeared he was. He withdrew long enough to pull on boots and a jacket, and then he was back again.

"Hurry," Wren muttered, beginning the long, painful climb back up. She had knotted the rope to make for an easier grip, but her legs were burning and her hands fumbling by the time she reached the top.

Leo was not far behind, and despite the sweat coating his brow and his heavy breaths, he looked delighted at being sprung from his room. "Not exactly the thrilling destination I was imagining," he mused, running a finger along the dusty window ledge. It had evidently been a while since this room had been in use.

"Shut . . . up," Wren panted, leaning against the wall.

The smile on Leo's face faltered. "Has something happened?"

Wren blew out a breath and straightened. "Yes."

She told him first about Odile, about her father's role in it, and how Galen was currently locked up and set to pay the price.

"I can't say I feel sorry for him," Leo said, his expression hard. "Still, he's not a murderer."

"But my father *is*. He was the one who paid Galen. He sent me here on purpose, as part of a deal with the regent, only . . ." Wren shook her head. "That Corpse Queen. She's my m-mother," she faltered, swallowing thickly. "That's why she wanted me and no one else. She's a ghostsmith, and that must be why I could . . . why I'm able to . . ." She didn't understand how it was possible. How she could have both bonesmith *and* ghostsmith powers. Was it the well's doing too? Did it amplify her magic so forcefully that it turned latent abilities into dominant ones? And was her brother the same? Maybe he would have the answers she sought and could explain what was happening to her. Or maybe he would betray her too. "My father wants to seek her out, to try to use the power in the well himself. . . . We can't let him."

"We won't," Leo said at once, before the shock of it all settled on him. "Your father . . . your *mother* . . ." Wren stared at him, at a loss for what to say or how to explain her own reaction. "*Family*," he said eventually, his tone dismissive, but his eyes were kind.

"Family," Wren agreed, nodding, utterly relieved at his unwavering acceptance. "Speaking of, we're not the only ones who've been betrayed by our families recently."

Leo perked up. "You don't mean . . ."

"I do," Wren said, and he grinned.

While springing Leo had been relatively straightforward, if physically challenging, freeing Julian would be another matter entirely. Not only was he in a proper cell with real guards, but he currently hated both of them and might turn on them the first chance he got.

It was a risk Wren was willing to take.

Apparently, Leo was too. "After what we did to him . . . if he wants to barter me for his people, maybe I should let him."

"We'll come up with something better—together."

While Galen was being held in the upper-floor dungeons for "important prisoners," as Odile had put it, Julian—though more noble than Galen—was being held in the high-security dungeon on the floor below, where dangerous criminals were kept. It was fully underground: dark, dank, and oppressive.

As such, they couldn't just walk in and ask to see him *or* climb in through a window. In fact, they'd be lucky if they were allowed to catch a glimpse of him in his cell, never mind spring him.

"Even if we get in," Leo asked, "how do we get out?"

"Leave that to me," Wren said, Odile's key clutched tightly in her hand.

Her plan to get into the dungeons involved the scraps of corre-spondence she'd stolen from her father. It took some doing, but she managed to pry off her father's imperfect seal, then reheat the back of the wax with the help of a lantern and attach it to a fresh page. Luckily, Leo was better with a pen than her and did his best to forge a letter allowing them both permission to visit Julian in his cell.

It would get them down there, but the rest would be up to luck, timing—and just how much damage Julian could do with Ironheart from behind bars. Wren's bone blades wouldn't hold up against Breachfort steel, and Leo was no fighter, though he'd surprised Wren in a scrap before. Still, his royal blood might cause the guards to hold back, even just for a moment.

She hoped it would be enough.

FORTY-ONE

Wren had barely poked her head into the hall when Inara's face appeared before her.

"*Gravedigger,*" Wren muttered, jumping a foot before grabbing her cousin by the shoulder and dragging her into the room. "What are you *doing here?*"

Inara was unapologetic. "Watching your back. Obviously *someone* has to. This one can't be good for much," she said, pointing a dismissive thumb at Leo.

He didn't look insulted in the slightest. In fact, he smoothed his hair and tugged at his jacket, flashing her a smile. "Some have called me a golden prize."

Inara ignored him. "Their meeting is wrapping up on the floor above. Commander Duncan is on the move. Vance is being held up with the steward, but I don't know how long that will last."

Wren narrowed her eyes at this useful information, suspicious at once. "Why are you helping me?"

"Stop being an idiot. I'm not helping *you*. I'm hurting *him*." She must mean Vance. Still, Wren wasn't convinced. Inara rolled her eyes. "If you don't trust me, trust Fell ambition. I'm more than happy to see the Graven family fall."

Wren smiled darkly. Fair enough. "We need to get to the dungeons."

"I can divert the commander, keep him away from the stairs."

"How long can you buy me?"

Inara tilted her head. "Five minutes. Seven, tops."

It would have to do. She nodded, but Inara paused.

"Getting you down there is one thing, but getting you up again . . ."

"Don't worry about that."

Inara studied her for several heartbeats, then shrugged. "If you say so."

Then she was off toward the stairs.

"Who was *that*?" Leo asked, sounding positively enamored.

Wren shushed him and watched from the doorway as Inara disappeared at the end of the hall, the sound of her footsteps receding as she climbed to the next floor. Voices echoed down to them, and while Inara's words were muffled and impossible to make out, they were soon met by Commander Duncan's low rumble of a reply. No additional footsteps came, which meant their progress was halted.

Wren and Leo were on the clock.

"Move," Wren hissed, following Inara's path to the stairwell and heading in the opposite direction, down to the lowest levels instead of up. Then it was a quick sprint across the empty main hall toward the stairs that led to the dungeons.

Once out of sight, Wren slowed her pace and affected her best casual stroll, though it paled in comparison to Leo's elegant, carefree saunter. They passed the floor where Galen was kept, the guards stationed there unconcerned with them as they continued by.

On the floor below there were four guards total—two by the door and two more seated at a table, though all of them stood to attention at their arrival.

Before the guards could voice a dismissal, Wren shoved their forged paperwork under the nearest one's nose.

As he unfolded the letter, she glanced surreptitiously toward the cells that lined the wall. There were three, and she had a feeling Julian was in the nearest one. She couldn't see inside from this angle, but there was a scuffing sound, like boots on stone, and then Julian appeared, leaning against the bars, watching them with hooded eyes.

His gaze burned into her, hot enough to scorch, and she fought the urge to flinch. Instead, she shifted her stance, drawing attention to the hilt of Ironheart tucked into her belt. Could his magic reach it from there?

"It says Lord-Smith Vance has given you permission to question the prisoner," the man read dubiously. "Why didn't you just come with him? He was here barely an hour ago."

Shit. He must have come here sometime after he killed Odile but before he holed himself up with the commander in his tower.

"I'm afraid it was my fault," Leo said, flashing his winningest smile. "I had other matters to deal with. Letters to send, you know. To my father. The king."

He was laying it on a little thick, in Wren's opinion, though the guard's skeptical expression faltered a bit.

"Let me see that," said another guard—one who'd been seated at the table. He wore the insignia of guard captain. She was relieved to see that none of her father's men were here, but the odds were still against them.

The captain's eyes narrowed. "Lord-Smith Vance gave us explicit instructions that there should be no visitors," he began, and Wren opened her mouth to explain that he'd changed his mind, hence the letter, when he finished, "*Especially* you."

She glanced at Leo, but it seemed he was out of charming excuses or names to drop. They both were.

She sighed. Their time was up.

"Take them both—"

Wren unleashed a cloud of bonedust. The nearest guards reared back, choking and blinking against their streaming vision, while Leo kicked out at the table, sending it careening into the last guard who was seated, trapping him against the wall.

The guard captain recovered from the bonedust first, reaching for his sword, but he had staggered backward and was inches from Julian's cell. Julian grabbed the guard's arm from behind, stopping him from withdrawing his sword, and the next thing Wren knew, there was a tug at her waist, and Julian had his other arm around the captain's neck, Ironheart pressed to the man's throat.

The rest of the guards stopped fighting at that point, allowing Wren and Leo to hastily disarm them. They bound and gagged all four, then dragged them into the cell at the end of the hall. They'd be discovered eventually, but Wren hoped it wouldn't be until the guard shift changed.

She removed the captain's key ring but was crestfallen to see that the one for Julian's cell was missing. She crouched before the captain and tore his gag free.

"Where is it?"

"Lord-Smith Vance has it," he said with an inordinate level of satisfaction.

"Of course he does," Wren muttered, shoving the gag back in place.

"Now what?" asked Leo from behind her.

Hands shaking slightly, she faced Julian's cell.

"I ...," she began, voice tremulous, but Julian ignored her. He was tugging off the black glove on his left hand ... a glove she'd never seen him remove before. And underneath ...

There were black lines sprawled across his hand, wrapping around the musculature like tendons or veins.

It was *iron*. Shards of iron embedded in his skin. Wren thought of what he had told her about amplifiers, about the combination of material, blood, and living matter.

There was bright-red scarring where metal met skin, and Wren flashed back to their kiss in the spring, when her fingertips had trailed over raised ridges across his shoulder, the contact causing him to hastily pull away.

The lines of iron disappeared under his sleeve, confirming that the implants likely went all the way up his arm.

Avoiding their stares, Julian crouched before the lock. Like the bars, it was made of steel—iron in nature, but an alloy, and therefore untouchable to his magic.

He couldn't manipulate or reshape the lock, but apparently, with iron reinforcement, he *could* crush it with his bare hand. Wren recalled the wooden shelf in the closet in Caston, the fact that he had accidentally crushed it to splinters suddenly making sense.

The metal screeched as his hand squeezed, damaging the lock beyond repair and peeling it away from the frame. Wren marveled at the intricate control involved to make the iron implants bend and twist and function within his living hand.

The door swung wide, and he strode through it, drawing his glove back over his hand.

He made directly for Wren.

She backed up until she bumped into the cold stone wall, then had no choice but to stand there and meet his gaze, his *fury*, head-on.

He looked slightly deranged, his hair askew, his eyes sparking dangerously. Despite how effortless it had looked, he was sweating from the exertion of crushing that steel lock. He kept shaking out that hand as if there was pain as well as fatigue.

He came to a stop bare inches in front of her. She raised her head. "I'm sorry."

His lip curled, disbelief etched across his features. She couldn't blame him. She had betrayed him willingly, however difficult it had been.

"He would have killed you. I couldn't let him."

"He. *Your father,*" he said, speaking the words with careful deliberation. She regretted he'd had to find out that way, but it was relatively low on her list of sins, so she decided against apologizing again.

"You were right," she said instead. His expression flickered, and she couldn't tell if he was surprised that she had admitted as much or annoyed that the words were so insufficient. "We never should have come here. And we need to leave. Now."

He continued to stare at her, hard, and then a rueful smile twisted his mouth. He chuckled darkly and stepped away, giving her space. A part of her lamented his absence.

She glanced around, then pointed to a locker on the far side of the room. "Your armor and weapons," she said. He stalked wordlessly toward it.

"I think that went well," Leo said brightly. "For me, anyway."

She glowered at him.

"What are you up to, little bird?"

Wren froze. Slowly she turned toward the stairwell, fear pinning her to the spot. Her father stood in the doorway with half a dozen of his personal guard ranged on either side.

Leo and Julian had also paused, and now both their heads swiveled to face her.

She swallowed. "I'm leaving," she said, her voice tight. "*We're* leaving."

"I see. I know you've been through a trying time—all three of you. And high-pressure situations like that can cause a certain . . . *bond* . . . to form between the unlikeliest of people."

Wren did not appreciate his condescending tone. "Like between you and my mother?"

He sighed, but in an indulgent—though still slightly frustrated—way. "Wren, your mother and I—"

"*Enough*," she cut in. "I don't want any more lies from you."

For the first time, her father's confident facade faltered. "I'm not sure what—"

"No. More. Lies."

He didn't know that she'd been eavesdropping on his conversation with Odile, but he could tell she'd discovered something she wasn't meant to.

"What did Odile say to you?" he asked, trying to figure out what she knew without exposing himself.

"She didn't say anything to me, but she said a good deal to you. I won't wind up like him. Like Locke. Odile was right. We have to destroy it."

Wren felt everyone's eyes on her, particularly Julian's. He knew nothing of her plans or what else she had discovered that night, but he undoubtedly knew she was talking about the well.

Vance's eyes fluttered closed, and he cast a surreptitious glance over his shoulder at his guards. "You don't understand—"

"I understand better than you!" Wren burst out. "I *saw*, okay? I saw the result of what happened that day. Hundreds of bodies, crushed to dust. Their souls forever trapped. I *felt* it when I touched the magic. I felt the danger. We can't—"

"Look around, Wren! The Dominions are safe and at peace, and that is also the result of what happened that day. Think of what else we could accomplish together! All *this* means"—he withdrew the ring as he slowly walked toward her—"is that you are more powerful than you thought. Capable of more than you can imagine. More than Locke. It means you are different. Special."

"I don't want to be," Wren said, staring at the ring.

"I know. But it doesn't change anything. You are still a bonesmith. And you are still my daughter, Wren, in all the ways that matter. I have loved you as a daughter, and so my daughter you will always be." His voice was constricted, his expression sincere, and it caused tears to fill Wren's eyes.

She reached for the ring, and he let her take it, thinking he had won. He tilted his head at his guards, directing them to apprehend Leo and Julian. The prince was unarmed, and Julian had yet to make it to the storage locker. Ironheart would not be enough.

But the instant Wren's fingers touched the ring, she felt the well's power within her stir. Apparently it *was* an amplifier, as Julian had guessed. She just hadn't noticed before with the well's power fresh and foreign and coursing through her. But now, with the passage of time and distance, she felt the way it reared up again, awakened by the ring.

She understood then what it might have been like to be Locke. To have what you needed right there at your fingertips.

And to use it.

"Don't touch them," she snapped—but these guards were living, not undead, and her commands had only the power her father gave her behind them. He frowned at her.

"Wren, darling, I thought we understood each other. We're on the same side, but I can't have you running around here disobeying me. They will not be harmed, okay? Apprehend them," he finished, speaking to his guards, while putting a restraining hand on Wren's shoulders.

One of them reached for Julian, arm outstretched.

Wren thought of the moment in the mill house when she seemed to have flung Julian against the pillar with more than just her muscles alone.

She stared at the guard's forearm, *willing* it to stop moving.

A sickening crack echoed in the dungeon, and the man cried out in pain and confusion.

Wren felt the blood drain from her face. She hadn't just stopped his arm.

She'd broken it.

The guards nearest to him drew their weapons, assuming Julian had somehow attacked him. Julian, meanwhile, was staring in shock at the man, hunched over his broken limb. Leo also looked stunned, the guards that had been edging his way halting in their tracks.

None of them knew what to make of it.

None of them except her father.

He had seen this kind of thing before.

Whirling around, he stared at Wren with equal parts fear and hunger. "Wren, did you—"

"Call them off," she choked out.

"Come now, little bird, you can't—"

"I said, *call them off*. Now."

He lifted his chin, studying her. He saw the sheen of sweat, the wide eyes.

She hated this.

And he saw that too.

"No." He turned to his guards. "I told you to apprehend them both. Do it. By any means necessary."

They were well trained—Wren had to give him that. His guards hesitated only a second before stepping around their prone fellow toward Julian again.

Wren gritted her teeth, reaching with her magic. She could sense their bones, standing upright before her, just like she might sense a skeleton in the dirt. She could reach for them as she might her weapons. Or she could apply pressure, as she had when she'd broken that bone.

Instead, she pushed.

With a surge of magic, she sent all six of them slamming into the wall behind them. Two cracked their heads audibly, while a third fell through the open doorway, landing somewhere on the stairs. The others moaned and muttered, heaps on the ground. None got up.

Wren turned to her father. "We're leaving. Do not follow us. I'm going to do what you should have done decades ago and destroy that well." He took a step toward her, and she raised a hand. "Don't make me."

He froze. Glanced at the men huddled on the ground, then back at Wren. "You're making a mistake. Let me help you."

"Like how you helped me during the Bonewood Trial?" she asked, grabbing Leo and pulling him toward the hidden door beneath the stairs. Julian, seeing her movement, hurried to the locker to retrieve his armor and weapons and then followed them. Vance's expression, which had still been colored with hope, slipped to resignation.

"I'm disappointed in you," he said softly, delivering the words he thought would be a blow to her heart.

They might have been. Once.

She smiled bitterly at him. "Then maybe I'm finally doing something right."

Turning her back on him, she withdrew Odile's key and unlocked the hidden door. She grabbed one of the torches from its sconce and led the way over the threshold. Once Leo and Julian had joined her, she slammed the door behind them and descended the stairs.

Her breath misted in the air as she reached the bottom, taking a moment to collect herself. Vance wouldn't be able to follow them through the passage, but she couldn't trust that he wouldn't hightail it up the stairs and send guards riding out the gate.

She strode into the cavernous space, halting when she realized the others weren't following. She looked over her shoulder. "You two coming or not?"

"Where?" Julian asked.

"Into the Breachlands. Where else?"

"To destroy the well?" he pressed.

"Do you have a better idea?" It would be no simple task, she knew. And she would have to face her mother and brother again to do it. Her stomach tightened. . . . Was that fear, or anticipation?

"It would stop the queen," Leo said. "The iron revenants, and your uncle."

Julian studied her for a long time—too long. Sweat beaded Wren's brow and made her hands clammy. Did he see the hidden desire there? The curiosity? And worst of all, the pull to that dark magic that still swirled in her veins?

"Why?" Julian asked finally, and Wren knew he wasn't just asking about their destination. He was asking about all of it.

"I . . ." Wren trailed off, looking at Leo, but he too appeared curious for her response. She'd yet to fully explain herself. "I was trying to protect you," she tried again, hastening to finish when his expression shuttered at what he perceived as a blatant lie, "but I was trying to protect myself more. I was everything you accused me of. Selfish. Reckless. I thought . . ." She shook her head. "It doesn't matter what I thought. I was wrong. My father paid the informant. He's working with your uncle, and he sent me to the fort on purpose, meaning for me to get kidnapped too. Except tonight he learned that the queen, who is a ghostsmith, is also my mother. And that boy? My twin brother."

The scowl on Julian's face shifted fractionally, surprise lifting his brows despite his determination to hate her. He glanced down at the ring, which she was wearing on her finger.

"My father knew about the well. Locke, his brother, used it to destroy all those soldiers. And now Vance wants to use it again. To use *me*. I won't let him."

Her chest heaved, not from a lack of air but from suppressed emotion. She would be damned if she let anyone use her ever again.

"So, are you in?"

Julian glanced at Leo, who scrubbed a hand through his hair. "My cousin set me up." He turned to Wren. "Your father set you up—and your uncle tried to have you killed," he finished, returning to Julian. "They sought to use us, to kill and capture and shuffle us around. I don't know about you, but I'm tired of being a pawn. I want to be a player. I'm in."

Wren smiled, then together, they looked at Julian. His expression shifted, skepticism turning into angry determination. It was better than disinterest. It was better than disgust. Anger she could use.

"I'm in."

Relief swept through her. Smiling grimly, she led the way through the subterranean chamber to the travel supplies. This was more than just a passage under the Wall, after all. It was a dungeon and a hide-out, a safe house, a black-market cache, and a storage room.

It was also an infirmary. Her attention shifted to the row of beds, and she thought of her mother.

Had Wren been born here in one of these narrow beds? Were those old bloodstains her mother's blood? Ghostsmith blood?

Wren's blood?

While facing her brother again filled her with dangerous hope, the idea of facing her mother felt far more precarious. Ravenna wanted to use that well, and Wren wanted to destroy it. They were in opposition, but they were also family.

Blood.

Would those ties prove a more powerful influence on Wren, who had always longed for a mother, or on Ravenna, who had lost a daughter? Did she truly care about Wren at all, or was Wren simply a tool to be used to further her own ends?

Or would it be as it had been with her father, a cruel combination of both?

Turning aside, she found some bags and tossed one each to Leo and Julian.

"Take whatever you can easily carry," she said. After Julian donned his armor, they loaded up on food, water canteens, and even weapons. Leo took a few pieces of golden jewelry and Wren, several jars of bonedust.

While Julian was examining a pair of iron throwing stars, Wren noticed that Ironheart had made its way back onto his belt. Of course he wouldn't want *her* to have it after her betrayal.

But it hurt all the same.

When they reached the end of the room, there was a wide hatch, large enough for barrels and a horse to be led through, and a smaller door more suitable for people. Wren bent over the bone lock, using the key once more, then carefully opened the door.

Ditching the torch, she emerged in a cavern of sorts, with natural stone concealing them from above and a tangle of bushes protecting them from wider view. Wren suspected that this place would be impossible to spot from the Wall or along the usual patrol routes, but they were still within the palisade's protections.

"Come on," she said, ushering the other two out and closing the door behind them.

Together they took in their surroundings, staring at the world beyond their small enclosure. All was darkness, save for the lanterns dotting the Wall above and the flash of bone-white bricks illuminated by the moon and stars. The palisade stood like distant specters, watching, waiting.

"Now what?" Leo asked, looking between them.

"We go back into the Breach," Wren said, casting her gaze northeast. "We destroy the well by any means necessary. After that, we deal with the rest."

The rest. Their respective families, their convoluted plots . . . and their army of revenants.

But Wren was ready, and she didn't need Ghostbane *or* Ironheart because *she* was a blade—a weapon to be wielded, a force to be reckoned with.

And she would defeat the undead.

ACKNOWLEDGMENTS

Thank you to my publishing dream team—my agent, Penny Moore, and my editor, Sarah McCabe—who have been the best partners I could ask for in this career. I'm so glad we got to do this again.

Thank you to everyone at Simon & Schuster and Aevitas Creative Management, who do so much work behind the scenes that I rarely see—but always feel—on the long journey from a messy manuscript on my hard drive to publication.

Thank you to my friends and family, who have supported me from the beginning, and who make those rare days I'm not working worth all the struggle in between.

Thank you to the First Riders Street Team alumni, who keep the love alive years after the series ended. I hope you enjoy the Dominions as much as you enjoyed the Golden Empire. Super special thank-you to my Rider Council: Alex, Brianna, Callum, and Megan, who helped me run things the second time around, and who continue to help with constant support, encouragement, and beta reads.

Finally, thank you to the readers, reviewers, librarians, book-sellers, and everyone in the bookish community for championing my stories. I couldn't do this job without you, and I couldn't be more grateful.

NICKI PAU PRETO is a fantasy author living just outside Toronto—though her dislike of hockey, snow, and geese makes her the worst Canadian in the country. She studied art and art history in university and worked as a graphic designer before becoming a writer full-time. She is the author of the Crown of Feathers Trilogy, and you can find her online at NickiPauPreto.com.